MY CALAMITY JANE

MY

CYNTHIA HAND

CALAMITY

BRODI ASHTON

JANE

JODI MEADOWS

HARPER TEEN
An Imprint of HarperCollins Publishers

HarperTeen is an imprint of HarperCollins Publishers.

My Calamity Jane

Copyright © 2020 by Cynthia Hand, Brodi Ashton, and Jodi Meadows

All rights reserved. Printed in the United States of America.

No part of this book may be used or reproduced in any manner whatsoever without written permission except in the case of brief quotations embodied in critical articles and reviews. For information address HarperCollins Children's Books, a division of HarperCollins Publishers, 195 Broadway, New York, NY 10007.

www.epicreads.com

Library of Congress Control Number: 2020934468
ISBN 978-0-06-265281-2

Typography by Jenna Stempel-Lobell
20 21 22 23 24 PC/LSCH 10 9 8 7 6 5 4 3 2 1

First Edition

For the boat rockers, the rulebreakers, and the troublemakers. No one ever became a legend by blending in.

When a man hits a target, they call him a marksman.
When I hit it, they call it a trick.
Never did like that much.
—Annie Oakley

I figure, if a girl wants to be a legend,
she should just go ahead and be one.
—Calamity Jane

Prologue

Listen up, y'all. We're gonna tell you the story of Calamity Jane. You might have already heard of CJ—she's one of the most famous names of the Old West. She was quite the character, if you believe the stuff that was written about her in the dime-store novels and newspapers of the day. They say she dressed up in britches like a man, shooting and swearing with the best of them; that she was a Pony Express rider, a stagecoach driver, a pioneer, a scout for the US Army, a spy, a showgirl, and the love interest of many a notorious gunslinger. "The Heroine of the Plains," they liked to call her, and if all this wasn't exactly true, well, it made a good story, so Jane never did try to set the record straight.

Historians, for their part, claim that in "reality" Calamity Jane was an illiterate, foul-mouthed alcoholic. They paint her as a lone wolf, a wanderer, a perpetual screwup who eventually drank herself to death and died alone and friendless, a tragic end after a lifetime of self-destruction. Not exactly a happily ever after.

We, your faithful narrators, think Jane had a good heart and deserves a better ending, so (as usual) we have a different tale to tell. Hold on to your hats, because we're going to take you back to 1876.

Now, we want to warn you that the America of this tall tale doesn't exactly resemble the history books. We've improved upon it, naturally. We changed people's names when it suited us, combined a bunch of guys named Bill into one, and messed around with dates and ages. As we do. In our story, Calamity Jane's been working in a theatrical production called *Wild Bill's Wild West* (say that ten times fast). The show was one part demonstration—sharpshooting and rodeo-type tricks—and one part storytelling, in which Wild Bill Hickok, America's first gunslinger and all-around stone-cold badass, thrilled audiences with accounts about his great adventures hunting garou.

If you're not familiar with the term *garou*, we can hardly blame you. It's an old word, derived from *garolf*, which had been, over centuries, modified from yet another, even older word: *werwulf*.

You see where we're going with this.

The garou had always been around, but they were good at hiding in plain sight. A garou looked like a human, walked and talked like a human, and really *was* a human . . . most of the time. But in 1876, garou bites were on the rise. There were whispers of an evil garou gang known as (wait for it) the Pack, which was headed up by a mysterious figure called (you guessed it) the Alpha. Understandably, the US government was concerned about all these people getting turned into werewolves, so they hired Wild Bill Hickok and his posse of undercover garou hunters to bring the Alpha to justice, a job that would lead to one of the wildest adventures in the history of the Wild West.

That brings us to the three not-so-typical teenagers this story is really about: a dashing young feller trying to follow in the footsteps of his famous father, an ambitious-but-charming sharpshooter determined to prove herself, and a hotheaded but tenderhearted girl who's fixin' to get tangled up in a few dangerous plots of her own.

Get ready to meet the *real* Calamity Jane.

PART ONE

Cincinnati

(In which things get
a little hairy.)

ONE

As usual, they caused a ruckus when they came to town. Wild Bill liked to make an entrance. He led the group right down the center of Main Street, Bill riding way out front on his gleaming black horse, Jane and the rest following behind. Within minutes of their arrival the streets had flooded with onlookers, staring and pointing and exclaiming things like, "Wowee, that there's *the* Wild Bill Hickok," and "He's the best sharpshooter in the West—no, the *world*," and "A genuine hero, he is!"

Bill waved grandly to the bystanders, tipped his hat at the ladies, and swept back the edges of his billowy black coat to reveal the matching pair of engraved, ivory-hilted, silver-mounted .36 caliber revolvers strapped to his hips.

"That Wild Bill's shot over a hundred men," Jane overheard

as they approached a gaggle of boys on the stoop of a barbershop.

Folks tended to exaggerate when it came to Bill.

"Well, I read in *Harper's New Monthly Magazine* that he killed ten garou in a single fight," said another boy. "With only six bullets in his gun!"

Jane heard an incredulous snort and glanced over her shoulder at the two men riding behind her: Charlie Utter, Bill's business partner, and Frank Butler, Bill's son. It was Frank who'd given the snort.

Jane crossed her eyes at him.

Frank responded by cupping his hand under his armpit and making fart noises.

Jane pantomimed vomiting.

Then Frank turned his head and pretended (at least we hope he was pretending) to slowly stick his finger up his nose.

Jane coughed to cover her laugh. Dang, he'd got her.

"Stop it, you two," Charlie barked. "So help me I will turn these horses around."

Jane sighed and swiveled to face forward again.

"Nellie, look!" cried a lady in a pink dress. "That's Frank Butler, the Pistol Prince."

"Oh! Isn't he handsome?" breathed a second woman.

"So handsome," agreed the first. "He's even more handsome in real life, don't you think?"

They must have missed the nose-picking. Jane peeked over her shoulder again at Frank, who weren't so comely as all that, even if he did comb his hair regular and have all his teeth. Still, she'd never be able to think of Frank in any romantical way.

"You see the white dog riding on the special seat behind him?" continued the woman in the pink dress. "That's George the Poodle. He's part of their show."

"I simply adore a man with a dog," cooed the second girl.

From his perch, George gave a low growl. Jane agreed. This part was just so stupid, dandying up and promenading through town to get gawked at and fussed over.

"Hey!" a young man yelled out from the door of a bank. "Ain't that Calamity Jane, the Heroine of the Plains?"

Well, maybe it wasn't *so* stupid. That word did have a nice ring to it: *hero-eene.*

"Nah," scoffed another fellow. "That can't be Calamity Jane. She's not pretty enough."

Jane could instantly feel them looking her up and down. She knew she'd never be what a man would think beautiful; her shape was downright squarish, both body and jaw, her face burned and freckled from the sun, her hair dark and tangly as a stack of black cats. But a recent article in the *Chicago Tribune* had described Calamity Jane as "a lovely, spirited waif," which had given folks certain erroneous expectations.

"That's a girl wearing man's breeches who's riding with Wild Bill Hickok," argued another man. "It's got to be Calamity Jane."

"I guess you're right." The first man laughed loudly. "Huh. She ain't much to look at, is she? I can see why they call her 'calamity.'"

Jane's face burned. She should brush it off—she knew that—but instead she brought her horse to a stop alongside the bank and fixed the men with a stare. They fell silent.

What she wanted to do was spit. Jane was an excellent spitter, and it would be thoroughly satisfying to send a clean arc of spittle right onto the face of the rudest man.

"Jane," came that warning voice behind her—Charlie, again. Gawl-darned Charlie, who disapproved of Jane spitting. It was bad for business, he always said.

Charlie spoiled all her fun.

So Jane swallowed down the impressive loogie she'd been working up (which we commend her for, as your narrators, but ewwww), cried "Yah!" and galloped ahead.

"You cain't lose your temper," Charlie scolded her later as they saw to the horses at the livery. "It reflects badly on the show."

She nodded dully. "I didn't. I won't." But she knew she probably would at some point. She'd never been skilled at holding back her temper, a trait she'd inherited from her hotheaded ma, God rest her soul.

"Folks can be mean as snakes, I know." Charlie finished oiling Wild Bill's saddle and gave Jane a sympathetic smile. "But at least they know your name. That's good, Janie. That's what we want. Recognition. Notoriety."

Charlie was always working on the fame thing—how to get it, how to keep hold of it once they got it, how to turn it into profit. Sometimes it was easy to forget that being their manager was only a cover for Charlie's true occupation: he was a Pinkerton detective.

(A little background information, dear reader, about the Pinkertons. By the time of our story, the Pinkerton agency was the largest private law enforcement organization in the United States. Pinkerton agents were mostly hired by businessmen to protect their interests, but they also served as bodyguards for Abraham Lincoln, spied on the Confederate army, and worked as "private eyes" sent to investigate crimes before we had the FBI. That last part brings us to Special Agent Charlie Utter, who'd been assigned to track the notorious garou known as the Alpha. Charlie'd been on the job for less than a year when he bumped into Wild Bill Hickok—who claimed to be retired from garou hunting but actually was an undercover US Marshal tasked with bringing down the Alpha. It made sense for the two of them to team up and start the Wild West show as an excuse to move from town to town, gathering intel. And the rest, as we like to say, is history.)

But the Alpha's trail had gone cold months ago, and even though being Bill's business partner was only a cover, today Charlie was all about the show. He pulled a tall stack of papers out of a box. "Be a dear, Jane, and put these up around town."

Jane scowled. "It's Frank's turn."

"Frank's off with his adoring public, I'm afraid."

"Simpering ladies, you mean," Jane scoffed.

"It's good for business."

"I guess."

"You know what else is good for business?" Charlie added good-naturedly. "You putting up these flyers."

"All right." She sighed and took the stack from him. "But you owe me."

He smiled. "Fine by me."

The trouble wasn't in people knowing or not knowing her name, Jane thought as she made her way back toward the main street with a hammer and a pocketful of nails. The trouble was that they knew her name but they didn't know *her*. Right now, for instance, people passing by assumed she was a man and didn't give her a second glance. They didn't think to themselves, *Now there goes a genuine hero-eene.*

"Hey, mister." Jane felt a tug at her sleeve and jerked back reflexively, but it was only a kid, come to beg, by the looks of it. Dirty face. No shoes. "You got a penny to spare?"

She dug in her pocket, produced two nickels, and handed the coins over. Not so long ago, she'd been that kid, doing whatever she had to do to fill her empty belly.

The boy took the money and ran off down the street without even thanking her. He'd never know that he'd been face-to-face with the famous Calamity Jane.

If you want to know the truth, dear reader, Jane wasn't sure she wanted to be famous. She was good at the hero-type things, if she did say so herself (and she did, quite regularly). But celebrity had come on her accidental-like, and she'd rolled with it, because she didn't have much in the way of options as a woman. It would be enough for her, she thought, to lead a simpler kind of life, get a bit of land someday, a small cabin to call her own, some horses to raise and sell, and a few people she could call friends, maybe even family.

She trudged up to a post and nailed the flyer to it, narrowly avoiding pounding her thumb. The word *family* was like a burr in her heart—it pained her to think on, but she kept thinking on it all the same.

She'd had a family once.

She walked to the next corner and absent-mindedly nailed up another flyer. Before she'd set off to make something of herself (at the tender age of eleven, we should mention), she'd left the youngest of her siblings, Hannah and Sarah Beth, in the care of a Mormon family in Salt Lake City. Her brother Silas had died of a fever earlier that year, another thing Jane tried not to think on. Lena and Lige, who weren't much younger than Jane, had gone to a boardinghouse. She sent money back when she could, which wasn't near often enough.

She hoped they all had shoes.

"Look out!" Right then, Jane was nearly run over by a passing carriage. At the warning she jumped back in the nick of time and ended up sprawled in the dirt in the middle of the street, the flyers strewn around her.

"Consarn it!" she blasted after the retreating carriage. "Watch where you're going, why don't ya!"

"Oh dear. Are you all right?" came a sweet voice.

Jane squinted up at the figure who was suddenly standing over her, silhouetted by the sun. The girl was wearing a white dress with lace at the collar. She had fair-colored hair and eyes and a pair of black wire spectacles perched delicately on her nose.

She was the prettiest thing Jane had ever seen.

"Gosh almighty!' Jane blurted. "You're the prettiest thing I've ever seen!"

"Oh. Well. Thank you," the girl said in an amused tone. "Here, let me help you up."

Jane stared at the unblemished white-gloved hand the girl offered. She jumped to her feet. "No harm done to me," she said. "Thanks."

Together they bent to gather up the flyers, which were a bit dusty but all right. As they finished retrieving them the girl straightened and read the paper in her hand out loud: "'Come one, come all, to *Wild Bill's Wild West*! Tales of Wild Bill Hickok's Most Terrifying Adventures with Outlaws and Garou! Exhibitions of Peerless Sharpshooting and Trick Shots by the Pistol Prince, Frank Butler! Wondrous Feats with the Bullwhip, Performed by Calamity Jane, the Heroine of the Plains!'" The girl pushed her glasses up on her nose. "Oh my goodness. You're Jane, now, aren't you?"

Jane waited for the girl's eyes to sweep over her and find her wanting, but the girl only smiled.

"Yep," Jane said at last. "That's me. Most days, anyway."

"I'm glad to meet you," said the girl. "I've been most eager to make your acquaintance since I heard you were coming to Cincinnati."

Jane nodded. "Uh, likewise."

The girl laughed. "I'm Miss Harris." She held out the gloved hand again. This time Jane took it and shook it gently.

"Jane," she said. She thought it best to omit the Calamity part.

"Now that we've officially met, I hope I will be seeing more of you," said Miss Harris. "I've read all about you."

"Oh yeah? Like what?"

"Like you're only sixteen."

"That's not true," scoffed Jane. "I'm twenty." (In truth, she was seventeen, but she always lied about her age. It suited her for folks to think she was older than she was, and she was so tall and brawny that they always believed her.)

"I see," said Miss Harris. "Well, in any case, I think it's admirable, what you do."

Jane scratched at her head. "I am decent with the whip."

"What I mean is, you don't let your gender define you," Miss Harris continued primly. "You walk about in men's clothes and go adventuring just like a man. You're not limited by the constraints of your sex. You're perhaps the most daring and progressive woman in America, and I find you fascinating."

Jane felt her face redden. "Uh, why, thank you, miss." She found herself suddenly tongue-tied. She glanced up at the sky, where the sun was almost directly overhead. "Shoot, look at the time. I better scoot. Nice meeting you."

"Likewise," said Miss Harris.

It *was* nice, thought Jane as she walked away. This kind of thing usually happened to Frank, not Jane. She'd never had an honest-to-goodness admirer before.

"Well, shucks," she whispered to herself.

* * *

She was almost finished putting up the flyers when she became aware that she was being followed by a man she didn't know. Jane took off her hat and wiped her brow as if she were catching her breath, and surveyed the man from the corner of her eye. He was shorter than she was by almost a head. Young, maybe twenty at most. She could take him.

She crossed the street for no good reason but to confirm that he'd cross the street after her. Which he did. She walked for a spell, then stopped. So did he. She started walking again, faster. He sped up, too. She broke into a jog and then ducked around a corner, upon which she stopped and spun to wait for the fellow. When he turned the corner, she grabbed him by the front of the shirt and bashed him into the side of the building. With her other hand she presented her six-shooter. It wasn't a fancy one like Bill's, but it would get the job done.

"What business do you have with me, sir?" she asked politely.

It took him a moment to answer, seeing as the wind had been knocked out of him. Then he smiled broadly, which caught her off guard. He did not have particularly good teeth.

"You're Calamity Jane," he panted at last.

"What's it to ya?" she replied.

"I'm Jack McCall. I got a message for Wild Bill Hickok," he said, still smiling at her. "It's about them woofs."

TWO
Frank

"I simply adore a man with a dog," the blonde girl gushed.

Frank had heard the same girl say the same thing earlier, when they'd been riding into town. But he didn't mind the repetition in the least.

"Do you?" He smiled, and three out of the four beautiful women gathered outside the theater pretended to swoon.

"Oh yes. Dogs are so cute," the blonde said. "And clever. I so admire cleverness. You're probably clever too, aren't you, Mr. Butler? Or should I call you Frank?"

He didn't get a chance to answer, because another girl said, "Oh, Mr. Butler, how do you shoot so well?"

"Lots of practice—"

But the third girl moved in.

"Is it Mr. Butler, or do you prefer Pistol Prince?"

"I—"

"Oh, Mr. Butler, your poodle is so adorable."

To which George replied with a growl, and all the young ladies backed off a step.

"I'm so sorry," Frank said. "George is afeared of the ladies."

I am not scared of ladies, thought George indignantly. *I'm a brave dog.*

See here, reader, Frank could hear the thoughts of animals—dogs, mostly, but sometimes wolves, wild cats, and the occasional angry badger. It was a skill he didn't advertise, for reasons we'll explain later.

Frank patted George's head. "I think you're a brave boy, George. The bravest." It wasn't so much that George was scared of women, it was more that he just didn't like them, plain and simple . . . and utterly mysteriously, because Frank adored them.

"Awww!" cooed all four ladies in unison. "Poor George."

George sniffed with disdain.

Overhead, the sun crawled toward noon, so Frank put his hands out, palms down in a calming manner, and said, "Thank you for your much-appreciated attention, ladies, but I have to prepare for the show."

"We'll be there," said the brunette.

"And we welcome your attendance," Frank said.

George growled, as if to say he would welcome anything *but* their attendance, and Frank nudged him with his knee.

"Toodleloo," sighed the blonde.

"Same to you," Frank replied.

The crowd of women reluctantly dispersed, and Frank ducked into the theater.

Why do you talk to them every time? George looked up at Frank, his dark eyes curious.

"Well, it's part of my job." Frank scratched the back of George's head. "I like talking to the ladies. I like ladies."

More than me?

"Of course not."

George huffed as if he weren't sure he believed Frank and trotted over to a crate filled with props. *But you don't* like *like them*, George thought. *Not any of those ladies.*

"I like them fine." Frank followed George to the crate and used a crowbar to pry off the lid. "But town after town, they all start to blend together." He carefully removed the paper-wrapped mirrors (for trick shots) and glass balls (for shooting). "It would help if you weren't so mean to them," he added.

I growl because they're not the right mate for you.

Frank coughed and almost dropped one of the glass balls. "Excuse-a-*what*?"

"Hey there, partner." Bill came in, walking stiffly. "Need some help?"

"Sure." Frank gave one last eyebrow raise to George, and then he and Bill set up the targets and other props. It all had to be placed just so, because in a sharp-shooting show where bullets were flying, attention to detail was crucial. Frank handed George an empty whiskey bottle, and the pooch took it and placed it on a pedestal on the opposite side of the stage.

Is this right? George asked.

Frank nodded. The bottle was for Jane's bullwhip act. She was so good with a bullwhip, she could . . . well, your narrators don't want to spoil it for you. You'll have to wait for the show.

Frank paused in the center of the stage, the familiar buzz of preshow anticipation filling him. And for that one small moment, he let himself imagine that show business was all he did.

The heat of the lights on him.

His gun in his hand, the bang of each perfect shot.

The audience gasping and cheering and calling his name.

"Frank Butler!" they'd cry. "Hooray for the Pistol Prince! Frank! Frank! Frank!"

He drew in a deep breath. Even the smell of the theater was something special, like velvet and sawdust and dreams.

"Frank!" Bill stepped in front of him. "Son, are you listening to me?"

Frank blinked a few times. "Sorry, I was lost in thought, I guess."

"What's on your mind?"

"The show," Frank admitted. "Do you think that someday—after we catch the Alpha, of course—the show really could be our job, not just a cover?"

Bill shook his head. "I'm tuckered out, kid. After we catch the

Alpha I'm going to retire. For real this time. From garou hunting and from show business, too."

"Oh." Frank felt a pang in his heart. "Maybe we could take a vacation," he suggested. "Rest up, then find a permanent place somewhere to do the show. A theater. Heck, maybe even this one."

"Nah," said Bill. "I'm done. You know it's not only me I'm thinking about. I've got Agnes waiting for me."

Oh yeah. Bill was married now. It was hard to remember sometimes.

A few months back they'd been doing a show in Cheyenne when Bill had run into an old flame named Agnes Lake. Agnes was in show business, herself. She owned a circus. She also walked the tight rope and trained the fiercest lions, tigers, and bears. (Oh my!) Bill was instantly smitten with her all over again, and in an impromptu move no one (or certainly not Frank) saw coming, Bill asked Agnes to marry him, right then and there, and she'd said yes. The honeymoon hadn't been long, since the gang still had shows to do and the Alpha to hunt, but ever since they'd left Cheyenne— and Agnes—Bill had been talking of settling down. Even so, today was the first time Bill had ever said the word *retire* like he actually meant it.

Bill patted Frank's shoulder. "I've had my time in the sun. But just because I'm done doesn't mean you are. The show must . . ."

"Go on," pressed Frank.

"Right. The show must go on. Without me."

"Yeah, well, then I've got some pretty big shoes to fill," Frank said glumly. It was hard to imagine *Wild Bill's Wild West* without Wild Bill. How could the show really go on without the world's greatest showman?

Bill chuckled and lifted a boot to go alongside Frank's. "Not so big as all that, see? You'll be a natural at it, son. I know you will. In fact, why don't you take over the show from now on, manage things, get a feel for it?"

Frank's breath caught. "What about Charlie?"

Bill pshawed. "He's a Pinkerton. Not a showman. I'm sure he'd rather focus on the Alpha. You think you can handle it?"

"I can do it," said Frank.

"Good. Can you finish setting up on your own?" Bill asked.

"Of course," Frank said.

"I'm gonna head back to the hotel and get us squared away on that end."

Frank watched him go. George sat at his feet.

It's good to think about the future, George thought.

"Maybe," Frank said. "But what if, when Bill leaves . . ."

The show falls apart? George supplied.

"Thank you for your confidence. I was going to say suffer, but sure." Frank scratched George's ears.

George's tail thumped.

Frank sighed and turned back to the set, which was almost finished. He missed the days when it was just him and Bill, going from town to town, living hand to mouth. Well, more like gun to bull's-eye.

From the beginning, life was always an adventure with his

dad. Bill's family farm had served as a stop on the Underground Railroad, and then Bill made a name for himself by joining the antislavery Free State Army of Jayhawkers, where he served as a bodyguard for General James H. Lane.

He fought in the Civil War and left Frank in the care of a family in Ohio. Those years were the longest of Frank's life, the longest he'd spent without his dad.

When Bill returned from the war, he vowed to never leave Frank for more than a couple weeks at a time. The two went on the road again, and Frank noticed that people along the way started to recognize his father. His gunfighting abilities had granted him even more fame.

But it was Bill's encounter with a bear where his legendary status really rose. The bear surprised him on the road, and Hickok shot it. The bear didn't die, and the two wrestled until Bill used a knife to slit the bear's throat.

Frank was with him at the time, hiding behind a tree, watching his dad in amazement.

As Bill's star began to rise, so did the threats against him. The man who killed *the* Wild Bill Hickok would stand to gain fame and possibly fortune.

Bill spent the next few years teaching Frank the ins and outs of a nomadic life, all the while dodging bounty hunters and opportunistic thrill seekers who wouldn't mind seeing Wild Bill dead by their hand.

Then, a few years back, Bill left for a scouting trip, and when he returned, he had a little girl in tow. Jane, her name was.

Jane took to their lifestyle like a fly takes to sugar. When Charlie joined up a couple years later, their gang felt complete. They had a good thing going, here. And now it seemed like they were all about to go their separate ways.

"I don't know if I can carry it alone," Frank murmured to the rows of empty seats.

George lay on the floor and put his chin against the wood. *Don't worry. I've been living this nomadic life for a while now, and if there's one thing I've learned it's—* George's ears pricked up. *Mail wagon!*

Frank could barely hear the hoofbeats outside. George barked enthusiastically for a few minutes, and then settled down again.

"You're a good watchdog," Frank said.

I know, George replied. *The mailman is dangerous, but I'll protect you.*

"Thanks. So what's the one thing you've learned?"

What one thing?

"The one thing you've learned after your nomadic life?"

I don't remember.

"Frank!" came a shout from the theater entrance. "Fraaaaaank!"

It was Jane. She ran down the aisle, spitting as she went.

"Try not to spit on the paid seats," Frank called.

"I have news." Jane put a hand up and leaned over, gasping for air.

George whined and cocked his head, and Frank walked to the edge of the stage so she didn't have to yell.

"Jane, what is it?"

"You gotta come right now to Bill's . . ." She lowered her head again, still struggling to catch her breath.

"Room?" Frank guessed.

Jane nodded.

"But, the show—"

Jane shook her head. "It's a garou emergency!"

Once Jane, Frank, and George got to Bill's room, Frank realized Jane's definition of the word *emergency* was a bit looser than his own. His was more like, a burning building or garou attacking children.

What he found was Bill, standing next to a man who looked vaguely familiar.

Frank glanced at Bill to get a sense of his old man's feelings about the stranger, and found the holsters of those beautiful ivory-handled pistols clipped. Bill didn't believe they were in danger here, or the clips would have been off; it made for a faster draw. Not that Bill shot as much these days—his eyesight wasn't the greatest anymore—but the clips worked as a secret code between father and son.

"Frank, this is Jack McCall," Bill said. "He claims he is a garou hunter."

"Woof hunter," Jack McCall said.

Woof hunter was a term lone vigilantes often used. Frank had a hard time taking them seriously.

"I was gonna hunt 'em by myself," Jack McCall boasted, "but then I heard y'all were comin' into town."

"Going to take who on?" Frank asked.

McCall ignored him. "Is your whole gang here?"

"Everyone but Charlie, but we can fill him in later. He's in charge of this outfit."

"But, I thought . . ." Jack pointed at Bill. "I thought you was in charge."

Jane took off her hat. "Bill's what you might call the face of the operation. Charlie's the head."

Frank nudged her. "Isn't the face part of the head?"

Jane shoved him back. "I think you've been sniffin' too much perfume, pretty boy."

"Are you two . . ." Jack McCall let his words trail off and grinned.

"Ew, no," Jane said, lurching away from Frank.

"You don't have to be so dramatic about it," Frank said. "Sorry, Mr. McCall. Please tell us about the"—he sighed—"woof."

"Well, I came into some information that the foreman at the old P and G factory is a super bad woof," said Jack McCall.

"That's interesting news," said Bill. "But I'm afraid I'm retired from garou hunting."

McCall gazed thoughtfully at Bill. "A woof hunter ain't never retired, is he?"

Bill didn't answer.

"Besides, this isn't some insignificant woof," added McCall. "This here's the Alpha."

The group went still. The general public was not aware of the existence of the Alpha. People were terrified enough by the thought of a regular werewolf, without adding a werewolf supervillain to the mix.

Jack McCall puffed out his chest. "Yeah, that's right. I'm in the know about the Alpha."

"How do you know that this man—this foreman at the P and G factory—is the Alpha?" Bill asked slowly.

McCall scratched at the back of his neck. "Well, I don't *know* know, exactly. I heard—through my various woof-hunter sources—that he's a leader in the Pack. A big boss. Like top tier. So I reckon he's probably the Alpha. And then I reckoned that if I'm gonna go up against the Alpha, maybe I need to bring along the best garou hunter in the world. That being you, Mr. Hickok, sir."

"I see. What's the man's name?" Bill asked.

"Mr. Badd. He's super bad."

"His name is Super Bad?" Frank asked. "What were his parents thinking?"

Jane snorted.

Jack McCall looked confused. "No, I'm just telling you how bad he is, but also, his name happens to be Badd, but spelled with two *d*'s." His face broke into a smile again.

Frank realized where he'd seen Jack McCall before—playing poker, in one of their previous towns. Possibly St. Louis? He didn't remember the place for sure, but he definitely remembered that smile, the constant show of teeth, and how he hadn't been able to tell whether Jack McCall was bluffing.

"Hmm," Bill mused. "I read something in the paper this morning about a series of strange disappearances at a factory. If it's the P and G, they could be missing because they've been turned."

Frank scoffed. "Who would turn a bunch of people in the same place? It would draw too much attention. The Alpha would know better than that."

Bill narrowed his eyes. "You'd think."

"We should go check it out," Jack McCall said.

Frank's pulse sped up. "But what about the show?"

"The show will go on as scheduled," Bill said. "We still have a few hours. Keep an eye out the window for Charlie. When he gets back, we'll investigate the factory."

While Bill continued asking Jack McCall questions—mostly about how he came by all this information—Frank leaned on the window frame and gazed outside. If this Mr. Badd fellow did turn out to be the Alpha, and they caught him tonight, that'd be it. Bill would retire. Frank would inherit the show.

Everything would change.

He spotted a blond girl down on the street in front of the general store, looking at her reflection in the glass. She was one of the girls from earlier—the one who *adored* a man with a dog—all prim and proper and pretty. She was pinching her cheeks when a stagecoach came by, splashing mud onto her fancy dress. She shrieked like she was mortally wounded, so loudly the shopkeeper rushed out to see what was the matter. The girl sobbed and gestured to her soiled dress. The shopkeeper put his arm around her and ushered her into the store.

Frank sighed. Maybe George had a point. None of these girls were right for him. But what girl would be? She'd have to be the type who didn't mind life on the road, and who didn't mind guns, and who got along with George. That seemed like a tall order.

He caught sight of Charlie coming up the front steps. "Dad," Frank said, interrupting whatever his father had been saying to Jack McCall. "Charlie's back."

"Good," Bill growled. "Get your things. We're going Alpha hunting."

THREE
Annie

Annie was a fairly regular young lady.

She loved her family, liked sewing pretty dresses, and wanted to build a good life for herself and those she cared for. But the way she went about those things was somewhat, ahem, not regular for a sixteen-year-old girl living in Darke County, Ohio, in 1876.

Back up a few days from the last two chapters and take this touching family moment for example:

Imagine a sprawling farm (deeply in debt, but still growing food—just not quite enough to get the family through winter), and a farmhouse (packed tight with siblings), and a mother and daughter working together in the kitchen, having what most folks would consider a pretty serious argument.

"I'm not getting married!" Annie glared at her mama, who was kneading bread on the table.

"Yes, you are!"

"No, I'm not!"

"Yes, you are!"

"You're not the boss of me!"

"I am so. I'm your mama."

Annie grimaced. Mama had a point there. But still, Annie's refusal stood.

"I'm not getting married." She shoved her hands back into the rabbit she'd hunted earlier and was cleaning now. "And you can't make me!"

"Don't talk back to me, young lady, and don't begin a sentence with a conjunction." Mama worked the dough harder and harder. The bread was going to end up a rock if she wasn't careful. "We all need to do what's best for the family, Phoebe Ann, and for you, that means getting married."

Annie finished quartering the rabbit, trying not to make a mess of the task simply because she was upset. These weren't Mama's words—well, some of them were. Mama had always been invested in her daughters' romantic attachments (or in Annie's case, the lack thereof), but lately, her mama's interest had turned into obsession.

"But you need me here," Annie insisted.

"I have Grandpap Shaw now," Mama said. "You know he loves to take care of things."

Oh, Annie knew her new stepfather liked to take care of things. Some might even go as far as to call it controlling. Those same people might even think it was weird that everyone—even

Mama—had to call him Grandpap Shaw, as though he were their grandfather. At age seventy-four, he was certainly old enough.

Annie clenched her teeth, caging her sharp retort. She didn't want to fight again.

It was just . . . Annie was supposed to be the one who took care of things. From the time that she was little more than a toddler her pa had brought her along when he went trapping and fishing. Annie was a fast learner and loved the outdoors, and after her pa had died in a sudden snowstorm ten years ago, Annie had been using those skills to keep her mother and siblings fed and clothed. And she'd been doing an excellent job of it.

"If I got married, I'd have to take care of my own family," Annie pointed out. She didn't intend to create her own family, but that was an argument for another day. "Then I wouldn't be able to help you at all. But with my game and the money Mr. Frost pays for what I send him—"

"All that shooting isn't feminine. Really, Phoebe Ann." Mama shook her head and continued kneading the dough. "You should be seeing about marrying that Mr. Frost, not selling him dead animals."

"Mama!" Annie turned around, horrified. "He's near forty years old! He's ancient"—(at this point, your faithful and likewise ancient narrators die inside)—"and he's already married."

Annie's mama bristled at the age comment (she'd recently married a man who was twenty-eight years older than her, after all), but then sighed and bustled out of the kitchen. Annie sighed, too.

She loved her family, she did, but no one—least of all Grandpap Shaw—seemed to understand how hard Annie worked to keep the farm. They still owed about a hundred dollars on it, and that wasn't going to change if Annie got married. What she needed was a job, a regular-paying, honest-to-goodness job, but there weren't many jobs for a girl with Annie's very particular set of skills.

"Annie!" Her sister Huldy skipped into the kitchen and laid a newspaper across the table. "You've gotta see this."

Annie washed her hands and hurried over to the paper. "A dog?" she asked, looking to the advertisement where Huldy was pointing. "I'm sorry, but you know we can't have one." Even thinking about dogs made her nose itch and her eyes water. She could almost feel a sneeze coming on.

"No!" Huldy moved her finger over a section. "I mean this one."

"Oh!" Annie sniffled in relief. "All right. Read it to me." Annie and her siblings might not make it to school every day—there wasn't usually enough time—but Annie liked to make sure they all practiced their numbers and letters, and the newspaper was one of the best textbooks they had.

"It says, '*Wild Bill's Wild West*: coming to Cincinnati at the Coliseum Theater! See the magnificent feats of Wild Bill Hickok, the legendary gunslinger, along with Frank Butler, the Pistol Prince, and Calamity Jane, the Heroine of the Plains.'"

A sharpshooting show! Starring Wild Bill! Annie had read everything she could get her hands on about Wild Bill Hickok.

Seeing his show would be a dream come true.

"What's all this?" Mama and Grandpap Shaw came in, followed by Sarah Ellen holding baby John, to find Annie and Huldy hunched over the paper.

Grandpap Shaw glanced at the advertisement. "Show business. Pah. It's one thing for a man to go out and shoot for his supper, but when he puts on a fancy hat and does it for entertainment? It's downright unseemly." He looked pointedly at Mama.

Mama nodded, quiet now that her new husband was here to do the talking for her. Annie felt a pang of yearning for the way life had been before. Sure, they'd been poor in material things but rich in other ways. There'd been late nights when Mama had taught Annie to sew by the fire, cozy hours spent making plans for what to plant in each field or how to get through the winter, laughing and joking and simply enjoying each other's company. But since the wedding, all that had changed.

Annie's jaw tightened. She picked up the newspaper and read the advertisement again. They wanted spectators, not another sharpshooter, but maybe . . .

"What are you thinking?" Huldy whispered. She always knew when Annie had something in mind.

"When I was out hunting today, I shot the cap off a mushroom from fifty paces. And I shot the fuzz off a caterpillar from twice as far."

Huldy nodded, her skinny face glowing with pride. "There's no trick you can't do, Annie. I bet you could outshoot that Pistol

Prince, no problem. You should join their show. Annie Mosey, the best sharpshooter in Ohio! All your shows would sell out."

The words stirred something inside Annie—a sense of adventure and importance she'd hardly allowed herself to acknowledge before. She really should be in the Wild West show, she thought. Why not?

"There will be no more talk of show business in this house!" Grandpap Shaw said. "If you want to help the farm, then you'll think about getting married, like your mama and I did."

Annie pressed her mouth into a line to trap her disagreement. People liked shows, and she *was* really—we mean *really*—good with a gun.

Mama moved to the counter to finish supper. "Sarah Ellen, set the table. Huldy, clear your newspaper away. And Phoebe Ann?"

Annie didn't suggest that she not start a sentence with a conjunction.

"Stop thinking about running off to join a show." She wrinkled her nose with utter distaste. "You can't get a man with a gun."

"I don't need a man, Mama. I have a gun."

"Quit your daydreaming right here," Grandpap Shaw said. "The show isn't even looking for help. They have a show. You'd only be in the way. No daughter of mine . . ."

But Annie had stopped paying attention three paragraphs ago. She was going to do it. She was going to join the show. She was going to make her fortune, and then they would never have to worry about money again.

She was already planning what to pack, how much game to leave with her family, and what she'd do if this didn't work out.

Wait, no. Scratch that. It *would* work out. Annie would *make* it work out. Because the only thing Annie didn't know how to do was take "no" for an answer.

Her plan was simple: take the train to Cincinnati, stay at the Bevis House, where she'd sent ahead word to Mr. Frost that she was coming, and go see the Wild West show for herself. After that, she'd know what they were lacking, and she'd figure out how to persuade the company what they were lacking was her.

Mr. Frost met her at the station. On the way back to his hotel he gave her a cursory tour of Cincinnati—enough to help her get her bearings. It was the biggest city she'd ever been to, but Annie had a knack for finding her way. Even as a child, on the run from the Wolves— Well, more about that later. Suffice to say, Annie was almost never lost.

The hotel was grand, lording its four stories over the corner of Court and Walnut Streets, and when Mr. Frost led her to a beautiful room on the topmost floor, she had to protest.

"This is too much!" A colorful rug covered the hardwood floor, the furniture was all solid oak and polished silver, and the bed was big enough for Annie and all three sisters. "I can't accept this." She couldn't *pay* for it.

"Nonsense, dear." Mr. Frost put her trunk down at the foot of the bed. "This is your first trip into the big city. Allow me to make it a memorable one."

Annie was so grateful she was at a loss for words.

"Now, I've acquired tickets for the show. We'll go this evening, at eight, if that's all right with you. And tomorrow, Mrs. Frost wants to take you to the local shops and give you a taste of city life. See if it's to your liking."

"That's very kind." Annie didn't have enough money to buy anything, but she would have fun looking. Well, maybe if she skipped a meal or two, she could buy Huldy some paints, or Sarah Ellen some fabric. And if she got the job—no, *when* she got the job—she'd be able to buy something nice for herself, too.

"I'll leave you to unpack. Come downstairs when you're ready for supper." Mr. Frost left the room, whistling.

Annie grinned and got to work putting her belongings away. Then she came to the gun case that held her father's old Kentucky long rifle.

Annie had taught herself to shoot at only eight years old. When she'd loaded and aimed out the window, the force of the blast had knocked her back and across the room. But she'd killed the squirrel she'd been aiming for, and that was what they'd eaten for supper that night.

She'd only gotten better from there.

She opened the case just to look inside. This was her ticket to a better life. This was the way she'd ensure her family's survival. This was the way she'd convince her mother of her ability to provide for herself—without a man.

Carefully, she closed the case and locked it, then laid a hand on the wood.

(Hey. It's us—your narrators. You may have noticed that our characters have what some might call an unhealthy obsession with guns. This was a symptom of the time—guns were becoming more easily available in America after the Civil War, shifting from the basic rifles that people used to hunt and defend themselves to flashier revolvers and six-shooters, a situation that, coupled with rampant alcohol use, lent itself to more of a gun-happy "shoot 'em up" mentality and a rise in death-by-gun violence. The problem was becoming so bad that many towns were demanding that people turn in their guns to the sheriff before they were allowed to enter. Well, thank goodness we've got that problem solved now. Right?

Oh. Wait.

Anyway, we, your faithful narrators, would like to reassure you that no real live humans were harmed by firearms in the writing of this book.)

After a while, Annie went downstairs for supper, but she wasn't halfway through the lobby when she spotted three very impressive—very recognizable—figures. (And two others standing with them.)

The first was Wild Bill Hickok, and she knew him because of the broad black hat, long hair, and signature coat he wore. He and another man were in discussion with Mr. Frost, asking about transportation. A third man—a scrawnier fellow with a permanent smile—stood apart from them but watched them closely.

Then there were the other two: Frank Butler and Calamity Jane. They were both tall and carried weapons, but the similarities ended there. Where Mr. Butler was put together—wearing a fine jacket and polished black boots—Miss Calamity looked intense with her mud-spattered buckskins and unkempt black hair. They made quite the interesting pair, Annie thought, gently elbowing each other, bickering in the same sort of friendly way Annie and her sisters did.

Annie stood there, starstruck. She'd come to see these people, and here they were. Mr. Frost hadn't said a word about them staying at his hotel. What were the odds?

"Your carriage will be around right away, Mr. Hickok," said Mr. Frost. He was smiling coolly, as though he met celebrities such as Wild Bill Hickok every day. And with this fancy hotel, maybe he did.

When Mr. Frost disappeared into another room, the group huddled together. "This is the best lead we've had in weeks," said the man who wasn't Mr. Hickok. "We absolutely cannot let Mr. Badd get away tonight."

Mr. Badd? That was a little on the nose, wasn't it?

Never mind the man's name. They didn't sound like they were talking about show business. But then what . . . ?

Everyone knew Wild Bill had stopped hunting garou years ago, so this couldn't be about that. Unless it was. Regardless, their tones suggested their imminent trip was important—maybe *adventure* important—and if Annie wanted to join the show, she needed to do what anyone else would do.

Follow them.

Quickly, she ran back upstairs, unlocked her gun case, and grabbed a pouch of ammunition. The group had already left when she returned to the lobby, but she was out the door in time to see them all climb into a carriage.

She looped her gun strap over her chest and kept low (which wasn't hard, given that she was five-foot-nothin'), and the instant the carriage jerked into motion, she jumped onto the back, keeping just out of view of their window.

Mama would be horrified. Grandpap Shaw would throw a fit. But this, Annie knew, was what she was meant to do. It was absolutely the most exciting moment of her life.

FOUR

"Nothing's happening," Jane complained. She'd been crammed in the carriage with Bill, Charlie, and Jack McCall for nearly an hour, watching the comings and goings at the aforementioned P & G factory down by the river. Only there hadn't been any comings or goings to speak of—no Mr. Badds skulking, no rogue garou creeping about. The place had been silent and still.

Jane was getting antsy. Her butt had fallen asleep some time ago, and Jack McCall was not the sweetest-smelling fellow to be pressed up against. That, and he would not stop smiling at her, which made her feel, well, antsy.

"Maybe if we got out for a spell, looked around?" she suggested.

"We could always come back tomorrow." Frank drew his

pocket watch out of his vest and checked the time. The show wasn't a cover for Frank—it was his life, his joy, his "raison debt," he called it. He'd been downright reluctant about hunting the Alpha lately.

"We should wait," barked Charlie. "Something will happen."

Across from Jane, Bill closed his eyes. Frank fidgeted with the watch. Jane's knee started to bounce up and down.

Jack McCall turned to look at her. "That sure is a nice shirt you got on."

She frowned. "You could get one near enough like it at any general store."

He smiled. Again. "No, I'm saying, I like it. On you."

"Oh." What was it with people complimenting her lately? She decided to change the subject. "Do you, uh, come here often?"

Jack scratched his head. "I ain't never been to Ohio before."

"But you're a garou hunter," she said. "So this kind of situation must be familiar."

He coughed and glanced out the window at the darkened factory. "Right. I hunt the woofs. That is what I do. Every day. Yep."

"And is this how you do it?" she asked. "You sit and wait for something to happen?"

He shook his head. "Most woof hunters just run into a place with their guns and start shooting at anything hairy. So that's how I do. Yep."

"But that's not how *we* do," Charlie said pointedly.

"Yeah, but it seems like we are not *doing* anything," Jane replied.

"Oh, but we are," Charlie argued. "I like to call this a 'stake-out.'" (This, dear reader, was the very first use of the term *stakeout*, but our heroes did not properly appreciate its novelty.) "You lay low, watch and listen, and eventually something will turn up. You have to be patient, is all."

"I like steak," said Jack wistfully.

Frank sighed and glanced at his watch again. Bill made a wheezy sound suspiciously like a snore. Charlie rubbed at his eyes. Outside, the street was still uninhabited. The factory remained dark. And nothing happened.

"I also like your hat," said Jack.

"That's it," Jane announced. "I gotta go."

Bill's eyes opened. "You have someplace better to be, Jane?"

"Yeah. I mean, no, but I gotta *go*, if you catch what I'm saying."

They all caught what she was saying.

"I told you to go before we left," Charlie admonished.

"I didn't have to then, and besides, we were all so busy 'gearing up for the garou hunt' that I forgot."

"Well, hold it," Charlie advised.

"I've been holding it. I can't hold it no more." With that, Jane exited the carriage.

The air outside was better. She looked up and down the street. At first, she thought she heard a rustling noise from behind the carriage, but when she looked there was nothing there. (Don't worry about Annie, reader. She had crawled underneath the carriage to avoid detection, and that was getting her dress dirty, which miffed her, but otherwise she was fine.)

Jane started walking toward the factory. Behind her, Bill, Charlie, Frank, and Jack popped out of the carriage like a bunch of circus clowns and followed her as she strode right up to the building. She tugged on the doors, but they were locked, so she headed around the side.

"Jane, stop!" Charlie hissed. "What do you think you're doing?"

"Looking for a place to water my daisies." She could see a smaller building in the background. Perhaps, with luck, an outhouse.

"Jane, I mean it!" Charlie whisper-yelled. "Get back here!"

She kept walking.

"Jane," came the calm voice of Wild Bill. "Jane, please wait for the rest of us."

She slowed. Stopped. Swore. "But I really have to *go*."

Then she noticed something in the dirt at her feet.

A footprint.

Or, we should say, a paw print. A set of paw prints, in fact. Jane dropped into a squat to get a better look.

"Oh come on, Jane," she heard from Frank. "No one wants to see that."

She waved him over. "No, silly. Look here. A clue."

The rest of the group hurried over and circled around.

"They're wolf prints," Jane said. "Big ones. Much bigger than your average wolf." She stood and pushed Frank out of her way to follow the tracks for a few paces. "And they come from a beast that walks upright, on two feet, not four."

"So it's a garou," Frank said flatly.

Jane, being the group's official tracker, continued to follow the tracks, which led directly to the small building she'd spotted earlier behind the factory. Sadly, it was not an outhouse. It was some kind of guard shack or foreman's hut, a boxy room with a table, a stool, and a window looking toward the main facility. But inside were some other interesting clues, like: a half-eaten leg of raw lamb. "Clearly torn at with sharp, pointed teeth," observed Jane.

"So, a garou," said Frank.

Charlie shushed him. "Let her work."

Jane moved on to the next clue: A copy of Ned Buntline's latest book, *Fearsome Garou and Where to Find Them*. "Look, a picture of a wolf on the cover," observed Jane.

"So, an introspective garou," said Frank.

Jane swept a hand over the little table and came away with— "Aha! Fur!" Jane rubbed her fingers together, sending the fur floating back onto the table.

Someone in the group sneezed lightly.

"Bless you," said Jane.

"I don't want to jump the gun, here, but I think we may be tracking a garou," said Frank.

"I think you may be right," agreed Bill.

"It's a woof, sure enough," said Jack McCall.

Frank sighed. "Where did this particular—I think we can all agree—*garou* go?"

Jane went back outside and picked up the tracks (which were quite clearly pressed into the dirt) leading straight from the shack to a back door to the factory. "It went this way," she said, and everyone shuffled after her.

The second door was miraculously unlocked. The group slipped into the building. It was still light outside, the sun sinking behind the row of buildings, but inside it was dark. There wasn't much to see anyway, except a bunch of wooden crates and boxes stacked up here and there, three enormous metal vats in the center of the room, and some complicated-looking machinery. At this point, Frank (seeing as he had the sharpest eyesight but mostly because he was in a hurry) took the lead. He navigated them smoothly through the maze of boxes and machines to two sets of stairs—one that went up, and one that descended into total darkness. Jane shivered. She'd never been too fond of the dark.

"Anybody think to bring—I don't know—a lantern?" Frank asked.

In answer, Bill removed the lid from the nearest box and pulled out a candle.

This was a candle factory, it turned out.

"Well, that's handy," said Jane as Bill distributed a few candles among the group and lit them with the matches he kept for his pipe. Then they turned again to the stairs.

"I vote we go up," said Frank. "They'll have the business

offices upstairs, I'm betting, and if this Mr. Badd fellow is the manager, that's where we're likely to find him."

The stairs still looked spooky to Jane. "Yeah, let's go up," she agreed.

Bill turned his face toward the stairwell and frowned. "No," he said. "We're going down."

FIVE
Frank

Downstairs they found a large metal cage in a back room, and in that cage were the missing factory workers. From the looks of it, they were all suffering from an infection. They each had a bandage somewhere that covered a nasty bite wound. Many of them were sweating and feverish, some even delirious, rambling on about the moon. Their eyes didn't look right: the pupils were an odd shape. A few of the people were sprouting hair in places they shouldn't.

At the sight of the whole gang coming downstairs, they cowered toward the back of the cage.

Frank swallowed hard. "Who would do this? I understand about accidental bites, but this . . ."

Someone in the group sneezed again.

"Bless you," said Jane.

"We need to get them out of here," said Bill.

Jane tugged at the door of the cage, but it didn't open. "Where's the key?"

"Mr. Badd had it," whispered a young man with eyebrows that had grown so furry they almost obscured his eyes. He couldn't have been more than fifteen or sixteen. "He's probably gone home for the night, but he might keep the key in his office. Upstairs."

"Told you so," said Frank. "Upstairs. Let's go."

"Wait. We should gather more evidence," said Charlie.

"We could split up," Jack McCall suggested.

Bill smoothed down his mustache. "Yes. We would cover more ground that way."

"We don't need to cover ground," Frank said. "We need to find the key, which could be in Mr. Badd's office right now. Where we might even find Mr. Badd himself."

"It's not enough to simply find Mr. Badd," argued Charlie. "We have to have grounds to arrest him. We can't simply march up to him and say, 'We heard you're bad, so you're under arrest.'"

Frank turned to the young man with the eyebrows. "Who bit you?"

"I'm not sure. It was a garou."

"Well, who locked you up in this cage?"

"Mr. Badd."

"So now we've established that Mr. Badd is bad," said Frank. "Let's arrest him."

"But why did he do these things?" asked Charlie. "What's his motive?"

"Uh, because he's bad?" ventured Jane.

"Because he's high up in the ranks of the Pack. Possibly even the Alpha." Frank swiveled to look at Jack McCall. "Isn't that what you told us?"

Jack nodded vigorously. "Yep. That is what I said. Yep."

"So why does the Alpha want to bite a bunch of random factory workers? It's not like these people volunteered to join," said Charlie.

"I don't rightly know," mumbled Jack McCall.

"Charlie's right. We need more information," Bill decided.

"Couldn't we get that after we arrest Mr. Badd?" Frank checked his watch. "Like, tomorrow morning, perhaps?"

"We could split up," Jack McCall said again. "One group could go look for the key in the office. And the other could poke around down here."

"That's a terrible idea," exclaimed Frank. (As your narrators, we're completely with Frank on this. In spooky places, never, *ever* split up. But our heroes had never seen a horror movie, so what happened was:)

"Yes. We'll split up," Charlie decided.

Jack McCall smiled toothily at Jane. "I'll go with you."

"Nah, me and Frank will go upstairs," Jane said quickly. "Seeing as how I'm the best tracker and Frank's the best looker."

"You mean best-looking," Frank said.

Jane punched his arm. "We'll search the office for the key. You three can stay here and talk to the workers. Look for more evidence."

"All right, you two go," said Bill. "And if you happen upon Mr. Badd up there, don't engage with him. Just hurry back."

And that's how Frank and Jane ended up on the second floor a few minutes later.

"There's got to be a place to go," Jane muttered.

"We're going to look for the key," Frank reminded her. "In the office."

"No, I mean, *go*."

"Oh." Frank glanced around. He had a prickly feeling he was being watched. "Still?"

"Of course, still!"

"You can't hold it?"

"I've been holding it!"

Right then, they heard voices from up ahead. They were coming from behind a cloudy glass door. An office, clearly. The name on the door was *Mr. Thaddeus Badd, Manager*, and by the sound of the voices, Mr. Badd was in there now.

Frank's heart was beating fast. What if this was it? The Alpha, at long last.

They crept toward the door, listening. Which was easy, because the folks inside were shouting.

"You're a fool!" cried a low voice, a man's voice.

"I'm sorry," pleaded an even deeper voice. "I was only doing what you said, and you said to bite as many as I could."

"Not all from one place, you idiot! And not from the factory! You were supposed to be discreet." As he moved closer to the door,

Frank could see that the man wore a tall top hat.

"You didn't tell me to be discreet," said the second voice. "I was only trying to do what I was told! I'll bite people away from here next time. I'll go to the other side of town."

"You won't bite anyone else," directed the top hat man. "You'll take the ones you've already infected to the train one or two at a time. There will be someone there to accompany them, and someone to pick them up on the other end and transport them the rest of the way."

"It'll cost," said the deeper voice. "I don't have much money."

"You'll be provided with the money for their fare, of course. But what's more, if you don't screw this up, maybe the Alpha will decide to let you live."

Frank and Jane exchanged glances. If they were talking about the Alpha, then neither of these men were the Pack's leader. Jack McCall had been wrong. What a shock.

Still, Mr. Badd sounded like he might be important, so they kept listening.

"The Alpha knows?" came the second voice fearfully.

"There was a newspaper story!" yelled the top hat man. "I'd be surprised if the Alpha hasn't already sent someone to take care of the situation. And by that I mean, to take care of you! I would dispatch you myself, but that would draw even more attention."

"I'm sorry!" whimpered the second voice miserably. "Please tell the Alpha I'll do better."

"How many do we have?" asked the top hat man.

"Fourteen. Three or four should be turning any day now."

"Good. Send the first along on Tuesday."

"Yes, sir," said the deep voice. "Thank you, sir."

Now, as the two men had been speaking, Jane and Frank had also been having a conversation, a silent one, communicated through looks and gestures. It had gone something like this:

Jane: Should we bust in on them now?

Frank: No. NO. I mean it. No.

Jane: I think we should bust in on them now. Time's a wastin'. Remember the show?

Frank: I know, I know. But let's keep listening.

Jane: Fine.

Frank and Jane: (listening)

Voices: Something about the Alpha. Something about Tuesday. "Thank you, sir."

Jane (lifting her pistol): Their conversation appears to be over. Now *can we bust in on them?*

Frank (also pulling out his pistol): Okay. You cover one, and I'll take the other.

Jane: OKAY! LET'S DO THIS!

Frank (grabbing Jane's shoulder): Wait. We have to take them alive. We're going to arrest them, remember. Not shoot them.

Jane: Okay, fine! LET'S DO THIS.

Frank: Okay. On my count. One. Two—

But before he could get to three there was a huge crash from somewhere below them, big enough to make the floor shudder.

Something had obviously gone awry with Bill, Charlie, and Jack McCall.

"What was that?" one of the voices from inside the office said.

Before Jane and Frank could get out of the way, the door opened, and the biggest, burliest man Frank had ever seen came bursting out. He plowed right over our heroes, knocking them flat.

"Who are you?" the big man demanded as they all scrambled to their feet.

"Uh, we were passing through, and I was wondering if I could use your facilities," said Jane. "I have to go. If you'll point me in the right direction . . ."

"What? You need a bathroom?" The man's gaze fell on their guns. He scowled.

"Don't move," said Frank. "You're under arrest."

"Kill them," came a cold voice from inside the office.

Then everything happened fast. The big man loomed over them. The other man slipped out of the office, still wearing the top hat. That was Mr. Badd, Frank was sure of it, but he didn't get a look at the man's face. Their much-larger problem was the big guy, who was stooping to remove his shoes. Apparently he was preparing himself to (gulp) kill them.

"I said, don't move," said Frank, but the man pulled his shirt over his head and tossed it to the floor. He seemed to grow impossibly bigger, taller, wider. Even his head was growing: his face elongated, his nose and mouth changed shape before their eyes.

Hair appeared all over his face. His fingers became claws. His legs snapped backward with a cracking sound and became haunches, like a dog's, and his pants tore away and dropped to the floor. His eyes glowed yellow in the dim light.

"So, it's a garou," Jane concluded grimly.

The beast sprang at them, all glinting teeth and claws. Jane raised her pistol and pulled the trigger, but her gun misfired. She threw herself to one side, out of the way.

It was up to Frank now. He took a deep breath, his finger tightening on the trigger. The beast leapt again, this time at him. No time to think. A shot rang out, and the garou howled, then collapsed to the floor in a hairy pile.

"Wow, Frank," Jane panted, scrambling to her feet. "Good shot! I know we weren't supposed to shoot them, but I think you were justified, seeing as how it was about to kill us."

Frank frowned and lowered his gun. "It wasn't me who— I don't think— Did I?"

"You killed it," Jane said softly.

He stared at his gun. Frank had never killed a garou before. Usually it was his dad or Charlie who handled that kind of thing. He had never really killed anything before. He typically just provided the backup and witty banter.

"He was bad," Jane said. "You didn't have a choice."

"Badd," Frank murmured. Then he remembered. "Mr. Badd! He's getting away!"

SIX
Annie

At that moment, Annie was perched on a catwalk above Calamity Jane and Frank Butler, staring at her rifle in much the same way that Mr. Butler had been contemplating his pistol, because here's what you've probably already figured out: it wasn't Mr. Butler who shot the garou, but Annie.

Unlike Mr. Butler, Annie had killed lots of things before . . . but never like this.

Before, when Annie had taken the life of a rabbit or squirrel or even a deer, she'd stopped and knelt next to the body, and thanked it for supplying her family with another meal, or a few dollars to help keep their farm running. She'd always been careful—so careful—to shoot to kill instantly, so that the creature felt no pain.

But this was different. It *felt* different, and she couldn't stop looking at her gun, at her hands, and the way everything trembled.

If she hadn't shot the beast, it would have eaten up Calamity Jane and Frank Butler. There was no question, not with the way it had lunged at them with its teeth snapping. Even Mr. Butler had seemed ready to shoot it, despite claiming he wanted to arrest it. Annie just happened to be faster, and so she'd killed it.

Her hands were still shaking.

There'd been a *garou*. Right. There. (It was still there, but now it wasn't moving.) Sweat trickled down Annie's face and neck, even though all her limbs felt cold and numb with shock.

Annie took several long, slow breaths as, below, Mr. Butler recovered himself as well.

"He was bad," Jane said softly. "You didn't have a choice."

"Badd," Mr. Butler repeated. Then: "Mr. Badd! He's getting away!" He jumped up and ran after the top hat man, and Jane started to run in that direction too, but Mr. Butler called back, "Check on Charlie and Bill! Something happened down there!"

On the floor below, Calamity Jane hesitated—she clearly wanted to go with Mr. Butler—but then she went back to the stairs.

Annie slung her rifle strap over her chest and followed Jane.

Jane descended to the first floor, where hazy sunlight from the ceiling-level windows barely penetrated. It was a gloomy place, dominated by three huge vats, large wooden crates, and other unidentifiable pieces of machinery. The second floor, where Annie stood now, was a platform against the outer wall—positioned so that supervisors could overlook the main floor—with catwalks crisscrossing the space. Control pedestals stood watch over each of the vats, and as far as Annie could see, there wasn't much in the way of railing to keep people from falling over the sides.

"How dangerous," Annie muttered.

Below, Jane was coming off the stairs and heading around to the basement steps—slower now. "Charlie?" Wariness filled her voice as she peered down into the dark. "Bill?"

Annie crept toward the stairs Jane had taken, keeping an eye on the motionless garou body. It was still hard to believe she'd shot it. Plus, all those things she'd overheard—something about a train, about Tuesday, and a person called the Alpha that everyone was afraid of—crowded her mind. Wild Bill Hickok and his posse were definitely not finished hunting garou. No, they were just doing it in secret now.

"Hello?" Jane called ahead.

No one answered.

"I really have to go," Jane muttered, and Annie felt a pang of sympathy for the other girl. She was alone (or so she thought), in the dark, and this was a really bad time to have to relieve oneself. (Is there ever a good time? Not really. There are only inconvenient times.)

Shoes scraped the concrete as Jane paced, glancing around until her eyes landed on a bucket. "Aha!" she said, but then, from the basement steps, a hulking figure emerged behind her.

The garou was fast. With a terrifying growl, it tackled Jane to the ground before Annie could either call out or shoot it. And now, there was nothing to shoot, because the garou and Jane had rolled behind a vat and out of Annie's line of sight.

"Drat," she swore, and scrambled for the stairway, whipping

her gun from its place around her chest.

Partway to the stairs, her toe caught on something, and she staggered forward a few steps before looking back. The garou. The one she'd shot. It was still there, while down below, the growling and scuffling intensified.

Which meant that there were two garou.

Two.

Annie ran down the stairs, loading her gun as she went, but it really was much darker down here and she was going to be too late to help Jane unless she did something *now*.

At the bottom of the stairs, she found a large red button attached to the machines. The label—barely readable in the shadows—read "ON."

Annie slammed her palm against the button, and immediately a metallic clanging filled the room and the vat began to heat. A sour stench rolled through, like warm animal fat.

"Grr!" cried the garou, and a moment later, heavy (but human) footsteps ran away from the beast—toward Annie and the stairwell.

Annie ducked out of sight as Jane threw herself up the stairs—*thook thook thook*—and back onto the second floor.

Heart pounding, Annie hefted her rifle and crept around the heating vat.

The machinery clanked and clattered, and the stink of tallow filled the factory, but Annie kept her footfalls quiet as she moved through the gloom.

A low growl was her only warning: the garou ran toward

her. Annie swung her gun around as the beast brushed past. She sneezed and reeled back, gripping her gun like her life depended on it (it probably did), but the garou didn't go up the stairs after Jane. Instead, an exterior door opened, and dim light fell across the garou as it ran out, away from the banging machinery and Annie and her gun.

Was it . . . running away?

Well, maybe it had heard what Annie had done to the garou upstairs. It *should* be afraid.

It surely wouldn't be long before Mr. Hickok, Mr. Utter, and Mr. McCall came to investigate the noise of the machinery, so Annie was about to sit on a crate and wait in the shadows when something above caught her eye.

Jane was moving, creeping toward an open window. But that wasn't the alarming part. No, behind Jane, a garou—the one Annie had killed—was sitting up and shaking its head like it was waking up from the most confusing nap.

Wait, the one Annie had killed? That garou shouldn't be sitting up at all!

And worse yet, as the wolf shook his head, fur drifted down to the bottom floor. Annie couldn't see it, but her nose sure knew about it. Tiny wolf hairs tickled her nostrils and—

"*ACHOOO!*" Annie sneezed so hard her eyeballs hurt.

"Bless you!" Jane said from above, because some things were drilled into a person, and she literally could not stop herself even when silence was important.

Annie rubbed her nose and looked up to see the garou swing around to look at Jane.

Jane let out a yelp and scrambled down one of the catwalks stretching over a vat, but it was too late. The (not-so) dead garou lurched to its feet and lumbered after her.

Quickly, Jane ducked beneath a control pedestal, hiding, but the garou stomped across the second floor and turned down the catwalk, moving straight toward her. The metal swayed beneath its weight, and even over the noise of the machines, Annie could hear it huffing and puffing—closing in on Calamity Jane.

"Well, drat," Annie muttered. How dare that garou come back to life? She lifted her gun, but there wasn't a good angle. "Drat," she swore again.

The garou clomped closer and closer to the control pedestal where Jane was hiding.

Annie did the only thing she could think to do: she whistled.

It was a good, loud whistle, one that pierced even through the banging of the machinery. The garou's head swiveled in Annie's direction, and—wasting no time—Jane kicked out with both feet, knocking the beast back just far enough that it lost its balance on the platform.

With a roar, the garou fell backward, and since there were no rails for safety, it dropped directly into the bubbling vat below.

Annie blew out a long breath as she slumped against a crate. Both wolves were gone and—how about this—she'd saved the day.

SEVEN

"You're under arrest," said Bill to the wax-covered man in the vat. The garou had almost instantly reverted into his human form upon coming into contact with the hot tallow, which was a good thing, Jane thought, on account of all that hair. The wax had been hot enough to bind him, but not really burn him, which was also lucky.

"Jane!" Frank panted, running up to her and grabbing her by the shoulders. "Are you all right?"

"I'm fine," she said. "I will have you know that I have single-handedly captured this here garou." A great feat of derring-do if she'd ever heard it. Minus the hiding and the cowering, but those details didn't matter. What was important was that she—Jane, not Bill or Frank or Charlie—had saved the day.

"Well done, Jane," said Bill, and she beamed.

"How about the other guy?" she asked Frank. "The one in the top hat?"

Frank sighed. "I couldn't catch him."

Jane turned to the man in wax. "Where's your friend?"

"He's not my friend," said the man.

"Where's Mr. Badd?" she yelled.

"I'm Mr. Badd!" he yelled back.

"You're Mr. Badd. Well, then who was the man in the top hat?" she asked, but Mr. Badd refused to say.

"What about the Alpha?" Bill asked. "What can you tell us about him?"

Mr. Badd laughed. "You'll never find the Alpha. Never."

Jane was getting awful tired of these cagey garou minions.

"Where's Charlie?" Frank asked. "And Jack McCall?"

"Charlie and I got separated from Jack McCall," said Bill. "Then later a huge pile of pipes came down on us. I was able to spring back, but Charlie got caught in it. He's hurt pretty bad—busted his leg and some ribs, and he's probably concussed, but I think he'll pull through. I got him outside and flagged down someone to fetch a doctor."

"Poor Charlie!" exclaimed Jane.

"Mr. Badd, if you'd be so kind as to give us the key to the cage downstairs," Bill said to the man in the wax. "It will go better for you at this point if you cooperate."

"It's around my neck," said Mr. Badd. "But I can't move my arms."

Bill retrieved the key. Then he left Frank to wait with Mr. Badd for the police to arrive and went with Jane back down to the basement, where they unlocked the cage.

"As I'm sure you're aware," Bill said, before they let the prisoners go free. "You folks have all been bitten by a garou, which means that you will become one yourselves. You must be thinking, 'Now what?'" He laid a hand gently on the shoulder of the boy with the bushy eyebrows. "I'm here to tell you, your life can still go on, almost as usual, as long as you're willing to follow a few rules."

Jane leaned against the wall. This was a speech she'd heard Bill give many times before. She called it: "SO YOU'RE A WEREWOLF—NOW WHAT?"

A man in back raised his hand. He was missing his trigger finger. "There are rules to being a garou?"

Bill nodded solemnly. "Well, these are more like guidelines. It's not illegal to be a garou. You can't help that. But there are some restrictions that come with it, the first being, *Don't bite anybody*. Makes sense, right? If you bite someone, enough to draw blood, you will infect that person, and they, too, will become a garou. That *is* illegal. So watch your mouth."

"What about the full moon?" asked the boy with the eyebrows. "Is that when we'll change?"

"Yes. That's rule two, in fact. *Beware the moon*," Bill affirmed. "I think it best if you lock yourself up during that time, to be safe, and remember that the moon is full three consecutive nights every month, not just one night. But that's not the only time you can turn, which brings me to rule three: *Be mindful of your temper.* If you lose your cool, you could change and do something you regret. Any strong emotion—but fear and anger, mostly—can bring the wolf to the surface. It's best to go off by yourself for a while. Don't spend time around people until you get the wolfy side under control. And that's the last rule: *Protect the people you love.*"

The group appeared to take this all pretty well. Maybe it seemed better than the cage and the uncertain future they had faced before they'd been rescued.

Jack McCall came loping up. He was out of breath, and his clothes were a bit raggedy, as if he'd been in a tussle himself.

"What happened to you?" Jane asked.

He smiled through his panting. "I got lost, is all. I have a terrible sense of direction. And then I got, well, scared. Sorry."

Jane had a feeling that Jack McCall wasn't being completely honest about being a seasoned garou hunter. But who was she to judge? She nodded. "It's all right."

"What'd I miss?" he asked.

Later, still with twenty-seven minutes to go before the Wild West show, Jane sat down at the bar across the street from the Coliseum Theater and allowed herself to take a breath. She'd finally found a bathroom, thank the Lord. Charlie was with the doctor, who'd said that he was going to be fine, eventually, but out of commission for a while. Frank and Bill had gone back to the hotel to gussy up before the show. But Jane just wanted to sit. It had been some day, and her entire body was hurting. Getting through the show would be a chore.

She rubbed at a particularly sore spot on her left arm. Then she frowned and rolled the sleeve of her shirt up to the elbow. What she saw there should have shocked her, but she felt oddly numb as she gazed down at it.

A bite.

She could see the exact outlines of the garou's teeth. It didn't actually look that bad, considering what it was, but it was scabbing. Which meant the garou had drawn blood.

When did it happen? she wondered dazedly. It must have been when the garou jumped her from behind. She hadn't felt it then, but that was the only time she'd been close enough to get bit.

She rolled her sleeve back down and gestured to the barkeep.

"I'll have a whiskey," she murmured when he came over.

He put the glass in front of her and filled it with the amber liquid.

(Your narrators here. We'd like to pause to admit that, yes, we're talking about a seventeen-year-old drinking whiskey, but this wasn't strange or—*cough*—illegal for the time. People back then drank alcohol because bottled water didn't exist yet, and the only available water was likely to be contaminated with things you don't even want to know about. Jane herself had been drinking for pretty much as far back as she could remember. She'd decided a long time ago not to let whiskey get its hooks into her the way it did with some—*cough*, her parents—but tonight was turning out to be a drink-it-up sort of night.)

Jane lifted her glass and drank the whiskey all in a gulp, the firewater burning a trail from her throat to her stomach. She gasped and nodded at the barkeep. "Make that two."

EIGHT
Frank

"Jane," Frank called. "Jane!"

Jane ignored him. She was sitting at the bar turning an empty shot glass over and over in her hand. He didn't know how many shots she'd had. Frank frowned. Jane liked to boast that she could drink any man under the table, but the thing was, Frank had rarely seen her drunk. It was another one of the rules of their gang: no drinking before a show or during a garou hunt. They had to stay sharp.

"Jane," he said. "You know we have a show, right?"

She kept on contemplating her glass.

"Jane!" Frank said again, loudly.

She spun to glare at him. "What? What's so all-fired important that you have to keep yelling 'Jane! Jane!' at me? I can hear perfectly well, can't I?"

"Remember the show?" Frank asked. "Across the street? In ten minutes?"

She blinked a few times, then sighed. "Yeah, 'course I remember. I'm coming."

"Good." He watched her closely as she got up from the barstool and grabbed her hat. She wasn't drunk—maybe a little tipsy, was all. He held out his arm, and Jane took it. Her body was tight as a bowstring, and she was even trembling. Preshow jitters? But that wasn't like Jane either.

Something else was troubling her.

"Charlie's going to be all right, you know," Frank said, patting her hand.

"That's what people always say," she replied mournfully. "They say, 'Things will be all right, you'll see.' But then they're not."

"It's only a broken leg," Frank said. "He really is going to be fine."

"I know," she grumbled.

"Do you want coffee? Or a barrel of water?" he asked, thinking both the coffee and a dunking would do her good.

"I want a barrel of coffee," Jane said.

"I'll get you one."

"Nah," she said. "Don't worry about it."

"So you want coffee, but you don't want coffee. Help me keep up here."

She pushed out the door. "What does it even matter anymore?"

"What do you mean?" Frank asked. "Aren't you supposed to be Calamity Jane, not Melancholy Jane?"

"I'm thinking about changing my name. That has a ring. Hey." Jane nodded at the line of people wrapped around the building. "Is that for us?"

"It's a sold-out performance," Frank said with a grin.

"Good." Jane swallowed hard. "That's real good, Frank. You must be over the moon."

"Getting there." He hurried the both of them to the back entrance—away from all the people in line to buy tickets. George met them at the door, tongue flopping out the side of his mouth as he looked up at Frank and Jane.

Is Jane hurt? George whined. *She smells scared.* George, for all his dislike of females, was very protective of Jane.

Frank shrugged—better to answer silently when other people were around—and followed his dog as he led them to the backstage area.

"Are you sure you've got this?" he asked Jane.

Jane wiped a hand across her nose. "I was born to got this."

Wild Bill opened the show. Frank's father was the epitome of a showman, as always: tall and weathered-looking, with a neatly trimmed mustache and long, tidy curls. When he drew the ivory-handled pistols, the audience cheered so loud it made Frank's ears ring. Of course, Bill didn't shoot those pistols, on account of his failing vision and not wanting any unfortunate accidents, but he did regale the audience with the enthralling tale of a particular garou hunt.

"Way back when, I found myself tracking a small pack of rogue garou. They'd been tearing through the country and leaving a trail of bodies behind them."

The crowd booed.

Bill nodded understandingly. "Well, I tracked them all the way to a cabin."

Frank rolled the cabin set onto the stage, then vanished behind the curtains for the next part.

"It was said to have been occupied by a good pioneer family— a ma and pa and two strapping young sons—but by the time I arrived, the whole family was dead. I was too late."

"Horrible garou!" one man shouted.

Bill pulled his hat low, giving the family a beat of silence. Frank swallowed down the lump in his throat. That part was always hard to hear.

"Well, I knew what I had to do. I readied my weapons"—Bill drew his pistols and bent his knees—"and crept up on the cabin. I was hoping to catch them unawares, but they'd picked up a friend on the road. I'd thought there were four—and I saw four shapes moving inside the cabin—but there was a fifth standing watch."

Frank lowered the paper garou down into the makeshift tree. Everyone in the audience gasped.

Bill pulled himself straight up and squeezed a trigger. "*Bang!*" he shouted (because the guns weren't loaded), and Frank made the paper garou flutter to the floor. Half the audience jumped in their seats.

"I shot it, and the garou went down, but the noise alerted the others to my presence. All at once, I was surrounded."

Frank worked the pulleys until four more paper garou descended, and on the far side of the stage, Jane started growling. Frank growled, too.

The crowd collectively gasped, and a child shouted, "Watch out, Wild Bill!"

Bill held his guns out to his sides, bent in a ready position, and slowly turned a circle as the paper garou menaced him. "This was it," Bill said, his voice low and ominous. "Outnumbered four to one. I knew I was done for."

Several audience members shifted in their seats, and worried mutters rippled through to the back of the theater. Frank smiled, even as he kept up his part of the growling.

"But then," Bill said, and a hush fell across the room, "we all heard the sound."

Nothing happened—the theater was quiet.

Frank looked at George. "Come on, boy," he whispered.

Sorry, George thought. *I like this story.*

Everyone waited, and Bill looked like he was thinking about repeating the line.

"George, now," Frank hissed.

George whined, loud enough for everyone to hear, but it didn't sound quite like a normal dog whine. No, it sounded like a baby crying.

"Yes," Bill said, "I heard a baby cry, and so did those garou.

It was clear by the way they were lookin' that they'd had no idea there was a baby in that cabin—that those pioneers had not two children, but three—and that the ma and pa had hidden their baby when that gang of garou came. And as I looked around at the beasts surrounding me, I knew I had to find that child before they did."

The paper wolves fluttered as though they were running, and Bill was running too, and everyone in the audience leaned forward.

"It was a race for the child," Bill said as they all moved toward the cabin. "But the garou weren't going to let me get there first. One ran ahead, and I tried to keep up, but garou are faster and stronger than a mere human. I knew it would take all my skill, all my daring, to get there first—and then a garou jumped me."

There was a tussle, and the audience was one part tense breathing and one part nervous laughing (because it was a paper garou, after all) as Bill battled the garou and then: "*Bang!*" he cried, and Frank released the paper garou to drift to the floor.

"Just then, another garou came for me, and another!" Bill spun and shot—"*Bang, bang!*"—and both wolves dropped. "But the fourth wolf, the one that had gone ahead, was getting away. I ran with all my strength, following him into the cabin."

Behind Bill, Jane opened the cabin set to reveal a quaint room with a cold fireplace.

"We could both hear the baby crying, the garou and I."

Bill waited, and George didn't miss his cue this time; he made that baby-crying whine again.

Frank maneuvered the last paper garou to leap toward the

sound. Bill aimed, fired—"*Bang!*"—and the garou went down.

The audience cheered as Bill holstered his pistols and bent over the stage's trapdoor. Everything went quiet as he reached in and drew a small bundle.

"I got to the babe first," Bill said with just enough volume to carry into the audience. "And when I picked him up in my arms, he stopped crying because he knew he was safe—that I would never let anything happen to him again."

On cue, George stopped whining, and Bill glanced over at Frank. They shared a look, like they did every time Bill told this story, and then Bill turned back to the audience. "That child lives, even now."

The whole crowd whooped and cheered as Bill strode off the stage, the bundle still in his arms. Frank and Jane hurried to clear the cabin set—and close the trapdoor—and then it was Frank's turn. He felt his shoulders relax.

Frank was the best trick shot this side of the Mississippi, and by that, he meant either side of the Mississippi. This was where he shined. He shot a glass ball from across the stage, sighting using a mirror, with his back turned. He shot a bottle that was right next to him by ricocheting the bullet off a metal plate in the rafters of the theater. He had a woman from the audience pick a playing card— the ace of hearts—put it in a vise, and shot straight through the tiny red heart from ten yards away.

The crowd cheered wildly.

And then he introduced *the* Calamity Jane.

Jane stomped onto the stage, carrying her bullwhip over her shoulder and a pistol on her hip. "Evening!" she called. "I'm gonna do some tricks now. You want to see some tricks with the bullwhip?"

"Yeah!" cried the crowd.

Jane uncurled her whip and leveled a glare on the corked empty whiskey bottle George had placed earlier that day. "Have any of y'all seen a cork popped out of a bottle by a whip?"

"No!" came the shouts.

She drew her arm back, whipped it forward, quick as a lightning strike, and . . . the bottle clattered to the floor.

Frank's breath caught. Jane never messed up like this.

"Whoops." Her face went red. "I was just practicing that time. The sun was in my eyes." The crowd laughed. "Let's try that again, shall we?"

George trotted across the stage and replaced the bottle on the stool.

Jane's eyes trained on the bottle. She exhaled slowly. Then with one loud snap, she removed the cork from the bottle—*without breaking the bottle.*

The audience applauded enthusiastically, but Jane wasn't finished yet. She snapped her bullwhip to the right and to the left, and then she snapped it toward the bottle again. The bottle flew up to the rafters, and Jane stepped forward and caught it as it came down. Then she picked up the cork and placed it on her own hat. She flicked the bullwhip, and the cork went flying while her hat stayed in place.

Frank clapped right along with the audience.

Jane smiled and bowed. Her part was done. "Now for the fi-nal-ee," she said. "Mr. Frank Butler will shoot an apple off George's head!"

George went to one side of the stage and sat calmly while Jane steadied the apple. The audience leaned forward in anticipation.

Frank took aim with his rifle. He held George's gaze. There was nothing but trust in his dog's brown eyes.

Frank squeezed the trigger. A shot rang out across the theater. The apple flew into the air, a neat hole through its center. George yipped and grabbed the apple in his mouth. "Frank! Frank!" the crowd cried. "The Pistol Prince!"

Frank waited for George to bring the apple to him, as usual, but the dog hopped off the stage and darted into the crowd.

"George, come," Frank called. But instead George trotted over to a girl in the front row and deposited the apple at her feet.

She reached down and picked up the apple. "Why, thank you!"

Frank squinted through the lights to get a look at her. She wore her hair down, while most young ladies pinned theirs up, and her dress wasn't the fashionable type, those huge silk gowns with sweeping bustles in the back. This girl wore a plain dress made from a simple blue cotton, but it fit her slender form perfectly.

"Here, boy." Frank tried again. "Bring me the apple."

George stayed right where he was.

The girl rubbed the dog's head. "What a good boy!"

Oh gosh, she was asking to lose a limb, but George licked her hand and then . . . laid his head in her lap.

Frank glanced over at Jane. Her mouth was hanging open in astonishment. Bill, too, seemed baffled.

The girl looked up and caught Frank's eye again. "Your dog has excellent taste."

"Yes, he does," Frank replied, and bowed to her with an exaggerated flourish, as if George's behavior was meant to be part of the show, because he didn't know what else to do.

The audience clapped and clapped. Jane stepped to one side of him and Bill to the other for the curtain call. Frank took their hands, and the three of them gave a final bow.

"You up for poker after?" Bill asked as the cheering started to die down.

"Yes, sir," said Frank. The two of them played poker most nights after the show. It relaxed Bill, and always provided Frank with extra pocket money.

"Good, good," Bill said quietly. "I need to do some thinking on this business with the Alpha. Poker will help."

Poker always helped, Frank believed.

"You gotta schmooze with the ladies first, though," Jane reminded him. "They're already forming up a line to meet you." She made her voice higher pitched and tried to flutter her eyelashes. "Oh, Frank! You're so manly we can't stand it! Whatever shall we do?" He expected her to keep on ribbing him, but she seemed to remember something sorrowful, and her grin faded.

"What's the matter with you?" he asked.

"It's not like you to miss your mark, Jane," commented Bill.

"Nothing. I'm fine." She let go of their hands and stalked off the stage and out the side door.

Frank shrugged at Bill. George finally returned to Frank's side, wagging his tail and panting like nothing was out of the ordinary.

"What was all that about—with the girl in the blue dress?" Frank said out of the side of his mouth as he waved one final time to the audience.

Did you smell her? George thought.

"Of course not. When would I have had a chance to smell her?"

I like her, sighed George.

NINE
Annie

Obviously Annie was the girl in the blue dress. You expected that, didn't you? (Whoooo's a good reader?) After the show she waited outside by the door with all the other young women—or, rather, stood slightly apart from them while they fawned over Mr. Butler, requesting his autograph and asking when he planned to take them out for supper. One even went so far as to ask whether he had plans *tonight*.

It was all so scandalous. Not a single one of those girls had chaperones. Or it *should* have been scandalous, because this was a wild level of impropriety she was witnessing with her very own eyes, but instead, Annie felt something akin to a thrill. Such independence and forthrightness these women displayed. They simply asked for what they wanted. Which was, apparently, Mr. Butler.

"Do all the young ladies of Cincinnati travel about without chaperones?" Annie quietly asked Mr. Frost.

"It depends on the young lady," he replied.

"Hmm." Annie watched Mr. Butler sign autographs and flirt with every single young woman who approached him. He was handsome, that much was undeniable. He had an easy smile, and was good with a gun, but what stuck in Annie's mind was the way his dark eyes trained on his target with such an intense focus it'd made her catch her breath. With a stage presence like his, it wasn't hard to see why all those girls liked him. *Annie* kind of liked him.

Then she went back and erased that liking, because she was here for a job, not a man.

"Do you think now is the best time to ask him about the job?" Mr. Frost checked his pocket watch.

"Yes, I'm going to ask him now. Any minute." Annie continued studying Mr. Butler as he worked his way through the press of young women.

A warm body bumped against her right leg and rolled onto the ground, and when she looked down, she found George the Poodle resting on top of her feet, his tail thumping happily as he gazed back at her.

"Hello, handsome." Annie would have bent to pet him, but he had both her feet pinned, and she couldn't bear the thought of displacing him. She'd always been good with animals, even the ones that made her sneeze. "But you don't make me sneeze," she whispered. "You're a good boy."

George yipped and rolled over, giving her a chance to kneel and pet him properly.

"Well," said Mr. Butler as the crowd of young ladies finally dispersed. "If you don't mind—I mean, that's my dog there—I hate to break this up, but I have somewhere to be?"

Annie stood and smoothed her dress. "Why, Mr. Butler, it's nice to finally meet you, too." She smiled widely. "Where do you have to go?" Goodness, she was being almost as forward as those other ladies.

"Poker, but I can cancel." He offered a lopsided grin, and Annie's heart performed a small flip. Gosh, he was cute.

But it was probably part of his act, so she kept her expression neutral and cocked her head. "Why would you do that?"

"Oh." His grin faltered. "Did you just want an autograph?" He pulled out his pencil.

"No."

The grin fell a little further as he put his pencil away. "In that case, I'm afraid I'm not sure what I can do for you."

"You can give me a job."

"A job." He arced an eyebrow.

"Yes," she said. "You have one. I want one, too."

"You want a job." He looked ridiculously (and some might say adorably) confused.

"That's what I said. Try to keep up, Mr. Butler." She couldn't stop her smile.

He laughed. "All right. Can we start over? What did you say your name was?"

"I didn't. But I'm Miss Mosey, and this is Mr. Frost, my chaperone."

"Yes, Mr. Frost and I have met. We're staying at the Bevis House." The men shook hands anyway. "Well, Miss—"

"Mosey," Annie reminded him.

"Miss Mosey, I'm afraid I'm not in any position to hire people."

She nodded. "Naturally I asked Mr. Hickok first, but he told me that you were the manager for the show now. He said I should ask you."

Mr. Butler coughed. "We don't usually stay in one place for very long, and we're not looking for an assistant." He glanced between her and Mr. Frost again, as though he couldn't understand why a fancy hotel owner would be chaperoning someone like her. "But thank you for your interest, I suppose."

"I'm not an assistant," Annie said. "I'm a sharpshooter."

Mr. Butler studied her more closely, making her skin flush all over as he took in her dress and stockings and buckled shoes. "You don't look like a sharpshooter."

"What does a sharpshooter look like?"

He coughed. "Um, me, I suppose."

"And me." She grinned as George bumped against her leg again. "Really, the only thing one needs to *look* like a sharpshooter is a gun."

Mr. Butler seemed at a loss for words.

Annie sighed impatiently. "Truth be told, Mr. Butler, I came to Cincinnati to see your show and to make sure I really wanted to join."

"And have we passed muster?"

Annie shrugged. "I'll consider your offer." In truth, she'd very much enjoyed the show, and she'd found his sharpshooting skills quite impressive. It didn't hurt that they also went around having adventures in candle factories.

The corner of his mouth lifted like he was trying to suppress a smile. "Wait, did I offer?"

Annie waved that away like it would be merely a formality.

"So you want to join the show, now that you've seen it. Because you're a sharpshooter," Mr. Butler said.

"That's right."

"Have you ever even held a gun?"

"Yes, Mr. Butler, I have. How do you think I've fed my family?"

Mr. Butler looked down at his feet. "I really thought you might just want to have dinner with me," he said. "Because my dog likes you."

"Maybe I should have dinner with your dog."

It might have been Annie's imagination, but George seemed to sit up straighter.

Mr. Butler gave an amused snort. "I think I'm doing this all wrong."

"Yes," she agreed. "I think what you meant to say was, 'Why

yes, Miss Mosey, we do have a job opening for you.'"

"Nooo," he said slowly. "I don't think that's what I meant to say."

"You should know," she went on, "that I'm a better shot than you."

His eyebrows lifted. "Is that so?"

"That's so," she said. "I'll prove it if you allow a demonstration."

Something sparked in his eyes. She wondered if he was used to being challenged—if after every show there was some fool who blustered that he was a better shot than the Pistol Prince. "I'd love to," he said, "but I'm busy tonight."

"When will you be available?" she asked in her most professional tone.

"Um," Mr. Butler said eloquently. "I really must be going, Miss Mosey." With that he tipped his hat at her and hurried across the street toward the saloon, taking his cute (and nonallergenic) dog with him. He probably thought Annie wouldn't follow him there.

Annie's eyebrows squeezed together in consternation. First the theater, and then a saloon? Her mama would be shocked.

But her mama wasn't here.

Annie turned to Mr. Frost. "I'm going in after him."

"What?" Mr. Frost looked nervously at the saloon door. "Why? He said no."

"He said *um*," Annie reminded him. "Which isn't the same

thing as no. He will say yes, once he understands that he needs me for the show."

"Miss Mosey," Mr. Frost said, his tone all reasonable, "perhaps your family is right. Perhaps the Wild West show isn't the place for you."

Annie shot him a look, one that always scared her younger siblings into doing what they were told, but Mr. Frost wasn't Sarah Ellen or Huldy or John. He just smiled.

"I'm only asking you to think about it. The theater is no place for a lady."

That was exactly what Grandpap Shaw had said before Annie left, while Mama stood quietly in the background, her silence as good as agreement.

Well, they were wrong.

True, the theater *was* rather dangerous. Upon entering the Coliseum, Annie had noted all the gas lamps, the curtains, the flammable props—and the disturbing lack of safety precautions. For example, there were no fire curtains, or fire exits, or axe cases marked "In case of emergency, break glass." There wasn't even a clear path to the front doors, to help people safely exit the building. In fact, Annie had rather felt she was risking her life simply by walking in.

But there was only one thing that really made Annie nervous, and she hadn't seen any real garou at the show. All that was to say . . .

"The theater *is* a place for a lady, if a lady is inside it." Annie glared up at Mr. Frost.

Mr. Frost sighed.

"I'm going to be part of that show," she went on. "You'll see." She knew she could do it. She just needed someone to believe in her.

The hotel owner sighed again and glanced at the saloon, bright with lights and noisy with laughter and music. "Very well. What can I do to help?"

Annie grinned and judged the distance between here and the saloon. "It looks like you have about fifteen—maybe sixteen—steps to teach me how to play poker."

Jane
TEN

Having returned to the saloon again pretty much the moment the show was over, Jane made an unfortunate discovery: she was out of cash. She didn't have so much as two nickels to rub together.

"I'll do some dishes if you can spot me a drink," she informed the barkeep.

He shook his head, and his eyes judged her. "That's not how it works here, sir."

He didn't recognize her. Good. Charlie disapproved of public drunkenness. It was bad for business, he said. (It seemed to Jane that everything she liked to do was bad for business.) But Charlie wasn't here now, was he?

She drummed her palms on the bar. Dang it, Charlie. It was rude of him to go and get himself hurt, and not by a garou, either, but by a random bunch of falling pipes. That didn't seem right. She wondered if Charlie would have to retire now. Maybe they would all have to retire. That'd be fine by Jane. She figured this might be exactly the right time to quit garou hunting for good.

She bit her lip. Her stomach swam with a combination of panic and good old-fashioned guilt, because in some ways she was relieved that Charlie had been injured, seeing as that meant he wasn't here asking her questions about what had taken place at the candle factory. She touched the sore spot on her arm, wishing that it was really Charlie she felt sorry for right now, but she had her own problems to consider.

One bite-sized problem, anyway.

She could almost feel the infection setting in. Her chest felt tight, her skin, hot and itchy. Which made her really, really want a drink.

"I'd muck stalls," she offered to the barkeep. "Give me a task, and I'll do it. Just give me a shot to wet my whistle."

"I'm sorry, kid," said the barkeep. "I can't do that."

"Then what are you good for?" she asked, louder than she meant to.

The barkeep gestured to the burly man in the corner who served as the saloon's bouncer. But before it could come to that, a well-dressed gentleman slid into the seat beside her.

"I'll buy the lady a drink," he said.

"Lady?" repeated the barkeep.

"Lady." Jane slapped her knee. "Ha!"

The barkeep reluctantly poured her a shot. Jane lifted the glass and turned to her sudden benefactor to toast his generosity. And then she groaned.

"Oh, rocks," she grumbled. "I'm not in the mood to deal with any writers tonight."

The man smiled that snake-oil smile of his. "Good to see you again, Miss Calamity."

She threw back the whiskey. "Thanks for the drink, but I've got nothing to say to you, Mr. Buntline. Find another source for your fictions."

"Rumor has it that there was some excitement out at the old P and G factory earlier tonight," he drawled like he hadn't heard her. "Word is, one of your party is in a bad way. What happened?"

How could he even know about such things? Jane had always wondered. Ned Buntline was like a bad penny—turning up every place you didn't want or expect him.

"Nothing interesting," she said gruffly. "We were there, sure, because, uh, Bill wanted to get himself some high-quality candles. For the show, is all. And then Charlie had a little accident, but he'll be fine."

"I see," said Buntline.

Jane wiped at her nose. "There was a copy of your new book lying about, now that I think of it, but I pity the fool who was endeavoring to read it, seeing as it's a load of bull plop." (Or so she'd heard. Jane had never actually read it herself.)

"You were a great help to me during the writing of that book,"

Buntline reminded her, "One of my best sources, in fact."

She frowned at her empty glass. She vaguely remembered him interviewing her, some night last year when he'd offered her money and she'd been low on scratch. She could only imagine what she'd told him. Something, she assumed, about fearsome garou and where to find them.

"I'm writing a new book," he continued. "This one will be called *Wild Bill's Last Trail*."

Jane snorted. "Gosh dang. You make it sound like Bill's dead. He was alive and kicking when I saw him not an hour ago."

As if on cue, the doors of the saloon swung open, and in sauntered Bill, walking that all-shoulders walk he did. Right behind him was Frank, who was smiling slightly, as if he were laughing at some secret joke. The pair went straight to the poker table.

Buntline caught sight of them and hopped off his barstool, preparing to flee. It was no secret that Wild Bill Hickok did not get on well with writers, in general, and Ned Buntline, in particular.

"Never trust a writer," was one of Bill's most well-used sayings. (Which Jane probably should have heeded before.)

"I can pay handsomely, you know, for anything useful you could tell me," Buntline whispered to Jane. "And who knows? Perhaps one day I'll write a book-length feature on you."

Jane scoffed. "You mean a dime novel, where you make up half the stuff that happens."

"Oh, come now," Buntline wheedled. "I'd always prefer to write the truth. You could set the record straight about Wild Bill, as you know him so well."

She turned her thoughts to Bill. He'd always been kind to her. He, unlike Charlie, didn't seem to care about how much she cursed or spit, and he didn't pester her to dress as a woman, but still looked after her the way he might if she were his daughter. Her own father hadn't taken care of her nearly so well. At heart, under all the legend and gun bluster and dandiness of his attire, Wild Bill Hickok was a decent man.

"I suppose I know him well enough," she grunted to the pesky writer. "But first, buy me another drink."

Buntline nodded at the barkeep, who filled her glass again. She downed it. "What I know about Bill is none of your business." She grinned at her own trickery. "Now scurry off before he sees you."

Buntline slunk away. The bite on Jane's arm flared with pain. Her smile faded. In all the cases they'd been on, tracking rogue wolves, chasing the Pack, Bill had only ever given them one solid rule when it came to dealing with garou:

DON'T. GET. BIT.

She should tell him. She trusted him. But she didn't know if she could bear to see the disappointment on the face of this man she so respected. Maybe she could tell Frank, who she also trusted, and Frank could break it to Bill gentle-like. But then what would they do?

They'd send her away. There was no place for a garou in a group of garou hunters. Her stomach rolled at the thought of being on her own again, doing whatever she could to make do. Tears pricked at her eyes. She shook her head fiercely, as if answering some silent question.

No. She couldn't tell them.

But the truth would out. Once you were bit, there was no stopping it. There was no cure for the garou. At least she had some time—a week, perhaps even two—to decide what to do.

Another gentleman stepped up beside her at the bar.

"Hello, Jane," he said warmly. "I saw your show. Can I buy you a drink?"

She nodded. The barkeep sighed and poured her another shot. Jane lifted the glass again and turned to toast the stranger, but this one wasn't a stranger, either.

It was the girl she'd met in the street earlier today. Miss Harris.

She wasn't wearing a white dress this time. She was, in fact, decked out in men's attire—jacket, waistcoat, a pocket watch hanging from a chain, even a little brown mustache. The long pale curls were hidden under an expensive-looking hat. But she had the same glasses. The same nose. And her eyes were the same honeyed green.

It was definitely Miss Harris.

"Huh," Jane said. "I must be drunker than I thought."

"Hello," Miss Harris said in a lower, gruffer voice than she'd had on earlier. "I'm Edward Wheeler. I don't believe we've met."

"All right, I'll play," said Jane with a confused laugh, and for the second time that day, the two shook hands. "A pleasure to meet you, I guess. You saw the show? It wasn't my best performance, but—"

"You were marvelous. You have the best command of the

bullwhip of anyone I've ever seen," said Miss Harris/Mr. Wheeler. "Consider me impressed."

Jane's face filled with heat. It was unsettling to hear someone say such things, as if Jane's strangeness in this life was something to be celebrated. Her heart started thumping like a mandolin plunking a tune. Her palms got sweaty. But that could be the whiskey. Or the garou, stirring to life somewhere inside her.

This was not a time for her to be making new friends.

"Thank you for the drink, Miss—ter . . ." She downed the whiskey and wiped at her mouth. "I don't remember the name you just told me."

Miss Harris smiled. She made a convincing boy, Jane thought, but she smelled of lemons and laundry soap. "Wheeler. Edward Wheeler. Actually, I'm a writer," she confessed. "I was hoping that I might interview you, if you could spare a minute or two."

"Ah," said Jane dully. "Okay."

Miss Harris produced a small notebook and leaned toward her across the bar. "What happened tonight at P and G? It is true that there was a man arrested? A rogue garou? Is Wild Bill Hickok still a garou hunter, and if so, why?"

Jane felt like she was going to be sick. So that's what all the praise and flattery had been about, then. This person wanted something from her, the way everyone seemed to want something from her. A way to get to Bill.

She shook her head. The room spun a bit. "Look, miss—I mean, mister. You want to know about Bill, he's right over there."

She pointed to Bill at the poker table. "Ask him yourself."

"Oh." Miss Harris pushed her glasses up on her nose. "I only thought that you might be more amenable to talking to me. Seeing as how we're both—" She stopped herself and took a breath. "I recently wrote a story about the disappearance of several workers from the P and G factory, so of course I'm interested in following up."

"You wrote a story," Jane repeated.

"I'm a reporter," said the girl. "I'm actually starting to make a name for myself."

"Well then, no comment," Jane said.

"But—"

"I don't talk to liars," Jane added.

"A liar?" the girl repeated. "I don't know what you—"

"I don't pretend with people," Jane said. "I'm not trying to fool anyone into thinking I'm something I'm not."

Miss Harris bit her lip, which looked odd with the mustache. Where she'd seemed so calm and collected before, now she seemed befuddled. "Of course. I understand. Miss . . . Jane . . . I'm very sorry . . . I . . . When I'm . . . this way"—she gestured vaguely to the jacket and waistcoat—"I have a job to do. I mean to be the best writer I can be. So I have to compete with—" She waved her arms around at the room full of men. "And for them to take me seriously, I find I have to—"

She looked so distressed that Jane felt bad for calling her out.

"I'm sorry. I get it. I guess we all wear a disguise at times, don't we? But I've never been much good at it."

"Thank you," said Miss Harris, sounding relieved. "I want you to know, I wasn't pretending to like you. I do like you. I mean, I don't really know you. Not yet, anyway. But I like what I know."

"Oh," said Jane. She'd had a lot of whiskey at this point, so she couldn't be sure, but this felt like it was suddenly turning into a Moment.

She'd never really had a Moment, before.

Then a man plopped into the seat on the other side of her and cleared his throat. "Hey, Jane, I'd like to buy you a drink," he said.

Crud. It was Jack McCall.

"I been looking for you." He was smiling. Again. "That was one heck of a show you put on, there."

"Hey there, Jack," Jane said. "I was just sitting here talking to . . ."

"Edward Wheeler," the writer said. She was standing up, buttoning her coat. "I need to be going. It's late."

Jane stood up, too, with the thought of walking her out, but the floor tilted like the deck of a rolling ship. She put her hand on the bar and took a few deep breaths. "Good evening to you, miss," she said to Miss Harris. "I mean, sir."

"Good night," Miss Harris said.

Jane watched the girl walk away, disappearing with the same sort of suddenness with which she'd arrived. As she slipped out, another girl came in, this one wearing a blue dress and a determined expression. There sure were a lot of unexpected females in the bar tonight, Jane thought. The girl looked around, then lifted her chin and marched straight over to the poker table. She obviously wanted to talk to Frank, but she didn't seem like Frank's usual type.

Jane sighed, suddenly exhausted. The bite on her arm started to burn. She rubbed at it.

"Hey, are you okay?" asked Jack McCall.

"I don't rightly know," said Jane.

ELEVEN
Frank

To say Frank *liked* playing poker was to say a horse *liked* galloping through a big open field, or—to keep the metaphor on theme—a dog *liked* gnawing on bones.

For Frank, poker was a whetstone. It sharpened his mind and honed his instincts, and if he won a bit of extra cash . . . well, the folks who played against him should just get better at the game.

Right now, Frank was in a high-stakes hand against Heck Hotfinger. Frank's dad was sitting to his left, his back to the wall as he mulled over his own cards, and Jane was at the bar, next to Jack McCall. Frank tried to catch her eye, but she quickly looked away—back to the glass of whiskey in front of her. Whatever was troubling her, she didn't want to talk about it.

The saloon door swung open and in walked Miss Mosey—the

intriguing girl in the blue dress, followed closely by her chaperone, Mr. Frost. Frank didn't know what to make of this girl. At first, he'd thought her wit and confidence charming, and George was right—she smelled wonderful, a mix of soap and gunpowder and daisies. Even from across the room, the scent tantalized him. But she didn't fit neatly into any of the categories of people who usually sought him out. She was a girl, but not one of the flirtatious girls who found him before and after shows (the term *groupie* didn't exist yet, dear reader, but it certainly didn't apply to Annie). At no point in their conversation had she simpered or cooed. No, she'd said she was a better shot. That certainly wasn't the first time he'd been challenged that way, but usually it came from men with something to prove.

What was this girl trying to prove? Frank didn't know, but he was definitely interested in finding out.

The dealer cleared his throat. "Your turn, Butler." By the man's narrowed eyes, this wasn't the first time he'd said it.

Frank yanked his mind back to the game. "Check."

"Isn't that the girl from the theater?" Bill said. "The one who wants a job?"

"I don't know, I barely looked at her," Frank said as airily as possible.

"Hmm. I thought you got a pretty good look." The corner of Bill's mouth turned up.

"Yeah, well, your eyesight ain't what it used to be."

The dealer turned to Hotfinger. "Action's on you, Heck."

"Reckon I already knowed that," Heck grumbled. "Check."

"Check," Bill said.

Heck put his cards down on the table and pointed at Bill. "Hey, ain't you Wild Bill Hickok?"

"Does that change your cards?" Bill asked.

Heck had been at the table with Bill for a good ten minutes and he'd just now noticed he was sitting across from the most famous gunslinger in the country? Maybe Heck needed to worry about *his* eyesight.

Frank glanced at his cards. One more round of betting left Frank and Heck heads-up. They were the two big stacks at the table. The rest of the players had dropped out. Everyone was waiting for Heck to make a move.

Out of the corner of his eye, Frank saw Miss Mosey standing in the background, studying the game. When she noticed him noticing her, she flashed a smile and ventured closer to the table. "So, if you want to stay in, you have to ante," she said under her breath.

Frank bit his lip to keep from smiling. What was it about this girl?

Wait, no, he was supposed to be playing the game. "Woooo," he breathed, not loud enough for anyone else to hear. They'd laugh at him if they heard, but saying *wooo* always helped calm his nerves. (It was like Frank's own personal form of meditation, which henceforth we will refer to as "the Wooo.")

"All in," Heck said around his snaggletooth. Heck shoved his whole pile of chips into the pot.

All in. If Frank made this call and he was wrong, he would lose all his money. It didn't help that Miss Mosey was peering over his shoulder, studying the hand at play. Gosh, she smelled *so* darned good.

"I was thinking about our conversation earlier," she said suddenly.

Frank jumped.

Miss Mosey went on as though she hadn't noticed. "Perhaps your hesitation in hiring me might come from you doubting that I, a young lady of good standing, could be seriously interested in associating myself with show business, an occupation that can have, as I'm sure you're aware, a rather lurid reputation." She slipped into the empty seat beside him. "I can assure you that this isn't a problem. For my mother, maybe, but not me. In any case, I honestly believe—and I'm nothing if not honest, Mr. Butler, which you'll come to know about me—that I should join your posse. I'm a fast learner. For example, I just learned how to play poker as I was crossing the street. I may not be exactly good at it *yet*, but I know what I am good at, and I'm good at shooting."

The dealer cleared his throat. "See here, miss. It's not right to talk so much during a poker hand."

"Oh, I didn't know there were rules about that."

Frank couldn't help but smile. She did talk a lot, but he found he liked the sound of her voice. He turned his focus back to the cards. He had three sevens and a four and a two. Not the world's best hand. (That would be a royal flush.) But three sevens was a strong hand, beaten only by a straight or a flush. Or a full house. Or four of a kind.

Okay, so there were five types of hands that could beat him.

"I'm buying in," Miss Mosey announced.

Everyone at the table looked up from their cards.

Miss Mosey pulled some bills out of her pocketbook. Mr. Frost sat down beside her, and the dealer pushed Miss Mosey's chips toward her.

"Thank you," she said, as if someone at a dinner party had passed the potatoes. "Now, can you tell me what the different colors of chips mean?"

Frank tapped her chips. "These are ones. These are fives. They represent your money in the game."

Her mouth twisted into a small frown. "Why don't we use regular coins?"

"Because—" Well, Frank wasn't rightly sure. "Because we use chips. That's how the game is played. Why are you playing poker, anyway?"

"Because it's the only way to get your attention."

His heart picked up its pace. She wanted his attention.

For the *job*, he reminded himself.

"She's persistent, that one," Bill said. "I like that in a woman."

"Oh, I know," Frank said. "Your wife is maybe the most persistent woman I've ever met." She had to be, to nab someone like Wild Bill Hickok.

Miss Mosey's mouth dropped open. "Mr. Hickok, you're married?"

He gave a slow nod. "For a few months now."

"Congratulations." She turned to Frank. "But *I'm* the most persistent woman you've ever met."

Heck sighed loudly. "C'mon, Pistol Prince. Make your move. Even the women growed beards by now."

"Call," Frank said, not looking away from Miss Mosey.

"That's a call," the dealer said. "Turn 'em up, Heck."

Heck turned his cards up.

"Two pair," the dealer said.

Frank flipped his hand.

"Three of a kind. Mr. Butler wins."

"That's not fair!" Heck's nostrils flared and his cheeks darkened. "The girl was distracting me."

Miss Mosey frowned. "It wasn't my intention to distract you, sir."

"It don't matter what your intention was. You did distract me. I think that hand shouldn't count."

"It counts," Bill said evenly. "A good player doesn't let himself get distracted." He turned to Frank. "Does he, son?"

Heck scowled. "She distracted me on purpose. I say that's cheatin'."

Frank ignored him and gathered his chips. But he kept Heck's hands in his peripheral vision, because when you wanted to stay alive at the end of a poker game, it all came down to hands.

Specifically, the ability to see hands. So when Heck's right hand twitched and then disappeared under the table, there was only one thing to know, and it was something Frank had learned from his dad: you draw or you die.

Frank drew. We could go into more detail than those two words: how his left hand flew to his holster and his thumbnail released the leather clip and his fingers clenched around the grip while his thumb simultaneously cocked the hammer and his arm whipped the gun out and drew a bead on Heck, but an explanation of that length would not convey the speed with which Frank drew.

In fact, as we were writing this explanation, Frank had already shot the gun out of Heck's hand.

"I reckon you weren't meaning to draw your piece," Frank said.

Heck shook his head, in no position to argue.

"I thought so." Frank twirled his six-shooter around his finger and then holstered it. Out of the corner of his eye, he saw Bill slip one of his ivory-handled pistols back into its holster as well.

"That was an amazing draw," Miss Mosey exclaimed. "Was that fast? I thought that was fast."

Frank felt a warmth in his cheeks. "Wooo," he murmured.

The game started up again (sans Heck this time, as he'd slunk off), and Frank soon learned that Miss Mosey, for all her boasting, was just plain terrible at poker.

"Check," she said.

"You can't check. You have to call or fold," Frank said.

"Oh. What if I want to raise?"

Frank cocked his head. "That doesn't make sense. You were about to fold."

"Let her raise," Bill said, because he liked winning money.

Frank sat back in his chair. Clearly Miss Mosey was going to do whatever Miss Mosey was going to do.

She glanced at her cards again, blue eyes sparkling. "Do you have any twos?"

He stifled a smile. "This isn't Go Fish."

"Fine." She tossed in some chips. "I bet . . . that many."

"I call," Frank said.

Bill folded.

"You know what doesn't make sense?" Miss Mosey said as the rest of the players folded. "Why you won't take me seriously about giving me a job."

Frank pressed his lips together. It was time to be, ahem, frank with her. "I'm sorry, but you're a girl, and our *posse*"—if air quotes had been invented at this time, he would have used them—"is not the place for ladies. It's a hard life. We're always on the move."

"Calamity Jane's a lady," Miss Mosey said.

They both turned toward the bar, where Jane was in the middle of a belching contest with a large man. She was winning.

"Sure," Frank said. At least Jane looked like she was feeling better.

Miss Mosey threw her cards into the muck. (In other words, she folded.) "I am the best sharpshooter you've ever seen."

"That can't be true, because I see myself in the mirror every day."

She smiled sweetly. "Mr. Butler, I assure you that I'm good at anything I set my mind to."

"Says the girl who just mucked her cards after she raised," Frank said.

"Your poker rules don't mean anything to me. But it doesn't change the facts. I was born to be a sharpshooter."

"You should listen to her," said Mr. Frost. "That girl sitting next to you can shoot the wings off a fly. She's a local heroine."

Miss Mosey sat up straighter, if that were possible.

"That's great, but we've got a full posse right now," Frank said.

Miss Mosey studied her new hand, shifting her cards one by one as if she were alphabetizing them. Everyone at the table looked at her quizzically. But Frank smiled.

The dealer asked, "Cards?"

Without flinching, Miss Mosey said, "None. Thank you for asking."

The quizzical looks intensified.

"I mean," Miss Mosey said, "I don't think I need any."

Frank immediately bet, and everyone at the table called, including Miss Mosey, who raised. And when she did, she tightened the bow in her hair.

That was when Frank realized he could not read this girl.

He arched an eyebrow at her, but she held steady in her resolve.

He narrowed his eyes, and she had the nerve to wink.

"Uh . . . I fold?" Frank said, but it sounded like a question.

One by one, every other man at the table folded.

Miss Mosey turned up her cards. She had nothing.

"Beginner's luck," Bill said. "Even a blind squirrel gets a nut sometimes."

Frank couldn't believe it, the nerve.

"I'm a betting man." Mr. Frost leaned forward. "I'm willing to give one hundred dollars to the winner of a shooting match between the Pistol Prince and Miss Mosey."

Miss Mosey clapped, then seemed to think better about it and put her hands in her lap. "I could be interested in a competition," she said demurely.

A hundred dollars. (A quick note from your narrators: $100 is quite a bit of money now, but back in 1876, it was even more. When you consider inflation, $100 was equivalent to about $2,400.)

This girl might be smart and charming and pretty—some might even say distractingly so—but she had another think coming if she thought she could best Frank Butler. He never referred to himself in the third person, but this was a special occasion. His reputation was on the line. Plus, Frank simply could not ignore a hundred dollars.

"I'm in," he said, although it would be a shame to take Mr. Frost's money. It felt like taking advantage. Frank wasn't being conceited about that, either. He'd just never met anyone who could shoot as well as he could. Especially not a girl.

Jane wandered over. "Did I hear something about a bet?"

"I propose a match this Saturday," Mr. Frost said.

Bill whistled. "I'm beginning to think you might be eating that hundred dollars."

"Why would he eat a hunnerd dollars?" Jane asked.

Miss Mosey leaned toward him. She tapped the collar of his jacket. "Come Saturday, I will shoot the buttons off your shirt, and I'll be a hundred dollars richer. And if I win, I get to join your posse."

Frank glanced over at Bill, hoping for some help, but his dad gave him the old familiar "handle it yourself" look.

"No one actually agreed to those terms," Frank said, but Miss Mosey was already gone.

Bill coughed. "She's a spitfire, that one, and if it were only for the show, I'd say you should consider her. But as it is . . ."

"I know," Frank murmured, staring after her.

TWELVE
Annie

Annie liked winning.

She liked it a little too much, people might say, but as far as Annie was concerned, no one got anywhere without some kind of ambition. And see, this wasn't the first contest Annie had gotten herself into. She had a very long history—for a girl of sixteen years—of entering contests and winning. The local turkey shoot had finally asked her not to come back, on account of all that winning; they simply gave her the turkey every year and held the contest for second place, with her first place assumed.

But this contest was different. One. Hundred. Dollars. That was a whole lot of money, and when she sent the winnings to her family, along with a letter saying that she'd gotten the job (obviously she planned to win *and* get the job), Mama and Grandpap Shaw wouldn't be able to deny that she was worth more as a sharpshooter than a wife.

In the hotel Saturday morning, Annie dressed up special for the occasion: a pink gingham dress that fell just below her knees, her hair in a single braid down her back, the end tied off with a pink ribbon. She'd sewn the dress herself and was quite proud of the work. Some people might think it too girly, too *ladylike* for a sharpshooter, but Annie looked how she wanted to look.

When Mrs. Frost knocked on her door, Annie got her gun and followed the woman downstairs where Mr. Frost, Mr. Butler, and the rest of the Wild West company were getting ready to go to the fairgrounds.

"Good morning, George," Annie said, bending to pet the poodle's head. "A pleasure to see you, as always."

George grinned, his tongue lolling out as he looked at Mr. Butler, and Mr. Butler sighed and shook his head. He looked as handsome today as he had before, in a fine wool coat, shiny black boots up to his calves, and even a bow tie.

"I don't like my dog betting against me," he said.

Annie greeted everyone else, and then the entire party took the hotel carriages to the fairgrounds, where they came upon a huge crowd of people in high spirits, bakers selling slices of pie, and balloons of all colors. Excitement rumbled through the audience as the contestants started toward the stage.

Calamity Jane slapped Frank on the shoulder. "Don't get yourself beat by a girl now." She gave Annie a crooked smile. "My money's on you, miss. Good luck."

She was a strange sort of person, that Calamity Jane, but Annie rather liked her.

"Are you ready to meet your match, Mr. Butler?" Annie asked as they reached the side of the stage. (It was really just a tall platform big enough for people to stand on, but Annie preferred to think of it as a stage, because these people were about to get the show of a lifetime.)

"I think I'm ready to win a hundred dollars." Mr. Butler grinned, making butterflies swarm through Annie's stomach. He really did have a nice smile.

Stop, she ordered herself. *Stop noticing his nice smile.*

"Welcome, welcome!" A man in a top hat was making his way across the stage, waving at the crowd. "We'll get started once everyone settles down."

The crowd settled down.

The man reached the center of the stage. "I'm George W. C. Johnston, the mayor, for those of you who don't already know me. And now that we're all friends, I hope you'll remember to vote for me next November."

Annie sighed. Next November was more than a year away. If he was spending this much time campaigning, when was he actually politician-ing?

But the crowd cheered.

"In the meantime, I'm happy to welcome you to this event. Thanks to Mr. Frost at the Bevis House, we have a high-stakes sharpshooting competition, and the winner will receive one hundred dollars!"

The crowd went wild.

Annie stared at the mayor intently as he began to introduce Mr. Butler. Sure, lots of people wore top hats, even during the summer, but ever since the factory, she hadn't trusted that particular sort of headgear. Top hats, Annie was coming to believe, were the ultimate way to disguise bad behavior. After all, who suspected a man in a top hat?

But she was sure the mayor was a fine man. Hat notwithstanding.

"You all know this young man from *Wild Bill's Wild West*, performing this week at the Coliseum Theater," the mayor was saying. "Associate of Wild Bill Hickok—"

"And Calamity Jane!" called a voice that sounded suspiciously like Calamity Jane's.

"And Calamity Jane!" The mayor tipped his hat. "Allow me to introduce the Pistol Prince, Frank Butler!"

More cheering. And in the front row, a group of young women fanned themselves and gazed up at Mr. Butler as he walked onto the stage, George the Poodle at his heel.

"And challenging, we have Miss"—the mayor checked his notes—"Phoebe Ann Mosey, from Darke County."

A few people cheered, including the Frosts and a handful of folks who were clearly trying to be polite, but a large portion of the crowd stared at her like they'd never seen a girl with a gun.

Well, she'd show them.

"A coin toss, to see who goes first." Mayor Johnston fished a silver dollar out of his pocket and nodded to Annie as he flipped. "Call."

"Heads."

He caught the coin and slapped it on the back of his other hand. "Tails. Mr. Butler goes first. Now, please take your places."

Annie hated losing, even a coin toss.

Both contestants moved to opposite ends of the stage, and Annie stuffed down her nerves. In spite of all the contests she'd done, she'd never shot traps before, although she knew the basics: when she shouted *pull*, someone would fire a clay pigeon into the air, and she'd shoot it.

Mr. Butler wasted no time. He called, "Pull!" and shot the red clay pigeon that spiraled into the air.

Red clay dust scattered.

Everyone whooped and clapped, shouting Mr. Butler's name.

Then all eyes went to Annie.

"Very good, Mr. Butler." She grinned, knowing it would unsettle him. Then, with the unloaded rifle butt-down on the stage, she simply said, "Pull."

Everyone gasped, but Annie knew she had this. See, Annie had seen Mr. Butler shoot at the theater, and then again in the saloon that night. She knew what he could do. But he had no idea what *she* could do.

As the clay pigeon flew into the air, Annie loaded.

It was a simple process: just carefully measure black powder, pour it into the muzzle, add the greased patch, add the lead shot, shove them deep into the barrel with the ramrod, prime the touch hole with yet more gunpowder, cover the flash pan with the steel-faced frazzle, and bam. A shootable weapon.

Annie had the load, cock, and fire down to under twenty seconds.

Just as the clay pigeon reached its peak of flight and was starting to descend, Annie lifted her rifle and fired.

Only red dust fell.

An immense roar filled the shooting grounds, all shock and disbelief.

On the far side of the stage, Mr. Butler stared at her as though suddenly seeing her for the first time, all warm and appraising and somewhat overwhelmed.

Something shifted inside Annie, too. There, below the stage, was that gaggle of young ladies all trying for Mr. Butler's attention, but he was looking at *her* in a way he hadn't looked at any of them. Every part of her felt tingly . . . and then she reminded herself (in a very stern thought-voice) about why she'd come here, and getting a man—even one as handsome as Mr. Butler—to look at her like that (internal swooning!) was *not* the reason.

She was here for a job.

But that didn't mean she couldn't enjoy herself. She put on her sweetest smile. "Anything you can do, Mr. Butler," she said, "I can do better."

"No, you can't."

"Yes, I can."

He grinned, and when the crowd quieted down for his turn, he performed the same trick.

She did it twice more, but she wouldn't beat him with such simple stunts. She needed to escalate if she wanted to win. So for the next round, she turned her back to the audience and shot the target using only a mirror to sight.

But then so did Mr. Butler.

Then she shot without the mirror.

Mr. Butler did, too.

She escalated again, this time standing one-footed on a rail.

He did it, too.

She did a spin.

So did he.

Annie swore under her breath. "Well, drat."

From that point, it was Mr. Butler doing the escalating. First, he shot while jumping over his dog. Annie shot while jumping over a child who'd crawled onto the stage.

He shot with one hand.

Annie considered shooting with no hands, but quickly realized that wouldn't work without more preparation. So she shot with one hand.

They went back and forth, each round growing more and more ridiculous, until the twenty-fifth and final round. That was when Mr. Butler missed.

Stunned silence fell over the crowd.

Mr. Butler looked shocked, too. He stared at the sky where the clay pigeon had fallen without a piece of hot lead inside it. Then, he examined his gun like there must be something wrong.

Annie said, "Pull," and shot the final target without any showmanship whatsoever. No need to humiliate the man further.

You could have heard a pin drop in the moments before the mayor said, "The winner is Miss Phoebe Ann Mosey!"

The crowd exploded with cheers and screams and people calling Annie's name. A girl—a country girl—had beaten the famed Pistol Prince.

She went to the center of the stage. The mayor shook her hand, and Mr. Frost gave her the hundred-dollar bill. It was more money than she'd ever seen in her life.

"Thank you." She pocketed her prize and turned to Mr. Butler. "You're a fine shot, sir. It was an honor."

"The honor is mine, Miss Mosey. I'm not afraid to admit that I underestimated you." He smiled and shook her hand, holding on a tad too long. "I won't make that mistake again."

A thrill shot through Annie. She had to admit (only to you, dear reader) that she liked the way his hand felt around hers.

Mr. Butler glanced down at George, who was sitting between them. George gave Mr. Butler what *some* might call a meaningful look.

Annie, however, didn't notice, because she was busy noticing the way Frank ran his fingers through his hair.

"I know, I know, you like her." Mr. Butler looked up from George. "I'll never forgive myself if I don't say something now. And worse yet, George will never forgive me."

"Oh?" Annie couldn't stop the smile bubbling up. "Then you'd better say it."

Mr. Butler pressed his hand against his heart. "Miss Mosey, will you marry me?"

Annie stood there in shock. Had he been talking to her mother?

Around the crowd, the cheers for Annie's victory became cheers of encouragement. "Do it!" someone shouted. A few folks whistled.

Annie scoffed. Then she scoffed again for good measure. But there was a gleam in Mr. Butler's eye, and a playful turn to his mouth. She decided to go along—at least for now. "Why, Mr. Butler. It takes more than a shiny gun and a cute dog to impress me."

Mr. Butler's charming smile widened. "I understand. A lady such as yourself must keep her standards high. I hope I get the opportunity to prove my worth." With a flourish, he kissed her hand. Then he led her toward the back of the stage, where Mr. Hickok and Jane were climbing up the stairs. "We'll see about the show. It's not actually up to me."

"Mr. Hickok had his chance, but he sent me to you," Annie said. "Remember?"

Before Mr. Butler could respond—although Annie assumed he agreed—they reached Mr. Hickok and Calamity Jane.

Mr. Hickok stuck out a hand to shake hers. "That was some

fine shooting." He looked at her appraisingly. (Annie was, as we'd say today, freaking out a little inside.) "I didn't think I'd see the day where someone outshot our Frank here."

"Thank you," Annie said, forcing confidence into her voice. "I'm glad you noticed, because I wanted to talk to all of you about becoming part of your posse."

No one said a word, so she kept talking.

"I've more than proven myself. I know I can be an asset. I can shoot an apple off anyone's head. I could probably shoot ten apples off ten people's heads with one bullet."

Mr. Hickok stroked his mustache. "Your talent is undeniable," he said, "but you're just a girl."

Both Annie and Jane gasped in outrage.

"That doesn't make sense at all," Annie huffed.

"Yeah, that's bull puckey!" cried Jane. "She shouldn't be restricted by the restraints of her sex."

Everyone looked at Jane, confused.

"I agree with Jane," Annie said. "Plus, I already know your secret—"

"What?" Mr. Butler asked. "What secret?"

"Yeah," Jane added. "We don't have no secrets. None at all."

Annie smiled warmly. "Oh, it's all right! You don't have to worry. I won't tell anyone else that you still hunt garou."

"Oh," Jane said. "That."

Annie nodded. "See? I already know. So now you don't have to worry about me finding out the hard way. I also know you're hunting someone called the Alpha, although I'm not quite sure what that means, but I'll find out, and you won't even have to tell me—unless you want to, of course, and I'd appreciate it, but I also want you to know that I can fend for myself."

"Mercy," said Mr. Hickok.

Jane stared at her. "Did you breathe in there at all?"

"No," Annie said, but she wasn't out of breath. She could speak the longest sentences of anyone in her whole family.

"And how did you come by this knowledge?" Mr. Hickok asked in a low voice.

"Through simple investigation." She wasn't quite willing to admit she'd followed them into the candle factory the other night. "I always thoroughly research a place of employment before I apply for a job. So I know that you still hunt garou," she said firmly. "I can prove it." (Reader, in no way could Annie prove it, but she'd learned something about bluffing at poker, and she figured this was a good time for a bluff.)

Mr. Hickok glanced around at Mr. Butler and Jane. "If you knew about hunting garou, you'd know that the hunt is no place for a girl."

"Excuse me?" Jane said loudly.

Mr. Hickok waved her off. "You know what I mean." He turned back to Annie. "We wouldn't want you getting hurt, my dear."

Annie's jaw tightened. A series of unbidden memories flashed through her mind. A dark winter night, losing feeling in her toes and fingers as she watched smoke rise from the chimney of a ramshackle cabin.

The burning in her face, after her captors had slapped her.

The smell, almost like a dog but so much darker and deadlier; the thought of it made the hair on her arms prickle. (And her nose itch.)

In spite of the hot summer sun beating down on the shooting grounds, Annie shivered. "I can handle myself with garou, sir. It was me who— I have some experience with— Just give me a chance."

Mr. Butler, who'd been listening quietly all this time, raised his hand. "We should vote on it."

"I vote yes," Annie said immediately.

"You don't get a vote."

Ouch.

"Well, I vote yes," said Jane. "Because I don't like nobody telling anybody what she can or can't do on the basis of being a girl."

"And I vote yes," Mr. Butler said. "A woman who can shoot like Miss Mosey would be a huge draw to the show. People will come for miles to see her perform."

"I vote no," said Mr. Hickok gruffly.

"Two to one, then." Mr. Butler's eyes smiled at her. Not that Annie was spending all that much time noticing his eyes. (They were brown with lighter flecks, framed by long dark lashes, and had a sort of warmth to them that would make anyone's heart squeeze.) "Looks like you're in."

"Wait a second," Mr. Hickok said. "I voted no, so she's not in. Because my vote is the only vote that really counts."

"That's not fair." Mr. Butler stared at Mr. Hickok. "Besides, you put me in charge of the show, so that means *my* vote is the only vote that really counts."

Mr. Hickok didn't get to respond, though, because Jane had started shouting.

"The system is rigged!" She slammed her fist on the railing. "The system is unfair! One person one vote!"

Mr. Butler stepped toward Mr. Hickok. "Dad, come on. You either trust me to handle the show, or you don't. And I think Miss Mosey is the right choice. For the show, obviously. We can see about the garou stuff."

Mr. Hickok gave Mr. Butler a long, searching look, and then shrugged. "All right. She can join the show, but she'll need training."

"I'll help her," Mr. Butler said, maybe too quickly.

"Me too," said Jane.

"How does ten dollars a week sound?"

"That sounds more than fair. Thank you, Mr. Hickok," Annie said. "You won't regret this decision."

He glanced at Mr. Butler, and his expression softened. "When can you start?" he asked Annie.

Her heart soared. "How about now?"

"How about tomorrow?" he said, the corner of his mouth lifting.

Annie smiled. She loved winning. "That'd be just fine."

Jane THIRTEEN

Jane dreamed of the moon. She was standing outside her parents' shabby house in Salt Lake City, and a huge yellow moon was rising against the skyline, so bright it hurt to look on. She felt strange, her limbs heavy, her skin hot and tingling under her clothes. She could barely resist the urge to strip naked right there in the middle of the street and run . . . somewhere.

Martha, said the moon. *Come*.

Yeah, the moon was talking to her. That was new.

Come on, it said, and the voice reminded her of her ma's, actually, in those rare times that her ma had been in a sweet temper and spoke soft to her. Jane felt like she knew where the moon wanted her to go, someplace far off from where she was now, *toward* a thing, she thought, and not away.

Her gaze was drawn again to the window of the house. She saw her sister Lena there, a scraggly little girl in braids, feeding Silas at the table. Her throat tightened at the sight. Her eyes prickled. She hadn't seen Lena in five years. Silas was dead. Ma was dead. Pa was—

Don't dwell on it, Martha, advised the moon. *Just come.*

Jane nodded and turned away from the house. If the moon knew her real name, she supposed she should listen. She pulled her shirt over her head, let it fall to the ground, stepped out of her pants, and removed her socks and shoes. Her feet looked funny, long and oddly jointed, hairier than usual. The moon, as it beamed down on her wearing only her undershirt and drawers, filled her with strength. She was sure she could run forever, under this moon. She took a deep breath and filled her lungs with the light. Her body ached to run.

"No," she heard from behind her, the rough-edged voice of her pa. He was dead, too, but this was a dream. His hand grabbed down on her shoulder so hard it burned into her flesh. She heard the slosh of the whiskey bottle he'd always kept.

"Get in there, girl," he said, and pushed her toward the house.

She woke up. Someone was knocking on the hotel room door. (This happened a lot in Jane's life, being awakened by knocking, and dang, but she never got to be the one who knocks.) Jane groaned and flopped over onto her stomach.

"Go away!" she blustered in the direction of the door. "I'm asleep."

A pause, and then more knocking.

"Consarn it, go away!"

No such doing. If anything, the knocking got more insistent.

She threw off the sheets and lurched to her feet. Happily she discovered that she was already wearing boots. And a shirt. She wasn't sure where her pants had gone. She grabbed the wool blanket from the bed and tried to wrap it around her waist. Then she stumbled over to the door and heaved it open.

"Oh good, you're up." It was the crack-shot girl from the shooting competition, the one Frank was mooning over like a lovesick puppy. What was her name, again?

"I'm Annie, the newest member of your show," the girl said. "Good morning!"

"I don't see what's so gawl-darned good about it." Jane had a taste in her mouth like she'd had supper with a coyote. Had she gotten herself sloshed last night? She didn't think she had. She swallowed queasily. "What can I do for you, Miss—"

"Mosey," provided Annie. She crossed over to the window and opened the curtains, flooding the room with light. "And I've been wondering what to call you. Is your Christian name Calamity, or Jane?"

"My Christian name?"

"Your first name. Like mine is Annie. Well, actually, my Christian name is Phoebe, but no one but my mother uses it. My sisters thought Phoebe was too fancy, and I'd walk around putting on airs with a name like that. So it's always been Annie."

"I don't go by my real name, neither," Jane murmured. *Martha, come*, she thought. She must have gotten drunk last night, to have such a dream as the moon talking at her.

"Oh, I see," Annie said. "Why'd you change it?"

Jane rubbed at her eyes. "I guess there came a time when I had to leave my other name behind." An image from that fateful day swam up in her head, Bill sitting down next to her on the street in Fort Laramie, asking her name. "I needed a fresh start, was all."

Annie looked puzzled. "And you chose to start fresh as . . . Calamity Jane?"

"Nah, just Jane at first. I got the Calamity later, when I saved Captain Egan from certain death in a skirmish with the Sioux a few years back. I saw him fall from his horse, struck by an arrow, so I turned around real fast and rode back to him, and then lifted him up on my horse and rode him to safety. And because of that he said—later, after he'd recovered some, of course—'I dub thee Calamity Jane, the Heroine of the Plains.'"

(Um, reader, we should mention that this entire account with Captain Egan was a fabrication—a stretcher, Jane would have called it—and it didn't even really make sense. But that was the official explanation she'd come up with a few years back, and it was a pretty good whopper, so we'll let it slide. For now.)

"That's an amazing story," Annie said.

Jane nodded. "You can call me Jane. Frank calls me Calam sometimes, but I don't like it much."

"All right. Jane. I bet you're wondering why I'm here so bright and early."

Jane had been wondering.

"Mr. Hickok says that I am to room with you from now on," Annie continued. "So here I am, all ready to move in." She crossed quickly back to the door where she dragged in a trunk and gun case that Jane hadn't noticed before, then glanced a bit worriedly around the room. "Um, may I have the bottom three drawers of the dresser, and some space in the armoire to hang my dresses? I have quite a bit to unpack. I like to be prepared, you see. Better to have it and not need it, than to need it and not have it. That's my motto."

"Uh, sure. Go right ahead." Jane did not have much in the way of extra clothing or lady things. It all fit in a jumble in the top drawer, in fact.

"Wonderful." Annie slung her trunk onto the extra bed and unpacked it, hanging and smoothing her dresses, folding each item carefully into thirds and stacking them upright, so she could see all the items in the drawers. She had a lot of blue and yellow, a bit of green, and not nearly as much red or pink as Jane had expected. Wait, was that dress pink? Jane rubbed her eyes.

"Why are you putting your clothes like that?" Jane asked.

"Because it sparks joy," Annie said.

"Huh?" said Jane.

Annie scooped a pair of pants off the floor and handed them to Jane like an offering. "Now, Jane, if it's not too much trouble, I'd like you to show me the ropes."

Jane kicked off her boots and struggled to fit her legs into her breeches. There didn't seem to be enough leg holes for the number of legs she had. "Ropes? I don't often use ropes. Unless I need to tie something up."

"I was being metaphorical." Annie grabbed Jane's pants from her, whipped them in the air once to straighten them out, and then returned them. "You volunteered to train me, remember? I thought we could start this morning."

Jane considered the request as she shimmied into the pants. She still felt . . . strange, and she suspected it wasn't from the drink. She was sweating, and her skin had that unsettling tingly feeling. "Um, sure I could. But maybe later? I think I need to get me some hair of the dog."

Annie rubbed her nose. "That sounds unsanitary. If you're feeling unwell, some fresh air might help. My father always said that the best way for a person to feel better is to move about out of doors, get the blood flowing." She nodded as if she were agreeing with herself. "But perhaps if you're too sickly to go out, we could stay here and talk."

Jane stared at her, aghast. "Talk? You want to talk . . . more?"

"If we're going to be working together and living together, we should get to know each other."

"We should get a move on." Jane put her boots back on and tied her mass of unruly dark hair into a ponytail. Then she crammed her hat down onto her head, grabbed her gun and whip from the nightstand, and headed a bit unsteadily for the door.

"A move on to where?" Annie asked eagerly.

Jane shrugged. "I guess I'll show you the ropes."

* * *

"This here's Black Nell, Bill's horse," she said a few minutes later, pointing to the biggest stall, where Nell stood knocking her front hooves impatiently.

Annie stepped forward with her hand out, wanting to touch. "She's a beauty."

Jane pulled her back before the girl could get bit. "She's wild, that one, what you'd call undomesticated. Won't stand for nobody but me or Bill."

Annie reached out anyway, and Black Nell pushed her big velvety nose into the girl's small hand. Within a few minutes the horse was actually nuzzling her. It was unsettling. Jane ushered Annie down a stall, where two horses were standing, tails flicking. "This here is Charlie's horse, and we call him, uh, Charlie's horse, and that one there is Ed, Frank's horse. Frank likes to call him Mister Ed. He's a clever one."

Ed stuck out his face and gave a cordial nod, almost like a bow.

"Oh, but aren't you such handsome fellows," cooed Annie to the horses. "How do you do?"

"The horses cain't talk," Jane said gruffly, and moved them down a stall again. "This here's Bullseye. She's mine. She's gotten me out of many a scrape riding for the Pony Express."

Annie turned to stare at her with wide eyes. "You've actually been a rider for the Pony Express? For real?"

"God's own truth." Jane nodded. "I were one of the best, if

I don't mind saying so. I used to ride some of the most dangerous stretches of road in this here America, but I never had any trouble. Any road agents thereabouts knew I never missed a shot, and they didn't bother me." (Again, reader, this was not exactly the truth. Or even a little bit the truth.)

"You never miss a shot?" Annie smiled. "You only used the whip in the show."

"Charlie says the show needs variety. And I'm the best with the bullwhip, but I'm an ace with a gun, as well," Jane bragged. "I never miss unless I mean to."

"I don't, either," said the girl.

"Well . . . good," Jane said. "I suppose we'll get along well enough, then."

"What was it like," Annie asked quietly, "fighting the Sioux?"

Now this was a topic Jane was squirrelly about. "Indian fighter" had never been a label she'd been terribly comfortable with (and one we as your narrators are terribly uncomfortable with), but if you wanted to be a famous adventurer in the Wild West, you were supposed to act like you'd spent half your free time "bravely fighting off the hostile natives." (Which is pretty awful, considering that they were fighting the land's rightful inhabitants.) Jane scratched at her head. "You heard about that, did you?"

"Yes, from you. You said you saved Captain Egan during a skirmish with the Sioux," Annie reminded her.

"Oh. Right. Right." Jane nodded. "Uh-huh. That's right."

"So what was it like?"

(The truth is, up to this point in her life Jane had never been in a skirmish with the Sioux. She had never actually met a Native American in person, let alone in any kind of combat. In her past adventures, as a scout or a driver, if Jane ever had reason to believe that an Indian was thereabouts, she'd turn right around and go quick as she could in the opposite direction.)

Jane used her sleeve to wipe her sweaty brow. "It was like fighting anybody else, I expect. You try to stay on the living side of things."

Annie looked thoughtful. "My family are Quakers. We believe that what's happening to the Native people in this country is wrong. Can you imagine, folks showing up unannounced at your house, saying it's theirs now, and you've got to leave? And no matter where you go, that keeps happening, you're forced from one place after another, starved and abused and set upon everywhere you go? It's no wonder if some of them are angry."

Jane frowned. She happened to have some experience in being forced from her home. "I never thought about it that way."

"Well, you should," said Annie.

"All right. I will." Jane scratched the back of her neck and then changed the subject by showing Annie the rest of the animals: Bill's donkey, Silver.

"He's a lazy ass," Jane said. "Puffs up his belly if you try to saddle him. He'll stop moving every five minutes if you let him. Won't go but the slowest of walks. Sleeps most all the time. I don't know why Bill won't sell him."

"He's cute," said Annie.

They petted him for a few minutes in uncomfortable silence. Then Annie fished a small book out of her pocket. "I also wonder if you could tell me about the garou."

Jane straightened in alarm. "Why would I know anything about garou?"

Annie cocked her head to one side. "Because you're a garou—"

"No, I'm not!" burst out Jane.

Annie blinked at her. "I know you're all garou hunters, you and Mr. Butler and Mr. Hickok and Mr. Utter."

Jane folded her arms over her chest. "And how do you know that, exactly?"

Annie folded her arms, too. "I just do."

Jane's heart was beating fast. Yesterday Annie had said she had "proof" that their posse was still hunting garou. She'd acted like she herself was eager to hunt them. And now, as Jane happened to look at her hand, which was up by her face on account of her folding her arms, a tuft of fur sprouted from her right knuckle. She was changing. It wouldn't be long now, and this could be her entire body. A hairy beast. Jane thrust her hand into her pocket.

"A-choo!" said Annie. "Oh dear."

"Bless you!" Jane said. Then (and yes, we know she should have done this a lot sooner) she finally put two and two together. "Hey! It was you!"

"Me?" Annie looked at her with round blue eyes.

"At the factory! You were there! You were the one who kept sneezing!"

"Oh, that." Annie pressed a handkerchief to her upturned nose. "Yes, that was me."

"You almost got me killed!" Jane exclaimed, so loudly that Silver tossed his head and brayed.

"Well, yes, that's true, but I also saved your life multiple times," explained Annie. "It was I who shot Mr. Badd outside the office, not Mr. Butler."

"Which is why Mr. Badd didn't die," Jane figured out slowly. "Because you didn't shoot him with a silver bullet."

"I didn't know you needed a silver bullet to kill a garou," Annie confessed.

Jane snorted. "Everybody knows that."

Annie's chin lifted. "Even if I had known, I don't possess any silver bullets. And even if I did possess one, I wouldn't have known to bring it along with me when I followed you that night."

"Aha! So you admit you followed us that night!"

"Yes! I already said that!"

"And you almost got me killed! I change my vote," said Jane hotly. "You're not in the posse."

Annie's mouth fell open. "You can't do that! I saved your life!"

"Did not! I would have been fine if you hadn't shot that garou," Jane retorted. She would have been more than fine, she thought. She would have gotten clear of the wolf some other way and never been bit. To Jane's way of seeing, this was all Annie's fault.

"I was also the one who turned on the machines when that second garou was trying to get you, providing a distraction at the crucial moment." Annie's dander was clearly up now. Her face was turning pink. Maybe pink. Jane's eyes were acting up again. "So I saved your life twice, really."

"You did not!" screamed Jane. Then: "Wait, what do you mean, that second garou?"

"Oh, you know." Annie tilted her head to one side.

Jane did not know. "What are you talking about?"

Annie stifled a smile, obviously pleased that she had some new knowledge to impart. "There were two garou that night in the factory. Mr. Badd, and that other one who came from downstairs and attacked you."

Jane stared at Annie. Then she grabbed the girl by the hand and started pulling her toward the exit. "I change my vote again. You can be in the posse."

"Why, thank you," said Annie. "Although I'm still only counting your original vote. You can't change your vote. Where are we going?"

They reached the barn door, and Jane flung it open, revealing Frank standing there. He was wearing his dandiest suit, Jane noticed. He was also holding a bouquet of yellow flowers, and he'd put the fine smelly stuff in his hair. His gaze passed right over Jane and landed on Annie. He smiled, and Jane caught a whiff of mint.

"Good morning, Miss Mosey," he said. "Fine day, isn't it?"

"Yes, yes it is," agreed Annie in a softer voice than she'd been using before. "How are you this morning, Mr. Butler?"

"Very well, thank you. Would you like to—"

"Stop! There's no time for that!" yelled Jane. "We gotta go see Charlie!"

"I told you, Jane. Charlie's fine," Frank said as Jane pushed past him, still with Annie by the hand. "I saw him last night. He's banged up, of course, but he was in good spirits."

"We gotta tell him that there were two garou that night at the factory!" Jane kept walking, towing Annie behind her.

The flowers dropped from Frank's hand. He jogged to keep up. "Two garou? Uh, I have absolutely no idea what you're talking about."

"There were two!" It was the second wolf who'd bitten her, Jane realized. "One of them got away!"

"Charlie!" Jane called as she, Annie, and Frank burst into the doctor's house where Charlie had been convalescing for the past few days. "Charlie, wake up! We got news!"

Charlie, it turned out, was not asleep. He was sitting up in his bed, his wrapped leg stretched before him, looking pale and peaked, but not from his injuries. He was staring tensely at the open window (or outside of it, we should say), where there was a figure peering through at him. A boy, a few years younger than Frank, who seemed familiar to Jane.

It was one of the bitten factory workers, she realized. The boy with the bushy eyebrows. He was trembling and, from the looks of things, crying, even. Which didn't make sense.

Because he was holding a gun. And he was pointing it right at Charlie.

FOURTEEN

Frank

Frank held his hands out, palms down. "Hey, there," he said, his voice cracking a bit, which was totally embarrassing in front of Annie, but that was definitely not what he should be focusing on right now. "What's going on?"

Jane leaned over and said out of the side of her mouth, "What's going on is he's got a gun pointed at Charlie!"

Frank woooed softly, keeping his eyes on the boy. This was no time to lose his nerve. "You look frightened, which makes me think you don't want to be doing this."

"I have to," the boy said in a shaky voice. His hands were trembling so violently that Frank was afraid the six-shooter would go off by accident.

"Why do you think you have to?" Frank kept his voice even,

but his heartbeat was thunder in his ears. In the back of his mind, so far back it was most likely reflex at this point, he imagined all the things that kept him calm: wind in tall grass, the gentle dance of fireflies, and the sun sinking lower in the sky.

Tears streamed down the boy's cheeks. "He said they would tell everyone I was a garou. And if that happens, no one will give me a job. My family will starve. I'm the only one able-bodied enough to earn money."

"Who said that?" Frank asked.

The boy shook his head.

"I recognize you," Frank said. He took a tentative step toward the window, and the boy flinched. Jane and Annie both flinched, too. "You were at the factory that night, right?"

The boy didn't respond. He just shook.

"I think you were. I know you're going through a very hard time right now."

"A hard time? A *hard time*?" The boy howled in despair. "A week ago, I was normal. Now I'm a garou. My life is over. There's no way to keep it a secret. My mother is a cripple. My father is gone. And I guess I'm about to commit murder."

"Or, maybe, as an alternative, you don't commit murder," Frank said. He took another step. "You saw us at the factory. You know we're the good guys."

"Yeah," Jane said. "We're, like, the revengers."

Frank's heart was breaking for this boy. He was so scared, so young, and had no one to take care of him. "We can help you," he said, soothingly. "But if you kill Charlie . . . well, there's no coming back from that. And what's to stop whoever from threatening you again?"

The boy's shoulders slumped, and he lowered the six-shooter. Frank closed the distance and gently took the gun out of the boy's hand. Without looking, he passed it behind him to Jane, who carried it out of reach.

"Come inside and talk to us," Frank told the boy. "We'll figure it out."

The boy started to climb through the window.

"Oh," Frank said, "I meant through the door— Oh, okay, you're in."

The boy sank into the chair in the corner of the room. Frank and Jane (sans six-shooter) went to his side. Annie stayed by the door.

"Who threatened you?" Frank asked.

"A man in a carriage. He stopped me on the street."

"Did you know the man?" Frank asked.

The boy shook his head.

"Did you get a good look at him?"

"He was wearing a hat."

"A hat?" Annie repeated. "What kind of hat?"

"One of those fancy hats. A top hat."

Frank and Jane exchanged a look.

"Did you see his face?" Frank asked.

The boy shook his head. "It was too dark."

Frank frowned. "I know it was dark, but hasn't it been said . . . that . . . garou can maybe see really well in the dark?"

"I don't know if that's true," the boy said.

"I think it sure sounds true," Jane said.

"I was just so frightened. I didn't even look at him."

"Well, that makes it more difficult on our end," Frank said. "Was he tall? Short?"

"I don't know."

Frank was beginning to think this boy wasn't going to make a very good garou. He pulled some bank notes out of his pocket. "I'm betting this nondescript man happened upon you on the street and seized an opportunity. But I'm here to tell you that you can live a good life as a garou. You can learn to master it. It is *not* the end of your life."

The boy pocketed the bills and nodded. "I guess I can try. Should I take the gun?"

Frank raised an eyebrow. "Uh, that's a hard no. You can take the door on your way out, though."

The boy shuffled toward the door, and Annie gave him a wide berth. He paused with his hand on the doorknob.

"The man did have a strange smell," the boy said. "Like peppermint mixed with . . . moonlight."

With that he left.

Annie looked incredulous. "You're letting him go?"

Frank nodded. "Just because he was bitten doesn't make him bad."

"He almost murdered your friend."

"He was scared," Frank said. "The more pressing issue is who was at this factory turning all these people, to what end, and what the heck does moonlight smell like?"

Jane raised her hand. "Oh, oh, the reason we came here. There was a *second* garou at the factory."

So she'd claimed before, but—

"How do you know?" Frank asked.

Jane scratched her chin. "Well, that's a mite difficult to explain."

"I was there and I saw everything and I shot the first garou," Annie said. "But I did not shoot the second one."

"So, maybe it's not that difficult to explain," Jane said.

"You were at the factory?" Bill's voice came from the doorway.

"Yes." Annie stepped aside to make room for him to enter.

"And to further catch you up," Frank said, "one of the boys from the factory was blackmailed into trying to kill Charlie. We talked him down. The blackmailer wore a top hat, but the boy didn't get any further description, except he smelled of peppermint and (ahem) . . . moonlight."

At this Bill tilted his head. "There are a lot of things going on here."

"I know," Jane said. "Lots of threads. We're not used to plots with any complexity."

Bill looked at Charlie. "You feelin' okay?"

Charlie nodded. "I mean, my leg hurts, and not five minutes ago there was a gun aimed at my head, but now we're back down to just my leg hurting." He gave a wry smile. "So yeah, I'm fine."

Bill sighed. "I want to go check out a new lead."

"What new lead?" Frank said.

"It's not something that's even worth talking about yet," Bill said. "I'll go at it on my own. Jane, look after the horses. Frank, you and . . . Annie"—at the sound of her name, Annie stood up straighter, as she always did—"go practice for the show."

"Okay," Frank said, standing straighter himself, because he had talked the boy out of killing Charlie and now he was going to practice sharpshooting with Annie, and ever since she'd beaten him in that contest . . . Well, let's just say his heart had gone boom.

As they walked to their homemade shooting range behind the livery, Frank said, "I can't believe you followed us to the factory. You've got to be more careful."

"Oh, I was very careful as I shot that garou who was about to kill you."

Frank was embarrassed to admit he felt relief that he hadn't killed the garou. So he didn't admit it.

"And I didn't get so much as a thank-you," Annie said with a grin.

Frank's pulse started to race, and he wasn't sure whether to attribute it to the fact that she'd saved his life or the fact he liked her smile.

"I'm so excited to be in the show," Annie said as they reached the practice area. "Oh, George!"

George was dashing toward them. Frank crouched down to welcome him, but the poodle darted around him and leapt into Annie's arms.

"Who's a good boy?" she said.

Is it me? George thought.

"You're a good boy."

Yay! It's me! George responded.

She set George down, and he immediately flipped over onto his back, exposing his belly for rubbing. Annie obliged, scratching him in just the right spot as to cause his left leg to twitch.

Up until now, George had only done the leg-twitch thing with Frank. But Frank wasn't jealous. Because George was a dog and Frank was a man and man had no reason to resent dog and George was like a brother and he was most loyal and why did he like Annie better than Frank?

But then Frank looked at Annie. She was wearing another simple, formfitting dress, with a matching bow in her hair and buckled shoes that boasted a recent shine job. Of course George had leapt into her arms. Right now, Frank wanted to leap into her arms.

Annie stood up and ran her hand over her skirt, even though Frank couldn't see one darn wrinkle.

They stared at each other in silence, Annie with a half smile and Frank with a full smile.

"Shall we begin?" Annie said.

"Gosh, sure," Frank said articulately.

They spent the next few hours coming up with a routine for Annie's act in the show.

"That's enough warm-up," Annie said when they were done. "Let's start the competition portion of the afternoon."

Frank considered this to be the best first date in the history of first dates. "How will we keep track of the score?" he said. "Should we make notches in that tree?"

"No need to harm a tree," Annie said. "Let's keep track another way. How about if each time one of us can't copy a shot, we get a letter of a word. And when one of us, mostly you, finishes spelling the word, he—or she, but mostly he—loses."

Frank chose to ignore her hubris on account of she was just so darn likable.

"What word shall we use?" Frank asked.

"Um . . ." Annie glanced at the stables. "How about *horse*?"

And thus, dear readers, the very first game of H-O-R-S-E was played. Of course, now the game uses trick basketball shots instead of trick gun shots, and this change is probably a good thing, because no one was as good at shooting as Frank and Annie, and therefore if other people tried to replicate the game, there would be blood.

Anyway, back to this delightful scene of a boy and a girl, flirting with the rules of propriety and shooting guns at each other.

It was a tight game. At one point, Frank did his signature move of standing on his head and shooting at the target using a mirror. Annie followed suit. So did her skirt. She made the shot, but not before Frank caught the briefest glimpse of her leg. The left one.

He got very quiet.

"What did you think of that?" Annie said triumphantly.

"It was . . . I mean . . . ," Frank stammered.

At that moment, bells rang from some distance away.

"I can hear the bells," Frank said.

"Me too," Annie said.

The longer they stared into each other's eyes, the louder, and clearer, the bells got.

"Do you remember that one time you did that flip thing and shot the gun with your big toe?" Frank said.

"The thing I did five minutes ago? Yes, I remember."

"I thought that was just the darndest thing."

The bells were really loud now. So loud that Frank began to wonder if maybe they weren't ringing for him and Annie. They were getting closer, and now they were accompanied by the sound of hoofbeats and the commotion of a speeding wagon.

Realization dawned on Frank. "It's the fire wagon!"

"Yes," Annie said, looking as if that were the last thing she'd expected him to declare.

"George loves them!" Frank exclaimed.

But it was too late. The truck rounded the corner and passed the range, and George went madly barking after it. Frank ran after him. He'd seen this happen before, and sometimes George ended up miles away. It was like fire wagons were dog hypnotists.

"Come back!" he shouted. But neither dog nor truck listened, let alone obeyed.

Frank ran and ran until he thought he'd collapse. He stood bent over on the dirt road, breathing heavily.

Annie caught up to him seconds later, not breathing hard at all.

"Mr. Butler, are you okay?"

Frank was still gasping for air. "It might take me hours to find him."

Annie cupped her hands to her mouth. "George! Here, boy!"

"That's . . . never . . . going . . . to . . . " Frank panted.

He didn't get to finish the sentence because George was back.

"It worked," Frank said.

"I have a way with animals," Annie said.

Frank had always thought *he* was the one who had a way with animals.

Annie patted Frank's back. She was either consoling him or trying to help him breathe.

There was just something about this girl that spun his head around. When he'd watched her shoot, he'd felt like he'd been struck by lightning. So proper, so accurate, so prim, and yet she could shoot the shell off a snail, and the snail would crawl away unharmed.

He liked her. He liked that fierce gleam in her blue eyes. That stubborn set to her jaw. The way her lips pursed slightly when she was making a decision.

Her lips were doing that cute thing right now, as a matter of fact.

(We pause here, dear readers, to acknowledge that insta-love is a literary trope too often used. But history is on the side of this particular connection. When the real Annie beat Frank Butler in that sharpshooting competition, his heart had skipped a beat, and he really did wonder if she was the girl he was going to marry. It was love at first shoot. You can look it up.)

"Mr. Butler?" Annie said, and for the first time since he'd met her, she sounded out of breath.

"Miss Mosey," he murmured. Her skin was like porcelain. Tan freckly porcelain.

"Can I ask you a question?"

"Ask me anything," he breathed.

"What is the Alpha?"

"Huh?" Frank felt like she'd dumped cold water on him.

"What is the Alpha?" Annie asked again. "You all seem very worried about finding it."

"Right." Frank struggled to redirect his brain to the job. He wasn't sure about how much he should share with her. But as long as she was part of their group, he supposed it was all right. "The Alpha popped up a couple of years ago, organized the garou into the Pack, and now they go around biting people. As you've seen."

"All this time and you haven't caught him yet?" Annie frowned, as though she'd have found him the instant she heard the name.

"Most people don't know anything about him—not even most garou. Trying to find information about the Alpha is like trying to find . . ." He paused, failing to come up with an apt simile.

"Like trying to find a needle in a haystack?" Annie provided.

"Yes. That's precisely it."

"Thanks." She smiled broadly. "I'm the best at coming up with similes in my whole family."

Frank believed that.

"So this Alpha," she prodded.

"Well, we've been chasing him for a while, but the trail went cold a couple towns ago, so we came to Cincinnati to do our show and make some money. It was pure luck that Jack McCall happened to have information on the Alpha. Well, sort of. He said Mr. Badd might be the Alpha, but clearly that wasn't true. Still, we have leads now."

Annie nodded thoughtfully. "Very interesting. So this Alpha is bad, but not Mr. Badd. And the Alpha's not the top hat man either, although the top hat man seems to be more important in the Pack than Mr. Badd."

"Exactly."

"But the top hat man might lead us to the Alpha."

"That's the hope," Frank said tonelessly. Yes, it would be great to have this hunt over with, and the evil Alpha off the streets, but that meant Bill would leave the show—and therefore Frank—to settle down with Agnes.

Bill deserved to settle down.

But if they found the Alpha and put an end to the Pack, it would be a bittersweet victory.

Annie didn't notice his melancholy. "So tell me more about the garou."

"Oh, okay." Frank could hardly believe she had more curiosity left in her after that interrogation.

"Just for research," Annie went on, "since I intend to pull my weight in hunting the Alpha. Do garou have exceptional eyesight?"

"Yes, from what I've seen," he said warily.

"And do they have unprecedented hearing?" she asked.

"Yes, that's what I've heard, if there is something interesting they want to listen to," Frank said.

"So, this book I've read three times—*Fearsome Garou and Where to Find Them*—says that garou have a kinship with wolves. It speculates that garou can communicate with wolves, and maybe even dogs."

George glanced up at Frank, his tongue lolling out. *Is she talking about me?* he thought.

Frank squeezed his eyes shut and scratched the back of his head.

"I wouldn't know about that."

"Also, it says garou are colorblind."

"Um," Frank said. "I think they can see some colors, but not like humans see them."

"Right!" Annie nodded enthusiastically. "So a garou wouldn't be able to tell what color dress I was wearing."

Frank really hoped she wouldn't ask him what color her dress was. It looked sort of gray-yellow, with some blue in there, but who could say, really?

Annie whipped a short pencil out of her pocket and a blank book. She started scribbling everything down.

"The book claims garou can run fast," Annie said.

"Now *that* I can answer: not all of the time."

"Hmm," Annie said. "I guess the book was wrong about that. There's one other thing. Jane told me that it's really hard to kill a garou, and that it takes special kinds of bullets. Silver bullets."

"Oh." A pit formed in Frank's stomach. This conversation was definitely taking a dangerous turn. "Yes, that's true."

"That sounds expensive!"

He nodded, imagining sunsets again. "That's why we put on so many shows: to pay for the silver."

"Ah," Annie said, writing that down. "Good time to own a silver mine, I suppose."

"That's dark," Frank said.

"I bet it is dark in mines, yes. But the silver is undeniably needed now. I should get some silver bullets of my own. Where do I buy them? Or will I have to make them myself?"

Frank's heart kicked. Sunsets weren't really working. Why couldn't they go back to talking about bells? "Charlie can help you with that. Or Bill."

Annie nodded and made another note. "Great. I'll talk to them."

"Annie?" He meant to call her Miss Mosey, but her Christian name slipped out. It felt right.

She looked up, her eyes expectant. "Yes . . . Frank?"

"You seem really excited to hunt garou," he said.

"Oh, I am." She closed her notebook and put it in her pocket. "They frighten me, Mr. Butler—I mean Frank." Her cheeks darkened. Were they pink to other people? "Garou are so much more powerful than we are. It's terrifying what they can do. I don't trust them."

"I see." Frank knew as well as anyone how dangerous garou could be. After all, he'd been hunting garou for years—and helping them, too. Like that boy in Charlie's room, and the others from the factory. Those garou hadn't done anything wrong. They'd been scared. But Annie wanted to hunt all of them. "Why?"

"Why what?"

Frank steeled himself and forced out the question. He didn't really want to know the answer, but he needed it. "Why do you want to hunt garou so badly?"

FIFTEEN
Annie

Why did Annie want to hunt wolves?

Because she hated them.

She'd been eight years old the first time she'd met a garou, although she hadn't known it at first. No one had.

Her family's financial struggles were nothing new. Her pa had died when she was only five years old, and even though Mama had tried her best to keep the family afloat, she'd been forced to send the children away. Annie had gone to live with a family friend, where she'd taken care of their baby. Then, after a bout with scarlet fever, she'd stayed in the county home and helped with the children there. She'd made something of a name for herself, fixing a sewing machine that usually required a mechanic from the city to repair, and then—because simply fixing the thing wasn't enough—she'd sewn two dresses each for all the girls in the home.

That reputation for being good at fixing things, and being good with children, earned Annie her first paying job: a farmer had come to the county home looking for a girl who could help take care of his baby. Annie *loved* babies, and it was agreed she'd give the farmer and his wife a trial run of two weeks.

Those first two weeks had been fine, as far as jobs for young children went, but as soon as a letter to her mother was sent—saying how happy Annie was there—the Wolves began to show themselves for what they were.

At first, it was small things: they made her wake up early to prepare breakfast for the family, which involved slicing ham or bacon—they preferred their meats rare, we should mention—and paring and frying potatoes, and sometimes frying cornmeal mush or biscuits. They also drank coffee, although Annie was never allowed any (a fact at least one of your narrators finds completely unforgivable).

It started getting worse after that, until her days looked like this: up before dawn to make breakfast, then milk the cows and do a bunch of other cow-associated chores, wash the dishes, care for the baby, tend the vegetable garden, get dinner ready, do more dishes, care for the baby more, prepare supper, do a third round of dishes, and then sleep for a few minutes to repeat it all the next day.

Reader, we asked someone with kids how much sleep a nine-year-old is supposed to get (Annie was nine by this time), and they said more than ten hours. Annie was getting three.

The Wolves (this wasn't actually their family name, but Annie never thought of them as anything else) worked her like this for months, but at least she was getting paid. Or so she'd thought. They claimed they were sending her mama fifty cents a week, but that was a lie. They were also supposed to send her to school, but that never happened, either. Who had time with all the chores?

It was hardly ideal.

Then the real trouble came.

It had been a frigid winter night when Mrs. Wolf threw a pile of stockings at Annie for her to mend. Somehow, the heels of every single sock had been torn out, as though by claws. That was weird, but Annie hardly registered it. She'd been working all day, so she was having trouble keeping her eyes open, but when Mrs. Wolf caught her starting to doze off, she slapped Annie so hard her cheek bruised.

Annie startled awake and bit off a scream, but Mrs. Wolf still wasn't happy. She tossed Annie outside, into the freezing-cold weather, and shut the door fast.

This was the snot-freezing, eyeball-chilling kind of cold, and as Annie huddled inside her threadbare dress, a heelless sock shoved over both feet, she knew she would die. Her pa had died like this, lost in a snowstorm on the way home from hunting, wandering the farm because it was too dark, and the snow was too thick, for him to see the house. He'd died just outside it, frozen, reaching for home.

And now Annie would follow him.

She tried not to cry, because the tears would freeze on her cheeks, but she couldn't stop herself. She was only nine, after all. So she hunched under her dress and half-darned stockings, watching smoke rise from the chimney, watching the cheery light from the fireplace bounce across the windows. And she thought about her pa, and how her mama needed that fifty cents a week, and what she wouldn't give to be able to defend herself from these Wolves.

As the cold stopped hurting and Annie started to fall asleep, Mrs. Wolf brought her inside again and stuck her in the attic.

For the next two years, the Wolves kept her prisoner, flat out refusing to let her visit her family. In fact, they kept writing letters to her mama, saying how happy she was there. Annie didn't know about those letters until much later, but she did see the replies from her mama, encouraging her to stay since she was doing so well.

When Annie asked about going home, the Wolves threatened to eat her liver.

She'd thought that was only a scary threat until the day some of their relatives visited, and that was the day she saw them . . . change.

Annie had been working in the kitchen for an hour, cooking a whole cow for everyone. (*Cooking* being a generous verb; remember, they liked their meat extra rare, so Annie was mostly just warming it up.) Anyway, she'd been heading into the parlor to tell everyone supper was ready, but before the door was fully opened, it happened: their faces elongated and grew fur, which shouldn't have been possible. But then their arms and legs bulked up and turned furry as well. And then their feet grew longer and burst clean out of their shoes and stockings.

That answered all her questions about busted-out socks.

She must have gasped, or made some other small noise, because one by one, Mr. Wolf, Mrs. Wolf, and their relatives looked at her, and all Annie could think was what big eyes they had.

What sharp teeth they had.

What long claws they had.

They didn't eat her liver, thank goodness. She somehow managed to squeak out that supper was served, and they sat at the table like this was normal.

The next day, when the Wolves were out doing whatever they did when they weren't tormenting her, she wondered what would happen if she just . . . ran away.

So she did.

At that point, Annie had no money, no clothes beyond what she wore, and barely an idea of where this farm was relative to her own family's farm, but even so, she left the house and started walking.

She soon found the train station and planned to ask the conductor if she could pay him back when she got home, but when she climbed onto the train, an old gentleman sitting across from her inquired about her situation. He had a shocking amount of facial hair, but Annie told him everything, too scared to think that someone might give her back to the Wolves if they knew she had run away. But the kindly gentleman—whose name was Oakley, he told her—said, "You're safe now, little one. No one's going to hurt you."

When the conductor came by, Mr. Oakley paid for her ticket.

"You didn't have to do that," Annie said. "I'd have— When I get home—"

The old man smiled. "It never hurts to show a stranger a bit of compassion. I hope one day you heal from all this." And then he gave her a peppermint candy from his pocket and talked with her for the rest of the ride to Darke County.

Annie never forgot that kind man, but neither did she forget the Wolves and how they'd treated her.

Why did she want to hunt wolves?

Because they'd nearly killed her.

"Annie?" Frank's voice was rough.

"Hm?" She looked up from her memory and shook off the sick feeling she'd had earlier, when the wolf-boy with the eyebrows had gone through the door—passing by her too closely. He might not have killed Mr. Utter, but that was only because Frank had bravely stopped him.

"Why?" He looked at her with those warm eyes. "Why do you want to hunt garou?"

She could tell him, and he would try to make her feel better. Or he would tell Mr. Hickok and perhaps that would be enough to get her kicked out of the posse, if Mr. Hickok believed it was too personal a reason to hunt garou. She couldn't risk losing this job.

And it *was* personal. She'd just met Frank. As much as she

admired him, as much as she wanted to grow closer, she'd been weak during her two years with the Wolves. She wasn't ready to share that with him yet (even though they were already on a first-name basis!).

"It's not that I want to hunt them," she said finally.

Somehow, his gaze warmed even more, and he leaned toward her a tiny bit. Maybe he wanted to kiss her? Maybe she would let him.

Right after she finished what she needed to say.

"It's that I have to," Annie continued. "They're a plague on the world. They're vile, monstrous creatures, and I hate them."

"Oh," Frank said, and then he turned away.

Jane SIXTEEN

Jane booked it back as fast she could to the hotel. All she was thinking about now was that poor kid who'd tried to kill Charlie, the tremble in his voice when he'd said his life was over. It made her want to hide away forever.

It also made her want to drown her sorrows.

She burst into her room, crossed to the dresser, opened the top drawer, and drew her pocketbook out from underneath her spare set of underpants. Inside there was ten dollars. She stared at the wrinkled money, thinking of Bill's rules for becoming a werewolf.

DON'T BITE ANYBODY. Her belly rumbled at the word *bite*. She hadn't eaten since yesterday. She should get a hot meal. She'd feel better with food in her stomach.

BEWARE THE MOON. It was going to be a full moon in a

couple of days. She should buy a length of chain.

BE MINDFUL OF YOUR TEMPER. She should have the hotel people draw her a bath. She couldn't even remember the last time she'd had one. The warm water might soothe the churning mess of anger and fear inside of her.

PROTECT THE PEOPLE YOU LOVE. Her fingers closed around the bills. She could eat, buy a chain, have a bath, and still have plenty to send to her sister in Utah. Make sure the little ones still had shoes.

Go off by herself, as Bill always suggested to the bitten.

Jane swallowed. She wasn't ready to go. The wolf hadn't taken over, not yet. She'd only seen a bit of fur so far. And colors playing tricks on her eyes. And those weird dreams. Nothing serious.

She could hold it off.

She stuffed her pocketbook down the front of her shirt and headed for the door.

"Fill her up, Johnny," she said a few minutes later at the hotel bar.

The barkeep poured her a whiskey. She lifted the glass to her lips and closed her eyes.

"Stop!" cried an indignant voice. "Stop it at once!"

Huh? Jane opened her eyes. On the other side of the room, near the front desk where folks were checking in, a young woman was struggling to retrieve her carpetbag from the grasp of a large, broad-shouldered man.

"Come on, missy," the man was saying. "I'll take it up to your room for you. It's too heavy a burden for a peach like you to bear."

"I can handle my own property, thank you very much," said the girl primly, pushing her glasses up on her nose.

Jane recognized her at once. It was Miss Harris.

The man still had hold of the lady's bag. Then he leaned close to her and took a sniff of her lace collar.

"You smell . . . purty," he said.

Miss Harris blinked. "I have no desire to be sniffed at by a strange man. Now, if you would kindly relinquish my bag—"

"As you wish," said the man. "But I just wanted to ask you—"

He didn't get the obviously indecent proposition out before he was interrupted by the slash of Jane's whip cutting across his knuckles. The brute dropped the carpetbag, howling in pain, and swiveled to see who had dealt the blow. In a flash Jane was up in his face, the business end of her pistol under his chin.

"Hello, there," growled Jane. She cocked the gun.

"I'm sorry," the brute said immediately. He had surprisingly fresh breath. Still, Jane didn't stand down. She kept close (which was easy, really, with the fresh breath) and locked her eyes with his.

"I think it's time for you to apologize," she said, and then realized that he had, in fact, already apologized. "To the lady, I mean."

"I'm sorry," he said again.

"Now I'm going to take a step back, and you're going to light on out of here, and you're not going to come back, ever."

He whimpered. "Ever?"

"Oh dear . . . ," Miss Harris said.

"Ever," Jane said, then pushed him out the door.

Then she turned back to Miss Harris with a smile, entirely pleased with herself. She'd gone and saved the day. Again.

Miss Harris looked weary. "I suppose I should thank you for rescuing me," she said. "But . . ."

"Oh, that's *great*," groaned Mr. Frost from behind the front desk. "Now I have to find a new bellhop."

"I was only trying to ask about her perfume!" came the brute's voice from outside the door. "Is it lemon verbena?"

". . . I didn't need rescuing," finished Miss Harris.

"Oh," said Jane. The entire place was staring at her. "I thought you were . . ."

"I know," Miss Harris said gently. "It was kind of you. Shall we go . . . someplace . . . else?"

That was a terrible idea, considering. But Jane nodded. She paid her tab with the barkeep (even though she hadn't had a chance to drink the whiskey he'd poured her), Miss Harris stopped off at her room to deposit the fateful carpetbag, and the two of them wandered about the city for a while until they found a charming restaurant along the river. Jane had never eaten at a charming restaurant by the river before. She found it suited.

"So," Miss Harris said when they were settled at a table. "How have you been?"

"I've been better," admitted Jane. "But I'm still fighting the good fight."

"As we must," said Miss Harris.

They chatted back and forth, ate a supper of roast chicken and greens, and drank sweet tea. By the time they got to the apple pie, Jane had told Miss Harris all about traveling west on the Oregon Trail when she was eight, and she had learned that Miss Harris was from Boston, where her father had hoped to make a go of it as a tailor, but then he'd died in a smallpox epidemic and left poor Miss Harris—whose Christian name, it turned out, was Edwina—all alone to fend for herself in the big bad world.

"I survived on the kindness of strangers," she said a bit sadly.

"And now here you are," Jane said, patting Edwina's hand on the table in a gesture meant to be comforting.

"Yes. Now I'm here." Edwina turned her hand over and took Jane's, just briefly, mind you, but it was definitely another Moment, Jane thought, before they both pulled away.

"My pa also died," Jane admitted with a cough. "I was eleven." She did not go into the details, of course, but she told Miss Harris—Edwina—about the strain of becoming so suddenly responsible for her five younger siblings.

"Whatever did you do?" Edwina asked.

"This and that. I tended children, cleaned hotel rooms, washed and pressed laundry," Jane said. "And I dressed as a boy sometimes and shoed horses and helped with branding and roping cows and rode for the mail, whenever I got the chance. I was better at the boy jobs, plus they paid more."

"How resourceful of you." Edwina was impressed, it seemed, and not at all judgmental that Jane had tricked people into believing her to be a boy. But then of course Edwina would know all about the advantages of posing as male.

After the meal had been cleared away, the two of them stood. "You've been good company for me today," Edwina said. "I'm so glad you assaulted that bellhop."

Jane blushed. "Should I escort you back to the hotel?"

"That would be wonderful."

Jane led them on a meandering route along the riverbank. They were almost back when she had a thought. "Why are you staying at the Bevis House now? Don't you live here in Cincinnati?"

"Oh, no," Edwina said with a smile. "I've only been here for a few weeks, working."

"The P and G factory story," Jane guessed.

"Yes, among others."

"And what have you found out?"

Edwina laughed brightly. "Oh, you want *me* to tell *you* about it?"

"Maybe we can help each other," Jane said. She wanted to give this girl something nice, like a flower or a fancy watch, but she could guess that the thing Edwina liked best was information. Maybe it was possible to give her only a little of what Jane knew. Heck, maybe what Edwina had discovered could help Bill and the group.

Edwina nodded. "Maybe. I know you were involved. I know Wild Bill made an arrest, which means he's still a marshal, isn't he?"

"I got no comment about Wild Bill," Jane said. "But I was there, and the man arrested was a Mr. Badd."

"Yes, yes, he was the foreman at the factory," Edwina said, nodding because she obviously already knew all of this. "He was also a garou who bit dozens of his workers, many of whom are still missing. But he's not really the person of interest in this story, is he?"

"Nah, there's somebody higher up, right?" Jane agreed. A boss. The man in the top hat. And he—the top hat man—would lead them to the Alpha.

"I suppose that's true, and that does indeed interest me, but I meant you," Edwina said. "Are you a garou hunter, Jane? On top of being a show-woman and an inspiration to women everywhere?"

Jane met the girl's inquisitive eyes, and then stared off at the river. "I don't know what I am, these days," she admitted. "I'm still figuring that out."

"I think you're a marvel," pronounced Edwina.

Jane blushed again. She had never blushed this much in her life. She didn't know what it meant, but Edwina was such a nice girl, the nicest Jane had ever met, even counting Annie, who was pretty nice but also talked far too much and was bossy. Edwina, though, was like a china pitcher in a glass case—she seemed to shine with a certain kind of fineness.

"Edwina—" Jane started, but then a growl rolled out of her, unbidden. She tried to play it off as a belch, which was only slightly less embarrassing.

Uh-oh.

"Call me Winnie," Edwina said, as if she didn't notice.

"All right," Jane said. "Winnie. Can I ask you—" But she

couldn't finish the sentence on account of a scratch in her throat. She held up a finger and walked a few steps away, where she proceeded to cough violently.

"Jane? Are you all right?"

"Fine," Jane answered, but it came out more like a bark. She nodded that she would be okay, she just needed a moment to hack up a lung.

Finally she gagged, and then dry-heaved, and then out of her mouth popped a disgusting brown mass of . . . something.

"Oh dear, you should really watch how much you are chewing," Winnie said.

"Right," Jane said, staring at the lump on the boardwalk. Jane couldn't remember the last time she'd chewed, let alone swallowed that much tobacco. She had a sinking sensation of what it really was.

A hairball.

"I do apologize, Miss Harris," she murmured.

"You had no control over it. Let me fetch you some water."

Winnie slipped into a general store, and Jane sank down onto a bench. She put her face in her hands and felt a tuft of hair on her jaw.

Hair. On her face. Hair.

Oh, consarn it, Jane thought. *Not now!*

Winnie dashed back with a ladle of water. "Here you go."

"Thanks." Jane gulped down the water, grateful to get rid of the hairball taste. Then she stuck her furry chin into the collar of her shirt and walked back toward the hotel, at a much faster pace this time. The bellhop, reinstalled, it seemed, eyed Jane warily from the doorway.

"I better leave you here," Jane said. "I got someplace I gotta be."

She was sitting at the bar again when Bill found her, Frank and Annie both trailing him, wearing their guns and looking antsy. Jane wondered if she'd messed up and there was a show tonight. She was pretty sure there wasn't. But then she wasn't altogether sure what day of the week it was.

"Good grief, Jane, you look terrible," said Frank. "It's barely even five o'clock."

But she was actually feeling somewhat better. There was no hair on her chin anymore. No hairballs working their way up her throat. No hair sprouting between her toes. She was back to the usual amount of hair.

She lifted a glass to toast him. "It's five o'clock somewhere."

Bill stilled the glass before it got to her mouth. "We know who the man in the top hat is. I'm going to need everybody when we go to arrest him."

That perked Jane right up. "Arrest him? When?"

"Now," Annie said brightly, like she had never been more ready for anything. "We're going right this minute."

"Simmer down," Bill said. "You're here to observe, not get into the action."

Jane jumped to her feet. "I'm in."

She wasn't drunk, but Frank put his arm around her anyway, like she needed the support, which she thought nice but unnecessary. "Who is it?" she whispered as they swerved out onto the street. "Who's the top hat man?"

Frank cleared his throat. He seemed uncomfortable. "You're not going to believe this."

"I'm pretty sure I will."

"It's George W. C. Johnston," Annie burst out, her blue eyes dancing with excitement. "The mayor!"

SEVENTEEN

Frank

"The mayor," Jane said incredulously.

"Turns out moonlight does have a smell," Annie said, "and Mr. Hickok recognized the pairing with peppermint from the shooting competition."

Frank shoved his hands into his pockets and remained silent.

"Well, what do you know," Jane said. "Frank, you okay? What's wrong?"

Frank smoothed the frown off his face. His conversation with Annie kept rolling over in his mind, made worse every time she looked up at him with those bright eyes and flashed a smile, as though they were best of friends now—or maybe more. He'd wanted to be more, and for a short, magical time, Frank had thought that Annie was *the one*. Until it became glaringly obvious that she hated wolves.

Hated *him*. She just didn't know it yet. (Frank was a garou, in case you didn't catch that in his last chapter. He'd been one ever since he could remember.)

"Frank?" Jane pressed.

"Yeah." He pushed a false cheer into his voice. "It's good news. I'm just figuring out how we're going to handle him quietly."

"Or kill him loudly," Annie said. "Lest we forget, he's probably responsible for turning lots and lots of people into bloodthirsty wolves."

An eager light shone in Annie's eyes. Frank had to look away.

Bill put his hands out. "All right. We have no evidence of that. Plus, we need to interrogate him." He turned to the rest of the group. "Now, I've arranged a meeting with the mayor under the pretense that we have some information about the night at the candle factory."

"But we do have information," Jane said. "Why would you tell him that?"

"Because if he knows who Charlie is and who he works for, then he knows who we are, and he knows we still hunt garou. But he doesn't know that we know who *he* is."

"That's a lot of *know*s," Frank said, because that kind of commentary was expected of him. His heart wasn't in it, though.

"So if he thinks we have information we want to share, then he won't be wanting to ambush us and kill us," Bill said, like it was the most obvious thing in the world. "When we get there, we'll place him under arrest. Then we'll interrogate him."

"But if we know he's turned a bunch of people—and *killed*

people—why wouldn't we kill him?" Annie asked, sending another dagger through Frank's heart.

"That's not how we do things," Bill said, a disappointed-teacher tone in his voice. Then he addressed everyone else, too. "No one's drawing unless it's absolutely necessary, understood?"

Frank and Jane nodded. Annie stared at Bill, seeming to deliberate, but finally, she nodded, too.

"Let's go," Bill said.

Jack McCall met them outside the hotel, even though no one had invited him or even warned him that they were going somewhere. How the heck did this guy always know where to find them?

"Hey, guys! Where are we going?" he asked brightly.

Frank rolled his eyes. "We're going to practice for the show."

McCall frowned quizzically. "There's no show tonight."

What, did he carry around a schedule?

Jack McCall pointed his finger at Frank. "You guys are doing . . ." He looked right and left and then cupped a hand next to his mouth. "You know, a woof thing."

"Of course we're not," Jane said. "We're doing the opposite of that."

"So then you won't mind if I come with ya."

"Oh, we mind," Frank said.

McCall frowned. "I guess that's okay. I have plans to meet that reporter, Buntline, for a drink."

Alarm rolled through Frank. The last thing they needed was

McCall telling a reporter his own version of what happened at the P & G. What did he know about it anyway? He'd gotten scared and had run off, not doing anything useful. But they didn't need any of it in the papers.

"Fine," Frank said, blowing out a long breath, "you can tag along, but don't get in our way."

The group departed for the mayor's house.

It was darker than it should've been for five o'clock. Thunder clapped as the gang stood at the entrance of the mayor's mansion.

Bill raised the knocker and banged it on the large oak door.

After a few moments, it opened, creaking loudly, and there stood a butler wearing a drab uniform and an even drabber expression.

"You know, you can grease them there joints," Jane told him.

He looked her up and down and didn't answer.

Jane jerked her head toward Bill. "Wild Bill Hickok, here to see the mayor."

The butler gave a single nod. "The mayor is expecting you."

The gang started forward, but the butler put up his hand. "He is only expecting Mr. Hickok."

"Mister, we're all coming in." Jane pushed the side of her jacket out of the way and let him get a look at her gun.

"If you'll follow me," the butler said, turning around and raising a lantern. It was weirdly dark inside, but Frank figured maybe that was because of the dark skies outside, and the dark wood paneling on the walls.

The butler led them down a hallway and into a parlor. "Please sit. The mayor will be along in due time."

The gang sat down, except for Jane, who opted to stand. "Haven't they ever heard of more candles?" she asked.

"Maybe there's a shortage after the factory thing," Frank suggested.

"Ha," Jane said unenthusiastically.

Suddenly there was another candle. "I never go anywhere without an emergency candle," Annie said.

Right then, the door to the sitting room opened, revealing a silhouette wearing a top hat.

Everyone jumped, and Annie whispered, "I knew it!" even though Frank had no idea what she thought she'd known.

The silhouette held the lantern closer to his face. It was the mayor. "My apologies. I didn't mean to frighten you."

"Not at all," Frank said as his heart made its way from his throat back to his chest.

"Please excuse the lack of lighting. I'm afraid we have been hit by the candle shortage."

Jane snorted, and Frank shot her a look.

The mayor crossed the room and sat in the largest chair near the fireplace. "Now, what is this information you have for me?"

Bill stood up. "Well, Mr. Mayor, our information involves you."

"Is that so?" the mayor said.

"We think you could shed some light on the happenings at the P and G factory."

"How can I shed light when there's a candle shortage?" The mayor smiled at his own joke.

"Look, we're not here to waste time. We know you're a garou, and not only that, we know you were involved with the tragedy at the candle factory. I'm still deputized, and you're under arrest."

"Am I?"

Bill stroked his mustache. "But I'm willing to work with you if you—"

Suddenly the room fell into darkness, except for Annie's tiny emergency candle. There was a scuffle, a muffled yelp, and the squeak of a door opening and then slamming shut.

"Don't let him get away," Jane shouted.

Bill lit the mayor's lantern and turned it all the way up. Light flooded the room.

"He's gone," Jane said.

"Well, let's split up," Bill said. "Jane, you and McCall take the front of the house. Annie and Frank, the back. I'll search the attic."

Frank glanced at Annie, wishing he'd told Bill he didn't want to be paired with Annie. Sure, on one hand, she was really good at everything, and going with her meant they'd probably catch the bad guy ten years before everyone else caught up. But on the other paw, she hated wolves and was it any surprise that he was wildly uncomfortable being alone with her now?

It was too late to argue.

Frank and Annie held their guns at the ready as they ran toward the back of the house. They found a secret door through the kitchen, but it was locked. Frank didn't hesitate, nor did he think of the damage it would do to his shoulder: he threw himself against the door, and he and Annie burst outside.

But there was no sign of Mr. Top Hat, er . . . the mayor.

"You go that way, and I'll go this way," Annie said. "We'll meet at the front." And because they still had not learned their lessons about horror-movie tropes, they split up, each of them covering half a perimeter of the house.

They met in the front, but neither of them had spotted the mayor.

"I got him." Jane was coming from off the street, the mayor in front of her, his hands tied behind his back. "He was halfway to who knows where when I caught up with him."

Jack McCall was trailing behind her. "He was more like half a block away."

"He was not," Jane said with a scoff. "He was practically to the train station." She turned to Annie and Frank. "Don't listen to Jack. He's got, like, no depth perception, and he obviously can't judge distance."

"Ffffffft," McCall said.

Jane led the mayor back into the house. "Hey, servant guy, get us some gawl-durned candles!"

A few minutes later they were in the parlor again, which looked much less scary in the light. Frank lit a few more candles for good measure.

"Now look, Mayor," Bill said, his hat in his hands. "You're headed for a hangin'. But I can lessen your sentence if you help us."

"I'll never help you," the mayor said.

"Frank, shoot a toe off."

Frank tried not to flinch as he drew his gun.

"Okay, maybe I'll help you." The mayor shifted his tied hands. "What do you want to know?"

"Why did you try to kill Charlie?" Bill asked.

"Isn't it obvious? I found out you all were still hunting garou and that Charlie was heading up the whole operation. Of course I'm going to try to get rid of him."

Frank tried to hold himself back from striking the mayor.

Bill leaned forward. "If you're running the Cincinnati area, then who's running you?"

The mayor narrowed his eyes and smiled. "If I told you that, I might as well hang myself."

"Why?"

"Because the Alpha would kill me," the mayor said. "Or send one of the thralls to do it."

"Thralls?" Jane asked.

But as the mayor opened his mouth again, Jack McCall stomped over and got in his face. "Tell us who the Alpha is," he yelled, spittle flying.

The mayor laughed and looked at Bill. "Boy, does the Alpha have it out for you."

"Tell us!" McCall raised his fist, and Frank and Bill lunged to stop him, but they were too late. Jack McCall punched the mayor, splitting his lip.

The mayor spat blood, and maybe it was Frank's imagination, but his teeth looked a little longer.

McCall struggled, but Frank wasn't about to let him hit the mayor again. "This isn't how we do things."

"Watch out!" Annie cried, as the mayor dropped his head and the veins on his neck bulged.

Frank and Bill both leapt back, releasing McCall.

"Calm down," Bill said soothingly. "Just stay calm."

"Wooo," Frank suggested, but it did no good.

The mayor growled as the bones in his feet and legs cracked, bending backward.

"You need to stop this," Bill said. "If you turn, you won't be giving us much choice."

The mayor took two deep breaths and the transformation slowed, but then a shot rang out. The mayor's body went limp, shifting all the way back to human.

McCall's gun was smoking. Beyond him, Jane's eyes were wide with horror, and Annie's fists covered her mouth. Even Bill seemed shaken.

Frank rounded on Jack McCall, as he lowered his gun. "What," Frank growled, "did you do that for?"

EIGHTEEN
Annie

That hadn't gone like Annie'd thought it would.

The next morning, she walked down the streets of Cincinnati, toward the post office, the sound of the gunshot still echoing in her head, and she couldn't help but wonder what the mayor had been about to say. She wanted the garou dead as much as anyone, but he'd been close to telling them something about the Alpha.

How stupid of Jack McCall to shoot the mayor right before he gave up important information.

Who was that Mr. McCall anyway? He wasn't even part of their posse.

Well, the city was down one evil garou, and no one would be biting any more innocent people in factories. The whole *shooting the mayor* might be an issue, but that was Mr. Hickok's and Mr. Utter's problem to solve.

She tried not to think about the way the mayor had shifted back into his human form as he died.

Because he was *dead*.

Because Jack McCall had shot him.

Was it still murder if the man had been transforming into a wolf right there? What about if he'd been responsible for a dozen innocent people getting bitten?

Annie put those and other uncomfortable questions away as, at last, she reached the post office, the letter—and her contest winnings—clutched tight in her hand. It was an awful lot of money to entrust to the postal service, but she didn't have time to take it home herself—not if she wanted to perform at the show tonight.

As Annie pulled open the door to the post office, she noticed a familiar figure at the butcher shop next door: Jane. She wasn't doing much of anything, just standing at the window like something interesting was happening inside.

"Jane!" Annie waved. "Jane, over here!"

Jane didn't seem to notice her.

"Jane, it's me! It's Annie!" They'd been roommates since yesterday, and if that didn't make them best friends, Annie didn't know what would. But at no point did Jane look over, although several other people gave Annie a wide berth as they went about their business.

Frowning, Annie stomped into the post office and waited her turn. "How much to send this?" she asked when she reached the front of the line.

"Three cents," replied the postal worker.

"Three cents?" Annie cried. "Are you kidding me?"

Three cents was the modern equivalent of about *seventy*-three cents—for a simple first-class letter! Annie, who hadn't sent many letters before, was outraged.

Of course, she paid the exorbitant price, carefully counting out three pennies in the slowest possible manner, and released the letter containing a hundred-dollar bill (*one hundred dollars*, people!) into the hands of the postal worker who no doubt hated her by now.

Annie marched back outside, feeling as though she'd been robbed, and found Jane still gazing into the butcher shop.

Annie walked over to her. "Hi there, Jane."

Jane jumped and spun to look at her. "Annie Mosey! Lord, you should wear a bell. Where'd you sneak up from?"

"The post office."

"Oh."

"Are you all right? You seemed deep in thought."

Jane glanced at the butcher shop one last time, then started walking away. "I was thinking about those poor folks from the factory. They didn't deserve what happened to them."

Annie couldn't disagree with that. They were garou now, but it wasn't as though they'd asked to get bitten. They were victims of circumstance. But if Annie knew anything about the garou (and she rather thought she did), it was this: they would soon be monsters.

"It's a shame they'll probably do something terrible someday, and then we'll be right back in Cincinnati so that Mr. Hickok and

Mr. Utter can arrest them," Annie said at last.

Jane looked curiously at her, but before Annie could ask if the other girl disagreed, Jane said, "What were you doing in the post office?"

"Sending a letter to my family. Did you know stamps cost *three* cents?"

Jane nodded disgustedly. "It's robbery, that's what it is."

"That's exactly what I was thinking!" Annie grinned at the other girl, happy to have something in common with her at last. "Do you send many letters? I expect I'll be sending plenty to my family as we travel the country. Plus, I want to send them some of my wages; the contest winnings will almost pay off the farm, but they still have to eat."

"I send lots of letters," Jane said gruffly. "Tons. And I send money to my family, too."

Annie's grin widened. "Mother? Father? Siblings?"

"Siblings," Jane said. "Parents died a long time ago."

Annie's heart clenched, and she nodded. "My pa, too. It's his rifle I use, in his memory. Mama just got remarried. It's been . . ." Well, she didn't really want to talk about how her mama had been since marrying Grandpap Shaw. "I have lots of siblings, though. Three sisters. A brother."

Jane's smile was more like a grimace. "Yeah, me too. Three sisters and a brother."

"Oh my gosh," Annie squealed. "We're the same!"

(Poor Annie. She's trying so hard.)

Jane shook her head. "They rely on me. It's a lot of responsibility. Weighs on me sometimes."

"I know exactly how that feels," Annie said. "You know, we should write our letters together. And go to the post office together. Maybe we can get a group discount on postage."

"I, uh, don't think it works like that."

But Annie wasn't listening. Already, she was imagining the two of them sitting at a table, their papers neat and orderly, and the scent of ink on their fingers as they penned detailed letters to their siblings. How wonderful it would be to have something to share with Jane. They were the only two girls in the posse, after all; they needed to stick together.

Little did Annie know, but Jane's mind was far, far away from letter writing. "I have to go," Jane said, peeling off as they passed a saloon.

"Wait," Annie called, but it was too late. Jane was gone, and Annie was alone.

Annie wasn't one for paranoia, but it seemed like people were avoiding her.

First Jane had abandoned her for the saloon, and then Frank claimed he was teaching his dog new tricks. Annie had offered to help, reminding him that she had a way with animals, but he said he had everything under control and didn't want George to get distracted by her.

But she could not ignore the unusual coolness to his tone. Or maybe it wasn't unusual, and she'd misunderstood the connection she'd believed they were developing.

Alone, Annie practiced for the show, reread *Fearsome Garou and Where to Find Them* to brush up on her garou knowledge, and started sewing a new dress she could wear on the stage. She also finished that dress, because she had no one to talk to or go on a walk with.

The new dress was pink, fell to the middle of her calves, and had an embroidered flower up the skirt. It was perfectly girlish, and she loved every stitch of it.

She didn't have anyone to show, though.

Finally, it was time.

Annie pranced onto the stage at the Coliseum Theater, her rifle resting on her shoulder, and the crowd cheering as she reached the center.

"Welcome, ladies and gentlemen!" Mr. Hickok waved for everyone to quiet down. "Before we get started, the Wild West show has a surprise for you all tonight!"

Everyone cheered again.

"And I suppose you've already seen her."

The cheering crescendoed.

"Because she couldn't wait to come up here and give you the performance of a lifetime. Please welcome the newest member of the *Wild Bill's Wild West*, Annie!" Mr. Hickok stepped aside and motioned to her.

Annie smiled and waved.

Jane stood on Annie's left side, clapping too, while Frank stood to her right. He was working the crowd, urging them to cheer even louder, and when he glanced her way and their eyes met, and his were so warm and inviting, Annie's heart lifted into her throat and her foot actually popped back.

The audience *screamed*.

He'd been too busy for her earlier, but maybe it hadn't meant anything. George *did* love her, and it was probably easier to train him if Annie wasn't around.

So everything was fine between her and Frank. Good. That settled, she threw herself into the show they'd rehearsed, giving it everything she had.

The first act was a retelling of Annie's introduction to the Wild West show, including the competition, although it had been thoroughly revised to include a lot more George the Poodle, Jane and her bullwhip, and even some singing. The vote had been left out, which was probably for the best.

After that, they moved on to trick shots, aiming for smaller and smaller targets—like playing cards and thimbles. The audience ate it up, a few even offering items out of their own pockets. At one point, Frank was given a lady's hairpin. He tossed it into the air, Annie shot, and Frank handed the bent pin back to the young lady with a flourish.

Finally, they reached the grand finale, tense with a fictional garou hunt, which Mr. Hickok narrated. This animated, excited man was a mask he put on when he was onstage, she realized, because this was certainly not the Wild Bill she was coming to know. And then there was George: he was the "garou," and no one could take him seriously, because every time he was "killed," he rolled onto his back and wagged his tail as his tongue lolled out of his mouth.

By the time Mr. Hickok swept back to the center of the stage, the audience was roaring with laughter and applause. "Thank you, all!" He waved his hat around. "Thank you so much for coming to our show."

If Annie had ever had any reservations about show business, she would never admit to it after this. As the applause escalated and everyone from the company took a bow, Annie knew this was where she wanted to be. Up here, on the stage, with these people— her heart felt full with happiness.

"And let's hear it one more time for our newest member, Annie!" Mr. Hickok shouted over the din. "You've just witnessed history with this one!"

Annie curtsied, smiling so hard her face hurt.

Then, the curtain fell and the audience began to filter out, and the mood backstage shifted.

Frank, who'd been his normal warm and charming self during the show, abruptly pulled away from her. "I have to help clean up."

"I'll help, too!" Annie trotted after him. "The show was amazing," she said, reaching for a nearby broom. "All those people! I can see why you love it."

"Yeah, it was amazing." But Frank didn't sound excited, only irritated. He took the broom from her and nodded toward the door. "Go meet your adoring public."

She tilted her head and frowned, but she was new around here, and maybe he was always moody like this after a show? (He hadn't been before, when she'd demanded to join the posse, but . . .)

"Is everything all right?"

"It's fine." He motioned for her to go, then started sweeping bits of paper and glass and shotgun shells without another word.

Stung, Annie got her gun and headed over to the door and found a dozen young women (the same unchaperoned young women who'd been fawning over Frank after every show), and even a few reporters.

"Annie!" one of the young women called. "Annie, come here!"

Annie smoothed her dress and smiled, suddenly imagining a class for women in which she taught gun safety, how to shoot, and more gun safety. If they were interested in her performance tonight, she'd be happy to teach them.

"What's it like working with Frank Butler?" one asked.

Annie groaned.

"You must have a very close relationship by now," another said. "But *how* close?"

Annie glanced over her shoulder, where she could see Frank pause his sweeping and lean over to say something to Jane. He did not look at Annie.

"Well?" the young woman asked. "How close?"

Not as close as Annie had thought. Not as close as she *wanted* to be.

The truth of that feeling bloomed in her stomach, and then

sank with the understanding that Frank was (probably) being cold to her for a reason, and she didn't know him nearly well enough to be able to guess what that reason might be. Except . . . she did know the *Wild Bill's Wild West* was his great love, and she had just received an immense round of applause on the stage he'd worked so hard to build.

Was he . . . jealous? Threatened?

"You'll have to ask him how close we are," Annie said with a wink, even though a sharp pain sliced through her heart. She'd liked him. *Really* liked him. She'd been ready to kiss him, after all, and then he'd pulled away. Now, here he was—well, over there, but you know what we mean—feeling threatened by her success simply because she was a girl. Didn't her success make the show's prospects better for everyone?

Some of the young ladies groaned. "Annie, please. He'll never tell us. All he does is sign autographs and say nice things about our hair, and then he goes off with Wild Bill and Calamity Jane."

Annie shrugged. "Then I guess you'll never know. But I will tell you this." She leaned forward. The young women leaned forward, too. "There's no business like show business."

"Miss Annie!" A reporter pushed his way through the throng of young women. "We want a photo for the paper!"

Annie lifted her rifle to rest on her shoulder and smiled as the camera flashed, and she blinked away stars.

"What's it like performing with *Wild Bill's Wild West*?" the reporter asked, pencil poised over a notebook. "Where did you grow up? How did you learn to shoot like that? And what's your last name?"

Annie worked through the assault of questions, starting to answer the last one first, but she paused.

Mama and Grandpap Shaw didn't approve of her joining the show. Her sisters and brother were supportive, but still, she needed to protect them from newspapers and anyone else who might bother them. They liked their privacy.

She couldn't give the reporter the name Mosey. She needed a different name for the stage. Something strong and memorable, but mostly something meaningful to her.

She'd been thinking about that elderly man from the train lately, the one who'd reminded her that people could be kind and compassionate, the one who'd cared for her when he had every right to take her back to the Wolves after learning she'd run away.

Annie wanted to be like that: good-hearted and thoughtful, helping people who weren't as fortunate as her.

"Well?" asked the reporter.

"Oakley," she said. "My name is Annie Oakley."

Jane NINETEEN

"Get in there, girl," her pa said, pushing her. Jane did as she was told. (Although her name wasn't Jane but Martha, and this was obviously a dream, since she hadn't been Martha for a while.) She scurried into the house and took a quick look around: Lena was at the stove making dinner, a stew made of mostly onions. Elijah was nowhere to be seen, probably off begging or stealing, she didn't even want to know. Silas was coughing. (Silas was always coughing.) Hannah was sleeping, because Hannah could sleep through anything, and Sarah Beth was crying, because that, too, is what Sarah Beth always did.

But at least the moon wasn't talking to her. It had been haunting her dreams a lot, lately.

Her pa shuffled in behind her and slammed the door. His

cheeks were red, his eyes bloodshot and swollen-looking. Her heart sank. He was fall-down drunk. Again. "What is that you're wearing?" he slurred.

"One of your shirts." She did not mention that she was also wearing a pair of boys' breeches that she'd stolen off a clothesline a few houses over.

"You're dressing up as a boy?"

"So I can do the manly work. I'm strong enough." She dug into her pocket and produced a handful of coins. "I can muck stalls and dig ditches and run a message across town twice as fast as any dumb boy. I made almost a dollar today."

"You're a little girl," he said with sadness in his voice. "You should be at school. Not digging ditches."

She nodded. They should all be going to school, but then who would take care of things?

Her pa reached for the money, but she pulled her hand back. "We're buying flour for bread. Butter. Some cloth to make Lena a dress." Lena had been wearing their mother's old dresses, which were far too big and bold for Lena, and Jane couldn't stand to look at them one more day.

Her pa grabbed her wrist and slowly uncurled her fingers from around the coins.

"Don't," she said, but he did anyway. "You'll just drink it up."

His expression darkened. "I'm doing the best I can, girl."

"It's not good enough. We're hungry." She glared up at him.

"It's not my fault," he growled. "I didn't ask to be stuck here with a half-dozen children."

"We didn't ask it, neither," she retorted. "But it's your job, seeing as you're our pa."

"I don't got a job no more," he said.

She took this to mean he'd lost his position at the livery, which he'd only been working at for a month.

"Why can't you keep a job for more than two minutes?" she accused him.

"The boss didn't like me."

Jane shook her head. "It's because of the gawl-darned wolf."

He went still. "What did you say?"

"The wolf you got inside you. Like Ma did that night she—" Jane swallowed, but then pressed on. "The wolf makes you drink. You got to stop drinking, Pa. You got to keep a job."

"The drinking's the only thing that makes the wolf bearable." His eyes narrowed. "Don't you talk that way, girl, like you think you're better than me. You're too much like your ma."

"I am not," Jane protested. Her ma had been a hard woman, the kind of mother who would laugh if you skinned your knee instead of kissing it better. Jane had loved Charlotte Canary, because she couldn't seem to help it, but she didn't want to turn out like her. "Take it back. I'm not like Ma."

"You are. Putting on airs. Telling me what to do. You think you're special, but you're nothing. You'll always be nothing. You're lucky I ain't already turned you out on the street. You look like a street rat, right enough."

A lump rose in Jane's throat. She knew he was right—she was

nothing. If for no other reason than because he'd said so. But instead of crying, she launched herself at her father, fists flailing, screaming loud enough to make Lena drop her spoon into the soup, and make Silas stop coughing, and wake up Hannah, and cause Sarah Beth to cry all the harder.

"Take it back!" Jane roared. "Take it back!"

He pushed her off so hard she slid across the floor to the far wall. The wolf in him rose to the surface, stretching his shoulders wide and hunching his back unnaturally. His fingers curled into claws. His eyes turned golden.

Jane went still, all her bravery vanishing like smoke.

Her pa stumbled away and breathed deep until he came back to himself. Then he said, "Get out, girl, and don't come back."

It was almost a relief to hear those words. She'd been expecting this. So she shoved out the door and into the street. She could hear Lena and Sarah Beth bawling inside, but she didn't let that stop her. She simply ran and ran, faster than any boy in town, until she came to the sheriff's office.

She'd had a run-in or two with the sheriff in the past year, and it hadn't been pleasant, but she thought he was honest. He was sitting at his desk, chatting with a tall man with curls and a big black hat, and a silver star on his chest.

She didn't ask who the second man was. She just said what she'd been practicing, over and over in her head for weeks.

"I'd like to report a garou," she said. "A bad one."

The words that changed it all.

* * *

Jane opened her eyes to moonlight on the wall. She could see the moon outside the window, like it was looking in on her. It was almost full.

"Not yet," she whispered. "Not yet."

In the bed on the other side of the room, Annie was sleeping, hard, by the sound of it, her breathing deep and even. Jane got up quietly and went to the basin on the dresser to splash cold water on her hot face. In the mirror her cheeks were flushed and her eyes were bloodshot and swollen. But that's not what Jane noticed when she looked at her reflection.

What she noticed was this: she'd grown a mustache. Overnight. And her eyebrows were bushier. And the backs of her hands.

She clapped one hairy hand over her mouth, then turned to check on Annie.

Still sleeping. Probably dreaming about hunting garou. The girl was surprisingly bloodthirsty when it came to wolf people. Which was going to be a problem, seeing as Jane was fast becoming a wolf person.

Jane rummaged in the top drawer for an old bandanna and tied it around her face, then hurriedly got dressed. She could see in the dark, she realized, as easily as she could see in the daytime, maybe even better. One good thing about becoming a garou, it occurred to her, was that she'd be able to sneak in and out of places more easily. A useful skill. Now she could be as quiet as a dog's fart, silent but deadly, a whisper in the—

BAM. She banged her big toe on the footboard of her

bed—loudly, and hard enough that it would surely be bruised come morning. Her eyes watered. She blinked over at her roommate.

Annie didn't wake.

Jane sighed in relief and put her boots on (which hurt, gawl-dang). Then she crept to the window. She pulled it open and stepped carefully onto the roof of the hotel—the room she shared with Annie was on the second floor. From there she climbed down to hang off the edge of the roof until she let go and dropped like a sack of potatoes onto the street. Something twanged in her ankle (the other one from the hurt toe). Jane couldn't help it—she swore up a blue streak that would have had your grandma looking for the soap. Then, once she'd determined that the ankle wasn't broken, she got to her feet and glanced up again at the window.

No light. No movement. She was clear.

Jane stuffed her hat onto her head and hobbled off down the street.

(We'd like to pause here to reflect that it would have been a great deal easier for Jane to have simply gone out the door of the hotel room and down the stairs and exited via the front door. It was the dead of night by this point and fairly quiet. But Jane thought of herself as sneaking out, and in order to sneak out a person had to go in a sneakier fashion than merely using the door.)

She made her way straight to her favorite saloon. At first the barkeep was quite alarmed on account of the bandanna around her face and how folks didn't much wear bandannas around their faces unless they were planning to ride somewhere dusty or rob somebody, but then he recognized her and poured her a whiskey.

After a shot or two, she didn't feel the mustache anymore. The hair on her hands was gone, too.

"Say, you don't happen to know when the moon is going to be full?" she asked the barkeep when she felt it was safe to talk again.

He shook his head. "Sorry."

She thought again about her pa. She hadn't meant to get him killed. She'd only wanted him to change—to be better than what he was. To take care of them. She hadn't wanted to become like her ma, and now she was turning out just like her pa. "I'm sorry, too," she murmured.

"Full moon starts tomorrow," said a voice, and of course, there was Jack McCall, sitting a few stools down, smiling his persistent smile.

Jane found she didn't even have the energy to give him a hard time about the way he always turned up out of nowhere. "Hullo, there, Jack."

"Hullo, Jane." He slid down to sit beside her.

"How do you know when the moon is going to be full?"

He stared at her blankly, as if he didn't understand the question. He was a mite puny in the thinker and trigger-happy—that was the essence of Jack McCall.

"Because I am a garou hunter. That's what I am. Yep."

Jane accepted this answer. "Full moon tomorrow, you say?"

"Yep."

Shoot. She was out of time. "Shoot."

"Shoot what?" he asked. "Are you all right? No one's bothering you, are they? Because I'll give them what for." He seemed to genuinely like Jane, accepting her as she was without judging, so she sort of liked him back. And right now he seemed downright concerned.

"I just meant shoot as in, that's a shame," she slurred. "Seeing as I have a . . . friend, see . . . who was recently . . . bit by a garou . . . and the full moon is bad news."

"That does sound bad," he agreed, but then he appeared to have an idea. He dug around in his pockets for a minute. "I got an idea," he said.

"Huh?"

"This." He pulled out a crumpled pamphlet and slapped it down on the bar. "This could help your . . . friend."

"What is it?" she asked.

"It's about the cure."

"The what now?"

"The cure for the garou."

She snorted. "There ain't no cure for the garou. Everybody knows that."

"Yeah, but there is. Some person off in Deadwood has been curing garou left and right. It's a special injection, and they stab it into a woof, and the woof ain't a woof no more."

"Get out," said Jane.

Jack McCall got up and started for the door.

He really wouldn't know dung from wild honey, she thought.

She waved him back. "No, I mean, not get out, get out, but I don't believe you."

He scratched behind his ear. "I wouldn't have believed it either, but I saw it with my own two eyes."

"You've been to Deadwood?"

Jane had been hearing about Deadwood, largely as a place men went to try to get rich off some new gold that had been found in the Black Hills. It was out in the Dakota Territory, a town that wasn't technically part of these United States seeing as how it was in Indian land (more on that later), and as such didn't play by the regular rules. It had always sounded to Jane like her kind of place.

Jack McCall nodded. "I was there, right before I came to be here. I saw a man turn into a garou, and then they gave him the shot—the cure—and he went back to being a regular man. Garou no more."

Jane felt dizzy at the thought. "Garou no more."

Jack McCall smiled. "So you tell your . . . friend to get herself to Deadwood, lickety-split. Get the cure. And then everything will be all right."

"Deadwood." Jane stood up unsteadily.

"Hey, why don't you take this?" Jack McCall pushed the pamphlet into Jane's hand. She pressed it to her chest.

"Thanks, Jack. I gotta go see about something just now," she said, and lurched off toward the exit. And after she was gone, Jack McCall kept on smiling. Because he had done exactly what he'd been sent to do.

* * *

188

On the way back to the hotel she tripped over a dog on the board-walk, which almost sent Jane sprawling face-first into the mud.

"Hey, I'm walking here!" she said to the dog.

And then the funniest thing happened. The dog said, *Sorry sorry sorry* with a wag of his tail. Then the dog said: *My master said,* Stay, *so I am staying, because my master said,* Stay. *He is a good and smart master.*

The dog was talking to her. With its mind.

That was new.

"Uh, okay, then I'm the one who's sorry," Jane said. "I'm sure your master is good and smart. You stay right there."

I know a joke, said the street dog. *A squirrel walks up to a tree and says, "I forgot to store acorns for the winter and now I am dead." It's funny because the squirrel gets dead.*

Jane roared with laughter. "That's a good one!" she cried. "Good dog!"

The dog's tail thumped against the boardwalk. *I just met you but I love you.*

She scratched the dog behind the ears. The feel of the fur under her fingers reminded her of something. Something hair-related.

Oh, yeah.

"I gotta run," she said, and strode off toward the hotel.

Two minutes later she was standing in front of the door of Edwina Harris's room. She checked for a mustache, but the skin under her nose was smooth. Hands, smooth. Eyebrows of the normal amount. She blew into her hand to check her breath, which bore the smell of whiskey. But that couldn't be helped.

She gathered her courage, and knocked.

A few minutes later Winnie opened the door wearing a gray dressing gown, her long pale hair braided over one shoulder. She looked bleary with sleep, and Jane remembered that it was the middle of the night.

"Sorry, I can come back in the morning," she said.

"No, it's all right. Come in."

Jane went in. For a minute, she stood silently, staring at the floor, trying to find the proper way into this important conversation, but then she thrust the paper at Winnie and said, "What does this mean to you?"

Winnie took the paper and went over to the nightstand to retrieve her spectacles. She put them on and sat down on the edge of the bed to read the pamphlet. "This is about the cure for werewolfism."

So it was true. "Yeah. That's what I thought."

Winnie's voice became gentle. "Can't you read this yourself?"

Jane kept her eyes focused on the floor. "Never learned. Do you think it's true?"

"I don't know. I would have to investigate. I have heard some rumors about garou flocking to the Dakotas. I assumed it was because the laws concerning garou don't apply there."

Jane nodded. "What else does it say?"

Winnie's green eyes scanned the page. "It says to go to a place called the Gem, and talk to a man named Al Swearengen. It also says that the price for the cure is one hundred dollars."

Jane sucked in a breath. (As we've already established, dear reader, one hundred dollars was a lot of scratch.) "Dang, that's a lot of scratch."

Winnie's brow rumpled. "Jane. Are you interested in this cure because you . . ."

Jane shook her head. "Me? No, no, no, I'm not interested for me. I've got a . . . friend . . . who was bit . . . recently."

"You're asking for a friend."

"Yep. That's what I'm doing."

"Well, I hope your friend is okay," said Winnie.

"She's fine. She's going to be fine, anyway. Thanks." Jane took the paper back and moved to the door. Then, she turned and stared ruefully at Winnie. "I, uh, I've got to take a trip."

"Is this because of your friend?"

"Could be."

"Oh. I'm sorry to hear that."

"I just wanted to say, in case I don't see you for a while, or, like, ever again, that I really liked you."

Winnie's smile was like a flower blooming. "I like you, too. So much."

Jane found herself smiling, too. "You're sweet."

"Why, thank you. I hope I do see you again."

"Me too." This was one of those times, dear reader, when Jane should have said goodbye and left but couldn't seem to bring herself to do it, so she kept babbling nonsense. But then she thought of something she really did want to say. "Can I ask you for a favor?"

"Of course. We're friends, now," Winnie said without hesitation. "Ask me for anything, and if I can do it, I shall."

Jane felt a pang of wistfulness at the word *friends*. It was nice, hearing Winnie say that, but it didn't feel exactly true.

"Can you not write about me?" Jane asked. "Can we be friends, without me being the subject of one of your stories? Ever? No matter what happens?"

Winnie seemed taken aback (which we, as the narrators, think is saying something, because she didn't even blink twice at the incident with the hairball), but she regained her composure quickly. "All right. Yes. I won't write about you. Not directly, anyway."

"Promise?"

"I promise."

"Thanks."

"You're welcome."

"Well." Jane tipped her hat. "I'll be seeing you," she said, and ran off before Winnie could say anything else to make her want to stay.

Getting back into her room was even trickier than getting out had been. First, she had to go outside again and climb a helpful tree next to the building to get up to the roof. Then she had to remember which window was hers and Annie's. Then, when she'd figured out which window (thanks to the gingham curtains Annie had sewed only yesterday), Jane had to work it so that she could swing herself gracefully back through the window. Except not gracefully, because she crashed through instead of swung through, and then she landed again on her sore ankle. Then she jumped to her feet and tried to act like she'd been there all along. (Again, we'd like to point out, she could have used the door.)

"What was that?" she said loudly. "It sounded like a crash. I hope nobody's breaking in. This would be the wrong room to try to break into, if you know what I'm saying. On account of all the guns we got."

In response, Annie turned over onto her back and snored delicately.

Jane had to go—*now*, she felt—but then she remembered that she didn't have any money. She'd drunk it all up. She was going to need money, for a train ticket, maybe, or provisions to get herself to the Black Hills.

She bit her lip, thinking it over. She knew where Annie kept her money—in a little calico purse on the bedside table. She slunk over and picked it up. Inside was twelve dollars and fifty cents. Not enough to get Jane to Deadwood, but enough to get her out of town.

She stared down at Annie's innocent sleeping face.

"Hey, Annie," she said quietly. "Can I borrow ten dollars?"

Annie's response was a wheezy rattle in the back of her throat. But that was good enough for Jane.

"Thanks, you're a pal," she said, and stuffed the ten into her own wallet. Of course she would pay Annie back, when she got herself straightened out. Sometime. Maybe.

"I wish I could give you that thing, where I say 'I owe you'? What's that called?" Jane shrugged and dug in her pocket for the prettiest item she owned, because she knew Annie had a liking for pretty things. It was a smooth piece of rose quartz she'd picked up along a trail a while back. She set it on top of the remaining two dollars and fifty cents in Annie's purse. Then Jane moved quickly around the room, stuffing the rest of her meager belongings into a satchel. She wished, for what felt like the thousandth time in her short life, that she could write. She would write a letter to Bill. To Frank. To Charlie. Heck, to Annie even. She would tell them all goodbye, and how much they'd meant to her. Especially Bill.

She didn't know what he'd do if he learned she was a garou. She prayed that one day she would not find herself on the business end of his pistol.

There was a light tap at the door.

"Jane," came Frank's voice. "Jane, open up."

"We need to talk to you," said Bill. "It's important."

Well, shoot. Jane knew she couldn't talk to Bill or Frank, not now. True, she had just been wishing that she could say goodbye, but a face-to-face goodbye would require too much explanation on her part. It was best if they didn't know about the bite. Or maybe they *did* know about the bite, somehow, and were here to confront her about it. In any case she thought the best course of action was to go off real quick, get the garou situation taken care of, and come back good as new without any fuss.

Yep. That sounded like a plan.

Jane ran to the window and slung her leg over the sill. (We concede that it was necessary for her to exit via the window this time.) She tipped her hat in the direction of the door, and then slid out into the night air.

"Goodbye, y'all," she said.

And then she was off to see about that cure.

TWENTY
Frank

Yep. Jane was a woof. Frank couldn't wrap his head around it.

Let's back up to when Jane was walking down the boardwalk earlier. What she didn't know was that Frank was watching her. She seemed lost in thought, obviously unaware of her surroundings, because before Frank could catch up with her, she tripped over a golden retriever.

And here was where it got weird. She yelled at the dog. And then promptly had words with it. Frank wasn't close enough to hear the dog's thoughts, but he knew a conversation when he saw one.

That's when things snapped into place. Jane's strange behavior after the factory raid. Her distracted conversations. Her bushy eyebrows, which Frank had assumed was just dirt. And now she was talking to a dog the way Frank talked to George.

Jane was a garou.

No wonder she'd been distressed lately. She probably felt so alone. Frank knew that feeling of bearing such a heavy secret, and he didn't know what he would've done without Bill's guidance.

It was Bill who had rescued him from the garou who had killed his family. (That part of the show was true, but Bill hadn't reached baby Frank before the garou had bitten him that fateful night, a detail they changed in the retelling of the tale.) It was Bill who had taught Frank to control the wolf.

They'd worked on it constantly when he was a child. Any time that Frank got angry, even at the smallest thing, Bill would practice the Wooo with the young boy, and stay by his side as Frank learned to settle the wolf.

Jane could learn to do it. With Frank's and Bill's help.

What she needed now was to know the truth about Frank. He had kept his secret for so long, he wondered how it would feel to say the words out loud to another person.

I'm a garou.

Another troubling thought emerged. If Jane was a garou, was it dangerous to keep Annie around? One garou could stay a secret, especially one as practiced as Frank. But a second one, who had arguably the biggest mouth this side of the Mississippi? (And by that, we mean both sides.) If Annie found out, people could get hurt.

He kicked at the dirt.

Bill would know what to do.

* * *

When Frank got to Bill's room, he found it empty. He went downstairs to see the manager, who was chewing on a toothpick.

"Hey, you seen Wild Bill?" Frank asked.

The manager removed the toothpick from his mouth and used it to point. "He's at the Kauffman Saloon."

Contemplating the best way to tell Bill the news about Jane, Frank made his way there. The poker room was saturated with smoke and the smell of whiskey.

Bill was sitting at one of the tables, but as usual, he was in his corner with his back to the wall, making it impossible for Frank to lean down and whisper.

"Hey, Dad. Can I speak to you?" Frank said.

"I'm in the middle of a hand. Is it important?" Bill kept his eyes on the pile of chips in the center of the table.

Well, of course Frank wouldn't interrupt poker if it wasn't important.

"It's about Jane," Frank said. "She needs some help with . . . that . . . book about garou."

"Jane's always been able to take care of herself," Bill said, checking his cards again.

"Yeah, I don't think this is one of those times."

A man across the table sighed loudly. "Are we gonna play cards, or are we gonna start a book club?" (Reader, this was before book clubs were a thing, so the man considered himself very clever.)

"I'll be done in a bit," Bill said.

Frank rolled his eyes. If Bill would only look at him, he could wink. "She's gone and gotten herself into . . . a *hairy* situation. With a bad batch of *moon*shine."

Finally, Bill looked up. Frank nodded.

"I fold," Bill said.

The entire way back to the hotel, Bill was saying things like, "Now don't scare her off. You know how jumpy Jane can be," and "We'll tell her how *you* handle the wolf," and "Don't be too critical of her behavior."

At this one, Frank scoffed. "I'm never critical."

Bill shot him a knowing look.

"Okay, okay," Frank said.

They got to Jane's room and knocked, but there was no answer.

"Jane." Frank could hear the urgency in his own voice. "Jane, open up."

"We need to talk to you," said Bill. "It's important."

From the other side of the door, they heard a thump and then a scuffle and then nothing.

"Stand back." Frank kicked open the door, but when they stumbled in, they found one bed full of Annie, and the other one empty. Frank felt a breeze. The window was open.

He rushed over to the window to see Jane jumping onto the back of a passing stagecoach.

"Darn it." Frank looked down at Annie, who was snoring lightly. And cutely, he might add.

"How did she sleep through Jane jumping out the window and us kicking in the door?" Bill asked.

"I don't know," Frank said softly, still gazing at her. "She must be a heavy sleeper."

Bill cleared his throat. "Um, Frank?"

"Yes?"

"You should probably stop staring at her now."

"Sorry," Frank said.

"We've got to find Jane," Bill said. "Where do you think she's headed?"

"Toward the nearest watering hole?"

"I don't think so." Bill had opened the wardrobe by Jane's bed, and there were only Annie's clothes inside.

Frank sank onto the empty bed. "Why would she leave? Where would she go?"

"Don't know. She's got siblings in Salt Lake City. Maybe she'll head out west."

Frank put his head in his hands and stared at the floor, where he saw the corner of a paper sticking out from under the bed. He picked it up, and read the headline. "Maybe she's not running away. Maybe she's running toward something." He held up the paper. "A cure for the wolf? In Deadwood? Jane wouldn't believe this, would she?"

Bill sighed. "Becoming a wolf can make a person desperate. But at least we know where she's going. Let's head her off at the station."

"What about Annie?" Frank said.

Bill smiled sadly. "She was fine before us, she'll be fine without us."

But would Frank be fine without her? His chest squeezed at the thought of leaving her without saying goodbye, but maybe it was for the best.

Bill's hand came down on his shoulder and squeezed. "Let's go," Bill said. "Time is of the essence."

A few minutes later they were standing outside the livery, where they discovered that Bullseye (Jane's horse, as you'll remember) was gone. Black Nell, Mister Ed, and Charlie's horse weren't in the barn either. Even the donkey, Silver, was missing.

They walked around to the back of the livery to the gated corral. Their horses and the donkey were scattered about. Bullseye wasn't there.

"That . . . She . . ." Frank was so mad he couldn't form words.

Bill tipped his hat. "You gotta admit, she can be shrewd when she wants to be. Let's round 'em up."

By the time they rode to the station, the train to Chicago (the most straightforward way to Deadwood) had already left. Presumably with Jane on it.

"Time to go pack our bags," Bill sighed.

As they were leaving the station, two men in the corner caught Frank's eye. One was Jack McCall, the other a man Frank didn't know. But he had the biggest handlebar mustache Frank had ever seen.

The hairs rose up on the back of Frank's neck. "It's Jack again."

"Don't alert him to our presence," Bill said. "I don't trust that Jack McCall."

"Why?" Frank asked.

"Just a feeling," Bill said.

They watched McCall as he handed the other man a roll of bills.

"Well that's not suspicious at all," Bill remarked.

"Why do you think he's paying him?" Frank whispered.

"I don't know." Bill tilted his hat lower over his face. "That's something we can look into, *after* we find our Jane."

TWENTY-ONE
Annie

Annie had been robbed.

Frantically, she searched through the drawers and wardrobe and even under her bed, in case her money had migrated to better climates, but everywhere she looked, her money was not there.

Oh, some of it was. There was still two dollars and fifty cents, along with—mysteriously—a pink rock about the size of her thumbnail. But a whole ten dollars was missing.

"Argh!" she cried, because money didn't just get up and walk away. Money certainly didn't change into rocks overnight.

It hadn't been much money, but it was all her earnings from the show—everything she hadn't sent to her family—and she'd been counting on it to get her through the next couple of weeks. Show business paid, but it didn't pay *that* well.

Someone knocked on the door.

"What do you want?" she yelled, digging through the trunk below the window. It had to be here somewhere. It *had* to be.

"Annie, it's me," Frank said from the other side of the door. "We need to talk."

That was never a good sign. Annie jerked up straight and hit her head on the windowsill. "Darn it to heck!" she swore, and somewhere in Darke County, her mama steamed up in outrage and didn't quite know why.

"Are you all right?" A note of urgency filled Frank's voice. "Can I come in?"

"Yes." Annie rubbed the back of her head as the door opened and Frank stepped inside. He wore his brown coat, tall boots, and a worried frown. Annie was suddenly grateful she'd dressed first thing, before she'd gone looking for all her worldly possessions.

"What happened?" Frank asked, looking her over for injury. "You're not bleeding."

"No," she agreed. "But I think I was robbed. I should check if Jane—" At last, she glanced around the room and realized that Jane's side was empty. "Where is Jane, anyway?"

"That's what I've come to talk to you about."

"About Jane?"

Frank nodded.

"What about Jane?"

"I'm sure you've noticed that she's gone."

"Just now, yes." This was going to be an awkward conversation. Annie could tell. "I was distracted by the realization that I've been robbed. Ten dollars is gone. Mr. Frost should be alerted to the presence of a thief right away."

Frank sighed. "It was probably Jane who robbed you."

"What?" It came out like a shriek. Annie took a breath and lowered her voice. "Why would she do that?"

"Because she wanted to go to Deadwood, but she drank all her own money away."

Annie scowled. "She stole my money so she could go to Deadwood?" That didn't make sense. Well, it did, sort of, because Jane had been drinking an awful lot. A worrying amount, really. But if Jane had needed money she should have asked. Not that Annie would have funded her drinking habit, but— The rest finally caught up with her.

"Wait, Jane is in Deadwood?"

"Yes," Frank said. "I mean no. I mean not yet. She's going there. She left this morning and we need to go after her. Not Charlie, obviously. He's in no shape to travel, and he needs to stay here to await orders, but yes, Deadwood." He caught Annie's utterly baffled look and dragged his hand down his face. "I'm not explaining this well."

"All right. Can you start from the beginning?"

"Probably not," he admitted.

"Mr. Utter is awaiting orders because . . ."

"He's a Pinkerton."

"Oh." Annie raised an eyebrow. How impressive. "I thought he was the show's manager."

"He's that, too. The show is the cover, as you already figured out." Frank said it in a way that made it clear he didn't want the show to be a cover—he wanted the show to be the job—but it wasn't his call.

"Oh, right." Annie scratched her head. "So . . ."

Frank sighed. "I think I should get to the point."

"The point being that Jane is going to Deadwood and we're all going after her, with the exception of Mr. Utter," Annie said.

"The point being that you're no longer necessary in *Wild Bill's Wild West*," said Frank.

It took Annie a moment to register those words. Then:

"*What?*" Annie quickly covered her mouth. "Sorry," she said, her voice muffled behind her hands. "I think I have a concussion. Did you say I'm fired?"

"I said it more nicely than that, but in essence—"

"Why?" Annie glanced around the room, as though she might find something to help her cause, but the only things she found were her gun, her pillow, and the shiny pink rock Jane (apparently) had left in place of Annie's ten dollars. She grabbed the pillow and brandished it at him. "Is this because Jane is gone? Or because you're jealous that the papers like me better?"

"I'm not jealous!" Annoyance tinged Frank's tone. "And they don't like you better. It's just that you're new and different."

Annie scowled. "*You're* different, and I'm not fired."

He shrugged. "Look, Annie, I'm sorry. I was hoping it would work out, but I don't think you're a good fit for the group."

Annie's scowl deepened, and she clutched the pillow so hard her knuckles whitened. "What does Mr. Hickok think?" The question ground out of her.

Frank eyed the pillow warily. "I'm afraid Bill and I are on the same page."

"He's not even here. How can he be on the same page?"

"We talked about this before I came over. And he agrees that you're not a good fit for the group. Remember, he voted against you to begin with. And now I'm afraid I have to change my vote."

Why did people think they were allowed to change their votes? "You can't change your vote."

"You don't make the rules."

"Someone has to make rules, and you're not doing a good job with it. So I'll make the rules, and I say the first vote stands."

"No."

"Yes."

"No."

"Yes! I'm in, and that's final."

Frank threw up his hands in exasperation. "Stop trying to change the rules. You're out of the group, Annie."

"Didn't you see me in the show? They loved me. They really, really loved me."

"Maybe so," Frank said, his voice more even now, "but as you know, the show isn't the only thing we do. We also hunt garou."

"And I'm good at that!" Well, she assumed she was, since she was good at most things.

"Yes," he said. "You're good at that, too. But you have the wrong attitude about it."

"How?" Her voice went embarrassingly shrill. "I have a great attitude. I have the best attitude of anyone in my whole family."

He closed his eyes and exhaled slowly. "You hate garou."

"Oh, should I love them? They're monsters!"

He took a step back as though she'd hit him. "That's the problem right there, Annie. You think they're monsters. I think they're people."

"How can they be? They change into wolves and they eat livers and they go around biting real people to make other garou."

"Real people?" Frank asked. "*Real* people?"

"Yes, real people!"

"You don't think garou are real people?"

"No! They're cruel, awful creatures." Tears stung her eyes. Why was he being like this?

His voice rose, too. "Then you don't think I'm a person."

"What?"

"I'm a garou!"

"*What?*" She could barely ask the question. All the air had been sucked out of her.

Frank's eyes went wide as he seemed to realize what he'd just admitted. And to her. But the words were out, and he repeated them carefully so there was no mistaking them. "I'm a garou."

"No, you're not." Now she spoke in a whisper, unable to stop herself from stepping away. Her hands shook, and the pillow—

which she'd intended to hurl at him later—dropped to the floor. "You can't be." Everything was spinning, and in spite of the morning sun pouring through the window, a sharp chill crawled over her arms and cheeks and throat. Suddenly, she couldn't breathe right; air kept getting stuck in her shut-tight throat, because if she could breathe, then she could scream, and if she screamed, then the Wolves would be angry and—

"Well, I am," Frank was saying, oblivious to Annie's terror, "and the fact that you suddenly think I'm a monster when you didn't five minutes ago is exactly why you aren't a good fit for this team. The problem is you, Annie. It's not me. You're not as nice of a person as you think you are."

With that, Frank turned and strode out of the room.

The door slammed, and Annie collapsed to the floor.

Annie didn't move for three hours. Well, she did move, but it was mostly small shudders from her crying and full-body quakes as she recalled the terror she'd experienced every day for two years at the hands of the Wolf family. They *were* monsters.

And Frank was apparently one of them. Sweet, kind, funny Frank.

He couldn't be a wolf. Clearly he'd been mistaken. Confused. Maybe it was a phase. But why would he say he was a garou if it wasn't true? No one would admit to that unless they were sure.

Frank wasn't like anyone in the Wolf family, but if he was a garou . . .

A hollow pit of uncertainty formed in Annie's stomach. Maybe she needed to talk to him again. But no, she couldn't, because he thought she was a horrible person for hating garou, and anyway, he was on his way to Deadwood.

Wait, he was on his way to Deadwood because of Jane? Why was *Jane* going to Deadwood? What was happening with Jane? Annie hadn't even had a chance to ask. Some best friend she was.

Then again, Jane had stolen ten dollars. Maybe Annie didn't know Jane as well as she'd thought, either.

After a while, Annie realized that huddling on the floor would get her nowhere. She'd been fired, and she had only two dollars and fifty cents (and a pink rock) to her name, which meant she needed to get a job so that she could get home.

And then what?

The idea of returning home was crushing. After everything she'd given up to come here, Mama and Grandpap Shaw would say they'd been right all along.

But it wasn't that Annie couldn't do the show. She was good at the show. It was that Frank was a garou and somehow *she* was the problem.

You're not as nice of a person as you think you are, he'd said.

She pushed that away.

First things first. She needed to find a job and get enough money to have options besides walking all the way back home.

Annie washed her face and headed out to the post office. With the outrageous prices they charged for stamps (*three cents, people*), they surely had enough money to hire her.

"We're not hiring anyone," said the man at the counter. "But we do have mail for you."

"You do?"

"Annie Mosey?"

Her chest squeezed up. She'd been Annie Oakley for only a day, believing that changing her name would change her life, but even that was gone now. "Yes," she said.

The man passed an envelope to her, and her heart sank. It was the one she'd sent to her family, addressed to them, with her return address here in Cincinnati. "I don't understand."

"It was refused," the man said. "So it was returned."

"Refused?"

He nodded. "Yep. Made it there, then got refused, and came right back. Do you know how much money returned mail costs us?"

"And that's why you can't give me a job?" But she didn't care about the job anymore. She was busy staring at her letter, the words *return to sender* scrawled on the back.

A lump formed in her throat as she imagined Mama scowling down at the envelope and then thrusting it back at the postman in disgust.

Annie had officially been abandoned by everyone she cared about. Frank and Mr. Hickok had left her. Jane had left (and robbed!) her in the middle of the night. And now her family wouldn't even take her letters.

Or her money.

Annie tore open the envelope to find the hundred-dollar bill she'd won in the contest. It was enough to get her wherever she wanted to go, but where was that?

She couldn't go home. She might have been able to endure the shame of getting fired, but now, with this stinging rejection in her hands, she knew she had no place there anymore. Her family didn't want her.

Frank and the Wild West show didn't want her.

You're not as nice of a person as you think you are.

Gah! Why *why* did she keep thinking about that? And why had *that* been the last thing he said to her?

What if it was true?

Annie turned her thoughts to Jane. Yes, Jane had robbed her, but she was the only person who hadn't *rejected* her. And there was the matter of that ten dollars and this shiny pink rock. Surely Jane wanted that rock back. Annie wanted her ten dollars back.

And if Deadwood just so happened to be where Frank was going, too . . .

Nope. Annie was going to Deadwood for *Jane.*

She'd help Jane with whatever Jane's problem was, and maybe Jane would have some insight as to what to do about Frank. If anything. Jane could talk him into letting Annie back into the show.

You're not as nice of a person as you think you are.

It was like a song she couldn't get out of her head, even though *he* was the garou all of a sudden. Him. He was the problem, not her.

Annie gave a heavy sigh and pushed out of the post office.

All right. She had to get to Deadwood. The train was gone for the day, but there was more than one way to get to the middle of nowhere.

Back at the Bevis House, Annie gathered her belongs and settled her account with Mr. Frost. Then she went to the livery. Black Nell, Mr. Ed, and Bullseye were all gone. But Charlie's horse was still there, as well as Silver, the cranky-looking donkey.

She looked between Charlie's horse and Silver, then back again.

Silver let out a long, squeaky fart.

Holding her breath until the stink cleared, Annie saddled Charlie's horse. But she wasn't a thief (unlike her only friend Jane, who was totally the reason Annie was going to Deadwood), so Annie picked through the change she'd gotten from Mr. Frost and tacked a five-dollar bill to the back of the stall.

Then she was on her way to Deadwood—and, um, Jane. Yeah. Definitely going for Jane.

PART TWO

Deadwood

(In which all heck breaks loose.)

Mid-Logue

If this story were a movie and not a book, this would be the part where you'd see a map of the Old West circa 1876, with a dotted line that starts at Cincinnati and follows our characters from Ohio to what is now South Dakota. Annie, because she was the most direct person, took the most direct route: her dotted line was a train from Cincinnati to Chicago, and then from Chicago to Bismarck, North Dakota, and then a long and dusty 242-mile trail that stretched from Bismarck to Deadwood. This was "the fast way," but then the wagon Annie was riding in got a broken axle. Then they lost half their supplies crossing a river and had to stop and hunt for a while to make up for it. Then there were a bunch of folks who came down with dysentery and a bunch of other folks who got bitten by snakes. Then the oxen just keeled right over and died. So the fast way wasn't really that fast.

Jane, on the other hand, had never taken the fast way in her life. True, she wanted to get to Deadwood and be cured of the garou, and the sooner she accomplished that, the sooner she could be back with Bill and the gang, doing the show again, and everything could go back to—if not exactly normal, then the way it had been before. Jane took the train to Chicago also, earlier than Annie did, but in Chicago Jane blew through the rest of Annie's ten dollars in less than a week, and therefore she had to stop here and there to work for some more cash before moving on. So Jane's dotted line to Deadwood was a mess of wiggles and curlicues, through some of the most rough-and-tumble places in the Old West, like Dodge (but Jane got the heck out of there), Kansas City, and the seedier parts of Nebraska.

Bill and Frank took the train to Chicago, too, and afterward their dotted line simply followed Jane's. They always juuuust missed her, and eventually they lost her trail. So they gave up the chase and proceeded on toward Deadwood, where they figured they'd eventually run into their friend.

All this to say, all three of our heroes made their separate ways to Deadwood, where coincidentally (or just because it makes things simpler for us) they all arrived in town at roughly the same time.

Jane TWENTY-TWO

Jane was so close she could practically taste it. (We're pretty sure Deadwood tastes like a mix of mud and whiskey, which would have been fine by Jane.) At long last she found herself in Crook City, which was only about eleven miles outside of Deadwood. Of course she didn't have anywhere near a hundred dollars saved up (or, cough, anything saved up), but she'd figure things out when she got there.

Along the way she'd found work as a scout, sometimes, and a messenger, at others, but as a bullwhacker, mostly. This was a job in which a person used a bullwhip (because Jane's skills in this area were, well, legendary) to drive animals down a trail. Along this particular stretch of road Jane had been driving a team of oxen pulling a wagon of wannabe miners, every single one of them sure he was going to get stinking rich on Black Hills gold.

There were garou among them, too, Jane suspected, on their way to Deadwood for the same reason she was. Every time there was a full moon a few of the men disappeared during the night. Herself included.

There was a full moon rising tonight, in fact. After seeing herself through a few of them, Jane could actually feel the full moon coming on. Every month it was the same. Jane did her best to keep to Bill's "SO YOU'RE A WEREWOLF—NOW WHAT?" guidelines. She found a safe place to stash herself—a room where no one would bother her, or, in tonight's case, a big tree a few miles away from town. She'd prepare for the change—she'd clear a room of breakables, for instance, and test the strength of the chains she'd bought that first night on her own to make sure there wasn't a weak link. She'd lock herself up as tight as she could manage. And then she'd wait.

She never remembered much about the nights she spent as a wolf. She always woke up sore and itchy, her throat dry, her wrists and ankles marked by the chains. But she hadn't hurt anyone, which counted for a lot.

She'd felt the moon coming all day. Her body felt bloated and tender in places. She'd developed a painful spot on one side of her nose. (*Spots*, dear reader, is the old-fashioned word for *pimples*, which means that Jane was experiencing your typical teenage breakout. Although maybe it's not so typical, seeing as she's a character in a young adult novel, but we're just going to put it out there: Jane had a zit.) She was cranky and craving something salty. That's when she figured out it wasn't only the garou stuff she'd been suffering from, but another condition that befell Jane every twenty-eight days or so. Especially in the Old West, this part of being a girl kind of sucked.

But the moon was still coming, so she headed out to the designated tree well before sundown to chain herself up. The next thing she knew, she was waking up in the middle of Main Street naked as a jay, right as the sheriff was coming out of his house in search of his morning coffee. She was arrested on the spot for indecency and public drunkenness (although she hadn't had that much to drink the night before, but she'd take it over any other explanation) and thrown in the Crook City jail.

This was a problem, seeing as the full moon is a three-night affair and she'd only made it through night number one.

"You got a cell way in the back, away from the prying eyes?" Jane asked the sheriff. "I don't want to be disturbed tonight."

He gazed at her thoughtfully. "You a woof, then?"

Her breath caught. "I'd appreciate if that didn't become common knowledge," she replied. "I haven't hurt anyone . . . have I?" Because she'd been loose last night. Who knows what might have happened?

"Not that I'm aware," he said.

She let out a sigh of relief.

"You're headed to Deadwood to get yourself sorted out?" he asked.

"Yessir."

He stroked his beard in a way that reminded her of Bill. "I don't know if I believe in this cure business. But I guess it's worth a try. I do happen to have a cell way in the back. You can be a guest there until the next party comes through that's headed to Deadwood, and then go along with them."

She nodded. "Thank you, sir."

She spent all afternoon in that cell in the back, glad for the solitude and the strength of the iron bars. She slept off and on. She had another dream. This one of her mother.

The dream was born from a bit of a memory from when Jane was four or five. Her mother was in one of her gentler moods and teaching Jane to ride, sitting behind her and showing her how to balance on the horse's back.

A good dream. Her ma's hands guiding Jane's hands on the reins.

Her ma's voice in Jane's ear.

"You're a natural," she'd said that day. "You're a natural horsewoman, Marthey."

But today, in this particular dream, her ma said, "Come to me, baby. Come on."

Which didn't make no sense.

Her ma was dead.

Which led Jane to another series of memories, these ones not so good. Her mother's rough laugh as her pa shouted at her not to be so careless—"If the neighbors find out, Char, we'll get run out of town!"

To which Ma said darkly, "Let 'em come."

They had gotten run out of that town, eventually. And the

next town. And the next, until her pa had decided to move them out of Missouri for good and off to a fresh start. Which in this day and age meant going west.

Then the worst memory of all, Virginia City, Montana. By then Jane had known her mother could turn into a wolf monster, but she hadn't known that turning into a wolf was brought on by a bite, or that there were other wolf people wandering about in this world, called the garou. At the time the wolf just seemed to be another one of the many facets of her ma's personality: one minute, smiling, stroking Jane's hair, rocking a baby in her arms, the next minute ranting and raving, throwing their only teacup to smash into bits on the floor, the next minute telling randy jokes around the kitchen table to a bunch of visitors, the next sprouting fur and fangs and ripping up the new curtains Lena had sewn.

But that last night in Virginia City, that was the worst.

And it had started with an argument over the moon.

"Come on, Char," Pa had pleaded with his hands full of rope. "We don't want a repeat of last month. Let's get you tied up."

"I don't want to be tied up," Ma said with an angry laugh. "I want to be free."

"You cain't," he said.

"Why cain't I?"

"Because you might hurt someone."

"If I hurt someone," she said coolly, "they had it coming."

"You don't mean that."

"Oh, but I do." Ma smiled a wicked-type smile. "It ain't

natural to tie me up. It ain't the way."

He shook his head. "What is the way?"

"The way is the wolf." Ma stretched her arms over her head and grinned. "I should run. I should hunt. If I kill someone, they were meant to die. If I bite them, they'll turn, and that's all the better."

"You will bring calamity upon us," Pa said mournfully. He wasn't drunk then, one of Jane's only memories of her father sober.

"No," Ma said. "I'll bring truth. Let me bite you, Robert, and you'll see."

"And what about our children? Have you forgotten them?"

"Of course not," she said. "I love my children."

Jane, who'd been hiding up in the loft even though her pa had told her to go with her brothers and sisters to the neighbors' for the night, smiled when she heard her mother say that. She loved her children. Which meant she loved Jane.

"When they're old enough, I'll bite them, too," Ma said.

Her father inhaled sharply. "Why would you do that?"

"Because then they'll be strong. They won't get diseases. They won't die like so many sheep. They will be wolves in a pack. They'll be part of the future, instead of stuck in the past."

Pa's hands tightened on the ropes. "You're not right in the head. It's not your fault. I should have protected you. I should have never let you get bit."

"I wanted to get bit," Ma said. "I asked for it."

"You *what*?"

"I always knew I was meant for better things than this. I was meant for greatness. I won't accept this is as the most I'm going to get—this shack in the mud. This life."

Her pa was quiet for a long time, and then he said, "I am your husband, so what I say goes. And I say I gotta tie you up."

Jane knew immediately that this was the wrong thing to say. Her ma never did like that "I'm the boss of you because I'm the man" kind of talk. Pa should know better.

"I'd like to see you try." Ma's chair scraped as she stood up. There was the tearing of cloth and a low, horrible growl, and Ma was the wolf.

Pa didn't act surprised. He dropped the rope and picked up a chair, like he was the lion tamer Jane had seen once at a circus. With his other hand he brandished a gun.

And that's when Jane knew he meant to kill her.

"I'm sorry," he said softly. "I'm so sorry, Char."

"No!" Jane cried.

Both heads turned to look at her, peering over the edge of the loft. Then the beast that was her ma stalked toward Jane, snarling. In her yellow eyes Jane saw no recognition, no love, only an intent to harm. To bite. Maybe to kill.

She scrambled back against the wall as the wolf leapt into the loft. A shot rang out, and the garou howled in pain as a bullet tore through her back. She fell heavily to the floor of the loft. Jane took the opportunity to run past her and jump off the edge.

Her pa caught her as she came down. He set her on the floor and said calmly, "You run now, Martha, straight to the neighbor house, and don't look back."

She ran. She tried not to hear the other gunshots behind her. She tried not to think about what they meant.

At sunrise, her pa showed up at the neighbor's house to collect the children. He was bandaged and bruised, his clothes in tatters. There was dullness to his eyes. But he was alive.

"Goodness!" exclaimed the neighbor lady. "What happened to you?"

"I took a tumble off my horse on the way over," he said. "I'm all right."

His eyes found Jane's.

"Is she . . ." Jane couldn't bring herself to say it.

"She's gone to the angels," her pa said.

"Oh my!" cried the neighbor lady, holding baby Sarah Beth tight to her chest as if to protect her from the news. "Was it the fever?"

"Yes. It was a fever took her," Pa said. "There was nothing for it."

Jane felt wetness on her cheeks. She opened her eyes. These dreams that had been chasing her were bad dreams, but there was a kind of relief in them. At least in these dreams, no matter how bad, she could see her parents again. She wasn't alone.

Outside the full moon was rising against the window.

Come to me, it said.

Jane threw back her head, and howled.

TWENTY-THREE
Frank

"Are you gonna write something, or are you gonna just hold that pencil above that paper until we get there?"

Bill was staring at Frank, who was staring at a blank piece of paper. The train rocked back and forth, and Frank and Bill rocked with it.

George whimpered.

"It's okay, boy," Frank said, scratching George's head. "We'll be there soon."

That's not why I'm whimpering. There are so many ways you can start the letter. Just write it already.

"Yeah? Like what?"

"Shall I compare thee to a summer's day . . ."

"Oh, shut up," Frank said. But actually that was pretty good.

There was no way he was going to use it, though, and give George the satisfaction.

Bill, who had given up on getting an answer from Frank, pulled his hat down over his eyes and tilted his head back.

Bill's own letter to Agnes was on the seat between them. Frank leaned over to read it.

My own darling wife Agnes,

I know my Agnes and only live to love her. Never mind, pet, we will have a home yet, then we will be happy.

Frank felt a pang in his chest. He picked up the letter to read more.

"Write your own darn letter," Bill said from under his hat.

"What am I supposed to write?" Frank said. "Something like, 'Hey, I thought we were getting along pretty good, until I turned out to be something you hated. But maybe we can get past that?'"

Bill sat up and put his hat back in its regular position. "Yeah, something like that."

Frank shook his head. "Annie's hatred of wolves runs deep. It's not something a letter can fix."

"But it might be something love can fix." Bill took back his letter to Agnes.

Frank turned away. "You're only saying that because you found the love of your life."

"Maybe," Bill said, sipping on a mug of coffee. "But love is strong."

"Strong enough to overcome hate?" Frank asked.

Bill shrugged. "Maybe." He lowered his hat again.

You could tell her how you feel, George thought.

"That's just it. I don't know how I feel."

Yes, you do, George thought again. *You just don't know what to do about it.*

"Oh yeah?" Frank said. "How did you become so smart?"

George buried his face against Frank's leg. *I've watched humans for years. And if there's one thing I've learned— Wait, is that a ball? It's a ball!*

George ran after a wadded-up piece of paper another passenger had thrown over his shoulder.

"Gee, thanks, George," Frank said.

He went back to staring at his blank page. And finally, after a month of traveling, he wrote words.

> *Dear Annie,*

"Okay, Frank," he said to himself. "Progress."

He tried to see the situation from Annie's point of view. What if he'd found out *she* was a garou? In that case, she'd probably have worked hard to become the perfect garou, best in her family, and then everyone would want to be a garou like Annie.

Maybe that was the answer. He should bite her.

George growled at him, as if he could read Frank's thoughts.

"I would never," Frank said.

Bill snored softly beside him, obviously content with his love life.

"What are you working on?" a voice asked.

Frank looked up to see a man sitting across the aisle. He was slight of build, but well dressed, with an expertly tailored suit and a pair of round glasses perched on his nose. A pencil and notebook rested on his lap. "I'm sorry, but who are you?" Frank asked.

"Edward Wheeler." The man held out his hand. "Pleasure to meet you."

Frank shook it. "Aren't you the one who's been writing all of those garou stories?"

The young man beamed. "Yes. I'm glad to hear someone's reading them."

"Well, excellent work," Frank said. "But I don't know anything about all of that."

"Don't you travel with Wild Bill and Calamity Jane?"

"We're on a hiatus," Frank said.

The man scribbled into his notebook.

"That's not something— There's no story in what I just said," Frank protested.

Mr. Wheeler nodded distractedly. "I know. But I take notes on everything."

Frank wasn't sure he felt very comfortable around someone who documented his every word.

Mr. Wheeler looked up. "I'm doing a follow-up piece after your successful string of shows in Cincinnati. What's next for your group?" He licked the tip of his pencil and held it poised over the notebook.

After a long pause, Frank said, "We're looking into retirement."

"Retirement?" Mr. Wheeler said incredulously. "At the height of your success?"

"Well, Wild Bill got married and is looking to settle down." Frank allowed himself a moment to feel sad. He had not talked to his dad about his apprehension over Bill's impending retirement. Bill deserved to retire in peace and not bear any responsibility toward Frank's utter despair about continuing the show without Bill and how could he do that to Frank??

"But what about Calamity Jane?" Mr. Wheeler asked, pulling Frank back from spiraling into pure terror at the thought of the future. "She's obviously not ready to retire. Where is she? Can I interview her?"

Jane's departure and subsequent travel to Deadwood was definitely not something Frank wanted in the papers.

"Jane is taking something of a sabbatical," Frank said. "So, really, there's no story to tell."

"That's not what I heard," Mr. Wheeler said. "I heard she's traveling to Deadwood for a particular reason."

Frank furrowed his brow. How could this reporter know so much? Then Frank remembered something his dad had told him about the press. Sometimes they pretended to already know something to get people to talk. Frank was not going to fall into that trap. "Who said she's going to Deadwood?"

"What's the reason for her sabbatical?" Mr. Wheeler inquired.

"She's traveling to Deadwood for no reason," Frank said.

"So she *is* going to Deadwood," Mr. Wheeler said.

Frank rubbed his forehead. "Can we be done talking now?"

Mr. Wheeler shrugged. "I think my readers would be very interested in knowing how Jane is doing. Have you at least heard from her? Is she all right?"

Frank studied Mr. Wheeler's face and thought that it wasn't just the readers who were interested in how Jane was doing. Sadly, he didn't know what was happening with Jane. Yet.

He was about to give a vague response, but then he noticed another man walking down the aisle, probably on his way to the dining car. He was the same man Frank had seen accepting money from Jack McCall when they'd followed Jane to the train station. Frank would have recognized that enormous handlebar mustache anywhere.

"Excuse me," Frank said to Mr. Wheeler, standing up.

"But wait, you were about to tell me about Calamity Jane," Mr. Wheeler said.

"Another time," Frank said, waving him off.

Frank followed the mustachioed man to the dining car and watched him order a dozen biscuits and a jar of jelly, which was definitely too much for one man to ingest.

Then Frank followed him through two more train cars before the man finally sat down. Frank watched from just outside the door as the man distributed the food among a half dozen other passengers.

"One at a time," the man with the mustache said.

The group formed a line.

Frank noticed that one of them was missing a finger—like the worker who'd been bitten in the P & G factory. He *was* that worker, Frank realized, which meant he was a garou.

Frank watched the group for a while. They all seemed dependent on the handlebar-mustache man, like he was in charge of them.

Frank's mind whirled. Mr. Handlebar Mustache had gotten money from Jack McCall, and now here he was taking the factory workers . . . where? Frank needed answers.

It was time to confront this guy, even though confrontation was one of Frank's least enjoyable pastimes. He would so much rather be shooting the ace of spades out of George's teeth in front of a paying crowd.

He entered the car.

Mr. Handlebar Mustache looked up at Frank, then down at his newspaper, then up again, with a startled expression. There were biscuit bits in his mustache.

"Can I talk to you?" Frank said. "I have some questions."

The man glanced around, surveying his cohorts. Then he nodded and motioned for Frank to follow him. They left the train car and stood in the corridor connection.

"What are you doing with these infected factory workers?" Frank struggled to be heard over the roar of the wind.

The man opened his mouth to speak, and then shut it.

"Why did Jack McCall give you money?" Frank shouted.

The man shook his head.

"Who are you?"

The man looked relieved. "My name's Jud Fry."

Finally, Frank had an answer to at least one question, albeit the most useless. "Where are you going?" he yelled.

"Deadwood," Jud Fry answered.

"Why?" Frank said.

"Because . . . because . . ." Mr. Fry seemed unable to finish the sentence. It was like every time he attempted to speak, something was choking him.

"Who's giving you orders?" Frank shouted. "How are you involved?"

Mr. Fry squeezed his eyes shut. "I . . ." He winced. "I can't . . . I can't say."

"I don't think you want to hurt these people," Frank said.

Mr. Fry, eyes still shut, shook his head.

"Then help me," Frank implored him. "Who are you working for? Does this have anything to do with the Pack?"

Jud Fry opened his eyes, forcing a nod. "I'm a thrall." His expression became desperate, haunted.

"A thrall?" Frank repeated. "What the heck's a thrall?" The mayor had said something about thralls too.

"I have to . . . do what they say," said Mr. Fry, with effort. "I can't . . . talk about it."

"Who put you under this thrall?"

"I said I *can't* talk about it."

"Was it the Alpha? Who is the Alpha?"

"I *can't*," Mr. Fry repeated. "If you want answers, find the cure."

"What? Why?"

Mr. Fry held up a finger.

Frank was patient, because the man obviously was going through something, and— Oh crap. With a yell, Jud Fry threw himself over the railing and off the train. For a few seconds, Frank thought poor Jud Fry was dead, but then he saw Mr. Fry tuck and roll and run off into the woods.

Frank stood there for a minute, staring at the spot where Jud Fry had disappeared. Then he returned to the train car to interrogate the factory workers. "Can someone please tell me what's going on?"

The men exchanged glances with one another.

Frank sighed. "Why are you on this train to Deadwood?"

The man closest to him shrugged.

"Are you under this thrall?" he asked another.

The man pressed his lips together.

Frank kept asking, but they stonewalled to the point that it seemed ridiculous. Eventually, Frank gave up and headed back to his own car to tell Bill what he'd learned, which wasn't much, except that when he asked about the Alpha, Fry had told him to find the cure. What if the person behind the cure was the Alpha? Or knew something about the Alpha?

Frank couldn't be sure. But one thing he did know, riding that train as it hurtled toward Deadwood: there was no turning back.

TWENTY-FOUR
Annie

You might recall that Annie had also taken the train as far as it would go and then joined up with a group of would-be prospectors who were on their way into Deadwood. It had been a nice time, as far as arduous journeys across dangerous terrain went, as Annie had spent her days getting to know the other travelers, keeping a wary eye out for bandits, and performing a few trick shots for everyone in the evening. She had to keep her skills sharp, and she liked serving as a walking, talking advertisement for *Wild Bill's Wild West*. (Shortly after leaving Cincinnati, Annie had decided she wasn't fired until Mr. Hickok himself told her that she was fired.)

Now, the caravan had stopped for the night, and everyone was checking the wagons and stagecoaches for broken wheels or snakes, or anything else that might set them back again. Assuming nothing else went wrong, they'd reach Deadwood tomorrow after-noon at the latest, and Annie was filled up with nervous energy. Tomorrow, she'd finally reach Jane. And—maybe—Frank.

You're not as nice of a person as you think you are.

Her heart twisted up at the thought of seeing him again. Why did everything have to be so complicated?

As the caravan set up for the night (Annie was already fin-ished, of course), she grabbed her gun (habit) and headed into the woods. A walk would help. A walk always helped.

Sunlight shone long and golden through the pine trees, and the tall hills cast deep shadows across the deer trail where she walked, but she kept moving deeper into the woods, letting her feet take her wherever they wanted. (No, she wasn't worried about getting back to the caravan; Annie had a great sense of direction, unlike some of your narra— Ahem, you know what? Never mind. Annie had a great sense of direction, and that's what matters.) Anyway, she was walking and thinking, thinking and walking, and letting the forest sounds soothe away the worst of her anxiety.

After about an hour, the sun dipped behind the hills and Annie stopped by a swiftly running stream to rinse the sheen of sweat off her face. The cool water felt good, and she almost missed the soft voice on the far side of the water: "You should know that I just peed upstream."

Annie yelped and scrambled away, scrubbing at her face as she tried not to wonder if she'd gotten any water in her mouth.

The voice, a girl's, laughed but abruptly cut off with a *meep*.

Annie looked up—past a dark nose, down a long muzzle, and straight into the golden-brown eyes of a grizzly bear.

The bear stared back at Annie, neither of them moving while they tried to figure out what the other was up to. "Were you just laughing at me?" Annie whispered to the bear.

With a roar, the bear drew onto its back legs and raised its front paws . . . which would have been cute if it weren't for the enormous claws, yellow from dirt and age and the blood of all its victims.

Quickly, Annie considered everything she knew about bears.

First, she knew this: bears were always hungry, and so it was wise to avoid acting like food.

Annie was currently on her feet and backing away from the bear, not looking like food at all. So that was covered.

Second, one was supposed to make themselves look bigger than they were, to discourage the bear from attacking.

Well, that was harder. Annie was quite petite, but she grabbed the skirt of her dress and held it wide.

All right, next.

The third thing she knew about bears was that she should use any weapon at her disposal, so long as she didn't have to bend down to get it, as that would make her even smaller and more vulnerable.

Well, drat. Her gun was on the ground where she'd left it to wash her face.

"Well, drat," she muttered. Maybe she should play dead. No, that would only make her look like food.

Darn it all, why hadn't she read more books about bears? Why had she focused solely on garou? After all, there was more than one kind of predator in North America, so skipping the books about bears had been really shortsighted of her.

Wait, weren't bears supposed to be nearsighted? In that case, all she had to do was get far enough away and she'd be saved.

(Reader. Hey, it's us. So that whole thing about bears and nearsightedness? It's a myth. Yeah. It turns out that bears have pretty decent vision—at least as good as humans', and likely better than two out of three of your narrators'—and bears have pretty good night vision, too. Like cats and dogs and garou, they have a reflective layer on the backs of their eyeballs, called tapetum lucidum, which makes them appear to glow. So yeah, bears can see just fine—better than your narrators, and if it sounds like we're taking this personally . . . well, you're not wrong. Anyway, let's get back to Annie making poor life choices.)

Annie darted for the trees, hoping to climb one and stay really, really still, but the bear was a lot faster than it looked. It crossed the stream in three long strides and circled around in front of Annie, teeth bared and dripping with slobber.

With her intended path blocked, Annie glanced left and right, looking for another escape, but there wasn't much in the way of climbable foliage and the craggy rocks looked as likely to slice open her hands as give her a height advantage.

Rustling sounded in the trees behind the bear. More deadly predators? It would be Annie's luck.

Behind her, at the bank of the stream, she heard the click of a gun being cocked. *Her* gun.

"Well, drat," Annie said again.

The bear roared in her face, lumbering closer.

"Do you want me to shoot it?" That was the voice—the same voice that claimed to have peed in the stream. It was not, Annie noted, coming from the bear. "I can do it, if you want."

"*ROAR!*" roared the bear, so loud Annie's ears hurt, and then it pressed its nose against Annie's stomach and took a good, long sniff.

Annie squeaked, feeling remarkably like food.

"Do you want me to shoot?" asked the voice with Annie's gun. "You're a few seconds away from becoming a midnight snack. Probably should let me know one way or another."

"It's not even close to midnight," Annie said, even though that was the least important thing right now. The bear snuffed against Annie's stomach, and teeth dragged across the front of her dress. She *was* about to be a twilight snack, if that was a thing. If it wasn't, the bear was about to invent it.

"Well?"

"Don't shoot it." Annie kept her tone as level as possible, considering the powerful jaws were a breath away from closing around her midsection. And speaking of breath, the bear's smelled like whatever it had eaten for lunch. Annie inhaled as shallowly as she could without passing out.

"Then do exactly as I say." The voice—and the girl the voice belonged to—moved closer. Strange, because Annie couldn't remember another girl on the caravan. "Don't make any sudden moves."

"I'm not." Annie sucked in her stomach as the bear gave another long *whuff* there.

"Don't make eye contact."

"That's the first thing we did," Annie admitted.

"Then I'm afraid I'm about to witness your untimely death."

"Really? But I haven't found Jane yet."

"Who's Jane?"

"My friend who stole money from me. She was going to Deadwood."

"That sounds complicated."

"It is." Annie gazed down at the bear's round ears. They were really cute, considering they were attached to the same creature as those teeth and claws. "So, my untimely death . . ."

"Try backing away slowly and try not to look like a threat."

Annie backed away slowly, looking as nonthreatening as she could manage. (Which was pretty darn manageable, considering she was teeth to tender juicy guts with a *grizzly bear*.) "If only we had some sort of spray," Annie said, sounding calmer than she felt. "Something that could disorient the bear while we escaped."

"Good idea," said the other girl. "We could call it bear spray, to keep its purpose clear."

"That's really smart."

"Thanks."

"I'm Annie, by the way."

"Many Horses."

"I like horses."

"Me too."

"Grrr," said the bear, drawing their attention back, which was pretty self-centered seeing as how they all just wanted the bear to go on its way. But Annie's heart thumped painfully as the bear—whose eyes she continued avoiding—gave a soft *oof* and glanced between the two girls.

Urgently, Annie worked to avoid looking like a threat but also not like food. It was far more difficult than she'd ever imagined.

"I think it's calmer now," said Many Horses, as the bear snuffed the ground in front of them. "Let's back away slowly and show it we don't mean any harm. . . . Uh-oh."

Somewhere in all that, Many Horses had lowered Annie's gun, and the metal clicked, drawing the bear's immediate attention. Or maybe it was the scent of gunpowder. Either way, the bear knew a threat when it saw one, or maybe smelled one, and abruptly it didn't matter how good its eyesight was: the other girl was about to get mauled.

The bear roared, front legs up and claws gleaming in moonlight. It was about to come crashing down on Many Horses when Annie did the first thing that came to mind.

She let out a roar of her own and jumped onto the bear's back.

Annie's breastbone hit the large hump at the bear's shoulders, and all the air whooshed out of her, but she shoved her hands deep into the bear's fur and hung on for dear life.

The bear screamed.

Many Horses screamed.

Annie screamed.

Wisely, Many Horses turned and ran. From between the bear's ears, Annie caught a flash of a tall figure and dark hair, but that was all as the bear lurched after the girl. Annie shrieked as the bear's body jarred her up and down, side to side, and vainly, she tugged fur this way and that, trying desperately to steer it away from Many Horses.

It didn't work.

"Run faster!" Annie shouted, but with the bear jostling her, her voice bounced and it sounded like "Ru-uh-uhn fa-ass-st-er-rrrr."

Many Horses ran faster, but she didn't have a lot of options as to *where*. Until suddenly, she was gone—and Annie was trapped on the back of the bear and no idea which way to go.

She made another choice. Possibly a poor one.

Annie pulled the bear's fur to the left. The bear twisted its head around as far as it would go (which was not very far) and roared, and before Annie realized what was coming, the bear slammed its back—and therefore Annie's back—against a large pine tree . . . and started rubbing.

"It's going to scrape me apart!" Annie yelled as her clothes started to shred against the bark of the tree.

"Let go of the bear!" The other girl's voice came from overhead now.

"Then it'll eat me!"

"Let go of the bear and lift your hands!"

That sounded like a horrible plan, but already Annie's back stung from the repeated contact with the rough bark.

Annie let go of the bear and lifted her hands.

Strong fingers wrapped around her forearms, and as the bear leaned forward—so it could slam Annie against the tree again—Many Horses pulled.

It took some effort and maneuvering of their body weight as leverage, but eventually they conquered gravity and Annie and Many Horses were both in the tree, climbing higher until they were out of the bear's reach.

If this had been a regular brown bear, the two would have been in even worse trouble. Those bears can climb. But grizzly bears have that big hump on the top part of their back and straight claws, which makes it difficult to climb very high. A fortunate thing for our heroine and her new tree companion.

Below, the bear roared and scratched at the tree, shaking it violently. Annie sat on the branch below Many Horses, keeping her feet tucked under her, determinedly ignoring the stinging pain in her back where the bear had slammed her against the tree.

"You're bleeding," Many Horses observed.

"It turns out that bears are really strong."

The bear grabbed at the tree again and shook.

"You'll probably live," Many Horses said, "but I'll look at the scrapes when we're not under attack."

"Thanks." Annie wasn't a fan of the word *probably* in there, but she didn't want to argue with the person who'd just offered to tend her injuries.

"What were you doing out here?"

Annie looked up through the dark tree to find Many Horses looking back down at her, and suddenly she realized why she hadn't seen the other girl on the stagecoach train: she was a Native girl. Lakota, probably. She looked about Annie's age, tall and pretty, with twin black braids and tawny skin, and a no-nonsense sort of expression.

"I'm going to Deadwood tomorrow—"

"After your friend Jane, who stole money from you."

Annie nodded. "Yep. After my friend Jane, who stole money from me, but I'm nervous about it, so I decided to take a walk through the woods. I didn't expect a bear to pee in the stream, laugh about it, and then chase me around the clearing."

"No one ever does," agreed Many Horses. "It wasn't the bear who said that, though. It was me."

"I figured." Annie started to smile, but then realized she had to ask: "Did you really—"

"No." Many Horses sniffed. "I was just seeing how you'd react. I've actually been following you since you left the stagecoaches."

Annie looked up. "What? I didn't see you."

Many Horses shrugged. "Pay better attention, I guess."

Annie bristled. She paid attention! She paid better attention than anyone in her whole family. But— "I was distracted."

"Yep. I noticed." Many Horses passed Annie's gun down. "This is yours."

Annie accepted the long rifle, looping the strap over her shoulder. It hurt, but she was glad to have her gun back. "Would you really have shot the bear if I asked?"

"No. I would have let her eat you."

Annie paled. "Really?"

The other girl shrugged. "Maybe not."

"That's comforting." Annie gazed down at the bear, who'd (good news) gotten bored of shaking the tree but (bad news) was now camped at the bottom, waiting for them to come down. This was far from ideal. "Why were you following me?"

"Because I wanted to see who you are. You're awfully good with that gun."

Annie got the sense that Many Horses had been following her a bit longer than she'd claimed. "Thanks," Annie said, because her mama told her to never let a compliment go to waste. "I'm Annie Oakley, by the way." (She liked the name. No point in letting that go to waste, either.) She reached up to shake the other girl's hand.

Many Horses glanced suspiciously at it. "No thanks."

"I saved you from the bear," Annie said.

"I saved you first."

"You gave me tips about not looking like a tasty midnight snack."

"In that case, I saved you last."

"I jumped on the back of a grizzly bear for you."

They stared at each other. "Fine," Many Horses said at last, and shook her hand. "I saved you, you saved me, but mostly I saved you, so let's not get into pesky details about who was braver, even though it was clearly me."

Annie glared up, because she really wanted to win this, but then she remembered Many Horses was going to look at her injuries later and that definitely counted for something. "All right, fine. I'll let you have this one, but know that I'm keeping track from now on."

"What makes you think there's going to be another time?" Many Horses asked.

"I just assumed bear hijinks makes us best friends."

"It's going to take more than bear hijinks."

"Oh." Annie frowned. All those people on the stagecoach trail had adored her, so why was she having such a hard time making people she liked like her back?

"But I figure you owe me now," Many Horses went on, "seeing as how I saved you extra, so there's opportunity in there somewhere."

Below them, the bear rolled over and went to sleep, and two smaller—although still plenty big—bears ambled up to the tree. Cubs. They made adorable baby bear sounds, and Annie was glad she hadn't asked Many Horses to shoot the mama bear, but one thing was increasingly clear: Annie was never getting out of this tree.

"Is it safe to assume," Annie asked, "that you have a way you want me to pay you back, and that it's connected to the reason you've been stalking me?"

"*Stalking* is such a strong word."

"There's a young man I really like—his name is Frank—and the first thing I did, before we met, was follow him through a creepy, dark factory, and then to the Wild West show."

"Ah, so you're familiar with the art of collecting information by long-distance observation."

"Very," Annie assured her.

"Then yes," Many Horses said. "There's a connection."

"You may as well tell me about it now," Annie said. "I don't think we're going anywhere until the bears finish their nap."

"It's kind of a long story."

"I think bears can sleep for a long time."

"That's during the winter. But all right. The short version is this: Deadwood is an illegal town. It violates treaties your government made with us."

Annie swallowed hard. "I'm sorry."

"That's nice. But not the point. All these Americans are here to rip open the land and settle down, like they didn't just sign a treaty saying they wouldn't do that. But they found gold, so here they are. Violating yet another treaty."

"Breaking treaties is unforgivable," Annie agreed. "Please note that I came after my friend Jane, who stole my money, and I have no interest in ripping up the land or settling."

"I believe you."

"You should."

"Right. Moving on. Deadwood's illegal. All these people are here illegally. And then there's Swearengen."

Annie's breath caught. Was she supposed to know that name? It sounded important.

"Swearengen is a garou—"

A chill worked up Annie's spine, and not only because her clothes were in tatters. A garou. Here in Deadwood. But Frank was a garou, too, and . . . Her thoughts started to spiral back to the confused mess they'd been since he'd fired her, said he was a garou, and stormed out of her life.

You're not as nice of a person as you think you are.

"Are you even listening to me?" Many Horses asked.

"I was thinking about something else. Sorry. Will you start over?"

Many Horses sighed dramatically. "Fine, but only because I want your help. As I was saying, Swearengen is a garou, which is fine. That doesn't bother me. What *does* bother me is that the Pack is out biting other people."

Annie gasped. "Like people who work in a candle factory in Cincinnati?"

"That's really specific, but yes, like that." Many Horses shook her head. "Swearengen has been having wolves bite people, including a lot of my people, and then taking them into Deadwood. Sometimes we see them again, and we try to help them, but they don't want to come back home."

"Why not?"

"They don't seem like they *can* want to come home." Many Horses's voice went tight, like she was trying not to cry. "They act like they might, but then they get flustered and confused, and then just say they have something they have to do."

"Are they being blackmailed?" Annie asked.

"No." Many Horses looked out across the stream. "No, I think it's something even more sinister. My father believes they're being controlled by Swearengen."

"Right. You said that."

"No, I mean"—Many Horses sucked in a sharp breath—"mind control. My father believes that Swearengen is an Alpha, capable of putting other wolves under thrall, and that is why my people cannot—will not—come home. Or, if they do, it's only to bite others and take them back into Deadwood."

"That's horrible." Annie had spent the last two months struggling to come to terms with Frank being a garou, but now, with this, it was easy to slip back into that cold hatred. What kind of monster would take control of other people?

"This is happening to garou from all over," Many Horses said. "They come here and fall under the thrall, and then go out and bite more people to create more wolves."

Annie shook her head, wishing she had something encouraging to offer but unable to come up with anything. Too easily, she could imagine the wolves who'd kept her captive involved in something like this.

"My father went west to meet with other Plains tribes," Many Horses went on, "but I would not go without my sister."

Here it was—the reason Many Horses wanted her help. "Where is your sister?"

"Swearengen's got her," Many Horses said. "They bit my sister and took her to Deadwood, and I haven't seen her since. I won't leave without her. She's my best friend. My confidant. My everything. And I won't go anywhere while there's still a chance she's alive."

Annie's heart twisted at the pain in Many Horses's voice. Oh, the lengths she would go to if Sarah Ellen or Huldy needed saving. "What can I do?"

"I know Walks Looking is in Deadwood," Many Horses said. "She must be."

"You want me to find her?"

"Yes." Many Horses peered down, and when the bears didn't move, she quietly lowered herself to Annie's branch. "I can't go into Deadwood. I'd be killed."

"What? Why?"

Many Horses gestured at her face and arms and everything else. "Hello. I'm Lakota, and I'm not under Swearengen's thrall. People in Deadwood would kill me the moment I stepped into town." Many Horses looked away, over the creek, but she couldn't quite disguise the grief choking her voice. "My father and the other tribes were attacked at the Little Bighorn River a month ago."

Annie's throat tightened. "Oh no."

"A general named Custer led his army into the village and tried to kill everyone there, but our numbers were superior, and we won the battle. We call it the Battle of the Greasy Grass. But because we won, white people everywhere are mad and trying to kill *all* of us, even people who weren't there. Reservations aren't safe, either."

Annie wanted to be sick. On the stagecoach trail, she'd heard talk of watching out for Natives, and killing any who were spotted. Many Horses had taken a great risk in following Annie. "I'm so sorry," Annie whispered. "I know it doesn't change anything to hear this, but I think it's horrible, what we've done to you and your people. It's not right."

Silence stretched between them, giving Annie time to think about how she should have said something on the trail, when the others were talking about killing Natives. She should have stood up and announced her dissent.

Next time, she promised herself—because she wasn't naive enough to think there wouldn't be a next time—she would do better.

Many Horses tightened her jaw. "I used to see some of my people in town, before the battle. I watched from the hills and could see Lakota men and women walking around Deadwood. White people pushed them around, but I could at least check on them. But ever since the battle"—her voice broke—"I haven't seen them. They're either in hiding, or dead. I don't know which."

Annie's heart squeezed for her.

"I don't know if it's possible to reach all the Lakota wolves, but perhaps my sister is still alive." Many Horses gazed westward, her expression heavy with sadness. "My father said he would return to the Black Hills. I would like Walks Looking to be able to greet him."

"I want to help," Annie said. "Whatever I can do."

Many Horses sat up straighter, surprise clear on her face. "You will help?"

Annie nodded. "I have sisters, too, and if anything happened to them . . . Well, I know how you must feel about wanting to be reunited."

"Thank you," Many Horses said after a few minutes. "If you hadn't agreed to help, I'd have had to push you out of the tree."

"Really?"

"No. But I'd have thought about it." Many Horses gave a strained half smile. "I keep thinking about how scared she must be, surrounded by people who hate her because of what she is. They don't know anything about *who* she is."

The words struck Annie closer to home than she'd been prepared for. After all, she'd known *who* Frank was before finding out *what* he was, and she hadn't been shy about badmouthing garou.

"I have something that will help," Many Horses said, producing a small vial from her pocket. A purple-tinted liquid sloshed inside. "This is wolfsbane, mixed with a few other herbs. Just a drop should sever the bond between Swearengen and anyone under thrall. Hopefully."

Annie didn't love the *hopefully* at the end, but she took the vial and put it in her own pocket. "So your sister should drink it?"

Many Horses nodded. "But be careful. She might resist."

This was sounding like a worse and worse plan, but if anyone deserved *something* going right, it was Many Horses. "I'll make sure she gets it," Annie said. "I promise."

Many Horses pressed her mouth into a line as she gave Annie a searching look.

A blush rose in Annie's cheeks. "I know you don't have any reason to believe me. White people have broken a lot of promises."

"Without fail, your people have broken *every* promise."

"I won't break this one," Annie said.

"We'll see." Many Horses gave a tentative smile. "But I've been observing you from a distance for a few days now, and I don't hate what I've seen. I want to trust you, Annie Oakley."

"I'll do my best to earn it," Annie said. "Will you tell me about Walks Looking? So that she knows I'm there to help her, I mean. She won't have any reason not to eat my liver otherwise."

"All right. But turn around so I can bandage your back."

Annie smiled and obeyed. "I think we're best friends now."

"You wish." But Many Horses was smiling, too.

Several hours later, the bears finally got up and left, but not before Annie noticed the mama bear shoot a dirty look over her shoulder.

When the bears didn't come back, the girls climbed down the

tree and washed the blood off Annie before she returned to the wagon train.

"I'll meet you here as soon as I can," Annie said. "Watch out for bears."

"I think you're the one who needs to watch out for bears, but I'll do my best."

By the time Annie made it back to the wagons, everyone in the group was waking up and getting ready for the last day of travel. She kept to herself, changing clothes as quickly as possible before climbing onto Charlie's horse.

At last, the wagons set off toward Deadwood. Everyone smiled while they worked, bright with renewed energy and eager to see the end of this journey, but a dark worry settled around Annie. Swearengen, the Alpha, the villain the Wild West show had been hunting all this time, was somewhere ahead.

Then, finally, they reached the town.

Deadwood was set in a narrow gulch, with steep hills rising like walls on either side of the main road. Clapboard storefronts advertised saloons, saloons, and more saloons—with a couple of shops for mining supplies sprinkled about for variety.

Mud—not the kind of mud made out of dirt—squelched under Charlie's horse's hooves, and a mighty stink flooded into Annie's nose. She blinked away the tears stinging her eyes and gazed around at the inhabitants, but they were as filthy as the town. Their faces needed washed, their clothes needed mending, and no matter how hard Annie tried, she couldn't find one person with a full set of teeth.

That's when the sign over a saloon fell and hit a drunk man on the head. He dropped face-first into the mud and all the people around him had a good laugh.

Annie flinched, wondering if someone should make sure the man was all right, but just as she considered climbing off Charlie's horse to do it herself, he rolled over and laughed. Mud from his face slid into his mouth.

Annie swallowed back the taste of bile. Never in her life had she been anywhere near this disgusting.

Hand sanitizer hadn't been invented yet, but if it had, Annie would have been pouring it all over herself and squirting it at the residents of Deadwood, because five minutes in, there was no denying it: Annie hated Deadwood.

Jane TWENTY-FIVE

Jane loved Deadwood. From the moment she arrived, she knew it was her kind of place. In Deadwood, everyone kind of looked like Jane, and everyone kind of walked like Jane, and everyone kind of talked like her, too.

"Hey, you!" said a man from the door of a saloon. "Come 'ere!"

"Yeah?" Jane stepped toward him.

"Come closer," he slurred, and when she did the man belched in her face.

She brapped right back at him. The man laughed coarsely and called her a name that Jane didn't understand the meaning of, because (in spite of what a certain popular TV show about Deadwood will lead you to believe) that particular dirty word didn't come into regular usage in America until 1890, and this is still 1876.

"Here!" yelled another man, and thrust a heavy white pot into her hands. "Have a free commode from Bullock Hardware and Supplies!"

A-yep. She was going to fit in here fine.

What was there not to like? Everything in the town was brown, brown, and more brown, which happened to be Jane's favorite color. On a related note, they gave out free commodes. And best of all, you could get a stiff drink pretty much everywhere you cast your eye to. There were four "theaters" (ahem—brothels), and five saloons: the Montana Saloon (even though they weren't in Montana), the No. 10 Saloon (even though there weren't nine other saloons), the Lone Star Saloon (even though they weren't in Texas), the Shaggy Dog Saloon (even though the owner only owned a bunch of mangy cats), and the Tully Saloon (which was owned by a man named Smith). Nothing was properly named in Deadwood. Which was just Jane's style.

But first: the cure. The pamphlet had said to go to a particular place in Deadwood, and talk to a particular person, only Jane couldn't rightly remember either one of those finer details. It'd been months ago, after all, that Winnie had read her that pamphlet, and Jane hadn't exactly written it down.

She asked around. One fellow said the cure could be found on Sherman Street, but all Jane discovered there was a shabby-looking bakery. Another man suggested the corner of Gold Street and Main, but at that juncture sat a log cabin–type grocery store owned by a man named Farnum, who wouldn't stop talking at Jane in a funny way she didn't understand. Farnum was the one who told her to try Old Doc Babcock's place, seeing as she was looking for a cure, so she should probably see a doctor.

The cure wasn't at Old Doc Babcock's, but the old man did know where to find it: the Gem. Once a day, around about one o'clock, there was a show at the Gem to demonstrate the cure of the latest garou to pay the hundred-dollar fee.

"A quack, though, that Swearengen," grumbled Old Doc Babcock. "What you need to do is take one of my tonics." He rummaged around in a cabinet and started lifting out bottles. "This one here is Tott's Teething Cordial, satisfies the baby, pleases the mother, gives rest to both. But it would work on the garou, too, I imagine." He saw that Jane looked unconvinced. "I also got Casseebeer's Coca-Calisaya, made from the very best Peruvian coca leaves." Jane shook her head. "How about Dr. Lindley's Epilepsy Remedy, for fits, spasms, convulsions, and St. Vitus' dance—that'd calm a wolf type right down, I reckon. Or here's Mixer's Cancer and Scrofula Syrup, which cures cancer, tumors, abscesses, ulcers, fever sores, goiter, catarrh, scald head, piles, rheumatism, and *all the blood diseases*. That would cover the garou, right enough." He turned to her, his arms full of bottles. "For one hundred dollars, you could have them all."

Jane took a step back toward the door.

"How about it, young feller?" said the doctor. "One of these is sure to fix your wolf problem right up."

"It's not for me. It's for a friend," Jane said hastily, and then beat it out of there. It didn't take her long to locate the Gem. When she got there people were getting the chairs set up for the show. A large metal cage had been placed on the stage next to a podium. For a minute she stood staring at the cage.

"Hello, there," said a lady, who by her dress and face paint Jane instantly knew to be a prostitute. "Come for the cure, have you?"

Jane found herself shaking her head. "I'm a garou hunter, see. That's what I am. Yep. So I've come to see if this cure business is true, because then I should probably look for another form of employment, don't you think?"

"All right," laughed the painted lady. "Well, the cure works, sure enough, but it won't get rid of all the garou. There's not too many of them that can afford the hundred dollars a pop."

Jane nodded thoughtfully. "That is a lot of scratch."

The lady smiled. "Enjoy the show."

Jane took a seat in the back.

At precisely one o'clock, another painted lady walked up to the front onto the makeshift-stage area and addressed the small crowd that had wandered in from the street. She motioned for them to settle down, and everyone went silent.

"What you came to see here today is a marvel," she began by way of introduction. "And the woman who brings us this marvel is no less than a miracle worker, in my estimation, a pioneer, an entrepreneur, an explorer, an inventor, and a—"

"A woman? Isn't it a doctor?" Jane asked loudly. This entire thing felt less legit if the cure-it-all person wasn't a doctor.

"She has come to clear this wolf plague that's cursed our fine country," the lady continued as if Jane hadn't spoken. "I give you, Deadwood's very own, Alice Swearengen."

Oh. He was a she, Jane surmised as a woman in a fancy dress took the stage. She was wearing a brown top hat with a length of silk tied around the brim, which trailed down her back like a bridal veil. She gave a graceful wave to the audience. Jane's heart started racing, her blood pounding all the way up to her head.

She really, really wanted the cure to be real.

"I am Alice Swearengen, the proud owner of the Gem, but call me Al," said the woman. "Some time ago I took an interest in this wolf epidemic that is raging across America. It affects so many people who cannot help what they are and would otherwise be good and upstanding members of society. There must be some way, I thought, to eradicate this affliction without destroying the garou themselves."

Jane clapped hard at that.

Al Swearengen continued. "After many years of trial and error, I came up with a serum that will, once injected into the bloodstream, attach itself to the part of the person that has been corrupted into a wolf, and quickly disintegrate the connection between the man and his inner beast. Any man—or woman, mind you—who wants to, can be cured."

Swearengen's eyes found Jane's in the crowd, and the hair on the back of Jane's neck lifted. There was something familiar about this lady. Jane couldn't put her finger on what. It was hard because the lady's face was partially shaded by her hat.

"Why so expensive, then, if you mean it for any man?" another member of the crowd called out—obviously another garou who couldn't afford the stiff price of the serum. "Why a hundred dollars?"

Swearengen had a ready answer: "The ingredients for my serum are top secret, and extremely rare, which necessitates the higher price tag."

"All right, then," called still another man in the audience. "We came here to see it, didn't we? Let's see it!"

This was Jane's kind of crowd.

"Of course," said Swearengen mildly. She turned back toward the painted lady who was her assistant. "Can you bring me Mrs. Hoagy, please?"

The lady dashed away for a minute and then returned escorting a little old woman. She walked in small steps to stand on the stage, so bent over it looked painful. She was wearing dark glasses and a hat that largely covered her face. As if the bright light was too much for her tired eyes.

Swearengen took her hand. "I'm so glad to see you, Mrs. Hoagy. Can you tell me about your condition?"

"Oh, Doctor, Doctor, Doctor," the woman said in a strange, trembly voice, even though nobody had actually confirmed that Alice Swearengen was a doctor of any sort. "I got the woof inside me, Doctor. Can't you help me?"

"Of course I can. But it will only work if you truly believe in it. Do you believe, Mrs. Hoagy? Do you desire with all your heart and soul to be rid of the wolf?"

"Yes, Doctor! I believe! I want to be changed!" She gave Al Swearengen a wrinkled hundred-dollar bill. Swearengen thanked her and tucked the bill into her pocketbook. Then she helped the old woman climb into the metal cage before locking it firmly. The assistant handed Swearengen a long stick and a whip.

Jane felt her body tense. The entire crowd drew in a worried breath.

Swearengen held out her hand. "No need for concern, ladies and gentlemen. Mrs. Hoagy here has agreed to let us see the wolf part of herself, so you can be assured that we are curing a garou here today. She will not be harmed. In fact, she will be freed from the constraints this life has put upon her until now."

Jane sat back again.

Swearengen whipped the cage. Mrs. Hoagy startled. Swearengen reached between the iron bars and poked her with the stick, then whipped at her again.

At such provocation, Mrs. Hoagy reared back against the cage, away from the bite of the whip, and then lurched forward again, collapsing onto the floor. The crowd gasped and sat up, straining to see her as she writhed and screamed at the bottom of the cage. There was the sound of clothing tearing and teeth gnashing. The old lady gave a loud, bloodcurdling howl, and stood up onto her back legs. And suddenly Mrs. Hoagy wasn't Mrs. Hoagy anymore. She was a garou, a shaggy brown beast with the head of a wolf.

People in the audience were standing up and pointing and exclaiming among themselves. Many of them had never seen a real-live garou before. It was exciting and upsetting all at once.

Jane waited—holding her breath—as Swearengen and her assistant quieted the crowd and urged folks back into their seats. The garou paced the cage, snarling. Al Swearengen stood at the podium like nothing had happened, perfectly calm.

"She's all right," she assured the crowd. "Now it is time to administer the serum."

Men appeared next to the cage. They opened a small window on each side and somehow managed to capture the garou's arms. Then Al Swearengen quickly produced a syringe (which Jane had never seen before, either) and stabbed the needle into the forearm of the garou. The wolf lady howled in rage.

Swearengen withdrew a watch from her pocket and looked at it. "Sixty seconds," she said loudly. "That is all it should take."

Sure enough, something began to happen to the beast who had formerly been Mrs. Hoagy. It gave a strange, strangled cry. Its body jerked this way and that, and suddenly flopped once again to the floor of the cage. For several heartbeats it didn't move. Then the crowd gasped again as Mrs. Hoagy stood up shakily where the garou had been.

She was human. Her hair was disheveled from all the tossing about, a wild mess around her face. She snatched up and put on her glasses, and clutched the remains of her tattered dress around herself.

Swearengen unlocked the cage and helped the old lady out from it, giving her a long robe to cover her torn clothing.

She was still bent and old and frail-looking, but she was definitely human.

Jane's breath whooshed out all in a rush.

"Oh, Doctor, Doctor, thank you," rasped Mrs. Hoagy.

"Come here, madam," Al Swearengen said. "I wonder if you might tell me something. We all know that one symptom of the garou's disease is color blindness. Could you differentiate color, Mrs. Hoagy, since you became a wolf?"

She shook her head. "I could not," she croaked, and then smiled.

There was something familiar about the old lady, too, Jane realized. Something about that smile.

Al Swearengen lifted a brightly colored handkerchief in each hand. "What color is the kerchief on the right?"

"Blue," the lady chimed sweetly.

"And the left?"

"Why, it's red!" she exclaimed. "Oh dear! I'm seeing red!"

Jane had no idea what color they were, of course, but by the dumbstruck reactions from the people around her, Mrs. Hoagy had named them correctly.

Al Swearengen said something about the old woman having been through so much this afternoon, and needing to rest now and recover fully. But she would, Al assured the audience, recover fully.

The painted lady led Mrs. Hoagy from the room.

All eyes returned to Al Swearengen.

"My friends, you've seen a miracle tonight," she said. "And you'll see many more if you stick around this place. If you have a family member—or a friend, or even a passing acquaintance—who's a garou, I beg you, for their sake and yours, tell them what you've seen here today. Spread the word. Help them save up the money to be treated. And wolf by wolf we shall wipe this plague from our great land!"

The crowd clapped and clapped, Jane more enthusiastically than any of them. She could hardly believe what she'd just witnessed. It was true. All that Jack McCall had said. The cure was real.

Jane's heart surged with hope.

The crowd dispersed, but Al Swearengen motioned to her assistant again, who nodded and took Jane aside after Swearengen disappeared into one of the back rooms.

"You're Calamity Jane, aren't you?" the painted lady asked.

"Maybe," Jane said. "What's it to ya?"

"We're so honored to have someone of your celebrity grace our humble establishment," said the lady. "Ms. Swearengen has asked to see you. In private."

Jane didn't think that sounded like a good idea. She'd meant to slip into town all incognito-like, find some work as a scout or a driver, save up the hundred dollars, get the cure without drawing any unnecessary attention, and rush back to Frank and Bill and Annie pronto. She didn't want it to be known that the famous Calamity Jane was or had ever been a garou.

She was pretty sure Charlie would consider such a thing bad for business.

But the painted lady was insistent that Jane go with her, and in short order Jane was ushered up the back stairs into a large, expensively furnished bedroom, where Alice Swearengen was seated at a vanity, her back to Jane.

"Calamity Jane, I presume," she said. "It's a pleasure to see you."

"Uh, likewise," said Jane. The hairs were standing up on the back of her neck again.

"What did you think of the show?" Al Swearengen asked.

"I found it mighty interesting," admitted Jane. In truth, she wanted to whoop. She wanted to sing and dance, even though she didn't know how to do neither. She wanted to get working straightaway on earning some money. "I should get going, though. I got some things to attend to."

"Stay awhile," said Al Swearengen, and then, still with her back to Jane, she took off her top hat and started unpinning her hair. Jane squinted at the reflection in the vanity mirror, but the glass was warped a bit. She knew this woman, she was certain of it now. Al's features had been shaded by the hat before, and the fancy dress and booming voice had been distracting, but—

Then Al Swearengen turned to face Jane, wearing a triumphant smile Jane knew as well as her own, and she said, "Hello, baby."

And Jane didn't know what to say, except, "Oh. Hello, Ma."

Because Al Swearengen wasn't Al Swearengen at all, but Charlotte Canary. Jane's mother.

"I've been waiting for you," she said, eyes shining. "I've been waiting for so long."

TWENTY-SIX
Frank

Frank's first impression of Deadwood was that it was dusty and crowded. The streets were lined with tents, with people selling everything from whiskey to mining tools to baths. Frank saw hordes of prospectors sifting through mud and rocks in metal trays, no doubt looking for gold. New construction was going up everywhere.

One merchant pushed a live chicken right in front of Frank's face. "Chicken, mister?"

"No, thanks," Frank answered.

By far, most stores and tents were selling prospecting supplies like picks, pans, and shovels. It was a street full of commotion, and Frank and Bill had to work hard to weave through the crowds without being accidentally struck by a pickaxe. There was obviously gold on the brain here. One man was even carrying a chamber pot, which Frank didn't know what to make of. A second man came by with a chamber pot.

"What's with the commodes?" Frank asked.

The man tilted his head back. "New hardware store running a special," he said. "You need a new commode?"

"No," Frank said. "But I need information. You know a fellow by the name Swearengen?"

"Everyone knows Swearengen, but she ain't no fellow. That's the lady who runs the Gem."

"A lady? The Gem?"

"Yep. It's right smack in the middle of town. You can't miss it. Just look for the painted ladies out front."

Unfortunately, there were painted ladies out in front of most of the buildings in town.

"Thanks," Frank said. He and Bill walked some more and sure enough, there was the Gem. And sure enough, there were the ladies, advertising their wares on a balcony out front.

And sure enough, someone was trying to shimmy up a post on the side of the building and sneak in through a window.

And sure enough, Frank would know that tailored dress and long brown hair anywhere. Even from behind.

"That. Is. Annie," Frank said. His heart leapt.

George snapped his head. *Where's Annie?*

"She's climbing up that wall. What in carnation is she trying to do?"

"Do you mean tarnation?" Bill asked.

"I always thought it was carnation," Frank said. "Anyway, it doesn't matter, because that. Is. Annie."

Bill tipped his hat up and squinted. "It can't be. What would a girl like Annie be doing in a place like this?" he said.

"I don't know. And how did she get here so fast?"

"Can't be her," Bill said, but we've established that his eyesight wasn't what it used to be.

The two men crossed the street and went around to the side of the building to get a closer look, where the girl was still shimmying up the post. She was most definitely Annie.

She hadn't made it very far. She sure as heck would never reach the window, at least not by nightfall.

"Annie?" Frank called out.

"Hang on, I'm almost—" She froze and then turned her head slowly to see Frank and Bill. "Frank!" she exclaimed. "Mr. Hickok! When did you get here?"

"Just now."

"Me too," Annie said.

"And you're already breaking and entering?" Frank couldn't help but smile.

"Not yet, but if all goes well, I soon will be," Annie said cheerfully.

"I've got news for you," Frank said. "It's not going well."

Annie looked up at the window and sighed.

"Won't you come down here and talk to us?" Bill asked.

"I can't. I have a job to do," Annie said.

Bill and Frank exchanged glances. What job could Annie possibly want at a brothel?

"Oh, calm down. It's not that kind of job," she said.

Well, that was a relief. But it didn't explain what she was doing here. "Please come down," Frank pleaded.

"Okay, fine." She shimmied down and dusted off her dress. "What would you like to know?"

"Start with why you're trying to break in."

Annie clasped her hands together. "So I was taking a walk in the woods, definitely not thinking about anyone in particular, when I ran into a Lakota girl, who made an unfortunate joke about pee, and then we ran into a bear, who, I might add, we fought bravely, although you can't really fault the bear for being aggressive because she had cubs with her."

Annie's eyes were bright, and she was gesturing animatedly with her hands. She was so cute when she told a story. Frank remembered why he had fallen in love with her in the first place.

Bill looked worried. "How did you fight off a bear?"

"Well, most of our efforts went into not looking like food, and not smelling like food, and there was a lot of waiting in a tree."

"Wow," Frank said. "I guess that bear really had it coming. So is she staying at the Gem? Is that why you're breaking in? To finish off the bear?"

"No, I—" Annie started to protest and then smiled. "I see. You're being funny."

Frank felt his face getting red. "I was trying to be funny, anyway."

"Yes. That was hilarious. So, back to my story, Many Horses—that's the Lakota girl's name—got to talking and she told me that there's a nefarious villain here by the name of Swearengen who's been turning people into garou and then mind-controlling them. I know, right? Swearengen is obviously the Alpha you've been hunting. And Swearengen is holding Many Horses's sister hostage. So she asked me to help, and that's why I'm here."

Frank and Annie stared at each other in silence.

"Wow, that was a long story," Bill said.

"I think it's safe to say I've solved the mystery of the Alpha," Annie said proudly.

Frank opened his mouth to tell her that actually *he'd* solved the mystery, back on the train, but he stopped himself. Annie loved winning.

"Anyway," Annie continued breathlessly. "It's good to see you."

Frank wanted to ask her if she was sure about that, considering how they'd parted ways, and considering that she knew he was a garou, but instead, he said, "Why don't you use the front door?"

She tilted her head. "A girl like me in a place like that? I'd stick out like a sore thumb." She gestured to her long sleeves and high-neck collar. "Not the thing you want to do when you're doing reconnaissance."

From what he'd seen of Deadwood, Annie would stick out

like a sore thumb everywhere.

"You have a point," Frank said. "How about Bill and I go in first and check things out? If we see any sign of your friend's sister, we'll let you know."

"You would do that for me?" Annie asked.

Frank nodded.

"We'd do it for us," Bill clarified. "We've been hunting the Alpha for a long time. If it's Swearengen, our job is almost done."

And then Bill would retire. Frank sighed and turned his attention back to Annie. "You never told us why you're here, though."

"I did tell you. I'm here to break into the Gem."

"He means why are you in Deadwood?" Bill said.

She glanced shyly at Frank. "Oh, um, I wanted to get my ten dollars back from Jane. Do you know where she is?"

Frank shook his head. "Not yet. But she's probably around here somewhere. Or she will be."

"Why would she even come here in the first place?" Annie asked.

Frank scratched the back of his neck. Annie had traveled all this way, and sure, she was being nice to Frank, but she probably hadn't changed her mind about the garou. After all, she came here for Jane. Or at least Jane's ten dollars. Which also didn't make sense, because she'd probably spent more than that getting here.

Maybe Annie just needed some friends. But if she found out the truth about Jane . . .

"Jane wanted some time away," Frank said. "She's done this

before—taken off on us. She calls it her restless soul."

Of course, this was a big fat lie. Jane had never wanted time away from the gang.

"Deadwood isn't that big," Frank said. "We'll run into her eventually. For now, Bill, let's go check out the Gem and see what we can find out about this Swearengen."

"We need to be very careful," Bill said.

"I'm always careful." Frank grinned at Annie. "I'm the most careful out of everyone in my whole family."

Which was not even close to true.

Ten minutes later, Bill and Frank sauntered into the Gem and quickly realized there was nowhere safe to look. Scantily clad women decorated every nook and cranny of every room. Annie was right. If she had come in, it definitely would've raised suspicion.

They snooped around for a while, but didn't see anything that was out of the ordinary for a brothel, or any obvious garou or outright villainy. "What now?" Frank asked.

Bill smoothed his mustache. "Let's see if we can locate this Swearengen fellow. I want to get a look at his face."

Frank's heart started beating fast. "Are you sure that's wise?"

"Wise? Nah. But I've come to this conclusion in life, son: The boldest plan is the best and the safest."

Frank wasn't sure he agreed. A few men had already recognized Bill. They were whispering excitedly among themselves.

"We need to move fast," Bill said. "It won't be long before the whole town knows I'm here."

"Maybe we should have sent Annie," Frank said.

One of the girls approached them. She was dressed in a white slip with a matching corset over top. "You looking for company, handsome?" she purred.

"Where would we find the owner of this fine establishment?" Bill asked.

Frank wondered if his use of the term *fine establishment* was a bit loose.

"Al's in the back," she said curtly, less friendly now that she knew she wouldn't be getting paid. She smiled at a man at the bar. "*You* lookin' for company?"

"I guess we'll find our own way," Frank said. They headed toward the back, to what looked like an office. Presumably Swearengen's office.

"You look in there first," Bill directed. A solid plan, since Bill couldn't see.

Frank paused by the doorway, his shoulders to the wall, and leaned over quickly to peek inside. Then he froze. Because he saw Jane.

"Jane!" he whispered. She was reclined in a chair, her feet up on the desk. Frank smiled, relieved. He would have walked in and thrown his arms around her right then and there, but Bill grabbed his sleeve and pulled him back. Bill put a finger to his lips.

"But it's Jane," Frank hissed.

"Jane and who?" Bill replied.

Oh, right.

Frank inched over a ways to get a look at who Jane was talking to.

"It's a woman," he reported to Bill.

Bill relaxed a little. "So not Swearengen."

"But she's wearing a top hat," Frank said warily. He'd learned his lesson about people in top hats.

"That's not helpful," scoffed Bill. "What else? Does it seem like Jane's a prisoner?"

Frank checked. Jane was smiling. He hadn't actually seen her smile like that since the night of the factory. "Nope, she looks pretty comfortable."

"Does she appear to be brainwashed?"

"How does a person appear brainwashed?" Frank retorted.

"Well, what's she saying?"

"Stop talking to me, and I'll listen," Frank said. Garou had excellent hearing, after all. He crept closer.

"That sounds very nice," Jane was saying. There *was* something different about her voice. It was higher-pitched, maybe? And her tone was more respectful than he'd ever heard Jane talk to anybody. Maybe she was under a thrall.

"You'll take a room upstairs," said the top hat lady.

"That would be delightful," said Jane.

Oh my gosh, she'd used the word *delightful*. Something was definitely wrong.

"And you'll take all of your meals with me," the woman said.

"Breakfast, dinner, and supper."

"Of course," agreed Jane. She was being awfully agreeable.

"And I'll have some tasks for you to do from time to time," continued the woman. "A few odd jobs."

"Whatever you need, Al," said Jane. "I'll do it."

Frank's breath caught. Al.

"I think the woman might be Al Swearengen," he muttered to Bill. "And Jane just promised to do whatever she wants!"

"What? A woman?" Bill frowned. "Let me see. Switch spots with me."

Frank didn't know what good that would do, but he obediently traded places with his father. Bill peeked into the room. Then he stiffened and pulled his hat down, shadowing his face.

"Do you know her?" Frank whispered.

Bill shook his head and backed away.

"I'm so glad you've come back to me," the top hat lady was saying warmly.

"I'm glad, too," said Jane.

"We need to get out of here," Bill whispered urgently. "Now."

"But Jane . . ."

"We'll figure out what's to be done about Jane later," Bill said. "Let's go."

The two of them stepped outside.

"What's going on?" Frank asked. "Was the woman Al Swearengen?"

"I think so," said Bill darkly.

"And you know her?"

Bill didn't answer. He was stroking his mustache again, obviously deep in thought.

"Do you think Jane already got the cure and she's in Swearengen's thrall?"

"I don't know," Bill said.

Right then the saloon doors swung open, and out stepped Jane with Swearengen.

"I'm gonna follow them and see what I can find out." Bill tucked his long hair, his most recognizable feature, underneath his coat.

"I'm coming with you," Frank said.

"No," said Bill. "You go keep an eye on Annie in the alley, before she gets herself into trouble." Then off he went to follow Jane and Swearengen.

Frank stared after him, puzzled. Then he returned to the alley where Annie, indeed, was trying to climb the post again.

"Annie, get down," Frank said.

"Did you find Walks Looking?" Annie jumped down and brushed off her dress.

"Well, no. But we did find Jane."

"Jane!" Annie exclaimed, her face lighting up. "How is she?"

"She seemed good," Frank admitted. "But she might be in cahoots with Al Swearengen."

Annie frowned. "What?"

"I don't know. I'm pretty confused. Bill went after them."

Annie seemed to make a decision. "Well, if Swearengen's not in there, it will be safe to go in and look for Walks Looking. Be right back."

Frank caught her hand. "You still can't go in there, Annie."

"Yes, I can," Annie said.

"No, you can't."

"Yes, I can!" Annie argued. "I was tasked with finding my friend, or at least the sister of my friend, and that's what I'm going to do. Don't worry. I'm the best finder of lost things in my whole family."

"Annie—"

"I've just got to figure out a way to get in without being noticed."

Frank sighed. Clearly there was no talking her out of this, but he couldn't let her go in there alone. "Wait," he said. "I have an idea."

TWENTY-SEVEN

Annie

It was the worst idea Annie had ever heard.

How bad was it? It made building a tower in Pisa on soft soil look intentional, and inviting the big wooden horse into Troy sound responsible, and Tesla's earthquake machine (which wouldn't be patented until 1898, but that's a minor detail) seem perfectly reasonable.

In short, Annie had never—and probably would never—hear of a worse plan.

Unfortunately, try as she might, she couldn't come up with a better plan, which left little choice but to go along with Frank's. Step one: get a room at the Marriott hotel. There had been a number of interesting lodging choices in Deadwood, but the Marriott was nice, and they could afford it.

"This is stupid," Annie said as she changed clothes. "I hate this plan."

Frank's voice came from the other side of the hotel room door. "You've said that at least a hundred times, but it's a plan that will work."

"No, it won't. Everyone will see through this costume. They'll know I don't belong."

"With an attitude like that . . ."

"Gah!" Annie fumbled with the bodice of the dress—*dress* being a generous word to describe it—and stared at herself in the mirror.

Here's what Annie Oakley, Miss Modesty herself, was wearing: a yellow "dress" that only went down to her knees, and was nothing more than a slip of silk. It had no sleeves and even less cover over her cleavage. And to make matters worse, while it did have a corset, the corset was—for some reason—on the outside, and threatened to force her upstairs assets right out of the dress and its ridiculously low neckline.

Yep. Annie was dressed as a painted lady. A lady of negotiable affections. A soiled dove. A shady lady. The oldest profession.

You get the idea.

Annie thought she might die from embarrassment, even alone in her room. (Alone aside from us, your narrators, and you, the readers. We all get to witness this strange and deeply uncomfortable moment of Annie's life.) Never had she worn so little with the intent to go out, and now, not only was she expected to leave the room (wearing this!), but she had to do it in front of Frank.

"This is a horrible idea!" Annie called again. "I don't even have pockets!"

"Don't forget your hair." Frank tapped the door. "You have to pin it up."

"How do you know so much about this?"

"Uh." Frank coughed. "Well, obviously I had to go into the Gem to get a look around, and I'm just telling you what I saw."

"How closely were you looking?"

"I'm extremely observant. It's not a skill I can turn off."

"And where did you get these clothes?"

Weirdly, Frank didn't answer that.

Annie finished pinning her hair and peered into the mirror again. If she'd have seen herself on the street, she'd have assumed she was very cold and offered herself a jacket. Maybe a whole coat. Maybe a sheet to drape over her head. Now there was an idea. "If I put a sheet over my head, can I go as a ghost?"

"Ghosts aren't real. Are you finished yet? The day's not getting any longer."

And she certainly *would* be cold once the sun went down.

Annie gave a deep sigh and opened the door. Frank stood on the other side.

His Adam's apple jumped as he engaged his powers of observation. "Wow," he said.

"My eyes are up here." Annie pointed at her eyes.

"Right." Frank shook himself a little. "Right, okay. Should we go?"

"We can't stay here," she said. "I'll catch a chill and die."

Frank winced. "I'd offer you my jacket, but we need people to see you."

Annie died inside. No chill necessary. "You have the vial Many Horses gave me?" No pockets meant she couldn't carry it herself, which made her uncomfortable.

"For the eleventh time, yes, I have it." He showed her the inside pocket of his coat. "It's right here. What is this for?"

She didn't have time to explain. "Let's go."

"Okay," Frank said, but he just looked at her. (Her face, we should add. He was smart enough not to get confused about the location of her eyes twice.)

"Annie," he murmured, "I—"

"I know. We need to hurry. I've been telling you not to dilly-dally this whole time." Annie pushed past him and headed outside. She knew very well what he wanted to talk about, or what he thought he wanted to talk about, but this was neither the time, nor the place, nor the attire. No, when they talked about that fight in Cincinnati, she wanted to be fully dressed.

Frank followed along behind her, then offered his arm. "We should— I mean so that everyone believes you're— That is, I want to anyway but—"

"Please stop talking," Annie said, taking his arm to shut him up.

"All right, but—"

"Stop," Annie begged. "Not now." She couldn't bear to think of it again—his parting words back in Cincinnati: *The problem is you,*

Annie. It's not me. You're not as nice of a person as you think you are.

"I was just going to say that when we' go in there, you have to act like you like me."

"I do like you." Annie clamped her mouth shut so quickly she bit her lip. "Ow."

Frank glanced at her, worry in his eye, but he didn't say anything. He drew her closer and together they walked down the street toward the Gem.

It was a drab place, even though it had been built only a few months ago ("reputable" sources say it wasn't built until April of 1877, pfft), and it looked as likely to catch fire as the theater in Cincinnati. It was all clapboard and narrow windows, but it tried its best to appear like a friendly, welcoming place: a balcony on the second floor held a band, of all things, and their music spilled out onto the street.

Annie shivered. Beyond those doors was a garou named Swearengen, an evil man who sent his wolves out to bite others. Someone who ripped apart families. (Clearly Frank hadn't enlightened Annie with the details about Al Swearengen and her relationship with Jane.)

"Cold?" Frank pulled her closer, and for a moment, Annie forgot all about him being a garou, too. He was just Frank. Sweet, wonderful, charming Frank.

They entered the Gem, and it took everything in her to keep from cringing. The noise: raucous laughter, glasses slamming against the bar, and a fellow playing the piano in the corner. It was an assault on Annie's ears. Not to mention the stink of unwashed bodies and too much perfume.

At first, it was similar to the saloon she'd visited in Cincinnati, but then she noticed the women. They wore heavy makeup and light clothing, and they were perched on men's laps, laughing at jokes that probably weren't funny, and roaming the main floor searching for customers. A woman wearing a white slip looked at Frank, then noticed Annie on his arm; she drifted away with a scoff.

These were the painted ladies of the Gem, the women Annie was attempting to impersonate. And while she was a show-woman now, it had only been the one show, and she'd been doing something she was good at: shooting things.

"Where do you think we'll find Walks Looking?" Annie asked as they moved around the room.

"Hard to say. Probably not upstairs. That's where the, um, business takes place."

Anne jerked her head up and stared at him. "And how would you know that?"

"Because I read the sign?" Frank nodded toward a sign that did indeed read, "Buy yourself and your lady a drink before you go upstairs."

"Oh." Annie wished she had read the sign first. "Powers of observation. Right. So she's not upstairs, and she's probably not on this floor."

"Which means you were climbing up the outside of the building for no reason."

"I had a plan."

"To get upstairs where the business goes on."

Annie's face went red. "I was going upstairs so that I could go downstairs to the basement, which is obviously the only place they'd keep someone prisoner."

"Right," Frank said. "Downstairs it is. But we can't go straight there. We have to blend in first."

Annie tried not to wonder whether he was trying to keep her in this dress longer. The room was warm, at least, but there were dozens of people in here, and they could all see her looking like this. But if Frank wanted to be near her again, and he was helping her find Walks Looking, then maybe he could forgive her for all the horrible things she'd said to him.

Of course, he was still a garou, but he was also Frank, and which one mattered more?

He looked at her again, and her whole body flushed.

They spent only a few more minutes wandering the floor. Frank bought them drinks, but Annie was a Quaker and never drank alcohol, and Frank's hands were shaking too hard to take a sip. Why? Because of her? Because of what she'd said in Cincinnati?

Finally, they wandered off the main floor, toward the back of a short hallway, and found a door marked "Cellar" at the end.

"This is probably it," Frank said.

"I'm in awe of your powers of observation."

"Tell me again how you bravely fought off that bear." He tried the handle. "Locked."

Annie turned the bolt. "Lock's on this side, genius."

"Well, that's just suspicious. Why would—" He looked at her. "Right. Because you don't want prisoners getting out."

"Hey!" a voice called from the other end of the hall. It was the same woman who'd looked at Frank earlier. "What're you doing back here?"

Annie froze. Frank froze.

Then, with no better ideas about what they were going to do now that they'd been caught, Annie kissed him.

The move shocked both of them, and there wasn't much to it beyond pressing their faces together and hoping that the woman on the other end of the hall didn't realize Annie had no idea what she was doing.

Buuuut apparently Frank did. He wrapped one arm around her and pulled her close, and touched her face with his free hand, gently tilting her head.

Annie gasped as his mouth moved against hers, soft but strong, and suddenly it didn't matter that she'd previously had no idea what to do here, because instinct kicked in as she echoed him.

Warmth spread through her, beginning everywhere he touched: her waist, her cheek, her lips. She listed toward him, wanting more and more, but a noise at the end of the hall snapped her out of the moment.

"No need to show off," muttered the woman. "Anyway, you know that belongs upstairs."

Did she? "All the rooms were taken." Annie's heartbeat raced.

Frank was still near her, close enough to kiss again.

"We won't be long," Annie said.

The woman gave her a look Annie couldn't hope to decipher, but she did leave them in peace.

Frank's face was red as he stepped back and opened the cellar door. "Did you have to tell her we wouldn't take long?"

Annie went first, taking the rail as she stepped down the stairs. The kiss had made her a little dizzy, but she wanted to do it again. But not here. Not like this. They had a job to do. "Why?" she asked stiffly. "Do you think it's going to take a long time to rescue Walks Looking?"

"I meant because—" Frank heaved a sigh and closed the door behind them. "Never mind. Let's go and you can finish emasculating me later."

Annie smiled, pleased there would be a later for them.

Then, as she looked around the cellar, which was lit only with the light from the high, narrow windows, her smile fell.

There was no sign of Walks Looking—or any other nefarious activity—in the cellar whatsoever. It was a normal cellar, filled with boxes and trunks, and walls lined with racks of whiskey and other beverages Annie couldn't identify but likely didn't approve of.

"She's not here." Annie slumped. "Many Horses said Swearengen had her, and I assumed she'd be somewhere in the Gem, but . . ." What if she was dead? What if Annie had to go back to Many Horses with the worst sort of news?

Frank touched her shoulder; his palm was warm against her

bare skin. "Someone is here. I can hear movement."

"How—" Oh. Right. She bit her lip. "Where?"

Frank drifted ahead of her, face lifted and head cocked, and paused a beat. Then he faced the western wall. "There. A hidden door. It has a draft coming from under it."

They went over and found a sizable gap between the whiskey rack and the wall, big enough for a person to squeeze into. It was too dark back here for Annie to see, but Frank went right to a spot on the wall and felt around.

"There's a seam," he murmured. "We just have to . . ." He pressed the wall and it swung open, revealing a secret room all in darkness. "I'll go first."

"Because you're a man?" Annie frowned.

"Because I can see in the dark?"

"Oh. Yeah. Thank you." Annie forced a smile, certain it looked more like a grimace.

He turned away before she could see his expression, then ducked into the other room.

"Who are you?" asked a girl whose voice was very, very similar to Many Horses's.

"I'm Frank," Frank said. A light flared, and a lantern swung into view. "And this is Annie. We've come to rescue you."

Annie glanced over her shoulder, through the rack of whiskey, but the cellar was still empty. Quickly, she hurried through the secret door and pulled it shut—but not all the way. She slid a shoe between the door and the wall, just in case.

The floor was cold on her bare foot as she turned to face the room.

Walks Looking—she had the same face shape and uneasy expression as Many Horses—sat in the far corner, all four limbs caught in shackles that had been bolted to the wall.

"Many Horses sent me," Annie said. "Walks Looking, I presume."

The girl's eyes widened. "You presume right. But why are you here?"

"Because Many Horses asked me to help you?" Hadn't that been clear?

"I know, but why did you come?"

"Because you need help. Obviously." Annie glanced at Frank. "Should we try the wolfsbane?"

"Why?"

"Do you think she's enthralled?"

"She's chained up," Frank said. "I don't think she's enthralled."

"I'm definitely not enthralled," Walks Looking said. "It didn't work on me. Hence the chains."

"Oh. Right. That makes sense." Annie hesitated, then pulled a hairpin from her hair and went to work on the locks.

"When did you learn how to pick locks?" Frank asked.

"I'm the best at picking locks in my whole family," Annie said.

"That doesn't answer the question."

Annie smiled and pulled the first cuff off Walks Looking. "I'm going to get you back to your sister. I promise." A knot of missing her own sisters welled up in Annie's throat, but she pushed the feeling aside.

Walks Looking rubbed at her wrists as the cuffs fell away. "Thank you."

"So Swearengen did this to you?" Frank asked.

"Yes." She pointed across the room, where a long table held glass vials and measuring cups and other alchemical tools. "That's where she makes the serum that enthralls the garou. But like I said, the serum doesn't work on me."

"She?" Annie asked. "Swearengen is a woman?"

"Oh, did I forget to tell you?" Frank said. "I already knew that," he said smugly to Walks Looking.

"Well that would have been helpful information to have. But how did you resist the serum?" she asked Walks Looking as the last cuff clattered to the floor.

Walks Looking climbed to her feet. "Just stubborn, I suppose. I'd seen what happened to the others ahead of me—how she gave them the injection and they changed. They became passive and followed any order she gave them, even when she told them to shift between human and wolf. I decided I would not be like that. I held on to my hatred even when I could feel the serum pulling at me, and it didn't work."

"So she locked you down here?" Annie said.

Walks Looking nodded. "She was trying to decide what to do with me."

Frank edged away from the worktable. "How strange that she

has two serums to give out," he said in the sort of tone that meant he knew he was wrong but didn't want to be. "One to cure, and one to enthrall."

"No." Walks Looking's expression went hard. "She has one serum."

Frank closed his eyes. "One to enthrall."

"That's right. The only reason the 'cure' appears to work is because she tells them to change into their human forms." Walks Looking studied the worktable a long moment, then heaved it up and over. All the vials and tools crashed to the floor, and liquid ran in shiny puddles. "She calls it a cure, but it is the opposite. Now"— she looked at Annie—"take me to my sister."

"You need a disguise first," Annie said, motioning for Frank to give up his hat and coat. "It's not safe for your people to be seen in town right now." She pressed her mouth into a line. If Walks Looking didn't know about the Battle of the Little Bighorn (what Many Horses had called the Battle of the Greasy Grass) and the murders following, Annie wasn't going to be the one to tell her. Many Horses could explain.

Walks Looking scowled. "What about the other Lakota wolves?"

"I don't know," Annie said softly. "I'll keep an eye out for them, after we take you to Many Horses."

"You can get back there on your own, right?" Frank asked, removing his hat and coat.

Annie nodded, enviously watching Walks Looking put on

Frank's clothes. Not only because it would have covered every part of Annie's body and then some, but because it was Frank's and probably smelled like him.

"Good. You should go back to our hotel first and change into something a little less comfortable."

"This isn't comfortable at all," Annie said.

"I know." He gave her a tight smile.

"What are you going to do?"

Worry flashed across Frank's face. "I have to find Jane."

Jane TWENTY-EIGHT

"I've been here since the very beginning of this town," the woman who called herself Al Swearengen said as Jane chowed down on a huge plate of steak and potatoes at the Shaggy Dog Saloon, which her mother claimed had the very best food in Deadwood. "I knew this was the place where I would make a name for myself."

Jane wiped her mouth on her sleeve. "For coming up with the cure?"

Al smiled and patted Jane's hand across the table. "The cure, of course, my dear, and other things. This is a town of opportunity."

It was a town of surprises, too, but good ones, Jane reckoned. She couldn't stop gawking at her mother. All these years, she'd thought Charlotte Canary was dead and buried, but she'd changed, was all, as Jane herself had changed. A new name. A new life.

"By the end of my first week here I had a dance hall up and running," Al was boasting now in that new, more-refined voice, too, different from the Missouri country talk that Jane had known. "By the end of the first month, I'd built a tavern—so small I called it the Cricket. I held prizefights there for the miners. And now I have the Gem. The papers described my theater as being 'as neat and tastefully arranged as any place of its kind in the west.'"

"It sure is nice," Jane said, remembering all the polished wood and velvet seat cushions. "You've done right well for yourself, Ma."

At Jane calling her "Ma," Al's expression shifted, almost a wince, and Jane thought she knew why.

"I understand," Jane said, a lump springing up in her throat. "I'll keep our family connection to myself."

"Oh, no, my darling, you misunderstand," Al said, laughing. "I want people to know that you're my daughter." She squeezed Jane's hand. "I'm simply emotional. This is all I've ever wanted, you know. A piece of this world to make my own. My precious daughter, by my side, sharing in my legacy."

Jane's chest filled with something like relief. Her mother hadn't been nearly so affectionate when Jane was a child, but now her ma seemed (gulp) proud of her.

"Not to overlook that you have your own legacy," Al said. "My daughter, Calamity Jane, the Heroine of the Plains. Everybody's heard of you. You're a legend."

Jane coughed and muttered that she had something in her eye.

"Well, I figure if a girl wants to be a legend, she should just go ahead and be one."

Al beamed at her. "Quite right. Take the world by the horns." Her eyes focused on Jane's tangled hair that was half loose from its ponytail, the dirty work shirt and worn buckskin vest. "We should get you cleaned up."

"Cleaned up?" Jane didn't know if she liked the sound of that.

"You may be a legend, but you look like you've been dragged through a pigpen."

That was more like the Ma Jane remembered. And that's how, ten minutes later, Jane found herself in a private room at the Gem that Al said would be hers, now, buck nekked, staring down at a steaming bathtub. She took a tentative step into it, lowered herself into the water, and then shot up again.

"Ah!" she screamed. "I just burnt my butt!"

"Well, wait a bit," her mother advised from the other side of the room, where she was laying out what looked to be a dress. "It'll cool."

Jane had never been good at waiting. She slipped down into the water again, wincing at the blistering heat, but she forced herself to stay this time, crossing her arms over her breasts because her ma had never seen those before and it didn't seem proper. She stayed that way for several minutes, steeping like tea as the layers of dirt floated off her.

(At this very moment, dear reader, Frank and Annie were breaking into the cellar of the Gem. If Jane had known about the kissing she would probably have laughed herself sick. But she didn't know. At this point Jane didn't know a lot of things that would have been useful.)

After a while Al came over, poured some of the water over Jane's head, and started to scrub her hair with a bar of castile soap.

"I'll rinse it with a wash of vinegar and rosemary," she said. "You'll shine up like a pretty penny."

But Jane knew deep down that her being pretty was not a matter of being clean.

They were quiet for a while, Jane holding still while Al scrubbed at her. Then Jane worked up the courage to ask the question that'd been on her mind all day.

"Ma," she said, because they were alone now, so she was pretty sure it was safe. "What happened?"

"What happened when, sweetheart?"

"When you died."

"Oh." Al stopped scrubbing. "Did your father tell you I died?"

"He told me . . ." Jane swallowed. "He told me you went to be with the angels."

Al laughed, a hard, tough-sounding noise. "The angels. How droll. No, I went to be with the wolves. My pack. I suppose I can understand why your father lied about it. You were a headstrong thing. You would have come after me, I think."

"Yeah, I guess I would have. I thought he killed you."

"Your father wasn't a killer. Ironically, that's what killed him."

Jane gazed at her feet in the water. She knew there was no

happy, surprise resurrection of her father in store. She'd seen Robert Canary laid out in his coffin, stiff and gray. She'd put flowers on his grave.

"I killed Pa," she whispered. "It was me."

Her mother stopped scrubbing her hair. "What's this nonsense? Your father was killed by a garou hunter."

"I know. But I was the one who outed him. I told the sheriff he was a garou."

Al stared down at her thoughtfully. "Now you listen," she said after a minute. "It wasn't the sheriff who killed your father."

"I know, but—"

"You don't know," Al said sharply. "I know, because I was there that night. I saw it happen."

"You." Jane's breath whooshed out of her. "You was there."

"*Were* there, my darling. Yes. I came back. It had been a year since I bit him." Al smiled with a touch of bitterness. "I thought maybe he would be thinking differently now that he was also a wolf. I hoped he might change his mind about how things should be."

"And did he?"

"No," Al said sadly. "But that hardly mattered, in the end. As soon as I left town, I was hunted and made to fear for my life for simply being what I was. There was one particular garou hunter who was relentless in his pursuit of me, this man who would not stop in his determination to destroy me and my kind. I thought I'd lost him, but that night he tracked me down again. Your father took the silver bullet meant for me. I myself barely escaped."

Jane hadn't known about any of that. She'd come back to the house that night to find herself an orphan. "But why didn't you come for us, after? We could have been with you. This whole time, I could have—"

But Al was shaking her head. "It wasn't safe. The hunter was always two steps behind me, until I was finally able to lose his trail, years later. I changed my name, changed my life, and became so powerful he could not touch me. But until now I've had to stay away. To keep you safe."

Jane shivered. The bath had gone cold. Her mother helped her out and slung a robe around her, then toweled off her hair. She made Jane put on silk undergarments, a petticoat, and a corset with whale bones in it.

"This ain't my style," Jane tried to protest. "I like to . . . you know . . . move a bit."

Al sniffed. "No daughter of mine is going to be walking around in Deadwood dressed like one of those filthy miners."

Jane didn't see how she was going to be walking around in this getup, period.

"You're Calamity Jane, 'a lovely, spirited waif,' the heroine of this story," Al said. "You should look the part."

Hero-eene, Jane thought. "What's a waif?"

"Never mind." Al helped her into the dress she'd picked out. It was a rich forest green with a lacy white collar at the top and a neat line of pearl buttons down the front. Then the fabric of the skirt swooped around to the back, where there was a large bustle.

"Doesn't this make my butt look big?" Jane asked doubtfully.

"It gives you a shape," Al pronounced. "And it makes you look female, which is a vast improvement."

She made Jane sit (which was difficult, what with the bustle), and brushed out her hair until it did indeed shine, and then she pinned it up in a simple, loose chignon at the nape of Jane's neck. By then Jane felt like a china doll, and she didn't much like it, and she certainly didn't feel like herself, but Al stepped back and smiled approvingly.

"There. That's so much better. You'll never be the beauty that I was when I was your age, but you're presentable." She pressed a finger to the side of her chin, thinking, then spritzed Jane with perfume. Lemon verbena, she said it was, and it reminded Jane of someone.

Edwina Harris. Winnie. She had worn this same perfume.

Al took a hat box off the bed. Out of it she drew a tall straw hat with silk flowers on it. "Here's the finishing touch."

Jane stood up and backed away. "Now, see here. Nobody said nothing about no flowered hat."

"Come here," her mother ordered. "Martha. Come to me, baby."

Jane felt a jolt of panic, enough to bring the wolf to the surface for the briefest of moments. A growl vibrated in the back of her throat. Her eyes flashed golden.

Al tilted her head to one side, smiling, unafraid. "Ah. So. There is a wolf in there. I wondered when I would see it."

Jane fought the urge to grab her flask from her things and drink the wolf down. The corset choked her. "You knew? You knew I was bit?"

"Of course. Why else would you come to see if the cure really worked?" Al said.

"Yeah, about that . . ." Jane was still eying the hat warily. "When can we do it?"

"Do it?"

"I want the cure," Jane said hoarsely. She cleared her throat. "I don't have no hundred dollars, but maybe you could spot me, seeing as I'm your daughter and you're proud of me and all?"

Al walked over and held Jane by the shoulders. "The cure is not for you," she said. "There are those who benefit from the injection, no doubt, those for whom the blood of the wolf is more than they can handle. But not you, my darling. You are strong. You've always been strong."

"But I'm becoming a . . . beast," Jane said.

Al scoffed. "You are perfect. You should be proud of the wolf, as I am. Instead of searching for some cure to fix you, you should be thinking of all the ways in which the wolf part of you can help shape your future. You could be unstoppable. You could change the world. We could, together."

"I'll think on it," Jane said, "but the cure still sounds awfully nice."

Al's hands dropped from Jane's shoulders. "The cure is not for you," she said again matter-of-factly. "It would break my heart to give it to you." She picked up the flowered hat again. "Now, no more talk of that. Hold still."

The cure is not for you. The words rattled around in Jane's brain as she came down the stairs a few minutes later with Al, who once again wore the accessorized top hat and the bearing of the benevolent ruler of the Gem. Al announced in front of the entire place that this was her long-lost daughter, the one and only Calamity Jane, and everyone clapped and cheered. A few men even asked Jane to dance, but she told them to get lost. She wanted to be alone, to sort out the events of the past few hours.

She wished Bill were here. He'd always been good at talking things out, making her see the situation clearly without making her feel like he was telling her what to do. She bit her lip, then blinked as she saw a boy who looked remarkably like Frank (good teeth and all) slipping out from a back room, escorting a prostitute who was the spitting image of Annie. But it couldn't be them. Jane knew darn well that Annie wouldn't be caught dead in a place like this, wearing a dress like that. It was wishful thinking, wanting these people to be Frank and Annie, who were surely back in Ohio, performing the show.

Would she ever get back there, now that her ma was alive and wanted her? Jane supposed that was the hundred-dollar question. She sighed and swiveled to look for her mother but couldn't locate her, either, so Jane took a seat at the bar and ordered a drink. Brandy, because ladies in fancy dresses drank brandy.

"What do I owe you?" she asked when the barkeep put the glass in front of her.

"Your money's no good here, Miss Swearengen," he said. "Everything's on the house."

"Is that right? Huh."

You could change the world, her mother had said earlier. Jane had never given much thought to changing the world. She'd been too busy trying to survive it.

From the stage, one of the painted ladies drew out a violin and began to play a lonesome tune. Jane sipped her drink, because ladies in fancy dresses sipped.

"Hello, miss," said a random gentleman, sidling in next to her. "May I—?"

"You may not," Jane said. "Go on, now."

A few minutes later another one tried. "Pardon me, miss."

"Git," was all she said.

He got.

And there was still one more. "Hello, Jane," this latest fellow said.

She glanced up, half expecting it to be Jack McCall. It struck her as odd that Jack McCall hadn't popped up in a while. (Wait. Or had he?)

But this time it was Ned Buntline, that no-good, stinking writer.

"Oh, rocks," she grumbled. "Not you again."

"I must say I am surprised to find you here, Miss Calamity.

You're looking . . ." He looked her up and down, smirking. "Well-rounded."

Jane jumped to her feet. She really wished she had the bullwhip on her, but the darned dress had no pockets. So she grabbed Buntline by the shirt front. "Say that to my face," she snarled.

"I, uh, did," he stammered. "I didn't mean any offense, truly."

"Well, consider me offended," Jane said.

Buntline smiled. "Why are you in Deadwood, Jane? Did you come looking for someone? Or some*thing*, perhaps?"

Her skin prickled at the idea that he might know her secret. She let go of his shirt and turned away in disgust. "I said it before, and I'll say it again, Buntline, slower, since you don't seem to catch my meaning. No. Comment."

"Isn't it obvious why she's here?" came another voice from a person who'd been standing on Buntline's other side, a slender fellow with green eyes and glasses. "She came to be reunited with her mother, Miss Swearengen. For Pete's sake, Ned. Pay attention."

"Hello, there," Jane said, delighted. It was like Winnie was here by magic, conjured from Jane's previous thinking about her.

Winnie's eyes sparkled behind her glasses. "Why, hello."

"It's good to see you, Mr. . . . ," Jane said. "Oh shoot, I forgot your name again."

The side of Winnie's mouth quirked up. "Wheeler . . . Edward Wheeler."

"Mr. Wheeler." Jane could not keep herself from smiling.

Buntline glanced back and forth between them. "You two know each other?"

"We met in Ohio when I was there working on a story." Winnie smiled and stood up. "Might you take a walk with me?" She offered Jane her arm.

Jane downed the rest of her brandy in a single swig. "Sure."

Buntline and the barkeep were laughing as Jane and Winnie walked away. "Now that there's a small man with a big woman!" she heard Buntline exclaim. "Woof!"

"Ignore him," Winnie said.

"Oh, I do," Jane said, but her cheeks were turning pink. "Buntline's the worst. Plus I don't much like writers."

They pushed out onto the street and started toward a better (but only slightly better) part of town. The sun was sinking below the steep Black Hills, but it turned all the brown of the streets to shades of gold and rose. Dust floated in the air, catching the light like sparkles. Jane felt as if she'd slipped into some kind of improbable dream.

"Wait. Are you following me?" Jane asked.

"In a manner of speaking," Winnie replied, and Jane didn't understand what that meant, but she didn't really care. They stopped in the doorway to a bakery, and the smell of bread washed over them.

"Now, what's this about you not liking writers?" Winnie said.

Jane's hand tucked into the crook of Winnie's arm felt strange and awkward. She pulled away. "I didn't mean you. I guess I don't really think of you as a writer, because I can't . . . you know."

"I could teach you," Winnie said. "Then you can read my work and tell me what you think. I'm a decent writer, too, at least my editor seems to think so. But he doesn't know my big secret."

It took Jane a few seconds to catch on. "Why do you have to be a man to be a writer?"

"It's just easier." Winnie shrugged. "Why do *you* so often pose as a man?"

"Well, it's more comfortable, for one thing." Jane pulled at the starchy lace collar of her dress. "So, yeah. Easier. I guess." It was easier, in almost every situation, she'd found, to be a man.

Except perhaps this one. With Winnie.

Winnie was gazing at her with the intent expression she often had, her eyes inquisitive. Searching. And very close, Jane realized. They were standing so near to each other that their faces were mere inches apart.

"Well, you don't seem quite yourself dressed this way," Winnie said. "But you are undeniably pretty."

"Shut up," Jane said immediately.

Winnie threw back her head and laughed, and when she stopped laughing she was even closer.

"You're pretty, too," Jane got out after a long pause. "But not so pretty as people would know to look at you, that you're a female sort."

"Thank you. I think." Winnie stifled a smile, her bottom lip caught in her teeth in a way that Jane found oddly distracting. "It is so good to see you again, Jane."

"Likewise," Jane murmured.

Then, seized by an impulse, she bent her head to kiss Edwina Harris. Their lips touched gently. Sweetly. Jane couldn't have said how long the kiss lasted—an instant and also an eternity in which everything Jane thought she knew suddenly shifted.

(She'd never really even wanted to kiss a person before. She'd never had what she would call a romantic interlude with anyone, boy or girl. But Winnie was good and kind and beautiful, and Jane wanted to kiss her. And so she did.)

Then she was gazing down at Winnie again, suddenly aware that she had just kissed a woman on the mouth. On the boardwalk in Deadwood. In public.

"I'm sorry," she blurted.

"Please, don't be sorry," Winnie said, but took a small step back. She touched her hand briefly to her lips and then smiled. "Well. We should . . . walk."

Jane glanced around, but no one was looking at them. Then she realized why. She was dressed as a woman, for once, and Edwina a man. Jane was six inches taller than Winnie, but height didn't matter. Only the clothes.

She took the arm that Winnie offered her again. They strolled down the boardwalk like they were promenading in some fancy city like New York. Jane could not think of what she should say then, and Winnie didn't speak, either. They quietly ambled along, night falling around them. Crickets literally started to chirp.

Jane coughed. "Do you want to know a secret?"

"Always," Winnie replied.

"My name isn't really Calamity Jane."

Winnie pretended to be shocked. "Is that so? Is it Jane Swearengen? Because I don't think that's exactly a secret anymore."

"Ugh, no," said Jane, her nose wrinkling. "Not Swearengen. How she even came up with that, I'll never— Anyway, my name is Martha."

Winnie's eyebrows lifted. It was satisfying, Jane found, to tell her something she didn't already know.

"Martha Canary. Like the bird."

"How do you do, Martha Canary?" Winnie held out her hand, and Jane shook it, holding her hand a little longer than was absolutely necessary.

"Fine. Nice to make your acquaintance," Jane said, and laughed nervously.

"So I wonder if you would tell me something," Winnie said then.

Her expression was suddenly, inexplicably mournful, in such a way that Jane wanted to give her a hug, to ask what ailed her, even if Jane was the problem. Even if Winnie had felt differently than Jane did about the kiss, Jane wanted to fix it. "I'll tell you anything."

"Al Swearengen isn't really your mother, is she?"

Jane's heart sank. She'd meant to tell the truth just now, but her mother's secrets were not hers to spill. "My mother went to the angels when I was a kid, like I told you. Her name was Charlotte

Canary." It wasn't a lie, she reminded herself. But it wasn't the whole truth, either.

"Why does Swearengen say she's your mother, then?"

"It's an arrangement we have" was all Jane could manage.

"Because you want the cure," Winnie filled in. "And Al Swearengen has it."

Jane's breath caught. "How did you . . ."

"Oh, come on. You had me read you the pamphlet about the cure, and about it being in Deadwood, and then that very night you left Cincinnati to make your way to Deadwood. I'm not a genius, but I can put two and two together. You're a garou, Jane, aren't you?"

"Oh." Jane looked at her hands. "Yeah. I guess I am."

She waited for Winnie to pull away from her, horrified, repulsed, but there was only sadness in the girl's expression. That and something else Jane couldn't read. Winnie reached up and touched Jane's cheek, which Jane felt through her entire body. Jane even thought that Winnie might be the one who would kiss her this time.

But then Winnie said, "I'm writing a story about it. That is to say, I already wrote a story. It may be the best thing I've ever written so far, but . . ."

The words were like an ice bath (and Jane had had enough of baths for one day). "You wrote a story about me being a garou," she said, hoping she'd heard it wrong.

Winnie's hand dropped. She nodded. "Yes."

Jane shook her head. "But you promised. You said you wouldn't write about me."

"I can't keep that promise."

"Why, because I'm a garou?"

Jane felt her shoulders expanding. Her fingers curled into fists; her nails felt sharp against her palms. She ran hot, then cold, then hot again. She was sweating. She could change, right there, on the street, and give Winnie the proof she needed. It was all Jane could do not to explode into the beast on the spot.

"No," Winnie was saying, but Jane wasn't hearing words at this point. "No, it's not like that. I can explain. It's—"

"You lied to me!" cried Jane. "You promised!"

Then she turned and ran, as fast as she could, leaving Winnie calling after her in the street.

She managed to stay mostly human until she was back in her room at the Gem, the door slammed and locked behind her. She tore off the stupid flowered hat, and then the dress, popping a few pearl buttons as she struggled to get out of it. The corset, however, had been tied from the back. She was trapped. She ran to the vanity and splashed water on her face, then saw, in the mirror, that her teeth were fangs. Her nails were claws. Her face was changing shape, her nose and ears elongating, hair sprouting up all over. In a flash she was completely hairy. The bindings on her corset broke and the contraption fell away from her. Her legs bent and snapped backward. "Geeze Louise," she cried.

There was a knock at the door.

"Go away," she said hoarsely.

Another knock. A familiar voice. "Jane?"

It sounded like Frank, but it couldn't be. Frank was in Ohio.

"Go away," she roared.

"Jane, it's Frank. Can I come in?"

It *was* Frank. How was it Frank? It didn't matter. He could definitely not come in. "Uh, no, Frank," she said. "I'm doing something in here."

"Jane, just open the door," Frank said. "Whatever it is, you can tell me."

"No, you don't want to see this," Jane moaned. "No, no, no!"

Frank's voice became gruff. "Jane, you open this door. I mean it. Right now."

She knew that tone. When Frank got like that he was like a dog with a tooth in a towel. There was no use resisting. He'd get his way.

"Okay, Frank. You asked for it." She lurched over to the door, unlocked it, and then threw it open.

Frank was standing on the other side. At least she thought it was Frank. He was wearing Frank's clothes, but his face was entirely covered with fur. His ears were pointed, too. His eyes, which were normally brown, were golden.

Frank was a woof.

"An explanation is probably long overdue," Frank said.

TWENTY-NINE
Frank

"Wha—? How?" Jane stumbled backward. She obviously hadn't practiced talking with her mouth in snout form, which was not an easy skill. "You," she got out with great difficulty. "Woof?"

Frank pushed her inside and closed the door behind them. He locked it and turned to face her. "I'm the same Frank you know," he assured her. "But yes. I'm a garou."

Her eyes, which were still recognizably Jane's eyes, widened. "Me . . . ," she said slowly. "Too." Then she let out an agonizing wolfy howl.

Frank rushed over to introduce Jane to the Wooo. He grabbed her hands in his. "Wooo," he said softly. "Say it with me, Jane. Wooooooo."

She met his gaze. "Wooo?"

He nodded. "Wooo."

They woooed together for a few minutes, exhaling in unison, until the hairs covering their bodies shrank back into their skin, and their claws retracted, and their slobber . . . well, stopped slobbering. And once they were both human again, and once Frank had wrapped a blanket around her (to cover up her lady bits), Jane sank to the floor.

"I know," Frank said, sitting down beside her. "I know."

"How'd you figure it out?" she asked.

"I saw you talk to a dog."

Jane pulled the blanket more tightly around her. "He told me the funniest joke about squirrels. There was this one, see, who didn't save up acorns for the winter, and he—" Her mouth dropped open. "You can talk to George!"

(Where was George, anyway? We haven't seen him since they encountered Annie on the street two chapters ago. He was probably off picking her flowers or something. But George could take care of himself.)

"Yes," Frank said. "Sometimes being a garou comes in handy."

Jane looked unconvinced. "Since when?"

"Since always. Oh you mean, since when have I been a garou?"

Jane snorted. "'Course that's what I mean! Why else would I ask ya?"

Now she was sounding more like the old Jane.

"For as long as I can remember," Frank answered.

"What, and you didn't tell me?" A long, curly hair popped out of Jane's knuckle.

"Jane, please stay calm. We need to talk as humans."

"Wooo," Jane said. The hair went away.

"Good," Frank said. "You're getting it." He took a deep breath. "You know that story Bill tells of him rescuing a baby from a garou attack?"

"Yeah," Jane said. "What about it?"

"He skips a part."

Her brow furrowed. "What part?"

"Bill changes the story so he reaches the baby first. Guess he wishes he had, you know? But the truth is that the garou got there first."

"Oh, rocks," said Jane. "Did the garou eat the baby up?"

Frank closed his eyes. "No. I'm the baby, Jane."

"You're a baby *and* a garou? That don't make no sense."

"Okay, let's try this again," Frank said patiently. "I was a baby, when I was younger."

"Yes. Go on," Jane said.

"And my family got eaten up by a garou."

Jane looked stricken. "Ah, Frank, I never knowed that."

"I know," Frank said. "That's why I'm trying to tell you."

"But you're a garou."

"Correct. You've got it. I'm a garou."

"I don't follow," said Jane.

Maybe the third time would be the charm. "I'm the baby who Bill saved from the garou that night. But I'd already been bitten before Bill got to me. But he took me in anyway."

It was quiet. Then Jane said, "Bill ain't your real pa?"

Frank swallowed. "He's the only pa I've ever known. That's real enough."

"I can't believe you never told me that," Jane said in a hurt voice.

That was a pang to Frank's heart, because he'd already felt so guilty for not sharing his secret with her. "I'm sorry. Bill thought it would be best if no one else knew that I was . . ."

"You told Bill but not me?!"

"Yes, Jane!" Frank yelled. "Bill's the one who saved me! Try to keep up!"

Then he had to wooo for a minute.

"Sorry," Jane said after he'd calmed down, shaking her head as if to clear it. "My head's so muddy right now. You don't even want to know the day I've had."

Now they were getting somewhere. "What happened?" he asked.

"I said you don't want to know."

"But I do want to know. After you put some clothes on." He waited, back turned, while Jane got dressed, and then sat with her on the bed. "Tell me."

Her lip quivered. "I . . ."

"Yes, Jane. I'm listening."

"I just got . . . I . . ."

Oh, rocks. She clearly had just got the "cure," and now she was in thrall, like poor Jud Fry on the train, and she couldn't talk about it.

"I just got my first kiss!" she blurted out.

That was not what Frank had expected her to say. "What?"

She sighed. "It was really nice, too. But now my life is over. My first kiss is probably going to be my last."

Frank was momentarily distracted by the thought of his kiss with Annie. Which had been, in a word, amazing. But then he remembered that this wasn't about him. "Why would it be your last kiss, Jane?" he asked.

Jane shook her head. "Right afterward, I found out that she—I mean, that writer, what's his name, Edward Wheeler—knows I'm a garou. And he's gonna publish a story about it."

"What?" Frank said. This time, a hair sprouted out of his elbow. "Does he know who you are?"

"I think *that* is what you might call the hook of the story," Jane said bitterly. "The hero-eene of the plains is a garou."

"Well," Frank said, "there's got to be something we can do. I've met Mr. Wheeler. He seemed like a reasonable fellow. I'll talk to him."

"Bad idea," Jane said immediately. "I don't want you to do that. You know what Bill says: Writers can't be trusted."

"Maybe Bill could talk Mr. Wheeler out of it," mused Frank.

"Don't you see? That's even worse," Jane said. "*The* Wild Bill Hickok, world-famous garou hunter, was stupid enough to employ a garou. That, as Charlie would say, would be bad for the show." Her jaw set. "I'm not draggin' Bill farther through the mud."

"But—"

"I said no!" Jane interrupted.

Frank held up his hands. "Okay. Wooo. Wooo with me, Jane."

"I don't need to wooo." Jane stood in a superhero pose: hands on hips, chest out. "There's only one course for me, Frank. I need the cure."

Frank rubbed his eyebrows. "Yeah. About that. I've got some bad news."

"I don't know if I can take any more bad news," Jane said. "So just give me the good news."

Frank felt a pit in his stomach. "I don't have any good news."

"Shoot. Well then, give it to me straight."

"Jane, the cure—"

"I know it's a lot of money," she said before he got out more than a few words. "But maybe that don't matter. I've got connections, you see."

"It's not that. The cure doesn't work."

She stared at him. "Sure it does. I've seen it."

"I don't know what you've seen," Frank said. "But the cure's a fake."

"What?" She scowled. "No. You're—You're wrong."

"I'm not wrong. There is no real cure for the garou. You're going to have to learn to control it. But I'll help you. And Bill will teach you, the way he taught me."

Jane's right arm shifted, sprouting hair and claws. "I don't need to be taught to control it," she said hotly. "Some people would even say it doesn't need to be controlled."

"We both know that's not true."

She really started to wolf out again then. Frank held up his hands. "Jane, calm down. Wooo."

"I don't want to wooo!"

"Jane, your neck is covered in fur," he pointed out.

"I don't care! I'm getting the cure!"

"The cure is fake!"

"You lie!" Jane roared.

"I don't!"

"How do you know?" Jane's left arm shifted, too.

"Thorough investigative work!" Frank exclaimed. "Wooo," he said to himself. This conversation was really starting to test his own control.

"I don't believe you! I believe Al Swearengen!"

"But Al Swearengen is the villain of this story," Frank said. "It's so obvious."

"That's impossible," argued Jane. "Al Swearengen is my mother!"

The words reverberated through the room. Frank's eyes widened. "*What?*"

Jane's hands balled into fists. "Besides that, she's an innocent garou, who was relentlessly hunted her entire life! She told me."

"I don't know about any of that," Frank said dazedly. "But Swearengen is not who you think she is. If you'll let me explain—"

"You know nothing, Frank Butler!" Jane cried.

With that, she jumped toward the window and smashed clean through it.

Why can she never use the door? Frank wondered.

* * *

Of all of Jane's problems, there was only one Frank felt that he was capable of solving.

He went from hotel to hotel, asking for a guest named Edward Wheeler, and finally hit pay dirt at the Checkmate Hotel. Mr. Wheeler was staying in room 203.

But when Frank knocked at room 203, a petite blond woman answered.

"Can I help you?" She looked strangely familiar, but he couldn't place her.

"Um, hi, I'm looking for Edward Wheeler," Frank said.

She tilted her head and studied his face. "And what do you want with him?"

"I need to talk to him about a matter of urgent . . . um, urgent matter."

"Mr. Wheeler isn't here right now," she said. "But if you'd care to leave a message after this sentence . . ."

Frank's shoulders sagged. "Please just tell him to . . . not print the article, about a girl named Jane."

The blond woman frowned. "I'm sorry," she said in a soft voice. "But whatever Mr. Wheeler was set to print, it's already being printed. From what I know about the business, there's no way to stop the presses."

Frank closed his eyes and sighed. "Thank you for your time." He tipped his hat and turned away.

"Is she okay?"

Frank turned back. "What?"

"This Jane of yours. Is she all right?"

Frank sighed. "Not really."

He trudged around Deadwood until he located Bill, who was watching the Gem from across the street, his expression cloudy.

"I been pondering over what to do about our Alpha problem," he said when Frank came up beside him.

Frank gazed up at the Gem. "It's worse than we thought."

THIRTY
Annie

Weirdly—or maybe not weirdly—Walks Looking didn't wolf out once on the way to the stream where they were supposed to meet Many Horses.

There wasn't even a hint of wolfiness. She remained a girl for the entire duration, albeit a girl clothed in Frank's coat and hat, and Annie tried again not to be jealous that someone else got to smell Frank's scent the whole way.

"Are you nervous about seeing your sister again?" Annie asked.

"No. Should I be?" Walks Looking led the way uphill, even though Annie was supposed to be the one doing the rescuing.

"I just thought if you haven't seen each other since you were bitten, you might be worried she . . ." Annie wasn't sure how to finish that question without hurting Walks Looking's feelings.

The girl gave Annie a serious side eye. "My people don't care about that as much as you seem to. Garou are given as much respect as anyone else, and they make excellent warriors and scouts." She paused a beat. "We, I suppose."

"It's very new to you," Annie said.

Walks Looking nodded. "I am not afraid, though. I'll learn to control the wolf, as others do."

"Do you think it will be hard?"

"For some it is. For others, it isn't. Your friend Frank is very good at controlling his wolf."

So good at it that Annie hadn't had a clue he was a garou.

"Does it bother you?" Walks Looking asked. "Him being a wolf?"

Tears stung Annie's eyes, but she blinked them away. "It did, because I didn't know, and I said some really mean things about garou that I shouldn't have—"

"You wouldn't have said them if you'd known he was a wolf?"

"Well, no." Annie frowned.

"And you don't see a problem with that?"

Annie's shoulders dropped. "I didn't think he could be a garou. He's so kind, and the only garou I'd ever known were horrible. They threatened to eat my liver. And then the garou I saw at the factory tried to kill him and Jane . . ."

Walks Looking nodded. "And now there's Swearengen, who sends her wolves to bite others, and then enthralls them."

Annie swallowed hard as they moved higher up the hill. "Yeah. I don't know a lot of good wolves."

"You know Frank," Walks Looking said. "And you know me. You probably know a lot more good wolves than you realize, but you've had your eyes closed to them. Open your eyes, Annie Oakley. Wolves can be good and bad, like anyone else. Most people are both. The world is complicated."

"You're right," Annie whispered.

They walked for a ways longer, not speaking as the night deepened and even the birdsong faded. When they found the stream and started following it up to the meeting point, Annie said, "I didn't mean to talk about me. You're the one who just escaped captivity and has to learn how to live with a new part of yourself."

Walks Looking shrugged. "It benefits me if you learn to accept wolves. It benefits Frank, too, and all the other wolves who did nothing to harm you."

At last they reached the clearing where Annie and Many Horses had fought off the bear, but the clearing was empty. There was no sign of Many Horses (or the bear).

Annie turned to Walks Looking. "She was here yesterday."

"I'm still here!" Many Horses emerged from inside a small, cleverly hidden tent. She ran to throw her arms around her sister. "You're safe!"

The girls hugged, laughing and crying, their emotions so raw that Annie had to look away. Tears stabbed at her eyes again and she couldn't help but wonder where her own sisters were. A wave of missing them swept over her so strong and fast that she worried she might drown.

Many Horses and Walks Looking wiped the tears off each other's faces, laughing in sharp relief. They spoke a few times, but in their own language, so Annie couldn't follow, but we, your narrators, can say for certain that they spoke of that unbreakable bond of sisterhood and how they held on to it any time they were scared or worried, and that they had always believed they would be together again. And here they were.

Annie couldn't understand the words, but she understood the emotions just fine.

After several minutes, the sisters pulled apart and turned to Annie.

"Thank you," Many Horses said.

Annie's voice was tight. "It was the least I could do." The last of the day's heat had faded, and Annie shivered.

"Oh, here." Walks Looking removed Frank's coat and hat. "Your friend will probably want these back."

Annie shrugged into the coat, then pulled the vial from the inside pocket. "And this is yours," she said, offering it to Many Horses.

"You didn't need it?" she asked.

"Nope. Not a drop."

Many Horses smiled. "Good. I was curious if it would work, though—if the bond between Swearengen and the thralls could be interrupted and broken."

"We may never know." Annie folded the sleeves back to her wrists. "I should go back to Deadwood."

"Do you want to camp with us tonight?" Walks Looking asked, motioning toward the tent. "You can go back in the morning."

Annie did want to stay with the girls. They were fun and friendly, and she really wanted to get to know them better. But she shook her head. "You should catch up. Still, I hope we see each other again."

Both sisters smiled. "You can count on it," Many Horses said. "Just try not to get eaten by any bears."

The next day, back at the Marriott, Annie sat down at her desk and began a letter. She was tired, but her conversation with Walks Looking had made her realize she needed to say something to Frank, not just run around Deadwood rescuing people with him. She'd hurt him before—hurt him a *lot*—and now she needed to apologize. Hopefully he would forgive her.

Dear Frank.

She crossed it out.

Dearest Frank.

She sighed and tried again.

Dear George.

There. That was better. She wrote the date across the top:
August 2, 1876

There's something I want to tell you, but it's hard to talk about. Something happened to me when I was young—something with garou. I've never shared this with anyone outside my family, but I think I should tell you—not as an excuse for my behavior, but as an explanation.

The short version is that a family of garou nearly killed me when I was a child, and for years they were the only garou I'd ever known. I thought all garou were like that, and I held on to my fear for so long that it turned into hate. I allowed that hate to shape my views of all garou.

I know now that I was wrong. Garou are not all the same. In fact, ~~you are~~ Frank is one of the kindest, warmest people I've ever met.

Recalling some of the things I said about garou . . . I can only imagine how I hurt ~~you~~ Frank. I shouldn't have said them, not only because Frank's a garou, but because it wasn't right.

I was wrong. And I am sorry.

I don't know if there's anything I can do to make up for this, but I am going to try my best. I want to start with taking down Swearengen. Not only is she biting people who did not ask to become garou, but she is exploiting their fears of everyone else. It's attitudes like mine that make so many garou desperate for the "cure"—desperate enough to spend a hundred dollars on something they know nothing about.

I will help make this right.

Yours, if you want,

Annie

Annie read her letter over again, feeling raw and revealed, and wildly uncertain what he would think when he read it. A letter by itself wasn't much—it wasn't nearly enough to make up for the way she'd been—but maybe it was a start.

Maybe.

She folded the letter and put it aside for now. There were more people she needed to write to.

Dear Huldy and Sarah Ellen,
I have so much to tell you about what I've been doing . . .

She kept writing until she ran out of paper, telling her sisters about the show, about the scandal in Cincinnati, and finally about how she had met Many Horses and Walks Looking.

Seeing them together made me miss you more than ever, and I want you to know that no matter what it looks like, I didn't leave you. You have been in my thoughts every day, and I will write to you so often you get tired of reading my words. I'll keep trying even if the letters continue getting returned to me.

Maybe soon I'll be back in Ohio and see you again.

Annie sighed and folded up this letter, too, and stuck it in an envelope. She was worn out and ready for a nap, but the sun was working its way toward noon, and below Annie's window, the streets bustled with activity. She wouldn't be able to sleep with all this noise.

(Narrators here: yeah, we remember that Annie is a heavy sleeper and that she could sleep straight through a tornado, but Annie didn't know that. She still had a few more things to discover about herself.)

She put the letters in her pocket and headed outside.

It was even louder down on the street, cacophonous with people shouting about gossip and mining tips, someone pushing toilets (not—we shudder—even new ones) at people, and the splat of horses leaving their marks on the street.

This was truly the worst town. But then she heard it: Calamity Jane.

Now what had Jane done? Annie followed the sound of her friend's name, hoping the worry knotting in her chest was for nothing. But then, like a scene from the not-yet-invented moving picture, the crowd parted and revealed the front of a newspaper.

The headline stood out, dark and daring:

CALAMITY JANE IS A GAROU!

Jane THIRTY-ONE

Jane stared up at the ceiling, listening to a bed creak rhythmically from the room above hers, which is how she remembered where she was: the Gem, her mother's "theater," which was actually a brothel. Which was supposed to be Jane's new home sweet home.

So why didn't it feel that way?

She sighed and rubbed her eyes, which felt swollen from crying. Last night Frank had told her that Al Swearengen was the bad guy of this story (or, to be more accurate, bad lady—ladies can be bad guys, too), but that couldn't be true. It was a misunderstanding, was all. People had obviously been misunderstanding Charlotte Canary her whole life, as people had always been misunderstanding Jane. She just needed to talk to her ma, sort things out, get them straight. There was an explanation for everything, Jane was sure.

Which led to her first dilemma of the day: what to wear?

The fancy dress was lying where she'd left it on the floor, a crumpled mess with several popped buttons. Her own clothes—the buckskins she normally wore—were in an unpleasantly fragrant pile next to the empty bathtub, and she remembered her mother saying something about a pigpen and something about "no daughter of mine" being dressed as a filthy miner. This left her painfully short of options.

On a whim she walked over to the wardrobe in the corner and opened it. Inside she found a row of dresses, shirts, and skirts, neatly hung. Al must have had the clothing sent over—it all looked like it was Jane's size. None of it was so highfalutin as the dress she'd worn last night, but that was a good thing. Jane didn't need fancy. She needed to be—what had Ma called it?—presentable.

She picked a simple, dark brown skirt and a white button-up shirt, bypassing the corset and lacy pantaloons in favor of a simple petticoat underneath. Over top she donned a dark gray jacket that accentuated the strength of her shoulders. She looked—if we as the narrators may say so—nice, and more important, she looked like herself.

As for her hair, well. There was no way to replicate the updo her mother had done. Jane found the brush on the armoire and spent a good twenty minutes removing the remaining pins from last night and brushing out the tangles. Then she awkwardly braided her hair in one thick plait and called it good. Her gaze fell on the bottle of perfume on the armoire. She picked it up and spritzed it into the air, filling the room with the scent of lemon.

Winnie.

"I'm sorry," she said to the empty room. "Winnie. I need you to know—"

But what did she need Winnie to know? Winnie seemed to already know everything, which was the problem, wasn't it? Jane scoffed. Everything was spoiled between her and Winnie. If they'd ever had a chance in the first place, which she supposed they didn't. There was no point in having imaginary conversations.

"Never mind," she said.

She left her room and made her way into the main lobby of the Gem, which is when Jane knew, without a doubt, that something had changed about her situation. The male patrons of the Gem smirked and muttered to each other just out of her hearing in such a way that she knew they were talking about her. But it seemed different from the way they'd treated her last night after Al had announced her as her daughter. This morning there was something jeering about their smiles, and the painted ladies eyed her warily, even moving to one side as she passed to avoiding touching her.

She put a hand up to check the state of her hair, but nothing was amiss. She checked her shirt—no buttons askew, no stains or holes. Maybe they all thought she was ridiculous, trying to act a well-behaved woman, but last night, in front of her ma, they hadn't dared to show their disdain.

She wandered up to the main door, where the leader of the painted ladies—Ida, the woman who'd brought Jane to Al after the show—was sitting behind the desk looking bored.

"Have you seen my— Al?" Jane asked.

Ida fixed her with a no-nonsense stare. "Al is out attending to some business," she said in a monotone.

"What kind of business?"

"I don't see how that's any of *your* business."

Jane decided not to argue. "When's she going to be back?"

Ida shrugged.

"Well, thanks for nothing," Jane stormed, and then she, well, stormed out.

She went straight to the livery. Nothing calmed Jane like the company of horses. She immediately spotted Mister Ed and Black Nell in a stall next to Bullseye's, and the sight of them cheered her greatly. Bill was somewhere close by. And Frank. She took some time brushing all three horses down, checking their hooves, talking to them softly about how pretty they were and how much she'd missed them. Nell had a hot ankle on the back right, and Jane wrapped it in a poultice to leech out the heat. Then she stood for a long while petting Nell's gleaming black neck.

"Wooo," she said softly to herself. "Woooooooooo."

She felt a bit silly for how much she'd fussed last night. It had been a dark night, surely. It had felt like the world was collapsing in on her. But today the sun was shining. It would be all right, somehow. Maybe. She hoped.

She needed to clear things up with her ma.

After a few hours with the horses, Jane decided that enough

time had probably passed for Al to finish up whatever business had been occupying her, so she headed back to the Gem. She was almost there when something hit her in the back of the head.

A rock.

She touched her head and came away with a streak of blood.

She didn't even get a chance to look around before the second rock struck her in the back. This time she saw who did it: a little boy. Couldn't have been more than seven or eight. He wasn't wearing any shoes. Reflexively she reached into her pocket for some nickels, only she didn't have nickels. And she didn't have pockets.

Women's clothing sucked.

And oh, yeah, he'd thrown a gawl-darned rock at her. "What's your problem?" she yelled at him.

The boy's lip curled. "Get on out of here, you dirty rotten garou," he sneered. "We don't need the likes of you in this town."

Jane was speechless as she watched him run away. She glanced at the back of her hands to see if they were hairy. They weren't. They were clean, actually, even under the nails. She checked for a mustache—nothing. So how had he known? And why did he care enough to throw a rock at her, when this town must be teeming with garou, all come for the cure? It didn't make sense.

That's when she noticed the newspaper lying in the mud in front of her. She leaned over stiffly and picked it up.

Now Jane couldn't read, but she did know the shape of her own name. And she did know what her name on the front page of a paper meant, too. She'd known there was a story coming, after all.

But she hadn't guessed that it would be so soon.

"Oh, Winnie," she murmured. "Why'd you have to be that way?"

A man stumbled out of the Gem and caught sight of her. His face broke into an ugly grin. "Hey, Calamity Jane! Ha-roo!" he howled at her. "Ha, ha-roo!"

That got her bristles up in more ways than one. She bared her teeth and reached for her bullwhip, but she didn't have it on her. Curse this female getup! The man skittered away, laughing.

"Wooo," Jane muttered to herself, and hurried into the Gem.

Her mother still wasn't available, on account of the cure-show going on.

"She wants to talk to you, after," a painted lady named Trixie informed Jane in such an ominous tone that Jane's stomach became an instant pit of dread. "She said not to let you go anywhere."

Jane sat in the back to watch the show. Al was saying, "After many years of trial and error, I came up with a serum that will, once injected into the bloodstream, attach itself to the part of the person that has been corrupted into a wolf, and quickly disintegrate the connection between the man and his inner beast. Any man who wants to, can be cured."

That still sounded pretty good to Jane. It actually summed up her entire plan for the talk with her ma. "Give me the cure, if you please," she'd say, and then the no-good writers could write about that and everything could return to normal.

"The cure *is* for me," she thought stubbornly, staring at her mother. "The cure *is* real."

Al turned to Ida. "Can you fetch Mr. Terminus for me, please?"

Ida disappeared for a moment and then came back with a middle-aged man who walked with a cane. The man shuffled up to stand next to Swearengen. He was wearing a wide hat and a brown bushy beard, so that a person could hardly see his face.

Al patted him on the shoulder. "It's good to meet you, Mr. Terminus. Can you tell me about what ails you?"

"Oh, Doctor, Doctor," the man croaked like he had a throat full of gravel. "I don't want to be a woof no more! Can you help me?"

Jane leaned forward. Something about the way he said the word *woof* struck a warning chord in her. "No," she whispered.

Al nodded gravely. "Yes, I can help you, sir. But this life-changing procedure can only work if you truly believe it will. Do you believe, Mr. Terminus? Do you desire with all your heart and soul to change?"

"I believe!" The old man handed Al a heavy bag of coins that contained what Jane assumed was a hundred dollars, which Al handed to Ida.

Jane stared hard at the man as they put him into the cage and proceeded exactly as they had with the old lady she'd seen in the earlier show. They whipped and poked him until he turned into a garou, they gave him the injection, Al counted off the time with a pocket watch, and then Mr. Terminus became a man again. Al unlocked the cage and gave him a robe to wear, scooping up his hat so the man could put it on.

"Oh, thank you, thank you," wheezed Mr. Terminus, smoothing his beard back into place.

"You've only got yourself to thank," Al said. "Well, all right if you insist, you're welcome."

They did the color test with the handkerchiefs. Mr. Terminus passed with flying, er, colors.

"Well done, sir," Al said, clapping him on the back.

Mr. Terminus smiled and smiled.

Jane realized she was standing up. She was walking forward, her eyes fixed on the man who'd been cured. And his smile. "I know you!" she said. "It's you! And it was you in the first show, too! It was you all along!"

"Uh, time for you to rest now," Al said quickly, catching sight of Jane. Ida and the man calling himself "Mr. Terminus" glanced at each other and then practically ran off the stage, so quickly that the man forgot his cane. But then he no longer seemed to need it. Because he no longer had a limp.

Jane was standing right below the stage now, staring up at her mother with wide eyes.

Al cleared her throat. "What you've seen today is a miracle," she said, looking deliberately away from Jane. "I beseech you, if you have a family member or a friend who's a garou, tell them about what you've seen here today. Spread the word. And wolf by wolf we shall . . . ahem . . . cure this great land."

The crowd was clapping. Jane found herself clapping, too, at the sheer audacity of what she'd just witnessed, at how easily she'd been duped.

It was true, she realized, all that Frank had said. The cure was fake.

Al was sitting at her desk reading that gawl-darned newspaper article when Jane rushed in, breathless with outrage and shock. Her mother didn't pause in her reading when Jane arrived; she simply said, "Sit," in such a cold authoritative voice that Jane plopped into a chair, and then, after what felt like the longest five minutes of Jane's life, Al lowered the newspaper, folded it carefully, and laid it on the desk.

"Well, this story about you is troubling," Al said. "But nothing we can't deal with."

"Why would you do it?" Jane asked. "Why would you tell people you've got a cure if you don't? What do you stand to gain by lying about it?"

"Money," Al answered. "And control. There are two types of people in this world, you see, sweetie, the weak and the strong. Even among the garou, this is true. The strong follow me of their own volition. They understand that the wolf in their blood makes them superior to human beings in every way. They recognize that they are the future. We're going to make this a country of our own, you see. A country of garou. Through the moon I call the wolves, and when they arrive I give them a task to prove their loyalty, and once they've proven themselves, they are welcomed as part of the Pack."

"The Pack?" Jane repeated hoarsely. Shoot. She wished she could run straight to Frank and Bill, wherever they were now. She'd tell them she'd figured out who the leader of the Pack was. She'd finally solved the mystery. But she doubted they'd be pleased, seeing the mess it left them in. Especially her. "So what about the cure?" she asked.

Al scoffed. "The weak ones come to me and desire to be as they were before: insignificant, puny humans. To these people, I offer the cure, at a price, of course. And then I give them the serum, which compels them to obey me. If they insist that what I am is a disease, I cannot help them. I can only make use of them in other ways."

A shiver ran down Jane's spine. She thought about all those men along the trail to Deadwood, the ones who would disappear during the full moon, making their way here to such a fate, so full of hope, as she had been until tonight.

There was a gentle knock at the office door. "May I come in now?" said a familiar voice, and Al said, "Yes, come," and just like that, Jack McCall was standing before them, smiling his creepy smile.

"Hullo, Jane," he said.

She felt like she was going to be sick. "Hullo, Jack."

"You recognized me this time. I wondered if you would,

seeing as we're such good friends. I was a bit offended, the first time you saw the show."

"Yeah, well, sorry," Jane said numbly. "You're a pretty good playactor, Jack. You sure had me fooled."

"Thank you, kindly, miss," he said, and gave a bow. "And now you're reunited with your ma. Ain't that something to celebrate?"

"That's something, all right," Jane agreed.

"Yes, Jack, thank you," said Al. "For helping my daughter find her way, I am forever grateful. Now you may go. We've much to catch up on, she and I."

Jack's smile faded, but he nodded briskly and shuffled out.

"He helped me find my way?" Jane asked, her jaw tightening.

"Jack McCall is one of my most loyal and dedicated disciples," Al said. "He believes in the way of the wolf. I have never given him the true serum, for all the 'cures' he's taken for me on stage. But even without the serum, he's always followed my orders to the letter, without question. He's my Beta, in fact."

"He's your what now?"

"It's the Greek alphabet," Al explained. "I am the Alpha, which means I'm the first, the boss, the leader of the Pack, and the second in line is called the Beta."

Jane shook her head in awe of what a fool she had been.

"I'd like that to change, though, now that you're here," her mother added.

Jane stared at her. "Huh?"

"I'd like you to be my Beta," Al said. "That's why I sent Jack to find you and to bite you, so I could call you to me. This way—don't you see—we can rule this new country together, as mother and daughter. We can be together always. I'll even send for your siblings, once we're better established. We'll be one big happy family again, as we were meant to be. And we will unleash hell on this sad world and come out shining like stars."

Jane was frankly getting a bit sick of her mother's metaphors. She'd never been one to enjoy purple language. She rubbed a hand over her eyes. "Ma," she said. "Come on, now. You had Jack McCall bite me? Couldn't you have—I don't know—sent a message? I would have come if you'd asked me to."

"I cannot make an exception for you, however," Al went on seamlessly, as if Jane hadn't spoken. "You will have to prove yourself, same as the others." She stopped and gazed at Jane with a calculating gleam in her eyes.

"What do you want, Ma?" Jane asked wearily.

Al folded her hands in her lap. If she'd had an evil cat, she would have been stroking it. "I've recently been informed that a particular garou hunter has arrived in town—the one I told you about, that odious man who chased me for a thousand miles and tried to end me at every turn, but I outsmarted him. There is nothing I wish so much as to kill this man, to gut him first, to see him suffer and squirm and know that I have beaten him, at last. I'd do it with my bare hands, if I could."

Jane swallowed. She knew who her mother was referring to. She'd known for a while, she realized. She could feel the choice she was about to be asked to make roaring toward her like a runaway freight train, and she did not want to make it. "What—what does this hunter have to do with me?"

Al smiled. "He has everything to do with you. He's the reason we've had to be apart all these years. He killed your father."

"I know," said Jane. "He—"

"And that's not the worst of it," Al snarled. "Then he sought you out—he as good as kidnapped you, and then he made you his lackey. He tried to mold you into a hunter, too, to harass your own kin. And he put you on a stage for people to gawk at. My daughter, a laughingstock. But no more. No more, I say."

Jane couldn't breathe. "Ma— You can't mean—"

"You're going to kill him," Al said, lunging forward suddenly and pinning Jane's hand under her own on top of the desk. "I'd do it myself, gladly, easily, with a snap of my fingers—he's really so weak now, it's pathetic, it'll hardly be a challenge, but there's justice in you being the one. I knew, the instant I recognized you in the papers, standing right there next to my greatest enemy, that you would be the one to bring him down."

"Ma, no," Jane begged.

Al squeezed her hand so hard it hurt. "You have always been strong. You've always been loyal. You will do this, to become part of the Pack. To become my Beta. To fulfill your destiny."

Jane managed to yank her hand away and pull it to her chest. She shook her head wildly. "Ma, don't ask me to kill Bill. I can't."

Al stood up. She was a tall woman, as tall as Jane, but imposing in a way Jane would never be. Her eyes glowed in the lamplight. "You can. You must. You will kill Wild Bill Hickok. And then you will be free."

Jane's eyes closed. It was like time stopped, the world gone silent and still, awaiting her decision.

She could picture exactly what Al Swearengen was offering: Jane would never have to worry about being alone again. She'd always have nice clothes and good food and the respect of the people around her. No one would laugh at her anymore, because they wouldn't dare. Her brother and sisters would be with her at last: Lena in a fancy dress with curls in her hair, being treated right. Elijah in shiny shoes, his hair combed. Hannah and Sarah Beth laughing and playing and wanting for nothing.

Jane could have everything she'd ever really wanted.

But Bill. Bill was the price. She remembered the regret in his kind blue eyes when he'd confessed to her that he'd been the one to kill her father. She thought about the way he'd looked after her, even though he'd had nothing to gain by taking her in.

Jane's shoulders straightened. Her eyes opened again. She gazed solemnly at her mother.

"No," she said.

THIRTY-TWO
Frank

"I can't believe she didn't believe me," Frank said for the hundredth time. He glared into the shot of whiskey on the bar in front of him. "After all these years together, you'd think she'd trust me by now."

Beside him, Bill grunted. "People can be peculiar when it comes to family."

Frank was still having trouble with that idea, too. "Al Swearengen is not Jane's *family*," he insisted. "She's never been there when Jane's needed her, but we have."

"Well, that's complicated."

"I don't see what's so complicated about it."

Bill turned and studied Frank's face. Then he signaled to the barkeep at the No. 10 Saloon to pour him another whiskey. He threw back the shot and wiped his beard. "Frank, did you ever wonder why I took Jane in?"

"I thought you just picked up strays, like me. I thought it was kind of your thing."

Bill shook his head. "A few years back, when I was hunting full-time, and you were staying with the Browns, I was on the trail of the most vicious garou I'd ever come across. It stayed in wolf form for months on end, biting people indiscriminately, killing some, looting and robbing, and tearing places apart. It seemed dead set on bloodthirsty chaos. I was determined to find that monster and bring it down."

Frank had heard his father tell many a tall tale on the stage, but this was different. He'd never heard this story.

"At one point, I caught up with it in Cheyenne," Bill continued in a melancholy tone. "Townsfolk were running down the street, shouting about a garou attack at the butcher shop. When I got there, the garou had the butcher and his wife cornered. The garou was toying with them. It had already cut up the poor wife's face with its claws, to mar her and terrify her. The butcher was begging the garou to stop. The garou made like it was backing off, but then it raised its arm to strike the butcher down. I drew my pistols, but the garou knocked me over with a slab of beef."

Frank raised his eyebrows. "Beef, huh?"

Bill pshawed. "It was a big slab of beef. Once I was down, the wolf came over the counter at me, teeth snapping, but I got a shot off. Not a killing one—just through the shoulder—but enough to make it think twice about eating me. It dropped to the floor, yelping and whimpering, like a hurt dog. Then it went quiet. I figured it knew its time was up." He paused, his eyes troubled. "I took aim to shoot it, through the heart this time, but right then, the garou began to change back to a human, and I saw it was a woman."

"A woman?" Frank echoed.

Bill nodded grimly. "I admit that I hesitated. I'd never shot a woman. She was beautiful, too, tall, dark of hair, proud. She stood up and held out her hand. There was blood on her fingers from where I'd shot her. She said, 'This is the only blood you'll ever get from me, Wild Bill Hickok.' I didn't know what to say to that, but it didn't matter. Faster than any garou I've ever seen, she was a wolf again and gone through the window. But first, she left me this." Bill tugged aside the collar of his shirt.

Frank had never seen the scar on Bill's chest up close before. It was deep, and it ran from his shoulder to his heart. Frank had always assumed Bill had gotten it during the war. "Then what happened?" he asked.

Bill sighed. "I continued hunting her. Came close a few times, but she always evaded me. It wasn't until Salt Lake City that I finally caught up with her again. Normally, she'd hit a place once, rob or bite somebody, and then move on, but this time, she stuck around town. She had to know it was dangerous. I couldn't figure out why she'd changed her pattern. I was working with the local sheriff, trying to nail down her location, but she always kept two steps ahead of me. Until this one day, at the sheriff's office, when in walked a little girl."

Frank's breath caught. "What little girl?" But he suspected he already knew.

"She was a scrappy thing, maybe ten or eleven, still in pigtails, but she was wearing britches like a boy. She seemed dazed." Bill stared across the bar, like he could still see her clearly. "She said there was a garou at her house. And the thing is, her house is pretty near the center of all the activity I'd been tracking, following this female garou. I thought, 'This is it. I've got her.' This time, I wasn't about to hesitate. If I had the chance to bring her down, woman or not, I'd take it.

"I rode out to the house. I saw the garou through the window. I shot her right through the heart."

Frank exhaled. "Okay. So you got the bad guy."

But Bill shook his head. "Inside the house, I heard screaming. Kids. I went in and told them they were safe now, but they kept sobbing and shouting at me. That's when I got a look at the garou I'd killed, who, in death had turned back into a human." He cleared his throat, then ordered and drank another whiskey.

Frank waited.

"It wasn't the woman I'd been hunting," Bill said finally. "It was a man. I'd just killed these kids' father."

Silence.

"I'm sorry," Frank said.

Bill stared into the empty glass. "I stayed in Salt Lake City long enough to make sure the children had places to go. I gave up the hunt for a spell. But I always wondered what happened to that little girl who told us about the garou, her father. She'd run off. She was all alone in the world. So I tracked her down. It took me a while, but I finally found her in Wyoming. She was teaching herself to be a scout. She dressed as a boy and took any odd job she could, but it was rough finding a living and staying safe at such a young age. So, eventually, after I went and got you from the Browns, I decided to take her in."

"Jane," Frank murmured.

Bill nodded.

Frank remembered when Jane had first joined them. She'd been skinny and dirty, her clothes not much more than rags. Frank had introduced himself and held out his hand, because the Browns had taught him manners, but she'd spit at his feet and walked away.

Later, Bill told him that Jane had a way with the bullwhip, and Frank had an idea. The next time they were outside, he took a piece of candy out of his pocket. "You ever had taffy before?" he asked her.

Jane didn't answer, but she looked at the sweet longingly.

Frank put it on the top of a fence post. "First one to snap it with the whip gets to eat it," he said.

Frank had never been any good with a bullwhip, so even though he tried to win (his father taught him to never throw a contest) it was Jane who ended up with the taffy.

She smiled and unwrapped the candy, took a bite, and then offered the rest to Frank.

"No, you won it fair and square," Frank said.

She gobbled up the rest and then held out her hand. "I'm Calamity Jane."

"How do you do, Calam?" he said.

Then they were friends, and after a few months, they felt like family.

"That's when I gave up hunting full-time," Bill said, pulling Frank back to the present.

"Does Jane know? That you killed her father?"

Bill nodded. "I told her. Apparently her pa was a drunk who couldn't hold a job and couldn't provide for his family. But that doesn't mean I don't regret it every day."

"You've given Jane a better life," Frank said softly.

"I don't know about that," Bill muttered.

But Frank felt like this still wasn't the end of the story. "What happened to the other wolf? The female."

Bill's jaw tightened. "A while back, I'd heard she'd been captured and killed. But yesterday, I saw her with Jane at the Gem."

"The wolf's Al Swearengen," Frank concluded.

"Yep."

Frank was starting to understand why this was complicated. "How come you never told me any of this?"

"Because it's Jane's story to tell."

Frank was a tad miffed that she'd never told him, then he remembered he'd never told her about being a garou.

"Jane had a rough time of it, and that leaves a wound," Bill said. "A wound that maybe makes a person overlook some red flags when they find out their dead mother is actually alive. But that's not something you can tell her. She's got to figure it out for herself."

Right then, the doors to the saloon opened and Annie rushed in. Frank's heart boomed at the sight of her, but her eyes were wide with fear.

Frank sprang to his feet. "What's wrong?"

"It's Jane."

Not again. "What about Jane?"

"She's a garou!"

Frank felt as though Annie had punched him. Jane was a garou, and that was *wrong*? Annie had been nothing but nice to him (that kiss, we're just saying), so he'd hoped she was coming around to the whole garou situation.

"I mean," Annie continued, "that Jane is a garou, and it's all over the newspaper, and now there's an angry mob, and it makes me so—so—angry!"

Frank's stomach dropped. "Oh."

"And the worst part is, they're going to force her to take the cure!"

Outside, the street was swarming with people buzzing about the news.

"Calamity Jane is getting the cure!"

"She's an abomination. The cure can't come soon enough!"

and

"She's finally getting what's coming to her."

Frank was surprised at how quickly people could turn on a person. How they could go from asking for an autograph to grabbing their pitchforks in the blink of an eye.

They started for the Gem, but there were too many bodies on the narrow street, and progress was difficult.

Annie, taking charge, as usual, tried to lead them and part the crowd by shouting, "Wild Bill Hickok needs to get through!" But no one could hear her over the ruckus.

So, being petite, she ducked and darted this way and that, narrowly avoiding hitting her head on the butt of someone's gun. She made it to the door of the Gem and waved to Frank and Bill, who were a ways behind. Then she felt at her back for the strap that she used to carry her rifle. It was broken. Somewhere in the crowd, she'd lost her gun.

A sea of people were entering the Gem by the time Frank and Bill made it to Annie.

"We better get in there," Bill said.

"But my rifle!" she cried.

"We've got this," Frank said. "Go get your gun. We might need it."

Then the press of the mob forced Bill and Frank forward, to where a line of guards stood outside the entrance to the theater.

"Hand over your weapons," they yelled. "No firearms allowed."

One of them recognized Bill. "Guns please, Mr. Hickok."

Bill opened his coat to reveal the ivory-handled pistols. "These never leave my side."

"Then you can't go in," the guard said.

Bill sighed, and he and Frank reluctantly turned over their guns. "What are we supposed to use to save Jane?" Frank hissed. "Harsh language?"

They entered into the back of the theater. Jane was already in the cage.

"No," Frank called out in despair. There was no way to reach her. There were too many people and too many guards. The audience was throwing stuff at her, everything from rotten food to rocks to shoes.

"C'mon," a man by Frank shouted. "Wolf out!"

Jane crouched in the corner farthest from the crowd. She was shivering.

"This is outrageous," Frank said.

"Well, if it isn't *the* Wild Bill Hickok," came a voice from behind them. Frank and Bill turned to see none other than Al Swearengen. She seemed to have been waiting for them. "I'm so happy you made it."

"Let Jane go," Bill said gruffly. "Your fight is with me."

Swearengen touched her shoulder. "You know, I still have the bullet you struck me with. I thought about selling it to the highest bidder, but then I decided to keep it with me always." She pulled out a necklace from inside her shirt. Hanging there was a silver bullet. "Here it is, right by the heart you missed, reminding me every day of your failure."

"None of that matters." Bill looked toward the cage. "That's your daughter in there."

"No, she's *your* daughter. But pretty soon, I'll have her back, and she'll forget she ever knew you." Al smiled wickedly. "Enjoy the show."

THIRTY-THREE
Annie

"Has anyone seen my gun?"

Annie pushed through the crowd, searching for the familiar Kentucky long rifle, but it could have been anywhere by now. Dozens of people crowded the street, and it seemed entirely likely that someone had kicked the rifle into a pigpen, or even picked it up to claim it as their own. It was a nice rifle, although probably mostly nice to her, what with the sentimental value.

"Heeeere, gun, gun, gun," she called, and then walked smack into her gun and the mustache bending to pick it up. (There was a man behind the mustache, but it took her an extra second to see him.)

"Excuse me!" said the mustache.

"Excuse yourself! That's my gun." Oh yes (oh yes) they both

reached for the gun (the gun the gun).

Annie got it first, hugging the rifle to her chest like it was a lost puppy that didn't make her sneeze.

"Are you all right, miss?" The man behind the mustache (it was as big as a push broom) looked to be in his late twenties, and though his face was mostly dominated by that mustache, she thought he had the look of a politician or a businessman. That was, he had cunning eyes and a quick smile, the kind that wanted everyone to trust him.

"Fine," she said, even though it was a lie. "I'm busy. I have to stop the cure."

"Why?"

"It's not a cure. It's—" Annie threw her free hand in the air. "Never mind. I have to go. Thanks for not stealing my gun, Mr. . . ."

"Bullock," he said. "Seth Bullock. And if you ever need mining hardware, I have a tent—"

"You're the man with the toilets."

"You've heard of me!"

"I've heard of your toilets. Good luck with that."

"Thanks, Miss—"

"Annie Oakley." Then she was gone, her gun finally in hand. Of course, at the theater door, the guards demanded her gun, saying she couldn't go in without disarming.

"Argh!" But she carefully handed her gun over, because the only other choice was not helping Jane at all. "I'll be back for this," she warned in her most withering tone. "And if it's not here when I get back, I'm blaming you."

The man, not withered at all, shrugged. "Enjoy the show."

"You too!" Annie said automatically, and then died a little inside when she remembered that (a) he wasn't going to see the show, and (b) she wasn't there to enjoy anything.

Face burning with anger and humiliation, Annie pushed her way through the crowd of shouting, swearing, and smelly townsfolk. Somehow, over a hundred of them had crammed into the theater in a matter of minutes, and now they were all jeering at Jane on the stage, locked in the cage. Shoes, tomatoes, and rocks flew at her, most bouncing off the bars to be picked up and thrown again. But a few sailed between the bars and hit the girl inside.

Jane was trembling. Oh, she tried not to show it, but Annie could tell that fear and adrenaline were flooding through her friend. If Jane really was a garou, then it wouldn't be long before she showed it.

Two other figures were standing on the stage. One Annie knew: Jack McCall, the man who'd been in Cincinnati with them, who'd always seemed to pop up at the worst time.

The other could only be Al Swearengen: tall with black hair, and the sort of smile that said she owned this place, this mob, this whole town. She even had a top hat, and we all know how Annie felt about people in top hats.

With a shiver, Annie hurried to Frank's side. "I don't even know what to say about all this."

Frank's jaw clenched. "You don't have to say anything."

"It's just," Annie went on, "Jane is suddenly a garou, which I only found out a little bit ago from the newspaper, and now she's up there getting rocks thrown at her."

Frank gave her a side-eye. "Sounds like you do know what to say."

"Not really," Annie said. "I'm babbling because I'm scared. What are they going to do to her?"

"Nothing good." Frank's expression didn't soften. "She didn't tell anyone she'd been bit. You weren't the only one she was hiding from. But given how you've felt about garou, is it really a surprise she saved you for last?"

"I found out from the newspaper," Annie reminded him.

"Right. So maybe she didn't intend to tell you at all."

That stung, but Annie figured she deserved it. She'd given Jane no reason to feel safe. "I'm sorry," Annie whispered.

Frank didn't respond.

"But what are we going to do?" Annie looked from Frank to Mr. Hickok. "How can we stop this?"

"We can't," Frank said. "Not without making it worse for her."

Then, on the stage, even without Annie and Frank trying to help, the situation actively got worse: Swearengen produced a whip, like the one Jane used. Maybe it *was* Jane's whip.

"Oh no," Annie breathed.

Crack. The bullwhip lashed on the cage bars. "You all know Calamity Jane as the Heroine of the Plains," Swearengen said. "And

I'm certain you've all heard by now that she's my own daughter."

A collective gasp sucked all the air out of the theater. Lots of people had known, yes, but hearing it again—and seeing the two of them like this—was a shock. And for Annie, who hadn't known because she'd been wandering around the Black Hills and reuniting the sisters, it was a punch to the gut.

"Swearengen is Jane's mother?" She could barely get the words out.

Frank kindly didn't remind her that Jane didn't have to tell Annie everything that went on in her life, or even *anything*.

"Because Jane is my daughter," Swearengen went on, "I need to set an example for everyone else. And I need to set an example for Jane, as well."

The crowd roared, booing and cheering with equal fervor. Booing for Jane, cheering for what they knew was coming. Annie felt sick. How could a mother do this to her daughter? Never, not in a thousand years, not even with all the disagreements they'd had before Annie left, could Annie imagine her own mama betraying her in this way.

"I can cure her," Swearengen said. "I *want* to cure her. Then she can go back to being a productive member of society."

Horror crept into Annie as the whip cracked again, missed the bars, and hit Jane instead. She screamed and lurched to the other side of the cage, but there was nowhere to run. "Ma, please! Let me loose!" Jane cried.

No one listened.

"Day after day," Swearengen said, "you've seen demonstrations of real garou being cured of the affliction from which they suffer. The affliction that terrorizes entire towns."

The crowd threw more random objects at the cage.

"And now we will cure Calamity Jane from this affliction. Wolf by wolf, we will cure the West of this plague." Swearengen whipped the cage again, then strode toward Jane, danger in every step. "Do you want to be cured of this plague?" she asked.

For the first time, the audience grew quiet, waiting to hear what Jane would say.

Jane pulled herself up tall, clenched her jaw, and stared at Swearengen. "No."

Everyone in the crowd gasped. Calamity Jane had admitted— in front of everyone—that she was a garou. And she wanted to stay that way.

"Well," said Swearengen, "I'm afraid what you want doesn't matter. You're my daughter, and you don't get to make your own decisions yet. You're also a garou, and that means you're a threat to society. You have no choice."

The crowd cheered in agreement, and Annie swayed with wanting to be sick. How could anyone do this to another person? To someone who'd never hurt anyone? To her own *daughter*?

Swearengen turned to the audience, speaking in the way a lecturing teacher might. "The cure works best if the wolf understands that she's dangerous and desires to be cured. I believe that Calamity Jane wants to be cured. She just doesn't know it yet."

Jane pressed herself against the back of the cage. "You don't have to do this," she cried.

"Wooo," Frank said under his breath. "Remember your Wooo."

"What was that?" Annie asked.

Frank looked over like he'd forgotten she was there. "What was what?"

"You said wooo."

"Oh." He glanced at Jane again. "It's how I control the wolf—and how I tried to teach her to do it. Saying wooo helps calm the mind. Sometimes I imagine a setting sun, too, because it's peaceful."

Annie bit her lip and gazed at Jane. "Can she do it?"

"I don't know," Frank said. "This is so much pressure."

The whip cracked again, closer to Jane.

Frank woooed some more, and then Annie joined in. "Woooooo."

But Jane was shaking inside the cage, her whole body rocked with fear and sudden change. Her face elongated, her feet grew, her arms bulked and tore the sleeves of her white top. Brown fur erupted from her face and arms and legs.

Jane was a wolf.

Annie gasped. She didn't want to be as shocked as she was, but in reality, she'd seen only a few garou before—the Wolf family, the two in the candle factory, and almost the mayor—and those wolves had all been tormenters or strangers. Not someone she cared about. It was easy to think *they* were evil, but now, she saw only her friend—albeit a much bigger and hairier version. It would have been terrifying if Annie hadn't realized that Jane was simply scared.

"Oh, Jane," Frank whispered. "Poor Jane."

Annie started to touch his arm, to offer him strength, but he shifted away from her and she let her hand fall down to her side once more.

Inside the cage, Jane snarled.

Swearengen nodded at McCall. "It's time."

McCall produced a rod with a loop on one end, and quickly, he dropped the loop over wolf-Jane's head and dragged her toward the side of the cage.

"No!" Annie yelled, stepping forward, but no one could hear her over the cheering crowd.

Frank took her shoulder and drew her back. "We can't do anything."

Annie wished she hadn't given up her gun. She could have shot the whip out of Swearengen's hand, or the rod out of McCall's. She could have shot the hinges off the cage to open the door and let Jane free.

"We have to stop this," she said. "We have to say something."

"Maybe the serum won't work," Frank said, although he didn't sound very hopeful. "It didn't work on Walks Looking, remember?"

Annie shook her head. "Walks Looking told me how hard it

was to resist, and I don't want to insinuate mean things about Jane but—"

"Swearengen is Jane's mother," he finished. "It's going to be hard for Jane to resist when there's probably a big part of her that wants to be with her mother."

Annie's heart sank. "Yeah."

That's when another man stepped onto the stage, a familiar figure in a long black coat. Everyone went quiet.

Annie looked to where Mr. Hickok had been standing a minute ago, to confirm that he didn't have a surprise twin running around Deadwood.

"Wild Bill Hickok." Swearengen touched the brim of her hat in greeting. "I'm honored you're so interested in the cure that you had to come see it up close."

Jane gave a faint growl, but she no longer fought; she'd strangle herself if she did.

"I'm here to put an end to this," Mr. Hickok said. "This business is no good."

The crowd gasped.

"You're going to put an end to Calamity Jane yourself?" Swearengen glanced at Mr. Hickok's empty holsters. "How do you plan on doing that?"

Mr. Hickok shook his head. "Of course I'm not going to hurt her. Calamity Jane hasn't harmed anyone in this town."

"She's harmin' us just by bein' what she is," said a man in the audience.

"Yeah!" someone shouted.

"Well, now wait," another man shouted. "This is Wild Bill Hickok. Maybe we should listen to what he says."

A few people muttered, and someone in the back shouted, "Can I have your autograph?"

"This isn't the USA, and you have no jurisdiction here," Swearengen said. "This is Deadwood, and Deadwood takes care of its own problems."

Lots of people nodded.

Annie pushed her way through the crowd. People might listen to Mr. Hickok because he was famous, but they were scared of Al Swearengen.

"You and I both know there's no cure for the garou," Mr. Hickok said evenly, "not because it's incurable, but because it's not a disease. It's not a problem that needs to be fixed."

A few miners and shop owners looked at one another and grumbled.

"Isn't it?" Swearengen grinned, showing the points of her eye-teeth. "After all, it's transmitted through a bite—through blood and saliva. It gives people chills and fever, and forces them to involuntarily change shape every month. That sounds like a disease to me. A very *dangerous* disease that needs curing."

Annie was in no position to agree or disagree with those claims, but it seemed incredibly hypocritical of Swearengen to make declarations like that, given that she was a garou, too, and sending her minions out to go make more. If there was a garou plague—and that was a big *if* as far as Annie could see—then Swearengen was the source of it.

But the crowd was shouting out their agreement, calling for an end to all the wolves. They booed and tossed more things at Jane. A hand clamped on Annie's shoulder. She jumped and spun around, but it was Frank. He'd followed her to the fore of the crowd, although his eyes never left the players on the stage.

"Thanks to me," Swearengen went on, "dozens of people have been cured of their garou disease. Thanks to me, the world is a safer place."

Mr. Hickok shook his head, slow and thoughtful even as the jeers continued to rise. "You, ma'am, have been pulling the wool over these people's eyes."

"Ain't no sheep in Deadwood," said McCall.

Before anyone could speak another word, Swearengen turned up the syringe and plunged it into Jane's arm.

"No!" Annie and Frank surged forward, but it was too late. The liquid pushed into Jane and that was that.

Everyone waited, watching the cage as the serum flooded through Jane.

"How long is it supposed to take?" Annie asked.

Frank shook his head. "I don't know."

They stood there, in the middle of the audience, watching as wolf-Jane howled and shook the bars of the cage, trying to escape, and as the minutes wore on, a dangerous grumble spread throughout the audience.

"It's not working," a man said.

"She's still a wolf," observed another.

"What if Wild Bill was right?" asked a third, but he was quickly shouted over.

"Down with wolves!"

Annie and Frank glanced at each other. Of course the "cure" for being a garou wasn't working, but what about the important part? What about the mind control?

Swearengen shook her head, deepening her voice. "Unfortunately, we have a difficult wolf," she said. "Remember, they don't all want to be cured. Some wolves love chaos."

The crowd booed.

Swearengen looked at Jane. "Come, dear. You know you want to be cured. You must become human again. So we can be together."

Jane growled and rattled the bars of the cage.

"Now, Jane. You should turn back to a human for what happens next."

Annie held her breath.

Jane lunged at Swearengen, growling loud enough to make Annie's stomach knot. This was the test. The real test.

"Turn back into a human," Swearengen commanded, but Jane roared and reached through the bars, claws sharp and gleaming. She didn't change back.

A fist loosened its grip around Annie's heart. Jane wasn't enthralled. She was still in control of herself.

Unfortunately, Swearengen knew it, too. She turned to McCall and nodded slightly. "Well, if she doesn't want to do what she's told, then we have no choice. Calamity Jane is a danger to society. And what do we do with folks who are a danger to society?"

"We toss 'em in the clink!" McCall said.

"Lock her up!" shouted the mob in frenzied unison. "Lock her up!"

"Stop all this," said Mr. Hickok. "It's not a crime to be a garou, and Jane didn't commit a crime."

Swearengen shot him a look of murder. "This land is lawless, except for the law we make. Besides, I gave her the cure in good faith that she'd pay for it once she saw the light, but now I'm out a hundred dollars."

"She's a crook!" McCall yelled. "She didn't intend to pay for the cure!"

That sent everyone into a frenzy.

As the chanting of "lock her up" intensified, Annie wanted to vomit. There was no reasoning with these people. They were all crashing toward the stage, taking the loop on a stick, and grabbing at the cage. Jane jerked back in horror, but it was too late. The loop went around her neck and they dragged her out of the cage.

"Shame!" someone shouted. "Shame!"

"We need to stop them!" Annie turned to Frank.

He pulled her close to keep her from being crushed by the mob. "How do you propose doing that? This isn't a room full of people right now. It's a room full of monsters."

Annie pressed her cheek to his chest. "I'm sorry. I'm sorry that I've been a monster."

He didn't say anything. Maybe he didn't hear.

After several minutes of people yelling and screaming and hauling Jane out of the theater, the only people left were Annie, Frank, and Mr. Hickok. Swearengen and McCall had led the charge to the jail, probably hoping to keep the residents of Deadwood as angry as possible.

"We should have stopped them from taking her," Annie said. "We could have."

"How?" asked Mr. Hickok. "At least they can't do lasting harm to Jane, not without silver."

Not all harm was physical, Annie wanted to say. Jane would remember this moment for the rest of her life. But Frank looked so distraught she didn't dare make it worse.

"How could Swearengen say those things about wolves?" Annie whispered. "Being a wolf herself, I mean."

Mr. Hickok sighed. "She's a con man. Woman, I guess. And those kind of folks like to project what they are onto other people, to make themselves look like the good guy. So Jane's a danger to society because Swearengen is. And wolves are a plague on this world because Swearengen knows that's what *she* is."

Annie bit her lip. "And now she has Jane."

"We'll get Jane out of there," Mr. Hickok said. "Don't you worry. I'll get the money to pay for her release."

"How?" Frank asked. "We spent all our money getting here."

"I have some," Annie said. "Not a hundred dollars, but enough to get us started."

Mr. Hickok nodded. "Good. Now, both of you make yourselves scarce." He glanced at Frank. "Last thing we need is someone finding out about you, son. You need to be careful—more careful than ever."

"I will be." Frank summoned up a smile.

Mr. Hickok touched Frank's shoulder, squeezed, and then turned and strode out of the building.

Annie looked up at Frank. "Are you—" Not okay. She couldn't ask if he was okay, because he clearly wasn't. "Do you want to talk?" she asked instead.

"Not right now," he said. "Can we just sit together for a bit?"

She hauled herself up onto the edge of the stage and patted the place beside her. He followed, and when she reached for his hand, he was already reaching back.

Jane THIRTY-FOUR

"You need a time-out here to calm down and think about your behavior," Al Swearengen said as her men dumped Jane in a heap in the back room of the blacksmith's shop, which served as Deadwood's makeshift jail.

Her mother's tone was almost sweet, parental-like, but Jane knew better.

"I'll come back tomorrow. Maybe by then you'll be ready to make better choices."

Jane scrambled to her feet and threw herself against the slatted iron door of her "cell," feeling the tight brick walls closing in around her. It was dark in there, even in the middle of the afternoon, the only light a narrow barred window at the far wall. It smelled like death. "Ma," she panted. "Don't leave me in here."

Al's eyes flashed. "Don't call me that unless you're ready to be a true daughter of mine. Not until you do what you're meant to do."

"I can't kill Bill," Jane said. "I don't want to kill nobody."

"Then you're weak, and I have no use for you," pronounced Al, turning away.

Jane wiped at her nose, which was bleeding from a blow she'd taken back at the theater. She hurt all over, but she tried to stand up straight. "If I'm so weak, why can't you control me?"

Al stiffened and pivoted slowly to face Jane again. "I believe it's because you're already under someone else's thrall," she said coldly. "But not for long."

Jane shivered. "Ma, please," she pleaded. "It don't have to be this way."

"You're a traitor to your own kind," Al said. "You need to be punished."

Jane's chin lifted. "We don't harm a garou unless that garou's hurting people or trying to hurt us. You act like you're helping the garou, but then you lie to them and make them your slaves. So which of us is really a traitor to our kind?"

Al made a sound like a growl and stepped forward with her hand raised, her lip curled into a snarl. Jane could see the sharp points of fangs in her mouth. But then her mother shook her head and smiled, the fangs receding, her hand closing into a fist and dropping to her side. "You always could rile me, girl. You're just like your father. He never did know how to see the big picture."

"I'm not like him or you."

Al sighed. "I suppose you're going to tell me you want to be like Wild Bill Hickok," she said in disgust.

Jane said nothing.

"To think, you chose to protect that tired old has-been." There was hurt behind the anger in Al's eyes, a jealous wound. "You chose him over me, your own mother."

"I don't want to choose," Jane murmured.

"That man shot me, nearly killed me, but you don't seem to care. What's worse, he killed your father, murdered him in cold blood in front of your brothers and sisters, no less. That's your hero."

"I know," Jane said. "He—"

But Al had started to pace and rave. "Why don't you want to take revenge? Don't you understand? That man ruined everything!"

"I know."

"He's a monster! He killed your pa!" Al cried.

"I KNOW!" Jane yelled, just to get her voice heard. Then, softer: "I always knew Bill killed Pa."

Al stopped pacing. "What do you mean, you knew?"

Jane swallowed. "He told me. Years ago. He told me what he did, and why, and I forgave him."

Al gave an incredulous laugh. Then she nodded, like she'd made up her mind about something. "You need some time to think about what's important here. Blood is thicker than water, my dear. You are *my* daughter, like it or not, and you belong with me. You could still have everything you desire. I would give it to you. A home here. Your family, by your side. Wealth. Prosperity. Why, I'm sure I could even find you a suitable husband, given time, and then you could have children of your own."

Jane said nothing.

Al glanced at her pocket watch. "As I said, I will be back in the morning to check whether you've seen the light. If not, the townsfolk are bound to be upset. Those mobs can get ugly, can't they, especially when they're scared, and nothing scares them more than a dangerous and uncontrollable female. They're like to want to hang you, and I don't believe even I could stop them."

"All right, then," said Jane.

Al sighed. "Being a good mother is so hard." She snapped her fingers at Jack McCall, who jumped to attention from where he'd been leaning casually against the wall. "Let's go. You've still got an errand to run for me."

"Bye, Jane." Jack smiled his usual smile, but this time there was something extra creepy behind it.

"Come, Jack," Al commanded, and swept from the room, Jack jogging along at her heels.

Jane sank onto the cold dirt floor. She tried to lie down and get comfortable, seeing as she was going to be here for a while, but there was no way to relax. It was cold. Damp. Smelly. She hugged herself for warmth. She wished for her man clothes—her buckskins and her breeches instead of this torn, flimsy shirt and cumbersome skirt. She wished she hadn't sassed her ma—that always made things twice as bad, in her experience, but she never seemed to learn that, did she? She wished . . . well, heck, she wished for a lot of things, but wishing was a waste of time, she thought bitterly. Wishing can't make a thing true.

She was a garou—everybody knew it now, everybody—and it turned out there was no magic cure that would make it not so. She was in jail, possibly about to be hanged by an angry mob come morning. But more than anything else, she was really, really hungry. Her stomach rumbled, and she clutched at her middle and groaned. She hadn't eaten or drunk anything since that steak she'd had the night before. (We'd like to point out that this wasn't that long ago, so Jane wasn't exactly starving to death. But still, she was hangry.)

"Hello!" she called into the rest of the blacksmith shop, hoping that there'd at least be some kind of guard. "Hey, is anybody there?"

Nothing. Folks trusted the strength of the brick walls and the iron doors to hold her. She rattled and pulled at the bars, but all that accomplished was making her arms more tired and her throat even more dried out. She licked her lips. "I need water!" she hollered. "I need food! Hey!"

No one came.

She dropped back to the floor. "Who do I have to bribe," she bellowed, "to bring me some grub around here?"

"You know, in order to offer a bribe, a person might first want to have something to barter," came a gruff but dear voice out of the darkness.

Jane sat up with a gasp. Her eyes searched between the slats of the door. "Bill! That you?"

"I'm here, Jane."

Jane was seized with worry. "You should get out of town," she warned. "Al wants you dead."

"Tell me something I don't know," he laughed.

"This ain't a joke," she said. "She will kill you, or send someone to do the job."

"Then we better leave town quick as we can, I reckon," Bill said, "but I'm not going anywhere without you, and you don't seem to be going anywhere, so that's a problem."

"I'm sorry, Bill," she lamented. "I've brought you nothing but trouble, haven't I?"

"This isn't your fault, Jane. It's mine." She could see him now, standing on the other side of the door, still a grand figure in his billowy white shirt with the laces up the front, his long auburn curls and carefully trimmed mustache. Jane crawled to the door and grabbed the bars to lift herself up. "It's going to be all right," he said. "You'll see."

"Ah now, you're just saying that." She swallowed back a sob. "Maybe you should . . . give me the silver-bullet treatment," she managed to choke out. "I'm a garou, and I cain't handle myself at all, as you've seen. It'd be a kindness, coming from you. You'd make it quick, Bill. Painless. Better than a mob is like to do." A shudder passed through her, but she braved on. "Best get it over, I think."

The thing was, though, she really didn't want to die.

"Oh, didn't I tell you?" he said pleasantly. "I'm not a garou hunter anymore. I have officially retired. For real, this time."

"Oh. That's nice. Good for you, Bill."

"Yep. So no one is going to be getting any more silver bullets from me. Least of all you." Bill placed his hand over hers through the bars. "Don't worry, Janey. I'll get you out of here."

She didn't see how. "I don't have the cash to pay for the cure, and I don't think they'll let me go, otherwise. I've got twenty-three dollars saved, in my boot back at my room, but it's not enough, and you cain't go into the Gem, seeing as they'd murder you before you could say howdy, and it's . . . it's only a matter of time before the people of this town get sick of waiting and come to get me."

Tomorrow, Al had said, and her ma wasn't the type to make idle threats. It was either her way or the—(uh-oh, highways didn't exist yet)—the way you took to get out of town.

"I'll get the money," Bill said. "I've got some of my own saved up, and I can win the rest at poker this afternoon—I've got a good spot staked out at the Number Ten. I'll have you free by supper-time, and then we'll light out of this cursed town and figure out our next move."

The idea that he would pay that much for her freedom—one hundred dollars—took Jane's breath away, but she shook her head.

"I can't let you do that, Bill," she said. "Why would you want to use your money on me? I ain't nothing. I've never been nothing. Not to anybody."

His hand tightened around hers. "How can you believe that?

All these years, you've never wavered in your lively spirit, your generous nature, your humor, your hard work. Besides, I ... You're ..."
He coughed. "You're my family, not by blood, perhaps, but in every way that counts. As sure as Frank is my son, you are my daughter."

Then he didn't speak again for several minutes, or maybe Jane was bawling so hard she didn't hear him. It wasn't a pretty cry, either. It was the full-out, swollen-eyed, snotty-sobfest kind of cry. But afterward she felt better.

"Oh, Bill," she sniffled finally. "Thank you for saying that."

"I meant it." He smiled that quiet smile of his that was mostly in his eyes. "Now I have to go scrounge us up some capital. I'll be back in a few hours, I promise."

"Remember, Al's gunning for you," she said, still feeling that the safest course of action would be for he and Frank and Annie to leave town as soon as possible. "Watch your back!"

He patted her hand, and she felt suddenly silly for advising him, *the* Wild Bill Hickok, the world's first gunfighter, the quickest eye, the fastest draw, on how to stay alive in the Wild West.

"I'll just wait here, then," she called after him as he swept away, his big black coat flaring behind him.

She wiped at her face with her torn sleeve. She might not have much, but she believed what he'd said to her. That she had people who cared. Bill. Frank trying to talk the mob down earlier. Annie crying "Stop!" when they'd whipped Jane in the cage. Which she reckoned was something to keep fighting for.

* * *

Time passed quick, because Jane took a nap. She woke when the blacksmith finally appeared and brought her some food—a fat hunk of bread and leg of what might be rabbit, a skin full of water that tasted of mud. She was in the middle of (if you'll pardon the expression) wolfing down her meal when she received another visitor to the cramped little cell.

It wasn't Bill come to spring her free, though. It was Edwina Harris.

She was dressed as a woman this time, in a dark gray skirt and fine white blouse, her corn-silk colored hair piled up in a mess of curls at the top of her head, some kind of fancy ivory brooch at her throat, and delicate white gloves.

Jane's heart thundered at the sight of her, but she wiped rabbit grease off her mouth with the back of her hand and conjured up a smirk. "Oh, good. So next it's to be torture, then?"

Winnie frowned and twisted her hands together in front of her. Ironically she seemed at a loss for words. "Martha, I—"

"I got nothing to say to you," sniffed Jane. "And my name ain't Martha, not anymore."

"Jane, then. Jane," amended Winnie. "I came to explain myself."

"No need." Jane put out a hand. "You wanted a story. You got one. That about sum it up?"

"You know it's more complicated than that."

"Is it, though?" Jane pulled her tattered shirt more tightly around her. She hated that she must look like a fallen woman, but she supposed that's what she was. "It feels pretty simple to me. You used me. Then you threw me away."

"No, that's not what I wanted to—" Winnie stopped and closed her eyes, then tried again. "I did it because of Buntline. He's been working on a story about Wild Bill, and he has this theory that all of you—Wild Bill, Frank, you, perhaps even Annie Oakley, are all garou. It's the perfect cover, see, as you're garou hunters. You're hiding in plain sight. Buntline thinks it will be the story of the century."

A chill trickled down Jane's spine. She thought about how careful Frank had been to keep that part of himself hidden. How the Wild West show, Frank's pride and joy, would crumble to nothing if people knew Frank was a woof.

"So you thought you'd beat him to the punch, huh?"

Winnie shook her head. "That's not what my story was about. Of course you didn't read it, but—"

Jane's jaw tightened. "Yeah, of course not. I'm dumb as a bag of rocks."

"Jane—" Winnie sighed. "I wrote about how you were bitten back at the candle factory in Ohio, how you were injured in the line of duty, so to speak. And I plan to write a follow-up piece, on how you came to Deadwood for the cure."

"Yeah and you saw how well that turned out." Jane gestured around herself.

"I think I can help you," Winnie said almost pleadingly. "I can write—"

"No, thanks. I think you've written enough." It was a lesson Jane would take to heart this time. Never, ever, ever trust a writer. As a whole, they're a no-good bunch. (Ouch. That smarts.) "Why do you care if my story has a happy ending? Will it sell more papers that way?"

"I'm sorry," Winnie said. "I know I promised you."

"Yeah. You did."

"I wanted to get the true story out there first, so Buntline wouldn't be able to spin it."

It made a fair bit of sense, but Jane could not forgive her. Not this time. "It wasn't your story to tell, though," she pointed out. "And now I'm here. Because of you."

Winnie nodded. "I didn't know how people would take it. I thought they would see how brave you were, how selfless, even, but all they saw was the wolf. I'm so sorry, Jane. I know you won't believe that, but I am."

They gazed at each other. Jane couldn't help drinking in the sight of Winnie, one last time, she told herself, just looking at her, and then she'd put what had happened between them away and never take it out again. She noted the sweep of her dark lashes, the slight upturned nose so small she had to keep pushing up her glasses. Those green eyes. The dainty, heart-shaped mouth that Jane had kissed.

Then Jane gave the girl a look made of iron. "Apology not accepted. Now get out of here. Get out of this town, if you know what's good for you."

"I meant what I said. I could—"

"Get out," Jane snarled, and turned to face the wall. "I never want to see you again."

When she looked that way a few minutes later, Winnie was gone.

More time passed, which felt like a year, and still Bill didn't come. Jane leaned against the wall and sang about bottles of beer until the blacksmith came and threatened to chain her up if she didn't stop.

He didn't get a chance, though, because right then there was a ruckus outside.

Jane went to the window and peered out. The first thing she saw was Jack McCall—her stomach twisting at the mere sight of him. But Jack was in trouble now. His expression was something akin to panic. He was holding a gun, but he suddenly threw it down onto the ground and kept on running, like he meant to run right out of town.

Jane tried to ask him a question as he sprinted past the blacksmith's shop, but he didn't even see her. That's when Jane noticed the mob behind him. They were coming with a cloud of dust, holding rifles and shovels and even some literal pitchforks, churning with noise and fury like a coming thunderstorm.

What is it with angry mobs today? Jane thought, feeling, in spite of her best judgment, a sudden flash of pity for Jack McCall, seeing as a few hours earlier these same people had been coming for her.

THIRTY-FIVE
Frank

"Miss Mosey wins," the dealer at the Shaggy Dog Saloon said. Frank and Annie were not making themselves scarce, the way Bill had told them to. Instead, they were playing poker, trying to raise the money to free Jane.

They had decided to sit at the same table, under the assumption that Frank would win all the money, and Annie would provide company, but it turned out that Annie was on a hot streak and Frank was card dead.

"Who, me?" Annie responded to the dealer.

Frank smiled. She really was good at playing the novice. At least, he hoped she was just pretending.

The next hand of cards was dealt, and Joe "the Player" Fletcher was acting as if his hand was the "nuts," which is a poker term for the best hand. (Incidentally, the term *the nuts* originated in the Wild West, because if a player wanted to bet his horse and wagon, he would have to remove the nuts from his wheels and place them in the pot.)

"All in," he said.

Frank folded, and the play turned to Annie.

"I don't know." Annie shrugged. "I guess . . . all in?" She said it as a question, and Frank knew then and there that Annie had a genuine hand.

But Joe didn't.

Everyone else folded, and the dealer called for cards up.

"Her first," Joe said.

"She called you," the dealer said.

And here's the thing, Joe just threw his cards into the muck.

"Why don't you want to show?" Annie said. "You were all in."

"*You* show," Joe said.

"I don't think those are the rules," Annie said. "And I've read the rules extensively."

The dealer shoved the chips toward Annie.

Annie leaned over to Frank. "Would you mind stacking my chips while I . . . ahem . . ."

"Of course," Frank said.

Annie excused herself, and Frank started stacking her chips. She had won thirty-five dollars so far. Frank wondered how Bill was faring. Perhaps with Annie's contribution, they were close to their hundred-dollar goal.

Frank thought about Jane, and her ordeal up on that stage. He couldn't imagine what she would be feeling now, alone in a cell.

George lumbered over and put his chin on Frank's leg. (Oh my gosh! George is back! Hey, George!) *Is Jane going to be okay?* George thought.

"I hope so," Frank said out of the corner of his mouth. He'd perfected the art of ventriloquism so no one knew he was talking to a dog.

Where's Annie? George thought.

"You mean your girlfriend?" Frank said. George's tail wagged. "I think she's doing her business."

Should we go to her? George said.

"I'm sure she wants to be alone," Frank said.

Frank thought of that one time (like, yesterday) in the Gem where Annie was dressed up and they'd shared their first kiss. The memory made him smile. Maybe if her feelings about garou had changed, for reals, Frank could see himself down on one knee.

Yes, Frank's thoughts turned this way. Because this was the Wild West, and life spans in the Wild West were short, and life spans in Deadwood were even shorter, and eighteen years of age was old enough to contemplate marriage . . . and then around twenty you could contemplate your own mortality.

Suddenly, there was a ruckus outside. Shouts and guns going off. Wails and screams. Frank and several other patrons went to the window. Dozens of men, and even some women, were chasing someone down the street.

"Don't let him get away!"

"Jack McCall's a murderer!"

Somewhere in the cacophony of sound, a name floated toward the poker room. Bill. And then Wild Bill. And then . . . *the* Wild Bill Hickok.

Frank stumbled backward, caught a heel on a broken slat of the floor, and fell.

He scrambled up and darted out the door.

Once on the street, he grabbed the first man he saw. "What happened?"

"Jack McCall shot Wild Bill Hickok!" the man said.

"Is he dead?"

The man shrugged and continued chasing after McCall.

It seemed the entire town was involved in the pursuit. But Frank ran in the opposite direction, toward the No. 10 Saloon, where he knew Bill had been playing poker.

He was barely aware of anything around him, until his wolf ears picked up the sound of delicate footsteps running in the same direction beside him. He turned his head to see Annie. Their eyes met. Neither one said anything, but their expressions held the same fear.

From the outside, the No. 10 Saloon was eerily quiet. Whatever had taken place there was over. The action was now on the other side of town, but Frank didn't care about that. He only wanted to find Bill.

He burst through the swinging doors. Annie slipped in behind him.

And there he was. Bill. Slumped over a table.

"Bill." Frank rushed to Bill's side. "Bill!" He stepped back and put a hand over his mouth. There was a ringing in his ear. A cold shock down his spine. "He's okay," he said.

Annie touched his arm.

"He's okay!" Frank said again, even though somewhere deep inside, he knew that wasn't true.

Annie's grip on his arm tightened.

"Everything's okay." Frank turned Bill over and shook his shoulder. "Dad. Wake up. Wake up!"

And then, there was a miracle. Bill's eyes slowly opened. "I'm okay, son," he said.

"Thank God." Frank scooped his father into his arms.

"Frank," Annie said. "Frank, he's gone."

"No . He's awake." Frank eased his grip on his father to show Annie that he was alive. But Bill's eyes were shut. He wasn't breathing.

"He just said . . . he just said . . ." Frank's voice trailed off.

"He didn't say anything," Annie murmured.

Frank gently lowered his father to the floor. He got up and ran to the corner of the bar and lost the contents of his stomach. Annie followed. She rubbed his back softly as he heaved and heaved.

"I'm sorry," she whispered.

"Don't say that," Frank said. "It's not done." He began to shake uncontrollably. He knew what that meant. "Annie," he grunted, doubling over. "The wolf is coming."

Annie paused for a split second, looking at him wide-eyed, and then burst into action. She rushed over to the windows and closed the shutters. Then she dowsed the brightest of the lanterns. The saloon became dark.

"It's happening," Frank groaned.

She took his hand and led him away from his sick, toward the back of the saloon.

"Get away," Frank warned her. There was no amount of wooo-ing that would help him now. The truth was sinking in. His dad lay dead on the floor. Murdered. No meditation could overcome that. "Please." Frank tried to push Annie away, but she stood her ground.

He looked at Bill again. There was a pool of blood around him. Frank could smell it.

His bones cracked and bent. His nose shattered and formed a snout. His shoulders cranked and cricked. His arms stretched, and claws sprouted from his fingers. For the first time in years, Frank involuntarily became the wolf.

He was suddenly so much taller than Annie. He could have picked her up with one hand if he wanted to, but he didn't want to. He wanted to tear the saloon apart, and then tear this godforsaken town apart, and then burn it all to the ground.

But he knew he couldn't. He simply stood there, at a loss for what to do, as his rage slowly melted into devastation.

Wolf-Frank loped over to the body and collapsed next to it. He put his arms around Bill's shoulders, laid his head on his father's chest, and stayed like that for a few moments.

Then he raised his head, arched his back, and howled.

THIRTY-SIX
Annie

All the hairs on Annie's arms stood up as Frank's howl carried through the No. 10 Saloon. Then, it was quiet, and Frank bent low over Mr. Hickok once again, sobbing.

It was the worst thing Annie had ever seen. The body. The wolf. The way blood dripped from the table and dotted the fallen cards.

Everything was horribly, horribly wrong, and she didn't know how to fix any of it.

"Frank?" Her voice was small. "Frank, are you—" Not all right. There was no all right.

But Frank's shoulders stiffened and he pulled upward, head cocked as he listened to her voice.

She tried to crush the trembling out of it. "Frank, when people get here, you can't be like this." They would haul him away to face the "cure," as they had Jane.

Annie swallowed a lump in her throat. He'd been so good at hiding it. He'd demonstrated such incredible control over his wolf that she wouldn't have ever guessed if he hadn't told her, but here he was: a wolf howling with grief.

"I know what you're going through," she murmured. It was true. She'd been the one to find her father when the snowstorm faded. It hadn't been a bullet that killed him, but still she understood the heart-stopping disbelief, the agony of hoping to wake up from this nightmare . . . Cautiously, she approached Frank. "I know it hurts," she said, avoiding looking directly at Mr. Hickok. "I know it hurts, but you need to change back, and we have to—"

The door flew open, slamming on the wall. Seth Bullock started in, saying, "What's all this—" but he stopped short when he saw the garou and the body.

Wolf-Frank jumped to his feet and spun, growling at the intruder as Annie staggered backward. His fur stood on end.

"Consarn it!" shouted someone coming up behind Mr. Bullock. "What's going on here? Another garou?"

By now, wolf-Frank's claws had burst through his boots and were digging into the floorboards of the saloon. His grief was terrible to watch. Quickly, he shifted back and forth, human then wolf again, like his body couldn't decide which shape would more effectively bear this sadness.

"Stay where you are." Annie fought to keep her voice level

as she moved to stand between Frank and the gathering audience. "Don't come in here." They'd only make the situation worse; they'd use guns with iron bullets, which would merely annoy Frank into mauling them, and then there'd be more dead bodies in Deadwood, and no amount of talking or bribing would persuade the townsfolk to spare Frank or Jane.

"I'll wait right here," said Mr. Bullock, moving to cover more of the doorway. "Back away, everyone. Slow steps. That's right."

Annie faced Frank, whose hackles were still high, and that low growl was rolling through the room like distant thunder.

"Hey, big guy." Annie held out her hand and met Frank's eyes. Wolf eyes, but still his somehow, too. "Sun's gettin' real low."

"Still hours 'til sunset," muttered someone outside. "How long's this girl been drinking?"

Annie ignored the audience, keeping all her focus on Frank as he reached out one paw. She traced a line down his inner wrist. "There we are," she murmured. "Sun's gettin' real low." That last part was just in case. One couldn't be too thorough when there was a giant garou within striking distance.

But Frank was finally beginning to calm. The tension in his shoulders eased, the fur lay flat along his body. And slowly, so slowly, the shape of his face began to shift.

Then, with barely a warning of screams outside, another garou burst through the wall and howled.

Then Frank howled.

All the hairs on Annie's arms stood at attention once more.

The two garou stared at each other, then Jane's eyes shifted beyond Frank to where Mr. Hickok's body lay. Immediately she became human again, gazing at Mr. Hickok. For a moment, she seemed frozen. Then she walked straight to the bar and took up the nearest bottle.

Five long gulps and she slammed the bottle back onto the counter, gasping.

Annie jumped a little.

But Jane just stood there, staring at the body like she didn't believe her eyes.

Annie glanced between Frank and Jane, the former still in his wolf form, slinking around uncertainly, while the latter listed back and forth as the alcohol hit her all at once.

"Jane," Annie said, stepping toward her friend.

"Maybe you shouldn't get so close," suggested one of the men outside. "She could bite your whole head off."

"Jane," Annie said again. "I think you should sit down."

"I'll kill him." Jane's voice was unusually soft. "I'll find him, and I'll kill him."

"Jack McCall, you mean." Annie matched her friend's tone.

"Yeah, I mean Jack McCall." Jane closed her eyes. "I saw him running, and the whole town running after him. He did it."

"Lots of folks saw it," said Mr. Bullock from the doorway. "Whole room full of people here, some at the bar, some playing poker, and all of them seeing Jack McCall shoot Wild Bill. Just shouted 'Take that!,' shot the gun, and ran out of here like he knew what kind of heck was going to rain down on him after that."

"I saw him try to steal a horse," another man said. "But he startled it, and it bucked him off before he'd got into the saddle."

"Then he ran," added another. "And everyone went running after him."

Frank growled, and Jane looked ready to follow him back into her wolf shape.

"Wooo," Annie breathed. No one outside moved as the two garou settled down again, and slowly, Frank began to shift back into a human.

He was on all fours, arms shaking as he struggled to hold himself up. He was, Annie thought, still too close to the body. Just a glance out of the corner of his eye might send him back into despair-filled howling. She edged toward him and rested her hand on his shoulder.

"Come this way." She nodded toward Jane, who'd turned to the bottle again. She didn't drink as quickly as before, but Annie could almost see Jane's liver quivering in horror.

Frank didn't move. Barely seemed to breathe.

"This way," Annie said, and at last he nodded and let her help him.

"Why?" Frank asked. "Why?"

But they knew that, too. Jack McCall had done it for Swearengen.

"My ma did this." Jane slammed the bottle onto the bar again, startling everyone. "She told him to do it, and like a no-good, slimy smiling, cure-peddling, lying lowlife, he did it. I may not be able to—" Jane swallowed hard. "Some people might be untouchable here, but he's not. And I'll—" Again, the alcohol seemed to get the better of her as she swayed and staggered backward. "I'm going to kill him."

With that, she transformed and threw herself through the wall again, creating a second wolf-shaped hole in the No. 10. Everyone outside scattered out of her way.

Annie moved quickly. First, she darted around to the business side of the bar and grabbed the shotgun that the bartender kept back there; she didn't know much about saloons and bars, but if stories had prepared her for anything, it was the fact that there was always—always—a shotgun behind the bar. Then, she hurried for the door, but all the people who'd moved for Jane were now pressed against the holes and door again, looking at Annie like they couldn't imagine what she intended to do.

"Make way!" she yelled. "Get out of my way!"

But they didn't pay her any mind. Several tried to squeeze themselves in to get a look at the body of Wild Bill Hickok. The rest kept crowding and scrambling and generally being in her way.

"Everybody move!" The booming voice belonged to Frank, but she'd never heard him speak with such volume. Then she realized he was halfway back into the wolf and had started woooing under his breath.

Nevertheless, it did the trick. The crowd parted at once, freeing Annie and Frank to run after Jane.

The presence of a garou running through Deadwood was causing a stir. People screamed and called for someone—anyone—with silver bullets, and at the sight of Annie with her stolen shotgun (which she fully intended to return with a thank-you note), they moved aside, assuming she was garou hunting.

"I don't see her," Annie panted.

Frank pointed. "That way!"

Together, they took off down the road, running at top speed until Frank's running-induced asthma caught up with him and he doubled over, gasping. "Come on," Annie said. "You're a wolf."

So Frank picked himself up and they ran again, and finally Annie caught sight of the large garou in a shredded white top and brown skirt.

She was clawing at the door to the butcher shop.

"Good girl." Annie stopped next to Jane and put her hand on her friend's . . . arm wasn't quite the right word, but neither was foreleg. "He's in here?"

Jane yipped.

"I can smell him," Frank agreed. "He reeks of fear."

Annie tested the door handle. Open.

Jane plowed in first, with Annie and Frank behind. It took a moment for Annie's eyes to adjust to the gloom of the shop, but Jane and Frank had no such problems. They went ahead, leading Annie to the back room where Jack McCall huddled under one of the counters.

Frank turned into a wolf. Then, both he and Jane stalked

forward and growled so deeply that Annie could feel it through the floorboards.

McCall shuddered. "Please don't kill me."

Annie hefted her shotgun.

"Or, yeah, if you're going to do it, do it fast."

"Like you did Mr. Hickok?" Annie glared and aimed at him. The lowlife. The murderer.

Frank and Jane prowled around the room, glancing back every now and then to see what Annie was doing.

"I know what I did was wrong," wheedled Jack McCall. "I know I deserve to go to prison for the rest of my long life."

Annie glanced at Frank, then Jane. Both of them looked ready to maul the man, but she couldn't let them do that—not as garou. She was maybe the only one in any position right now to think about the consequences of their actions.

The shotgun felt heavy in her hands. She could do it, though. She could do it quickly, before the wolves struck, and with relatively minor consequences. No one in town would blame her for executing a murderer. It was, after all, how things were done in Deadwood.

But she'd made a promise to herself that she wouldn't use her skills to hurt people, and no matter what this man had done, she was not the person to decide what his punishment should be. Wasn't that all part of the problem of Deadwood, anyway? People deciding they were outside the law, that they could do whatever they wanted?

No, she couldn't be part of that system. She wouldn't kill McCall—even though he was bad, even though he'd murdered someone she cared about.

"You're under arrest," Annie said.

"What?" Jack McCall looked up.

She glanced at Frank. "Wooo."

He snarled at Jack McCall again, then lunged, and for a heartbeat or two, Annie thought he wouldn't listen—that his pain was so great he couldn't control it anymore. But Frank only snapped at the man, pulling back just before his teeth connected with flesh, and shifted back into a human.

He shoved Jack McCall against the wall. "You'll go to prison, all right," he growled. "But I wouldn't count on it being a long time. You murdered Wild Bill Hickok. My father. The most famous gunslinger in the country. I'd say you'll hang for this."

Jane growled her agreement as she shifted back into her human form. "How do you feel about angry mobs, Jack McCall?"

Jane THIRTY-SEVEN

Night fell. Jane stood in the middle of Bill's empty room back at the Marriott, quietly taking stock of all she'd lost. Outside the window, the normally boisterous town had gone silent. She lifted her bottle of whiskey and drank deep, but the liquor was hardly taking the edge off her grief. From the moment she'd laid eyes on Bill on the floor of the No. 10, her body had felt heavy as lead.

She glanced around at Bill's things where he'd left them: his soap and razor at the washstand, the strap of leather he used to sharpen the blade, pen and paper laid out on the desk, a letter that Jane could not read but that read, "Agnes Darling, if such should be we never meet again, while firing my last shot, I will gently breathe the name of my wife—Agnes—and with wishes even for my enemies I will make the plunge and try to swim to the other shore."

She fingered his shirts hanging in the wardrobe—those dandy shirts she liked to give him grief about. Then she sat down on the edge of his bed and took another swig of the whiskey.

She'd tried to warn him. But it hadn't been enough.

There was a knock at the door, like someone rapping the inside of her skull. "Calamity Jane, I must speak with you," came a voice.

"I got no comment!" Jane yelled. "Let me be, gawl-darn it!"

The knocking continued, though, until she finally got up and opened the door. On the other side was a very nervous Mr. Marriott, the owner of the hotel. He tipped his hat and tried to smile.

"Miss Calamity, I heard you were in here. I hope you're getting by all right, considering," he said, like this was a social call. "How . . . are you?"

She held up the bottle. "Can't you see I'm busy?"

He nodded. "I hate to bother you, but I'm afraid I'm going to have to ask you to leave. Now normally we'd be quite happy to have someone of your . . . celebrity . . . as a guest of our hotel, but as it is—"

"What, am I not famous enough for you anymore?" she bellowed.

"Oh no, you're plenty famous. But you're an outlaw now," Mr. Marriott said. "You're hiding out here, aren't you? We can't have that."

She snorted. "How can I be an outlaw if there ain't no law in Deadwood? And even if there were, what, ezactly, was my offense? You tell me that. So the papers say I'm a garou. So what? Is being a woof a crime in Deadwood?" She took a step toward Mr. Marriott, looming over him. "Go ahead. Tell me you don't want woofs in your establishment. Say it to my"—she burped— "face."

Mr. Marriott tried to keep his composure, which was difficult considering the state of Jane's breath. He cleared his throat. "I have no quarrel with garou. My mother-in-law is a garou, in fact, and she's a pleasant lady . . . most days. But you, Miss Calamity, you haven't paid the hundred dollars you owe for the cure. Ms. Swearengen's saying that's as good as theft. There's a reward posted for your capture."

"The cure didn't work!" Jane burst out. "Why should I pay for something that didn't do me no good?"

"Nevertheless, Ms. Swearengen says you're to be locked up unless you pay up," said Mr. Marriott. "Around here we have to do what Ms. Swearengen says. Plus you broke our town's best jail." He tried to look her in the eye. "I'm sorry, but technically you're a fugitive. You should go straighten it out with Swearengen. Or just . . . go."

Jane took the deep breath she was going to need to tell him exactly where he could stick that hundred dollars, but Mr. Marriott had one more piece of business to see to. "Now, I don't wish to be insensitive," he said with a cough, "but Wild Bill Hickok will obviously not be requiring the use of this room any longer." He gave her a sympathetic smile. "I am sorry about that, too, Miss Calamity. I know it comes as a powerful loss."

His sympathy was more unbearable than any cruelty could have been. The fire of anger left her. "You don't know anything."

"Quite frankly, ma'am, I'm sorry to see you go," Mr. Marriott continued. "But we need the room, so as soon as you can be on your way, I'd appreciate it. And . . . here." He picked a box up from beside the door. "They brought this over from the Number Ten."

He held out the box to her. Inside was a familiar black hat, a folded billowy jacket, and—her breath caught—a pair of pretty silver .36 caliber pistols with ivory handles.

"Thank you," she managed gruffly. "Give me a minute, and I'll be out of your hair."

After Mr. Marriott was gone, she took the box over to the bed and sat down beside it. With trembling hands she drew the coat into her arms and smelled it, and it was all Bill—hair pomade and tobacco, the overwhelming scent of his cologne, behind which she could detect a hint of gunpowder and wood shavings and . . . blood.

"Dang it, Bill," she breathed.

She might have cried then, but she was all cried out. Instead, she took another swig of whiskey and wiped her mouth with the back of her hand, then investigated the box again, feeling a flash of gratitude toward Mr. Marriott. He could have sold all of this for a tidy profit—anything that had belonged to *the* Wild Bill Hickok would be considered the most precious of memorabilia now. Jane knew that a few blocks away folks were lined up all down the street outside the No. 10 Saloon, waiting to see Bill's body on display. Folks were already calling the hand of cards Bill had been holding (aces and eights) the dead man's hand.

Bill wasn't a man anymore. He was now only a legend.

Jane sighed and picked up one of the pistols, smoothing her thumb over the ivory handle. Suddenly, she smiled. She was remembering, see, an afternoon some three years back in Wyoming Territory and a fourteen-year-old girl named Martha Canary.

It had been three years after the death of her father. Martha'd pretty much been constantly on the move then, going from town to town, picking up cash by whatever means necessary, sending it back to her siblings. That day she'd been working at the Cuny and Ecoffey Hotel near Fort Laramie, taking bags and cleaning rooms and whatever needed doing, when at two o'clock in the afternoon, on a Sunday, no less, who should appear but Wild Bill Hickok.

At least that's what the owner kept prattling on about.

"That there's *the* Wild Bill Hickok," Mr. Cuny whispered excitedly as the man in the long black coat jangled his way into the lobby. "It's said he's killed a hundred men in gunfights, but never a one who didn't deserve it."

Martha had heard of Wild Bill Hickok, of course. She angled to get a better look at the man. There wasn't much wild about him that she could see. Even so, she felt a flash of excitement when he sauntered up next to her at the front desk. She'd never been up close to a celebrity before.

He tipped his hat to Mr. Cuny. "I'd like a room."

"Yessir, Mr. Hickok, sir," Mr. Cuny stammered. "It's an honor to serve a man of your quality."

Wild Bill and the owner began to chat about the weather, but Martha had stopped paying attention. She was staring at the matching pair of Colts strapped to Wild Bill's hips. Had this man really kilt a hundred men? He didn't look like a killer. He had kind eyes, she thought.

"All right, now, boy," Mr. Cuny was saying, "Take his bags up, won't ya?"

She nodded and grabbed a bag in each hand. It was a heavy burden, but she was used to it. She was strong. "This way," she said, and led Wild Bill up the stairs.

"Thank you," Wild Bill said when they arrived at the best room the hotel had to offer. "What's your name, kid?"

She blushed. *The* Wild Bill Hickok. Speaking to *her*.

"Son?" Bill said.

Oh right. Her name. What had she been saying her name was again? "Johnny," she remembered.

"Just Johnny?"

"Doe. John . . . Doe."

He gave her a silver coin. "You been working here long?"

"No, sir. A few weeks, is all. I don't mean to stay on long, neither," she admitted.

"Oh no? What do you mean to do? You want to be a soldier up at the fort?"

She shook her head. "I, uh— I'm going to be a scout."

He smiled. "A scout? You can't be older than fifteen, I reckon?"

Her chin lifted. "I'm seventeen, sir." (She was fourteen, remember, but lying about her age was a habit by now.) "Old enough to do anything you can. I reckon."

Wild Bill's kind eyes crinkled up at the edges. "Is that so?"

"That's so."

"Well, thank you for the help, John," said Wild Bill.

"Good day to you, sir." She pocketed the coin and went back downstairs, where there were dishes waiting to be washed. It was some time later, when she went to take out the trash, that she got jumped by a boy named Adam Pontipee and his six brothers. This bunch was always causing her trouble—thought they could just take what they wanted, off anybody. Lately, her.

"Lookee here, if it ain't little Johnny," sneered Adam. He was taller than Martha, which was saying something. All the Pontipee brothers were tall and redheaded, each named after letters of the alphabet, starting with Adam, then Benjamin, then Caleb, then so on. (This was actually how Martha learned her letters *A* through *G*, after which she always winged it.) Adam was the tallest and the meanest.

"This here's *our* trash barrel," he said.

She scoffed. "It belongs to the hotel."

"It belongs to us right now," said the bully. "If you want to dump your trash here, you're going to have to pay a toll."

"Uh-huh." Martha decided the toll she'd pay would be her fist to Adam's freckly nose. Then he was bleeding and howling, and she was running away, the trash scattered behind her. The nearest place of shelter was the carriage house in the back of the hotel, where Martha soon found herself surrounded by seven angry brothers.

But that's when her eyes fell upon a weapon:

A bullwhip.

She grabbed it and acted like she knew what she was doing. She did know how to use it, kind of—on the wagon train out west from Missouri she'd spent time with the bullwhackers, who'd let her play with their whips. She'd learned to shoot then, too, and ride as good as any of the adults. Now she spun the whip in a circle around herself and cracked it on the chin of the nearest boy—Adam. He went down like a sack of potatoes, bawling. She cracked it again—down went Benjamin, and—*crack*—Caleb.

But then the remaining four decided to rush her all at once.

Martha bit and punched and kicked and whipped with all her might, and she walloped those boys pretty good, considering she was outnumbered four to one. However, she also managed to knock over every single pile of tools and stack of saddles in the building, panic the horses, and light the carriage house on fire. Then she made a break for it and ran for the back door of the hotel, where her busting into the kitchen startled the cook into dropping a tray of glasses, which shattered onto the floor. Martha darted out of the kitchen and into the dining room, where she crashed into a waitress, who spilled a bowl of soup right down onto a lady in a fine silk dress, who shrieked, which sent Martha sprawling backward until she bumped into Wild Bill Hickok again, who'd been standing there watching the entire thing unfold.

She tipped her hat, "Good day, sir," and tried to run again, but that's when Mr. Cuny caught her by the ear.

"You, kid, are a walking calamity," Mr. Cuny observed.

She'd heard that before. "It weren't my fault," she panted. "I swear."

"Nevertheless, son, you're fired."

"I didn't want this stupid job anyway," she said, which is when he gave her the literal boot out the front door.

She was sitting alone on the boardwalk turning the silver coin over in her hand—her only money in the world now—when Wild Bill Hickok came to sit down next to her. At first he didn't say anything. He just offered her a bottle of sarsaparilla.

She gulped it down. Then she asked, "Could I hold one of your pistols, sir?"

He drew one of his guns and gazed at it fondly. "Yes. This is Susannah. The other one is Mary Ann. My lady loves."

"Um, sure." She wasn't certain how she felt about guns being named after ladies, but to each his own, she guessed.

"I'd like to offer you a job," he said then, handing her the gun.

She gave a disbelieving laugh. "You saw what happened. I'm a calamity."

"I saw that you can handle yourself when the odds are stacked against you," he said. "I could pay five dollars a week."

That was more than she'd made in a month at the hotel. She smoothed her thumb across the handle of the gun in her hand. "Why me?"

"I could use a girl like you."

Her breath caught. She'd been pretending to be a boy so long the word *girl* didn't even feel like it applied to her anymore. "Look, I don't . . . know what you're talking about . . . I'm not who you think I—"

He held up a hand. "I know who you are." Then he just came out and told her that he was the one who'd shot her pa back in Salt Lake City. That it'd been a mistake. That he was sorry, and he'd been trying to find her ever since, to set things right.

At some point she jumped to her feet and considered shooting him with his fancy gun, which would be justice, she thought, a famous gunfighter brought down by the girl he'd made an orphan. But then she sat next to him again and cried, and he put his arm around her.

"I know that saying I'm sorry doesn't make up for it," Wild Bill said gently. "Not even a little. I'll go to my grave with that sin upon my soul."

"Five dollars a week, you say?" she sniffled.

"Plus room and board, although we'll likely be bedding down in the open a fair amount. I'll also feed you and clothe you and provide all the necessary supplies."

"And what would I be doing?"

"This and that. Taking care of the horses. Cleaning and maintaining the equipment. I'm still a garou hunter, but I've a mind to turn my talents toward entertainment, some kind of show, maybe. We'll see. And you wouldn't be stuck with only me all the time. I have a son about your age. We'd get on all right together."

Maybe doing this would be betraying her pa. But when she

looked in Wild Bill's eyes, when he said he was sorry, she believed him.

"The way I see it, kid," Bill said, "you've come to a fork in the road."

"What's a fork doing in a road?" she asked.

He stifled a smile. "You've got two roads before you. One road you walk alone. You've been doing all right for yourself on that road so far, I reckon. I've been on that road myself, and it's nice to be so free. Nobody else to boss you around. But it's lonesome, and you've got to face all the problems life's going to throw at you by yourself."

Jane nodded thoughtfully.

"But there's another road, one where people walk with you, and you shoulder the burdens of life together, you help each other through the tough times. That's the road I'm inviting you on right now. To walk with me."

"All right," she said after a minute. "I'll walk with you." She gave him back the ivory-handled pistol.

"This will be a fresh start for you, kid," he said brightly. "I think you should own up to being a girl, but you should dress how you like. That kind of secret is hard to manage, I find. And you're going to need a new name."

She frowned. "My name's Martha."

He made a sour face. "No. That's not right at all."

"What do you mean that's not right? It's my name, ain't it?"

"If you're going to be part of my show, you want a name that will stand out, a name people will remember."

She scoffed. "Like Wild Bill Hickok?"

"James Butler." He leaned over to shake her hand. "Pleased to make your acquaintance."

"Martha Canary," she said stubbornly.

He shook his head.

"Martha . . . Doe?"

He winced. "What's your middle name?"

"Jane."

"Jane. That's it."

"My name's Jane?" she asked.

The edges of his eyes crinkled up again. "Nope," he said. "Your name is Calamity Jane."

Now, back at the Marriott, still smiling and crying a little, Jane put Susannah back into the box.

"I'm sorry, Bill." She would have reached for the whiskey, but then she saw the wallet tucked into the side of the box, fat with cash. It was what Bill had won at the poker table today. For her. And obviously some he'd been saving.

There was $128 there.

Enough for a new life. A fresh start.

She looked at the whiskey bottle, now nearly empty, and she knew there were two roads before her once again. One led her to the bottom of a bottle, drinking the pain away over and over until she ended up cutting herself off from everybody else. Her only real friend, in time, the amber glass. That road, she knew, had a bad end.

Or she could pick herself up now and walk with Frank and Annie, if they'd have her, and together they'd do what they could to set things right. Or maybe not right, as things would never be right again, not really, without Bill. But as right as they could make them. They could help one another through it and come out somewhere on the other side. This road was more work. It was harder. And it would hurt.

But she knew which one Bill would want her to choose.

"Oh, all right, Bill, all right," she complained loudly. Then she put the bottle in the trash and went about finding some gawl-darned boots.

Al Swearengen was surprised to see Jane when she strode into the Gem.

"Have you finally come to see reason?" she asked. "Ready to join the fold?"

"Nope." Jane slapped the money down on the bar. "Here's your hundred dollars. Even though the cure's a scam. Even though someday I'm going to see you pay for what you done, Ma, so help me God, but here you go, you . . . coward."

The room went silent.

"Did she just call Swearengen a . . ."

"Coward," piped up a man in the back. "Yep, she did. I heard her."

"You couldn't even face him, could you?" Jane accused. "You

had to send Jack McCall to shoot him while his back was turned."

Another hush. "Did she say Al sent Jack McCall?"

"That's nonsense," her mother said matter-of-factly. "What quarrel would I have with Wild Bill Hickok? I didn't even know the man."

Suddenly there were a bunch of guns out, all pointed at Jane. She swallowed. Maybe she shouldn't have called her mother yellow. She was still a bit drunk, she admitted to herself. But she was rapidly feeling sober. "You didn't even know him," she said softly.

Her mother smiled—the scariest smile Jane had ever beheld. "You'll come to see all this was necessary, my dear, in time. You've been sorely lacking in discipline, and bringing you to heel is going to require a bit of unpleasantness. But I have faith that you'll come around."

"You don't know me, either," Jane growled.

"You'll be glad to hear that I sent for your siblings," Al continued as if Jane hadn't spoken. "Now that there's no one hunting me, we can all be a happy family again. You'll want to set a good example, won't you, when they arrive?"

Jane stared at her, aghast, but before she could think of anything to say, Ned Buntline burst through the door.

"You again?" said Jane.

"I go where the action is," said Buntline breathlessly. "I've got news. The town's decided that there will be a trial for Jack McCall!"

"A trial?" said a man from the back of the room. "How can there be a trial when there ain't no law in Deadwood?"

"Just because there is no government here doesn't mean we can't make our own laws," said Buntline. "What happened to Wild Bill was a crime. You can't have people murdering celebrities in cold blood in your town—how would that look? So the townsfolk have appointed a sheriff—Mr. Seth Bullock, the man with the free commodes—who was a marshal back in Montana, and there happens to be a man—a Mr. Kuykendall, who rode into town today, who's a bona fide judge. What luck, wouldn't you say?" He glanced at Al Swearengen.

"Yes," said Al slowly. "What luck. And when's this trial supposed to take place?"

"Tomorrow morning, first thing," said Buntline.

Jane had been backing toward the door during this announcement, then slipped out and ran. She had to figure out how to stop her mother. She had to find Frank and Annie. But then somebody called her name.

"Janey!" cried the old familiar voice. "Over here, Jane!"

She turned, and there leaning on a cane in the middle of the street was Charlie Utter.

Jane almost bowled him over as she threw herself into his arms. "Charlie! When'd you get here?"

"Five minutes ago," he said.

She drew back, her lip trembling. "Oh, Charlie, Bill's dead."

He nodded grimly. "It's all anybody's talking about. Where'd they put the body?"

"It was my fault," she said as they walked down the street,

Charlie limping a bit. "I'm so sorry. My ma is Al Swearengen, and Al Swearengen's the Alpha, Charlie, and she hates Bill, and she set Jack McCall to straight-up murder him, and I tried to warn him, but he was trying to earn the money to get me out of jail."

"You were in jail? What for?"

"For being a woof."

"I see." He put his arm around her. "Where'd they take his body, again?"

"It's still at the Number Ten, I think. Oh, Charlie, I'm sorry. I'd trade places with him if I could."

He stopped and looked at her sternly. "Now see here. Bill has had a target on his back for who knows how long. He's a gunfighter. He knew this was likely how he was going to leave this world. He wouldn't have wanted it to be that way for you."

"But—"

"We need to regroup, figure out what to do now. I'll take care of the funeral arrangements," Charlie said, back all of five minutes but still the manager of the show in every sense of the word. "Where can we stay?"

"Frank and Annie still have rooms at the Marriott, I think."

Charlie's eyebrows lifted. "Annie's here, too? Well, good. I want to have a conversation with that girl about my horse. And we're going to need everybody we can get."

"But, Charlie—"

"It's going to be all right, Janey," he said gruffly. "You'll see."

But she didn't see how.

THIRTY-EIGHT
Frank

"Five dollars for a lock of hair from the legendary Wild Bill Hickok!"

The merchant tent had popped up outside the No. 10 Saloon almost before Bill's body was cold. It was late now, past midnight, but the main street was filled with rubberneckers, each wanting a piece of Bill's death.

Frank and Annie were watching the circus from the front steps of the Marriott, George at their feet, his head on Frank's knee.

Frank couldn't feel his hands. He couldn't feel anything, really, not since he'd changed back into a human after they'd brought Jack McCall into custody. But the numbness was better than the alternative. If Frank had been capable of feeling right now, he'd cross the street and flip the tables over. He'd scream and yell. He'd send the tufts of hair they were selling into the mud, even though he knew they couldn't possibly be Bill's. Bill's body was safe under the watch of Charlie Utter at his camp across the river. There was no telling what Frank might do to the vultures who'd descended to pick and nip and steal and merchandize what was left of his father.

But Frank didn't feel anything. Not rage. Not even sadness.

"Five dollars will get you a piece of history!" the merchants cried.

"That's so disrespectful," Annie said quietly. She hadn't left Frank's side since he'd wolfed out over Bill's body. She'd tried to convince him to go inside, get some sleep, but he was not having it.

So they sat there, together, watching. Waiting. Only Frank didn't know what they were waiting for.

George pushed his nose into Frank's hand. He wasn't saying much either, but his large brown eyes were mournful. Frank scratched behind his ear absently.

Just then an official-looking man in a suit walked out of the McDaniels Theater. With dramatic flourish, the man removed his hat and held it high. "Put your name in for the jury! A hundred names for jury selection!"

The man was instantly mobbed with merchants and miners alike, all scrambling to write their names on scraps of paper, clamoring to be on the jury.

"Trial starts tomorrow morning at nine a.m. sharp!" the man said.

"I wish they allowed women on the jury," Annie muttered. "I want to be on that jury."

Me too, thought George.

Frank didn't answer. A fresh wave of grief tore through him, from his head to his feet, and he doubled over. He couldn't breathe. He couldn't think. And then, as fast as it had come, the grief was gone.

George whined and licked his face.

"Are we going to go to the trial?" Annie asked.

Frank turned to her, numb again. "I want to be there when they tell Jack McCall he's going to hang."

Later Annie finally convinced Frank to eat something. She watched him while he nibbled halfheartedly on a biscuit and took a few sips of coffee. Frank felt like everyone in the restaurant was staring at them. Maybe they recognized him—the Pistol Prince. Maybe they were here to get a piece of him, too.

"Annie?" Frank said.

"Yes?"

"Thank you for standing by me."

Annie reached for Frank's hand, and then pulled back abruptly. "Of course." She smoothed the napkin over her lap.

Frank didn't know if she'd pulled back because of the onlookers or because she hadn't wanted to touch him. She'd seen him, he realized with a dull sense of horror. She'd seen him lose control. She'd seen his fur and claws and snapping teeth. How could she see *him* ever again?

But she was still here. With him. That was something. And she sat with him until the earliest morning hours, when Frank walked her to her room and reluctantly said good night.

The next morning, the McDaniels Theater was bursting at the seams for the trial of the century. Jack McCall sat at a table on the stage, alongside his counsel. At another table sat the prosecutor. They were arranged at an angle, so both audience and judge could see. Everyone was waiting for the judge.

"Oh dear," Annie said. Beside him, she scowled at the newspaper she was reading.

"What is it?" Frank asked.

"Nothing," Annie said, folding it.

"More stuff about Bill?"

She nodded.

Charlie wasn't there, because he wanted to guard Bill's body. Jane hadn't been able to bring herself to come to the trial, for fear that she would lose her temper and wolf out. George had opted to keep an eye on her. So it was just Frank and Annie and a few hundred people who'd come to watch the spectacle.

Frank studied Jack McCall's face. He closed his eyes and pictured walking up to him from behind, gun drawn. Would he be able to do it? Murder him in cold blood?

Frank wouldn't have thought so before, but this grief of his was a strange monster. This morning it was sitting heavy in his chest, occasionally swelling into violent urges to avenge his father.

If Annie hadn't been stuck to him like glue, he might have given in.

There were reporters all over the courtroom, their pencils scribbling furiously, even though the trial hadn't started. Frank recognized the writer he'd met on the train, Edward Wheeler. He wondered if any of this would have happened if it weren't for that article about Jane.

Ugh, reporters. That other loathsome writer—Ned Buntline— was sitting in front of Annie. She peered over his shoulder to see what he was writing. Then she gasped.

"'A small, sandy mustache covered a sensual mouth'?" Annie read indignantly. "Who is that supposed to describe?"

Buntline tilted his notebook so she could no longer read it. Annie poked his shoulder roughly. She contorted herself so she could read more. "You think Jack McCall's mouth was *supple* when he was pulling that trigger and killing my friend?"

"Easy," Frank murmured.

"Sorry." She righted herself in her chair. "It just makes me so angry, you know."

Frank knew. "It's okay."

"Supple lips," Annie grumbled loudly. "I'll supple your—"

"Please don't finish that sentence," Frank said.

"Point of order," the bailiff called and the crowd grew quiet.

Judge Kuykendall entered the room and sat in a chair that faced the two tables and the audience. The jury filed in afterward and sat in the front row of the theater.

Then, making a conspicuous entrance, Al Swearengen strode

in, walked down the aisle, and sat in the one seat left in the front row.

Frank made a move to stand, but Annie held him back.

The judge put up a hand. "I ask the good people of Deadwood to sustain me in the discharge of these duties. I am in the unenviable position to oversee the trial of Jack McCall, who is charged with the murder of James Butler Hickok, better known as Wild Bill."

Frank flinched at the sound of his father's name. The prosecutor rose to address the court. "We would like to call Charles Rich to the stand."

A man Frank didn't recognize stood and went to the chair next to the judge.

"Mr. Rich, you were at the poker table with Wild Bill. Can you tell us about what you witnessed?" the prosecutor asked.

"Man comes in and walks right up to Wild Bill and shoots him in the back of the head, and shouts, 'Take that!'"

Murmurs of outrage rippled through the audience.

"And can you identify the man you saw?"

Mr. Rich pointed to Jack McCall. "That's him."

More murmurs. More outrage.

The prosecutor brought two more witnesses who'd been in the No. 10 at the time of the shooting. They both had the same story.

"They have to find him guilty," Annie said. "They have to."

Frank nodded.

But then the defense called P. H. Smith.

"I know Jack McCall, and he is mild-mannered," Smith said. "I also had drinks once with Wild Bill Hickok, and he has a bad reputation. Always quick to use his guns and shoot people. I mean, think of all the people he's killed. Hundreds? Jack McCall probably saved lives killin' Wild Bill."

Frank's hands began to tremble.

"Wooo," Annie whispered in his ear.

Buntline was scribbling furiously, documenting the witness's erroneous testimony. Annie shoved his shoulder. "Don't write that down."

"Freedom of the press," the reporter growled back.

"Everyone knows Bill was a kindhearted man," Annie said. "This is fake news."

"Wooo," Frank said to Annie.

Finally the defense called Jack McCall to the chair. Frank could barely stand looking him in the face. That creepy smile. Those beady eyes. He'd sensed all along that Jack McCall was bad news.

"I'm going to murder his face," Annie said under her breath.

"Bill wouldn't want you to do that." Frank knew she wasn't serious. She'd already had her chance to kill Jack McCall, and she'd chosen not to.

"Bill is a better man than I," Annie said.

"*Was*," Frank corrected forlornly, feeling the pain in his chest.

McCall's counsel asked Jack why he shot Wild Bill Hickok.

Jack McCall straightened his spine (although your narrators don't know how he did it, considering we are pretty sure he was spineless). "Well, men, I have but few words to say. Wild Bill killed my brother, and so I killed him. Wild Bill threatened to kill me if I ever crossed his path. I am not sorry for what I have done. I would do the same thing over again."

"Liar!" a voice shouted out. It was a moment before Frank realized he was standing, and the voice was his voice. Everyone turned to look at him.

"Order!" said the judge.

Buntline was still writing away.

Annie rolled up her newspaper and smacked him on the head.

"Order!" the judge repeated.

Frank sank to his chair, glaring at McCall, and McCall had the gawl-durn nerve to glare back.

"Seeing as there are no more witnesses, court will adjourn," the judge said. "Please clear the theater while our fine jury decides the fate of Jack McCall."

Frank and Annie returned to the steps of the Marriott across the street. The wait was unbearable. Every second passed like a drop of sticky sap making its way down the bark of a tree. Jack McCall's fate was out of their hands now.

"Let's go for a walk," Annie suggested.

"I don't want to be somewhere else when the verdict comes down," Frank said.

"Well, then, let's just pace." So that's what they did, back and forth and back and forth on the muddy road in front of the McDaniels Theater, until the afternoon sun began to sink lower in the sky.

And then, out of nowhere, Annie reached out her hand, and Frank took it.

He couldn't hold in his question any longer. "Annie?"

"Yes?"

He stopped and faced her. "You saw me as a wolf."

"Yes," she said.

"Does that mean— Do you think you can—"

Annie looked up at him expectantly. "Yes?"

But before he could get the rest of his question out, bells rang on the street. The man in the suit emerged from the McDaniels Theater. "Verdict's in!"

Everyone rushed forward, but Frank remained frozen in place.

The man held up a piece of paper. "A statement from the jury. 'We the jurors find the prisoner, Mr. Jack McCall, not guilty.' He is free to go."

THIRTY-NINE

Annie

There was so much injustice in this world. Annie had believed there was a good chance that the people of Deadwood would go against Jack McCall and—by association—Swearengen. It had seemed reasonable to Annie that Deadwood might care more about the most famous gunslinger in the world, but Swearengen clearly held the whole town in her thrall, even if they weren't all garou. Annie had believed the truth would prevail.

She'd been wrong.

Now the four of them—Annie, Jane, Frank, and George— were sitting around in Annie's room at the Marriott (Jane had insisted on sneaking in through the window, even though she'd paid her debt), trying not to think too hard about the trial and Jack McCall's exultant expression when he'd been set free.

It was almost more than Annie thought she could bear.

(Ahem, narrators here. We know, we're supposed to be writing a comedy, and this whole part is pretty sad, but sometimes bad things happen and people are sad. That's the truth of life. Still, even the saddest of times can have moments of humor to help pull you through to the other side of grief. We'll get you there. We promise.)

"What do we do?" Annie asked.

"What *can* we do?" Jane countered.

Frank said nothing at all. Annie had liked Mr. Hickok, although she hadn't known him well, and Jane had loved him, but he was Frank's father. Frank wasn't turning into a wolf anymore, but his quiet grief was even more difficult to watch.

Annie started to reach for his hand again but stopped short. She didn't know what kind of comfort he wanted now—or if he wanted any at all.

"We'll have to tell Agnes," Jane murmured. "She needs to know what happened."

Right. Mr. Hickok's wife.

"I wish Charlie would come back here," Jane said. "He'd know what to do."

"What is he doing now? And can we do that, too?" Annie asked hopefully.

Jane flopped back onto the bed. "He's still watching over the bo—" She coughed a little. "You know. Him. Making sure no one cuts off pieces of his beard to sell and all that. And"—her voice caught—"preparing him, I guess. For the funeral."

"For the funeral," Annie echoed. It was so hard to think about. How would Frank endure it? Again, she started to reach for him, then shifted to make it look like she had meant to sit on her hand this entire time.

"Jack McCall is leaving town in the morning," Jane said.

"Yeah. I heard." Annie sighed. Maybe it was best that Jack McCall was leaving, but it seemed wrong that he got away scot-free while everyone else had to miss Mr. Hickok.

"Swearengen is making him," Jane added.

"I heard that, too," Annie said. Swearengen had stood up after the verdict and suggested that it was best if Jack McCall left, what with him being a no-good murderer, giving Deadwood a bad name. Which Annie found wildly hypocritical.

Jane wiped at her face, about as discreetly as Annie had sat on her hand earlier, and for several more minutes, they all just took up space and breathed stale air.

"There must be something we can do." Annie hated this—doing nothing when they should have been doing something—and taking action was the only cure. "There must be a way to make people see that Swearengen ordered Jack McCall to do it."

"It wouldn't matter if they did," Jane said. "They won't go against her."

"But what if they did?" An idea nudged at the back of Annie's mind. "People are afraid of her, but what if they were mad at her, too? What if we could turn the town against her?"

Jane frowned. "How do you propose we do that?"

"She's been putting all these wolves under her thrall." Annie popped up out of her chair. "But what if they weren't under her thrall anymore? What if everyone in town found out that she's been lying about the cure, that she's been enthralling wolves, and that she ordered Jack McCall to kill Mr. Hickok? What if—"

"What if you stopped with the what-ifs?" Jane said.

"Right," Annie said, "but what if we turned the town against Swearengen?"

"How," Frank said slowly, "do you propose we do that?"

A grin formed on Annie's face. "With the cure."

"The cure?" Jane sat up, scowling. "That doesn't seem right."

"I agree with Jane," Frank said. George, who'd been sitting quietly at his feet for the entire conversation so far, stood up then, and yipped.

"The cure for the cure." Annie bounced on the balls of her toes. "We'll get the cure for the cure and free all the thralls and they'll hate Swearengen and then the whole town will hate her, too. And this time they won't be shy about it."

"You have a cure for the cure to free all the thralls?" Jane asked.

"Not me. Many Horses. She gave me something for her sister. But Walks Looking resisted, like you did, so I gave it back to Many Horses."

"You didn't think we'd need it later?" Frank said. George tilted his head.

"It wasn't mine to keep."

"You didn't ask if you could keep it?" Jane asked.

"I didn't think we'd need it."

Frank frowned. George growled. "All right. So you want to find Many Horses again and ask for the cure for the cure to free all the thralls, and then turn the town against Swearengen."

"Exactly!" Annie grinned at him, excited now that there was something to be done. "When the townsfolk find out what she's really been doing, they'll be furious!"

"I think we've had enough angry mobs, though," Jane said thoughtfully. "What with all the angry mobs we've had."

Frank nodded. "They do like their angry mobs in Deadwood. But I agree that we need another approach."

"Like what?" Annie tried not to be miffed that her plan wasn't enough for him.

"We need to give them another source of information," Frank said.

"Like what?" Annie asked. "Like a newspaper article?"

Frank nodded again. "And it needs to come from somewhere they trust."

"Like where?" Jane asked.

"An unbiased reporter."

"Like who?" Annie and Jane asked at the same time, although Jane asked with a note of dread in her tone and believe us, Annie did not fail to notice.

"That Edward Wheeler fellow—"

"Ooooh, no," Jane said. "Nope. Not gonna happen. No way.

No how. No ifs, ands, or buts."

"Edward Wheeler wrote the article about Jane!" Annie pointed out. "Edward Wheeler is the reason for that angry mob that dragged Jane into the Gem in the first place."

"I agree," Jane said.

"Me too," Frank agreed. "And yet, that makes Edward Wheeler the perfect man for the job. The town knows him because of that article. The town will listen to him on this, too."

"Edward Wheeler is not the man for the job," Jane said.

"Why not?" Frank asked.

"Because she— I mean he, he's the one who—" Jane bit off the words and glanced at Annie, her face turning a soft shade of pink.

"Who what?" Annie frowned.

"We kissed!" Jane threw up her hands. "We kissed, but it doesn't matter! We're not talking to him!"

"You kissed?" Annie squealed, and her mind flew back to the day her older sister, Lydia, came home talking about a young man—the same young man she ended up marrying later. (Whoops, did we forget to mention Annie's older sister until now? Well, she had an older sister. Her name was Lydia. She'd gotten married and moved away years ago.) Lydia had been moody and contrary, going on about how much she hated the guy . . . followed by an ode to the color of his eyes. It had been a confusing few days before Lydia had admitted to liking the boy. "You have a crush on Edward Wheeler?"

(Reader! About the word *crush*. Around this time, people were using *mash* to mean a romantic infatuation, but Annie had never liked the way it sounded. Too icky. *Crush*, however—it just sounded better to her, so she was doing her very best to change hearts and minds and slang. Unfortunately, most folks thought Annie wasn't good at colloquialisms, and so they either ignored her perceived slipup, or told her, "Stop trying to make *crush* happen." It did catch on eventually, but not during the time this novel takes place. Anyway, etymology lesson over.)

"No!" Jane shouted. Then, softer, she said, "I mean, no, of course not. That would be silly."

"Jaaaane." Annie couldn't stop herself from smiling. "You have a crush! Since when? And how serious?"

"Not serious at all anymore." Jane crossed her arms. "So yeah, we kissed, the one time, and it was nice, but then she—he, I mean, Edward Wheeler—wrote that article about me and basically told everybody I'm a garou, and now my feelings are hurt, and everything else kind of hurts, too."

"Oh, right." That was a splash of cold water on the only fun news Annie had heard all day. "In that case, I'm on Jane's side. We can't bring Wheeler into this again. He broke Jane's heart!"

Frank gave Annie a measured look. "Perhaps he did, but he can help us, and maybe he deserves another chance."

Shame boiled up through Annie. Here she was, someone who'd broken Frank's heart, and he was still letting her help. "All right," she said. "As someone currently benefiting from a second chance, I think it's only right that I vote second chance, too, even if I'm still mad at him on Jane's behalf."

"Same," Frank said. "Except for the part about currently benefiting from a second chance. Unless I've done something I don't know about."

"Ugh," Jane moaned. "Uuuuuugh. You don't understand. That article was the worst."

"Did you read it?" Annie asked, pulling her copy of the newspaper out of her pocket.

"You've been keeping that on you?" Jane made a faint gagging noise.

"It's interesting. And he's a good writer."

"We can't trust writers," Jane insisted. "They're horrible liars and they like it when bad things happen to nice folks like us. 'Makes a better story,' they say. They *like* our suffering."

"Right," Annie said. "Back to the point. The title is a piece of horse dung, but Mr. Wheeler might not be responsible for that. He wrote the *article* in a way that's actually sympathetic to you. He makes you out to be some kind of heroine."

"Hero-eene," Jane corrected. "But go on. Tell me what it says."

Annie cleared her throat and began reading. "'We've all come to know Calamity Jane as a performer in *Wild Bill's Wild West*, along with the stories of her exciting adventures in the company of Wild Bill Hickok. But there's more to this woman than meets the eye. What makes Jane special is her ability to resist the traditional restraints and perceived requirements of her sex; Jane defies the

431

patriarchy by taking jobs typically held by men, and doing them with considerably more skill than most men.'"

Jane sighed dramatically. "Fine. That's pretty nice, I guess."

Annie went on to read the next paragraph, which was about how Jane had worked alongside Wild Bill and Frank Butler to investigate a series of garou bitings in Cincinnati, how she had fearlessly battled these renegade garou, and somewhere along the line ended up being bitten, dooming her to become a garou herself. The article ended with "It seems entirely likely that Jane will confront this new condition with the same grit and good-hearted humor that she has everything else. Get ready to meet someone who defies expectations and redefines what it means to be a garou: Calamity Jane."

Jane scratched the back of her neck. "I do like the part about defying the pantry-arch. A shame no one else in town read past the headline."

"I don't think Edward Wheeler meant for anything bad to happen to you," Annie said. "He was only doing what he thought was best."

"Well, it wasn't for the best," Jane said.

"No," Annie agreed softly. "Sometimes we think we know something, and then it turns out we know nothing at all."

"So about the plan," Frank interjected. "Annie will go ask Many Horses to give us the cure for the cure to free all the thralls, and we'll talk to Edward Wheeler—"

"I don't know where to find him." Jane crossed her arms.

Frank looked at Jane like he was reevaluating his own

expectations. "I know where to find him." He stood up and tugged his shirt straight. "All right. We'll go to Edward Wheeler and get him to write about Swearengen for this evening's edition."

Jane stood, too, although more reluctantly. "Maybe you can go by yourself, and I'll go with Annie."

"No, you need to tell Edward Wheeler the truth about Al Swearengen." Frank touched Jane's shoulder, and George came to lean against her leg. "It can only come from you, Jane. Come on. You can do this."

"All right. Fine. Have it your way." Jane lowered her eyes, but after a second, she straightened and dug through her pockets. "Oh! Annie! I have this for you."

Annie cringed, wondering what it could possibly be, but then Jane produced a crumpled ten-dollar bill.

"I thought you might want your money back."

"Oh, yes." Annie took the bill at the corner; it was damp with sweat. "Thanks. And I have this still." She pulled the rose quartz from her own pocket. "I think it's yours?"

Jane's eyes lit up. "You kept it!"

"Just holding on to it for you." Annie dropped the stone into Jane's cupped palm. "It's pretty."

Jane breathed on the quartz and polished it against her shirt. "Sure is."

"Are we ready to go?" Frank asked. "We need to move quickly."

Everyone nodded, and they all headed downstairs and to the

livery, where Annie saddled Charlie's horse. George rose onto his hind legs and put his front paws into the stirrup.

"Are you sure, boy?" Frank asked.

George yipped.

"Fine. If you insist." Frank lifted George into the saddle. "Looks like my dog is going with you, Annie."

Annie grinned. "Good boy, George."

George grinned, too, his tongue lolling out, and then he scrambled to the back of the saddle while Annie climbed onto Charlie's horse.

"Charlie's gonna want his horse back," Jane said. "Now that he's here."

"Whoops, sorry, didn't hear that, bye!" Without another word, Annie kicked Charlie's horse and galloped away.

It wasn't until halfway back to the bear clearing when Annie started to worry that Many Horses might not be there. She probably had a lot of other places she liked to hide out.

Annie urged Charlie's horse faster, and as she crashed into the clearing, she heard a voice say, "Hey, you!"

Annie reined Charlie's horse to a halt and looked up to find Many Horses and Walks Looking sitting in front of their tent. They both gave little waves.

"You're right on time," Many Horses said. "We've been waiting."

Annie frowned and slipped off Charlie's horse. George, for his part, remained perched on the saddle. He didn't like most girls,

Annie recalled. Well, maybe he should have thought of that before he'd decided to come along. She turned to Walks Looking and Many Horses. "What do you mean you've been waiting? How long have you been waiting?" Surely they had better things to do than sit around and wait for her to have some sort of crisis.

"Not long." Walks Looking climbed to her feet. "We were out hunting and Many Horses said she wondered if you were going to have some sort of crisis—"

Annie stamped her foot. "Well, drat."

"Annie Oakley, watch your mouth!" Many Horses said.

Annie pressed her hands to her mouth.

"Moving along," Walks Looking said, "my sister was right. I told her that you and Frank were clearly in over your heads with Swearengen but seemed determined to move against her anyway."

"We got to thinking about everything you told us, and I thought you'd probably be back for this." Many Horses held up a glass vial. The wolfsbane.

Annie's breath caught. "Okay. Good guess."

Many Horses flashed a pleased look. "I love being right."

"Things that are not news," Annie said, "that."

"It's not like I can help it."

Annie understood. "So, important question: do you have more?"

Many Horses tilted her head. "There's wolfsbane all over. But if you're asking whether I've made more cures for enthrallment, no. Just enough for my sister."

Annie rubbed her temples and considered. "All right. So our

plan is to cure all the garou in Deadwood so that they turn against Swearengen. But with a limited amount of the cure for the cure to free all the thralls—"

"Cure for the cure to free all the thralls?" Walks Looking wrinkled her nose.

"We needed to call it something."

"Wolfsbane is fine," Many Horses said.

"I need to figure out a good way to distribute the wolfsbane to break the garou free of the enthrallment. Maybe if I put it in the town water supply? I'll have to wait until nighttime and—"

"Wolfsbane is toxic," Many Horses argued. "Garou will survive a dose like this, but not humans. Not even if it's diluted."

"Oh, right." There were a lot of people in Deadwood, and Annie didn't want to kill any of them—even Al Swearengen or Jack McCall. "Well, in that case, I'll do some research and find out who the garou are. Once I'm certain I've found them all, I'll invite them to tea and dose them like that."

Many Horses looked incredulous. "What is wrong with you?"

"I'm trying to make sure I don't hurt any humans, like you said!"

"So you want to throw the werewolves a tea party."

"As if you have a better idea."

"You could, oh, I don't know, do it the simple way?" Many Horses raised an eyebrow.

Annie had never done anything the simple way in her entire life. "What do you mean?"

"Give it to Swearengen. The wolfsbane breaks the bond, remember? Bonds have two ends."

"Oh," Annie breathed. "That does make more sense than my way."

The sisters gave each other significant looks. "Yeah," Walks Looking said, and Many Horses rolled her eyes.

Annie clapped her hands, happy to have a plan. "All right, I'll make sure Swearengen gets this. But if it doesn't break the thrall, then we're in trouble."

"She'll be furious," Walks Looking agreed.

George barked.

"Oh." Walks Looking frowned. "Your . . . dog?"

"George is a poodle," Annie clarified. "Frank's."

"Ah." Walks Looking studied George again. "I've never seen a dog quite so . . . cute."

George growled.

"Well that's rude." Many Horses crossed her arms.

"He doesn't like girls, aside from Jane and me," Annie said by way of explanation for his bad behavior. "I don't know why he insisted on coming along. I think he just wanted to feel like he was doing something."

"Oh." Walks Looking seemed disappointed. "Well, he just told me something interesting."

Annie and Many Horses both looked at her.

"He said someone's died. Bill? Frank's father?"

Annie's heart sank. "Wild Bill Hickok. Swearengen had her

lackey, Jack McCall, assassinate Mr. Hickok yesterday. There was a trial this morning, and they let Jack McCall go."

"What kind of trial is that?" Many Horses shook her head.

"The kind they hold in illegal towns, I guess," Annie said. "Jack McCall is leaving on the first stagecoach out of town tomorrow morning. But before that, we're making sure everyone knows that Swearengen ordered the murder, and we'll suggest that Swearengen tampered with the jury. And when the garou she's enthralled are free . . ."

"Everyone will turn against her." An angry smile turned up the corners of Walks Looking's mouth. "Good. How can we help?"

"Don't you have anything better to do?" Annie asked.

"Of course we do," Many Horses said. "Your people killed all the buffalo in the area, trying to starve us out of the Black Hills. The two of us can make do on smaller game for now, but that means we spend a lot of time trying to feed ourselves. That and not get caught by all the white people roaming the woods looking for Lakota to murder. So we're avoiding death as well."

"But in addition to all of that," Walks Looking said, softer than her sister, "I'm not the only Lakota Swearengen tried to enthrall. She was successful with others. If we can free them, more families can be reunited in the way we were." She glanced at Many Horses and smiled.

"Thanks," Annie said. "I'm glad you're in."

"You said Jack McCall is leaving on the morning stagecoach?" Walks Looking asked.

Annie nodded. "So we want to get the article written tonight, before he even has a chance to pack his bags."

"In that case," Many Horses said, "if you can break the thrall, we'll meet the Lakota garou outside of town at sundown."

"I'll leave some coats and hats for you on the south end of town," Annie said. "In case you want disguises."

"Yes, thank you." Walks Looking cast a worried glance at her sister.

Annie's heart clenched. It was *so* dangerous for them to go that close to town, but maybe no one would notice them with everything else going on. . . . It was brave, though, and the Lakota wolves would have friendly faces to help them.

"Well, I need to get back." Annie climbed onto Charlie's horse, barely avoiding sitting on George, who was taking up more room than truly necessary.

Many Horses stepped forward. "Annie?"

"Yes?"

"I think you're forgetting something."

"Oh right. Where are my manners? Thank you."

"Not that. You already thanked us." Many Horses held up the vial of wolfsbane. "You'll want this. The cure for the cure to free all the thralls."

Annie took the wolfsbane and tucked it into her pocket. "Thank you," she said again, and blushed. "I'll see you soon."

FORTY

"That must have been some kiss," Frank said as they walked to the Checkmate Hotel.

"What do you mean?" Jane unbuttoned and then rebuttoned the top of her shirt—one of Frank's old shirts, actually, seeing as how most of Jane's clothes were back at her mother's place or tattered wolf-torn rags. It was nice to be wearing pants again, though, and she'd bought a pair of boots yesterday, new, calfskin boots, so soft they felt like hugs to her feet.

But these boots were made for walking. Yep, that's what they'd do. And in a minute these boots were gonna walk right over to where she was going to see Winnie. Face-to-face. When the last time she'd seen Winnie, Jane had said mean things like how she never wanted to see Winnie again. And then Jane was going to have to ask Winnie for a big favor.

She unbuttoned her collar. Best to be casual about it. Act like it weren't no big deal.

"I mean," Frank was saying, "that I've never seen you quite this nervous before, even for our biggest shows. So it must have been some kiss you had with this fellow."

She glanced over at him. He was trying to tease her about it, she thought, the way boys tease their sisters about beaus, but he wasn't smiling. He couldn't. Bill's death was too fresh.

Jane cleared her throat. "Yeah. About that . . ." How could she put this so he would understand? "Uh—you see, Frank—"

"Yes?" Frank prompted.

"I think I should go talk to Edward Wheeler alone," she said quickly. "Tell me what the room number is again, and I'll take care of it. No problem."

"No way," said Frank. "I'm not letting you go to some questionable man's room by yourself."

She stopped walking. "Excuse me? When have I ever not been able to look after myself?" Now, if she stopped to really think about it, there'd been several times in the past few months that she hadn't done the best job of looking after herself. But he knew what she meant. "And when did you get so prim and proper like? Do I look like I need a chaperone?"

He raised his palms in surrender. "I only meant, you could use some backup. Let's not forget that this guy has double-crossed you before."

"What was all that nonsense back there about second chances, then?" she barked.

"I believe that, but . . ." He sighed. "I want to have your back, Calam. We're in this together, remember? You don't have to go it alone."

He would simply not be talked out of coming along, so soon they were standing outside of room 203 at the Checkmate Hotel. Frank lifted his hand to knock, but Jane stopped him. She rebuttoned her collar (best to be as presentable as possible) and smoothed her hair down a bit. Then she nodded, avoiding Frank's eyes, and he rapped sharply on the door.

"Well, shucks," she said after about two seconds. "Guess he's out."

Frank grabbed her before she could run away.

"Okay, okay, I'm staying," she huffed, and unbuttoned her collar. Thing was choking her.

It was quiet on the other side of the door. She was kind of hoping that Winnie wouldn't be there, even though that would mess up their fine plans. She was also hoping that if Winnie were there, she'd be on the clock, dressed as a man, answering to the name of Edward Wheeler. That might make this entire exchange a tad less awkward, what with Frank around.

No such luck. The door swung open, and the person behind it was Edwina Harris, undeniably female in a pale green dress that perfectly matched her eyes. Those eyes grew wide when they saw Jane.

442

"Jane!" she gasped, and then her brows furrowed and her lips turned down in an expression that was utter sympathy. "Oh, Jane, how are you? I can't imagine. I'm so sorry about Mr. Hickok. It's terrible. And this business with Jack McCall—a travesty, is what it is."

Jane swallowed hard against the tears that threatened. It would be so nice to simply step into Winnie's arms and weep for all that had transpired. But instead she looked at the floor and blinked a few times and then said, gruffly, "I'm fine. I— We, that is, *we* need to talk to you."

Winnie tore her gaze away from Jane's face to acknowledge Frank. "Oh, hello."

"This here's Frank," Jane explained.

"Yes, I know. We've met," Winnie said a bit stiffly.

"Right. Well." Jane stared down at her boots. (Which were really nice—best boots we've seen in this book so far, and we've seen a lot of them.) But she couldn't seem to piece together the next sentence in her head. "I, uh— Well, you see— I know I told you I didn't want— But I was mad as a peeled rattler that day, and not thinking straight— But now I—well, I don't know how I feel, but I need to ask—I need to tell you. Oh, rocks, why is this so dang hard?" She could feel them both staring at her, Winnie and Frank, Frank like she'd just gone ahead and lost her mind.

"We need to speak with Mr. Wheeler," Frank explained for her. "It's urgent."

Winnie pushed her spectacles back up on her nose. "Oh. Well. I— Mr. Wheeler, he—"

"I need to tell you my story," Jane burst out at last. "The whole thing, all of it, so you can write about what really happened." She finally looked up and met Winnie's eyes. "You're the only one I'd trust to get it right."

"Huh?" said Frank eloquently.

Winnie nodded. "Come in."

Over the next hour Jane told Winnie about everything, from the Canary family being run out of every place they settled on account of her mother becoming a garou and refusing to behave, to her mother's faked death and her father's real one at Bill's hands. She described the years she had spent on her own and Bill finding her, becoming part of the group, learning to perform in the show, to hunt garou on the side, the way she'd kind of accidentally become famous and how those stories had finally reached her mother, who'd recognized her picture in the paper and wanted her back. Then Jane related what had truly happened the night they'd gone to the candle factory, how Jack McCall had been sent by her mother (who was now living as Al Swearengen), to bite Jane and send her along to Deadwood in the hopes that Jane would become Beta to Al's Alpha and help her fulfill her grand scheme to make as many garou as she could, to form a new country just for garou. She explained how the cure was made to enthrall garou, not to help them, and how Al Swearengen had demanded that Jane kill Bill, who Al saw as her greatest enemy. How, when Jane had refused, she'd forced the cure on her own daughter, but it didn't take. How her mother had sent

Jack McCall to assassinate Bill in Jane's stead, and how Al'd worked the trial so McCall would be set free.

"Wow," breathed Winnie when Jane was finally done talking. "Now that's a story."

"I'm going to need you to tell the world," Jane said.

"I will," said Winnie determinedly. "It will be my honor."

"Wait, *you're* Edward Wheeler?" Frank said at last. He'd been quietly listening to the entire tale, as rapt as Winnie had been.

"Geez, Frank, catch up, why don't ya?" said Jane.

Winnie's cheeks flushed charmingly. "Yes. When I write, I do so as Mr. Wheeler." She turned back to Jane and smiled a bit breathlessly. "And I will write this for you, Jane. Or do you want me to call you Martha?"

Jane thought a minute, then decided. "I think I've left Martha behind for good, this time. So it's Jane."

"All right. Jane," Winnie said, and Jane liked the way her name sounded being formed by Winnie's mouth right then, like Winnie was actually saying an endearment. "I will do my best with your story. I can tell you now, it's going to be quite the sensation. Al Swearengen a garou, luring and enslaving the other poor garou who come for the cure? That alone will rile up the entire country, not to mention the folks here in Deadwood."

"We're counting on it," said Frank grimly.

"Yeah, so let's get it printed," Jane said, slapping her hand down on Winnie's notebook, which she'd been scribbling in while Jane talked. "Daylight's wasting."

But Winnie was frowning. "Printed? What? When?"

"Before tomorrow. We have this plan, that if we can print the story and, at the same time, break the thrall Al has over the garou, the town will turn against her—arrest her—you see where I'm going? So we gotta get this out tonight."

Winnie's hand came down firmly on the notebook, keeping Jane from picking it up. "What's written here is not the story, Jane. This is just my notes. The story is yet to be composed."

"So compose it. Fast," Frank said.

Winnie was shaking her head in horror. "You want me to write it by when? And how many words does it have to be?" (We feel for you, Winnie. We really do.)

"About six words should do," said Jane. She held up her hand and counted off. "Al. Swearengen. Is. A. Bad. Garou."

"Oh, no," gasped Winnie. "Oh, no, no, no. A story like this takes time."

Frank drew out his pocket watch. "You've got, like, two hours."

Jane snorted. "That's loads of time. A person could write a whole book in two hours." (To which we, as the narrators, say no. A person can't. And now we're crying a little.)

Winnie's mouth opened and then closed again. "This could be the biggest story of my career, the culmination of everything I've been working on for months. I need to plot it out—how do I begin, in what way can I best hook the reader? I need to choose every word with the utmost of care. You can't ask me to rush this."

"You have to," said Frank.

"We've got to stop Al right now!" cried Jane, catching Winnie by the shoulders. "Please!" She realized that she was clutching Winnie too tightly, being too forceful, too strong. She relaxed her grip but didn't move her hands from Winnie's shoulders. Winnie met her gaze steadily. Jane wet her lips. "Please," she said again, more gently. "Do your best."

Winnie nodded. "All right." She took her notebook over to the desk and sat down. She stretched her arms in front of her and opened and closed her fingers several times, then rolled her wrists, first one way, and then the other. (An excellent prewriting habit, if we do say so ourselves.) "I can't guarantee anything, but I'll try."

"Excellent," said Frank. He crossed the room quickly to stand behind her, stroking his chin thoughtfully as Winnie dipped her pen into the bottle of ink on the desk and angled it to write on a fresh sheet of loose paper. Frank leaned over to squint at it. "*The.* Good choice. Start with the classics."

Winnie's delicate shoulders tightened, but she kept writing.

"What does it say?" whispered Jane, coming to stand next to Frank.

Frank leaned again. "'The town of Deadwood is quiet today.'"

"That's nice. Sets the mood," said Jane. (We, as your narrators, might have gone with "Listen up, y'all," but to each her own style.)

Winnie cleared her throat. "I'd appreciate it if you'd give me some space." She turned to smile at Jane tightly. "You could sit over there? Quietly?"

"Sure thing." Jane grabbed Frank by his jacket and pulled him over to the bed, where they plopped down on the edge and sat awkwardly. "These are real quality sheets you have here," she remarked, sliding her hand over the fabric. "Better than at the Gem, I'll tell you what."

"Yes, well, good," said Winnie.

"Let her work," whispered Frank.

"You were the one who was reading over her shoulder," Jane pointed out, but then she kept quiet. The only sound for several minutes was the frantic scratching of Winnie's pen. Jane could smell Winnie's lemon perfume all around her. It still made her heart beat fast. And she was sitting where Winnie slept.

She buttoned the top button of her shirt. For propriety.

Frank opened his pocket watch, checked the time, then clicked it closed. Jane started to bounce one knee. Then she bounced the other, and Frank rolled his eyes and scooted farther away from her on the edge of the bed. Winnie's pen was a flurry of movement, her lips pursed in concentration as she wrote.

After what felt like an hour (but was really only ten minutes), Jane made a show of standing up and stretching her back, and slowly walked around to stand behind Winnie again. There were many words on the pages now, a sea of words that seemed to roll like waves before Jane's eyes.

She pointed at a word that started with the letter *J*. "Is that my name?"

Winnie stopped. "No. It's the word *justice*."

"Ooh, that's a good one."

"Thank you."

"How about that one?" Jane pointed to another *J*. "Is that me?"

"Jane, you're bothering her again," Frank said.

"Am not," argued Jane. "I'm the inspiration, here."

Winnie sighed, put down her pen, and swiveled to face them. "All right, get out."

"Sorry. I'll be good. I promise," pleaded Jane.

Winnie shook her head, a tumble of pale curls. "I can't do this with you watching. It's too much pressure. You need to get out."

"But—" Frank and Jane said at the same time.

"It's dinnertime," Winnie informed them firmly. (Which, at this juncture in our history, meant that it was lunchtime, as they called lunch *dinner*, and dinner *supper*, back then. Super confusing, we know.) "Go get something to eat."

"I'm not hungry," Frank and Jane said at the same time.

"Okay. Then go sit outside somewhere. I will come find you when the story is done." Winnie stood up and ushered them both to the door.

"But when will it be done?" asked Jane.

Winnie gave her a tense smile. "It will be done when it's done."

An hour passed. Or maybe it was another ten minutes. Either way, Jane announced that sitting on the stairs made her butt hurt—it wasn't made to sit so long on a hard wooden step. Plus, she had to pee.

"Again?" said Frank.

"Yeah. I do it regularly," she snapped.

They went on a quick walk to find the nearest outhouse, which happily wasn't far. Then they walked around the block a few times, because walking felt good; it felt like doing something besides waiting. They kept close to the hotel, though, because they didn't want to be seen parading around the town by Al Swearengen's wolf minions, who mostly stayed nearby the Gem but a few of which were spread out around other parts of Deadwood.

"How many of them do you think are under the thrall?" Frank asked Jane as they slunk back toward the Checkmate with their hats pushed low over their eyes.

"Most of them, probably. The only one I know for sure ain't being directly controlled by her is Jack. So when we get that cure for the cure that will free all the thralls, it'll be all the thralls but Jack McCall." She grinned.

"Good," said Frank. "I want him to be held accountable."

Jane nodded, her smile fading, and the two of them fell silent until they reached the Checkmate again. They sat down on the steps without further complaint.

After a while Frank said, "This is a brave thing you're doing, Jane."

"Eh, my butt's okay now," she said.

He snorted. "No. I mean, this. Telling your story. Putting yourself out there."

She shrugged. "It's nothing."

"It's everything," he said. "You're telling the world your biggest secret."

She looked up at him gravely. "It's not my *biggest* secret."

He met her gaze for a minute, then looked away and scratched the back of his neck. "I won't tell. About who Edward Wheeler really is, I mean."

"I love her," Jane confessed. "At least I think that's what it is." She closed her eyes and took a deep breath. "I never felt like this before. My little sister Lena used to get spoony about boys, but me, I never saw the point. But with Winnie, this feeling's been building up inside of me so long, for months now, and I want to shout it from the highest hills, you know, how wonderful she is, how it feels like she really sees me, how I'm walking on wings whenever I'm around her, but—" She propped her elbow on her knee and then put her head in her hand. "What do you think Bill would have said, if he knew? Do you think he would have been ashamed of me? Would he call it unnatural?"

Frank looked thoughtful. "I think he would say something like, 'Oh, well. Love is love.'"

"Love is love," she repeated softly.

Frank nodded. "That's what he would say. And he did know something about love."

"So do you," Jane said. "Because you love Annie."

Frank muttered something like, "Yeah, well, that's complicated," and started to stand up, but Jane grabbed him and hauled him back down next to her.

"You do. You luvvv her. Your eyes go all mushy every time you look her direction. And your voice changes—it goes all soft like, 'Oh, Annie, fine weather we're having today,' and what you're really saying is 'I adore you, my darling. Won't you be mine forever and kiss me and hold me tight?'"

Frank shoved her, almost knocking her from her spot on the steps. His face was blotchy. But then he shook his head and sighed. "Okay, so maybe you're right. But it's still complicated."

"Tell me about it," said Jane.

The door then opened and Winnie peeked out. "I have a draft," she announced. "It's rough, but if we run down to the printer now, I'll revise it as we go. We can have it out by tonight if we hurry."

Jane and Frank jumped to their feet. Jane took off her hat and gazed up at Winnie. "Thank you. I can't tell you how much it means to me that you would—"

"Don't thank me yet," Winnie said. "I don't know if it's any good." She pulled a satchel over one shoulder and moved quickly down the stairs.

"If it's the truth, then it's good enough," Jane said.

A sharp whistle pierced the air. They all tensed as a horse galloped toward them up the street, but then Jane saw that it was Charlie's horse, trailed by George. Annie slid off the horse's back before he was even all the way stopped, and Frank caught her before her feet hit the ground. "Thanks," Annie breathed as he set her down gently. "Have you got the story from Edward Wheeler?"

"Right here," said Jane, pointing to Winnie's satchel.

"I don't know if we've met," said Annie, staring in confusion at Winnie. She extended her hand. "I'm Annie Oakley."

Jane and Frank exchanged awkward glances, and then Winnie laughed in a kind of resigned way and shook Annie's hand. "We have met. I'm Edward Wheeler, you see. But you can call me Winnie."

"Oh," said Annie. She looked at Jane. "Ohhhhh."

I already knew that, George said proudly in Jane's mind.

"You did?" Jane said. "How?"

She smelled like a girl. I don't know why it took Frank so long to figure it out. He never did know how to use his nose.

"Hey!" Frank protested. "I know how to smell girls just fine, thank you very much."

"Hey!" exclaimed Annie.

"Well, good for you, George!" Jane said. Then she became aware that Winnie was staring at her strangely.

"Are you talking . . . to a dog?" Winnie asked.

"It's a garou thing," Jane mumbled.

"Frank does it all the time," added Annie.

Jane glanced at her sharply. "Icks-nay on the arou-gay, Annie."

"What?" Then Annie covered her mouth with her hand, horrified by her slipup. "Oh, Frank! I'm sorry. I didn't mean to tell—"

"It's all right," Winnie assured her. "That can be off the record."

"Thank you," Frank said. "I guess it's a day for revealing our biggest secrets."

"Moving on," Jane said quickly. "Do you have the cure for the cure, Annie?"

Annie nodded distractedly. "Yes, and I have a better idea of how to free all the thralls."

"Good, we're on our way to the printer's now." Frank offered Annie his arm.

She clapped her hands. "I've always wanted to see a printing press. Is it true that you have to line up every single letter of the article individually?"

"We. We'll have to do that," said Winnie. "And then we'll have to proofread it before we print out all the copies."

"I'm excellent at spelling," said Annie. "The best in my whole family."

Jane groaned. She was not going to be remotely useful for this next part, she could tell. "All right, daylight's wasting. Let's go."

"I take it back," Frank said as the sun was going down. He and Annie walked Jane toward the Gem. They'd stashed George back at the Marriott. The next part of the story was no place for a dog. "*This* is the most nervous I've ever seen you."

Jane tried to stop her hands from shaking. "I don't know if I can do this," she admitted. "I've never been what you'd call an actress."

"You'll be fine. You're giving Swearengen what she wants," Annie pointed out. "Most people believe it when you tell them what they want to hear."

Jane nodded and then yawned. They'd been working nonstop for hours printing Winnie's article, which had felt unbelievably tedious to everybody but Annie. The papers were stacked and ready. Jane's story was about to be out there for the world to read, and there'd be no calling it back. Her stomach burbled nervously at the thought.

"This is where you better leave me," she said as they were about to turn the corner and come in sight of the Gem. They all stopped, and Jane took a few deep breaths.

"You got this," Frank said. "You have the cure for the cure?"

She nodded shakily and patted her sleeve, where the thin vial was tied to the inside of her arm, the cork against her wrist. "Wish me luck."

"Good luck," said Annie warmly, and reached to squeeze Jane's hand.

"We'll be waiting for you right here," Frank said. "Just get in, do what you got to do, and get out."

"Get out," Jane repeated. "Right." Then she flashed them what she hoped was a confident grin, tipped her hat back on her head, squared her shoulders, and marched toward the Gem.

As luck would have it, Al Swearengen was sitting at the bar when Jane sashayed through the door. At the sight of her, about a dozen of Swearengen's wolf minions jumped to their feet and drew their guns. She'd definitely beefed up her security since the trial. Jack McCall was nowhere in sight. He must be lying low until he could get out of town, which would have been a good idea seeing as how the townsfolk were still pretty mad that he'd killed Bill.

"Oh, relax, fellas," her mother said to the minions. "Are you here with another set of insults?" she drawled at Jane. "Or have you finally come around to my way of thinking?"

"Yeah, that second thing," said Jane.

Al turned to look at her. "What?"

"I seen the light." Jane climbed onto the stool next to her mother. "I'll be in your Pack. I'll be your Beta. You've got an opening now, right, if Jack's leaving?"

Al tilted her head to one side. "You'll be the Beta?"

"Yep."

"Why am I having a hard time believing that?"

Jane tried to keep her voice steady. "I can explain. But first, spot me a drink?"

Al frowned. "Are we going to have to have a tough-love talk about your alcoholism?"

Jane gave her a waiting look.

"Oh, all right," Al said, and nodded at the barkeep, who poured Jane a whiskey.

Jane turned to her mother without drinking it. "The thing is, you got me beat."

"I do, don't I?" An evil, triumphant smile appeared on her mother's lips. Jane suppressed a shiver of rage.

"You got rid of Bill. Frank and Annie are leaving town and going back to the show, but there's no place for me there, what with people knowing I'm a woof. I'm out of options," Jane said. "I got nowhere else to go."

"Poor baby," said Al.

"And like you said, blood's thicker than water. You're my ma, and my place is with you, I reckon. So I come to ask you to take me back."

"But what if I don't want you?" Al said. "You betrayed me. I don't take that kind of thing lightly."

"I was confused," Jane said. "There was so much happening, so many surprises, so much to think about, and thinking's never really been my strong suit."

"Indeed. Well," Al chuckled. She was clearly delighted by how all this was working out. Annie was right. People loved to be told what they wanted to hear. "All right. You are my daughter, after all. I'll give you another chance to prove yourself."

"I'll take it," Jane said. "What do you want me to do?"

"Charlie Utter's in town," Al informed her. "It's come to my attention that he's a Pinkerton agent, tasked with bringing me down."

"I know Charlie pretty well," Jane said.

"Yes, and he knows you. He trusts you. Which makes you the perfect person to take him out."

Jane's hands started to tremble again, but she clenched her fists and thrust them under the bar. "You want me to kill Charlie Utter?"

"You can do as you like," Al said lightly. "But if that man were to bite the bullet, so to speak, I'd see it as a favor done to me. I'd see the person who did me such a favor as a loyal member of the Pack. All would be forgiven."

Jane nodded. "Okay. I'll kill Charlie. I never did like him much. He was always spoiling my fun."

"That's my girl." Al put her arm around Jane. Jane fought a wave of revulsion. It was just so clear that her ma was evil, through and through. Anything that had been good about Charlotte Canary was long gone. It made Jane sad.

"Thanks, Ma," she murmured against Al's shoulder. "I won't let you down."

"I have faith in you, sweetie," said Al, drawing back and patting Jane's cheek. "You can do whatever you set your mind to."

Jane forced a smile and raised her glass. "I'll drink to that." Then she lowered the glass again. "Have a drink with me? I don't much like to drink alone."

"Oh, all right. Just one can't hurt, I suppose," Al said. "A celebratory brandy, if you please," she said to the barkeep.

"How about a whiskey, for my sake?" said Jane.

"Fine. Whiskey," Al said.

"I'll pour it," said Jane, reaching across the bar and grabbing the bottle of whiskey. In the same moment, she stealthily uncorked the vial that was up her sleeve, poured the wolfsbane and the whiskey into a shot glass, and set it in front of her mother.

Al smiled and lifted her glass.

"To family," Jane said, and she thought of Bill's kind eyes, now closed forever.

"To family," Al agreed.

They touched glasses and drank.

Al made a face. "That's nasty," she said. "Whiskey's never been my drink."

"It's an acquired taste, I guess." Jane wondered how long it would take for the wolfsbane to work. Would it be an instant thing? Was every enthralled wolf in town now suddenly waking up? She glanced over at the wolf minions sitting around the bar. They didn't seem any different—they were glaring at her exactly the same way they'd been before.

"Well, I should go see about killing Charlie," Jane said, hopping off her stool. She'd done what she came to do.

"Oh, and you should probably make it look like an accident," remarked Al.

"An accident?"

"I don't want to have to rig another trial."

Jane stared at her. Everybody in the room was staring at Al at this point.

Because Al suddenly had spouted a large, bushy mustache.

"What?" Al said, feeling the eyes on her. "What's everybody looking at?"

"Um, nothing much," Jane said as Al lifted her hand to her face and gasped in horror.

As suddenly as it had come, the mustache disappeared. But now Al's right hand had hair and claws. Al stared at it as her entire arm became that of a garou. But it was only the one arm. Then it quickly shifted back to its normal, human form. There was a crack from beneath her skirt, and Jane knew that one of Al's legs must be changing. Al's nose grew out into a snout. Then it receded, but her shoulders swelled, splitting the seams of her fancy jacket.

Her mother was losing control of the wolf, but one body part at a time.

Al stood up and whirled to look at Jane, her ears growing into points and sprouting hair. Comprehension dawned in her golden eyes. She picked up the empty whiskey glass and dashed it to the floor, where it burst into a hundred shards.

"What have you done to me, you stupid girl?" she snarled.

"What's going on, Al?" said one of the minions, and Jane instantly recognized his voice. He was wearing an eyepatch and had shaved his mustache off, but it was Jack McCall. "Are you all right? What should we do?"

The wolf minions, who Jane figured should be becoming unenthralled at this point, leapt to their feet and drew their guns again.

Oh, rocks, Jane thought.

Happily, someone burst through the door. It was Ned Buntline—that dirty, rotten, no-good writer. He was brandishing a paper over his head and waving it like a flag. He stopped short when he saw the men with their guns drawn. Then his eyes fell on Al Swearengen, who was still shifting back and forth to a garou. Her left arm was huge and hairy, and a tail was poking out from under her dress.

Buntline's mouth fell open. "So the story's true," he gasped. "Al Swearengen is a garou."

"It's not what it looks like," Al panted, thrusting her arm behind her back. "I've been poisoned."

"Poisoned?" repeated Buntline.

"Poisoned?" said Jack McCall.

"By her." Al lifted a clawed hand to point at her daughter. All the wolf minions spun to look at Jane again, lips curling up to reveal sharp, pointed teeth.

"Let's get her," said Jack McCall, smiling his creepy smile.

Jane really wanted to punch him in the kisser. But she was outnumbered twelve to one. So she just ran.

FORTY-ONE
Frank

"Poor Jane," Annie said. "She was so nervous."

Frank nodded. They'd found a bench that was far enough away from the Gem to be safe, yet close enough to watch for Jane, and now they were waiting for her to return.

"At least she can be comforted in the fact that her mother is an evil, no-good . . . I won't even say the word."

Frank smiled, because he was pretty sure she had no idea what word she was going to say. She probably wasn't even thinking it, because it would be improper.

"Yeah, her mom is pretty darn evil," Frank said. "But, when it comes to being an orphan . . ." Frank paused and scratched his forehead. "I don't know. I can only speak for myself. I grew up knowing that my parents were killed and Bill took me in and saved me. And despite all of that, there's always that thought. What would life have been like if my parents hadn't been killed? It's just the unknown. Jane thought her mother was dead, and then she found out she was alive, which meant she got this second chance with her. So even though Swearengen is, by every definition of the word, *bad*, I'm afraid this is going to be very hard for Jane."

They didn't speak for a while, Frank kicking at the dirt, Annie smoothing her dress. It was the quiet before the storm, at least it was as quiet as Deadwood ever was, which meant the low rumblings of prospectors rattling rocks and sand around in their tin trays, hoping for gold, and the occasional gunshot going off, gamblers missing spittoons, and painted ladies calling out to men passing by.

"What do you think will happen?" Annie said. "Will those poor enthralled garou remember anything after Swearengen gets the cure for the cure? Or what if the cure for the cure doesn't even work, and everything stays the same? Except for the news article will come out, and maybe everyone will think Edward Wheeler is a big fat liar? Oh dear." Annie placed her hand on her chest. "Wooo."

"I don't know," Frank said, but he was more interested in the fact that she'd called the garou "poor." He shifted on the bench so he was facing her. "Annie."

"Yes?"

"You probably drew your own conclusions on Edward Wheeler and Winnie and Jane . . ."

"Yes," Annie said, tilting her head.

"Well, she expressed concern about what Bill would think

about such an unconventional love. And I think I said something that was really smart."

Annie raised her eyebrows. "And what was that?"

"I said that Bill would probably say, 'Love is love.'"

"Then shouldn't Bill get the credit for being smart?" Annie said, a mischievous glint in her eye.

"What? No. He didn't say it."

"But you said he would have said it." Annie's lips turned up at the corners.

"Yes . . . No . . . Well that's not the point. The point is . . ." Frank cleared his throat. "The point is . . ." He looked into her eyes. And she looked . . . over his shoulder.

"Hold that thought," she said.

Annie stood and walked past Frank. Frank stayed perfectly still and whispered, *I love you* toward the spot Annie had just abandoned. He was like 90 percent there. She was *this close* to knowing how he felt about her. But close only counts in horseshoes. (Later the phrase would be amended to say, "Close only counts in horseshoes and hand grenades," giving it a little boost in cadence, but since hand grenades as we know them were not invented until 1914, the cliché had to remain slightly unbalanced.)

"Frank, look," Annie gasped.

Frank turned. A young boy was walking down the street with a stack of newspapers held together with twine. He took up a post on the street corner and untied the stack.

"Extra, extra! Read all about it! Al Swearengen is a garou!"

"It's starting," Frank said.

People began to migrate toward the boy.

"That ain't true," one miner yelled, and then followed it with a tobacco spit for punctuation.

"Them there are lies," another one hollered. And yet, they were lining up to buy the papers.

"Here we go," Annie said.

The news spread like the ripples from a rock thrown in a lake. Pretty soon, everyone on the street was walking and reading, sitting and reading, standing and reading, drinking and reading. And then the whispers started. Then the shouts of disbelief.

Frank could understand the incredulity. The unofficial town leader, the curer of garou, the hater of the abomination . . . a garou herself?

One man with an unusually dirty beard that looked more like a clump of dirt on his chin, crumpled the paper and threw it over his head. "It's lies. All lies. Who is this Edward Wheeler anyway?"

"Ain't he the one who outed Calamity Jane?" a man with a wooden leg said.

"So what? Now he thinks *everyone* famous is a garou? I'd like to see proof."

"Hmm," Annie said. "I'm not sure this is going to go the way we thought it would."

The mud-beard man eyed a few other outraged people and jerked his head, and they all headed off together past the hotel and around the corner to the alley.

"Jane hasn't had enough time to give Swearengen the cure, that's all," Frank said, trying to convince himself as well as Annie.

"You realize that if the cure for the cure doesn't free all the thralls, Swearengen could send every last garou after us," Annie pointed out.

Frank's shoulders tensed. He and Annie were good with their guns, Jane was good with a bullwhip, but there was no way they could fend off hundreds of garou if they decided to get organized. Perhaps they had not considered every possible outcome.

He grabbed Annie's shoulders. "Annie, if this doesn't turn out well for us, I want you to know . . . I need you to know . . ."

"Jane," Annie said.

Frank was thrown off. "What about her?"

Annie pointed. "Jane."

Frank turned to see Jane running top speed out of the Gem.

"Frank! Get the lead out! Annie! Get your gun!"

Frank and Annie stood bewildered for a moment, for it was only Jane.

Then the doors to the saloon burst open again, and out poured at least a dozen men, some in mid-transformation, and all of them chasing Jane.

"RUN!" Jane hollered.

"Annie, do you have your gun?" Frank asked.

"You said I wouldn't need it because we'd have the support of the town!"

"Haven't you learned yet not to listen to me?"

Frank and Annie started running as Jane caught up to them. "It didn't work," she said breathlessly. "It only made Swear . . . en . . . gen . . . like semi-woof out, but then . . ."

"Explain later," Frank panted, already winded from the running.

"Obviously the cure for the cure didn't work," Annie said in a voice that made it sound like she was out for a brisk walk.

"Annie, if you can run faster, go," Frank said.

"I'm not leaving you two behind," Annie said.

They ran and ran, past the Checkmate and the No. 10 Saloon.

"Does this mean you don't mind that I'm a garou?" Frank asked.

"Really, Frank?" Jane spit to one side. "*This* is when you choose to ask her that?"

"We might not get another opportunity," Frank said. "And I haven't had a chance until now!"

"Cow pucky!" Jane said.

"Yes," Annie said.

Frank turned toward her. "Yes, you do mind? Or yes, you don't mind?"

"Consarn it, Frank, she don't mind," Jane said. "Get it through your thick skull. Now will you please come up with a plan?"

"I've got one," Annie said. "I'm going to split off and get my gun. You two try to zigzag, and it would be helpful if you could lead them into a trap of some sort. Maybe double back. Then I'll try to pick them off one by one."

"Where are you gonna get a dozen silver bullets?" Frank asked.

"Where are we supposed to find a trap?" added Jane.

But by then, Annie was gone.

Frank and Jane tried to do as instructed. They zigged down one alley and zagged down another, went full circle around the McDaniels Theater and doubled back, and then, finally, one turn led them straight into a trap. Only, it was a trap for Frank and Jane. Because blocking their escape route at the other end of the alley was the man with the mud beard and the rest of his cohorts, who now outnumbered the group they'd been running from.

Every single member of this new mob drew their guns.

Jane and Frank reached for the sky.

"It's over," Frank said.

"I don't suppose that if we two surrender right here, ya might spare us?" Jane asked.

But the men's guns remained drawn. The minions from the Gem rounded the corner, and those who weren't garou drew their guns as well. Frank and Jane were officially surrounded.

The mud-beard man cocked his gun, and aimed.

"I love you, Frank," Jane said.

"I love you too, Calam. And Annie. I should have told Annie when I had the chance." Frank squeezed his eyes shut.

Bang! A shot rang out.

Then two more shots. *Bang bang.*

Frank had never been shot before, but he was surprised at how little he felt it.

The first shot had probably killed him instantly, thank the good Lord.

"Frank," Jane hissed.

"You're here with me?" Frank said, trying to hide the surprise in his voice that Jane would end up in heaven.

She punched him in the shoulder.

"Ow," Frank said. He didn't think there would be pain in heaven.

"Frank, we gotta run again."

Frank opened his eyes to see the townsfolk—who had previously been under the thrall—chasing the Gem garou, shooting at them as they went. They flew past Frank and Jane like a river going around two boulders.

Jane and Frank slowly lowered their hands.

"The cure for the cure must have worked," Frank concluded.

Jane nodded. "But why didn't it work on the Gem minions?

"Maybe the garou in the Gem didn't need the thrall to follow Swearengen. Maybe they only wanted the power. Speaking of Swearengen, where is she?" Frank said.

The two of them exchanged looks and then took off after the mob back toward the Gem. As the brothel came into sight, Frank saw a stagecoach at the ready, the door open, and Swearengen climbing on top, McCall clamoring inside.

"They're getting away!" Jane yelled.

Without a thought for the crowd of people spread through the street or even her own garou minions who were in front of the carriage, Al Swearengen whipped the horses. "Yah!"

The stagecoach trampled a few people, and Jane threw Frank to the side just in the nick of time.

Right then, Annie jumped into the middle of the street.

"Where did you come from?" Frank looked toward the sky as if she had fallen right from the clouds.

Annie didn't answer. She knelt on the road, took aim with her rifle, and fired.

But there was too much dust flying about the escaping stagecoach. It was barely visible.

Al Swearengen and Jack McCall were in the wind.

FORTY-TWO
Annie

"Well, drat," Annie muttered, lowering her gun. She'd hit some part of the stagecoach—she never missed—but it seemed unlikely she'd hit a vital part, because Al Swearengen and Jack McCall were long gone. "Drat, drat, drat." (Annie was really upset by this, if you couldn't tell.)

Frank coughed at the dust that still floated through the air.

"Are you all right?" Annie asked. "I'm really starting to worry about your pulmonary system. Are you allergic to anything? Being allergic to dogs, I can sympathize."

"My pul—what?" Frank's face went red, but that might have been because of the lack of oxygen.

"She means your breathing, you dope." Jane shook her head. "And she has a good point. You've been struggling. Are you okay?"

Frank crossed his arms. "We don't have time to talk about my running-induced asthma. The bad guys are getting away!"

"We'll never make it if we go after them on foot." Annie tilted her head. "Well, I might. But Frank would keel over just outside of town."

Jane nodded solemnly. "Frank can't run for plop."

"Can we continue mocking me after we catch Swearengen and Jack McCall?" Frank asked.

Annie turned about-face and pointed. "To the livery!"

"To the livery," Jane echoed, and they were off, with Frank trailing behind them.

Mr. Utter was already there, murmuring soothingly to his horse. "Yes, you are a good boy. I missed you very much."

Annie gasped. How dare he?! Well, technically Charlie's horse *was* Charlie's horse, but still! The gall. Her hands clenched into fists, but softened again when Jane patted her on the shoulder.

"Calm down there, spitfire."

At the sound of voices, Mr. Utter turned. "Oh, good! I've been looking for you three everywhere. I need to tell you about—"

"We don't have time!" Jane started grabbing saddles and tack. "Something big is happening, and we need these here horses."

"Maybe Annie could take this one," Mr. Utter said, stepping aside to reveal an angry-looking Silver, Bill's donkey.

"Hee-haw," said Silver.

"Oh, no." Annie grabbed her saddle blankets. "I would never leave my favorite boy out of this."

Frank made a sad noise, but there was no time for Annie to console him, because now Jane was telling Mr. Utter about the plan to expose Al Swearengen and how it had all gone horribly awry.

"And just as we got away from the angry wolves, we ran smack into the angry mob." Jane hefted her saddle onto Bullseye's back and tugged the cinch. "But thank goodness the angry mob wasn't after us this time. They ran at the wolves, and we ran along behind them." She gave the cinch one more pull and clipped it.

"So now you're going after Swearengen and Jack McCall?" Mr. Utter said with a frown. "Just the three of you?"

"The angry mob is busy at the moment," Annie said as she finished putting the bit into Charlie's horse's mouth. She hauled herself up onto the horse's back. "Sorry, there's no time to talk more. I can't wait to hear what it was that you wanted to tell us when we get back!"

Frank and Jane mounted Mr. Ed and Bullseye respectively. "And we're off!" Jane cried. "Ride like the wind, Bullseye!"

The three of them burst from the stables, this time leaving Mr. Utter coughing in the dust. Annie bent low over Charlie's horse's neck, letting him get as much speed as possible as they raced through the streets and straight out of Deadwood. Within minutes, they were galloping over ruts and tufts of scrub, urging the horses faster and faster.

Now, you may be thinking this was really dangerous, seeing as how it was dark out, and you'd be right, especially considering this was unknown territory for our heroes and horses, but back then,

473

the stars shone brighter because there weren't electric lights all over the place. As strange as it sounds, the horses and their riders cast shadows along the ground as they darted across the countryside, half flying after the stagecoach.

Soon, they caught sight of lanterns swinging in the distance, then the back of the stagecoach, and then the curtained window in the rear.

As our heroes started to close the distance, the stagecoach driver urged the team faster until the horses jolted into a run, making the stagecoach bounce along behind them

"They're trying to outpace us!" Frank cried.

"They're just a whip crack away!" Jane kicked her horse faster, ducking as a hot piece of metal zinged past. Someone had shot at them!

"Guns!" Frank called. "They have guns!" Sure enough, through the back window of the stagecoach, the muzzle of a rifle was visible. Then it retreated inside—probably to reload.

"Maximum effort!" Jane yelled.

"We have to do something!" Frank cried.

"I know! That's why I said maximum effort! We should flank them. Frank, you and me split up, one on each side. Annie, you stay back here, out of the way. Those bullets could actually hurt you."

Annie would have scoffed, but she didn't have time. Instead, she stood up on the back of Charlie's horse, one foot on the front and back of her saddle. The thrum of hooves beating the ground rolled through her, but she didn't lose her balance.

"What the blazes are you doing?" Jane shouted. "Didn't I just say—"

"Everyone knows there's a weakness to a stagecoach." Annie lifted her gun, steadying herself as Charlie's horse raced away beneath her. "It's a small part called the axle. The shaft leads directly to the wheel. A precise hit will start a chain reaction, which should destroy the stagecoach."

"What?" Frank was staring at her.

"The wheel will fall off," Annie explained. Then she took aim. And she fired.

In the midst of all this running and shouting and standing up on galloping horses, let's slow down a bit to really explain how incredible Annie's shot was.

Not only was Annie standing up on a moving horse, balancing herself, her gun, and her aim, but the stagecoach ahead of them was bouncing and weaving back and forth, and there was a light breeze coming from the northwest. Furthermore, even with all those stars shining above, it was still pretty dark.

So Annie squeezed the trigger and her bullet zipped out, and in spite of the running and darkness and pleasant breeze, the bullet struck exactly where she intended: right in that oh-so-delicate axle.

At once, the wheel flew off the stagecoach, making it drag along the ground as the team of horses tried very hard to keep going.

"What was *that*?" Jane exclaimed.

"That was amazing," Frank shouted.

"I know!" Annie called. "But weren't you going to flank them?"

Annie reloaded her rifle as quickly as possible, which was pretty darn quickly, because this is Annie Oakley we're talking about.

Meanwhile, Frank and Jane pulled away from her, kicking their horses into an even faster gallop. The stagecoach was limping, but Al Swearengen and Jack McCall weren't giving up. In spite of everything, the rifle appeared in the back window again, aimed straight at Annie.

Fortunately, Annie was really good at these things, as she was with most things, so when she heard the shot fire, she dropped into her saddle and ducked low as the bullet whizzed safely above her. Miraculously, Charlie's horse didn't shy once during all this. Maybe he was used to being shot at while running at high speeds.

Annie leaned off the side of Charlie's horse, aimed down the barrel of her rifle, and fired, this time on the front axle.

The stagecoach jolted as another wheel spun away. A bang sounded as a stray shot went off inside the compartment. Annie glanced at Frank and Jane to make sure neither had been hit, but they were each closing in on either side, and that was quite enough for the team of horses drawing the stagecoach. First the shooting, then the dragging, and now a pair of humans that smelled like wolves and growled like wolves and closed in on them like wolves. It was Quite Enough.

When Frank lifted his rifle and shot the yoke connecting the horses to the stagecoach, splitting it just enough for the horses to yank free, the team neighed and ran away as quickly as they could, leaving the stagecoach rolling to a stop behind them.

Annie had never been so attracted to Frank in her life.

"Great shot!" she called.

"Thanks!" he called back.

She sat down in her saddle again, allowing Charlie's horse to slow to a trot, then a walk. The poor creature was breathing hard, sweat gleaming on his neck, but she patted him and scratched his ear. "Good boy. And that's why you're my favorite."

Charlie's horse nickered.

Ahead, Jane and Frank swung off their horses and stalked toward the fallen stagecoach. "Come out with your hands up," Frank shouted. Then he turned to Jane. "I always wanted to say that."

Jane grinned and called, "Do you feel lucky, punk?"

Frank looked at her, confused. "Punk?"

Jane, as you might have noticed, was ahead of her time.

Annie was halfway to them when—out of nowhere—a wolf leapt from the stagecoach and tackled Jane.

Annie would know that wolf anywhere. It was the one from the candle factory. The one who'd bit Jane. Jack McCall, which she'd learned while the group had been typesetting Winnie's article.

"Jane!" Annie kicked Charlie's horse into a run, but the exhausted creature wanted none of it. He neighed and reared, and Annie held on for dear life as her gun slipped from her hands.

When Charlie's horse was on all fours again, Annie swung

herself off and scooped up her gun, but she was too late: Swearengen had stepped out of the stagecoach, and her rifle was aimed straight at Frank, while Jack McCall had shifted back into a human and found his own gun, which was aimed at Jane.

Annie meeped and gripped her rifle more tightly, searching for something to shoot that would allow her friends to go free. Maybe she could make the bullet ricochet, or . . . No, she'd seen Jack McCall shoot the mayor, and she had to assume Swearengen was just as fast. When Annie pulled her trigger, both would fire their own weapons.

"Don't do it!" she warned. Like she had a plan. Any plan at all. But she was down to the biggest lesson she'd learned from poker: bluff your way through a nothing hand.

"Don't make me," said Jack McCall.

"I hope you have a silver bullet in there," Jane said, eyeing Jack McCall's gun, and sounding really, really brave, all things considered. "You'll need silver to kill me. It's the only way to be sure."

"I always have silver bullets in all my guns," Swearengen said coolly.

"Um, oops?" Jack McCall looked at Swearengen, guilt written all over his face. "Mine just has regular bullets."

Swearengen sighed. "Fine. Swap me." Then, muttering, she said, "It's so hard to find good help these days."

The two swapped where they were aiming so that Jack McCall had his gun pointed at Frank, while Swearengen had hers aimed at Jane.

"Now you see that I'm serious," Swearengen said to Jane. "Of course, if Jack had shot you, you would live, but it would take you days to recover. You wouldn't like the experience."

Annie looked from Jane to Frank, who was cringing. Neither Swearengen nor Jack McCall knew he was a garou. Jane had effectively just saved Frank's life, if things went south. And they were looking pretty south at the moment.

"You, girl." Swearengen looked at Annie. "Put down that gun."

"No," Annie said. "I won't."

"If you don't," Swearengen said, "I'll shoot Jane."

"Are you serious?" Jane stared up at Swearengen.

"I already said I'm serious." Swearengen shook her head. "You need to pay better attention, dear. And really, this is going to hurt me more than it hurts you."

"You won't shoot her," Annie said, sounding braver than she felt. Swearengen had hurt so many people already, Jane included, and there was no reason to believe she'd stop now.

"I'll do it. And Jack'll shoot your boy here. Do you really want two dead friends?"

Jack's bullet wouldn't kill Frank, but it would hurt. A lot. And he'd come back to find that his best friend, his sister, was dead.

It wasn't fair, and Annie couldn't see any way that she could save both of them. She didn't have a choice.

Annie put down her gun.

Jane
FORTY-THREE

"Any ideas on how to get us out of this?" Jane struggled against the chains that bound her against Frank and Annie, the three of them back to back on the floor of the broken stagecoach. "Should we wolf out and see what happens?"

"No. We absolutely cannot wolf out right now," answered Frank sternly.

Jane examined the length of chain wrapped tightly around her wrists. There wasn't much wiggle room there. "Yeah, I guess that could make our hands pop off or something. Good call, Frank."

"The chains are around Annie, too," Frank explained. "If either of us became garou-sized, we'd crush her."

From behind them Annie made a muffled sound. (A few minutes ago Annie had insulted Jack McCall about a certain lack of hygiene she noticed as he was chaining them up, so he'd stuffed a filthy handkerchief into her mouth to stop her yapping.) Jane reckoned that Annie was probably trying to say something like, "Yes, I agree, no wolfing out, I'm quite fond of my ribs, thank you," or "Well, drat," which she'd been saying a lot lately. Right then the door of the stagecoach opened, and Al Swearengen leaned in.

"I hope you're comfortable," she said.

"Go to hell," Frank growled. His shoulders seemed a little bigger. Jane nudged him.

"Remember your wooo," she whispered. "No woof, right?"

Swearengen put a hand to her chest as though she were deeply offended by Frank's sass. "Now, now, we mustn't be uncivil. You're still angry at me over the death of Wild Bill, and I suppose I understand. It's a terrible thing when a man murders someone you love, isn't it? But the manner in which he died, well—Jack McCall lacked finesse, I admit, but the way I see it, your father got exactly what he deserved."

Frank glared at Swearengen. "Pretty soon the entire country will know you're a monster, a murderer, and a fraud. You won't be able to show your face anywhere. It's only a matter of time before you're caught."

Swearengen tsked her tongue. (This is a Western, remember. The villain always has to have a moment to twirl his mustache— and if Swearengen had still been sporting a mustache, she would literally have twirled it at this point.) "If there's one thing I'm good at in this world, it's reinventing myself," she said cheerfully. "I may be down, but I'm not out. But, all right, dear, go ahead, underestimate me. Your father did, too, and you see where that got him."

Annie made another muffled noise, which sounded vaguely like, "You won't get away with this."

Swearengen smiled. "I already have gotten away with it. You have cost me my stagecoach, which is a delay, I'll admit, a minor annoyance. But soon we'll be on our merry way again. On that note . . ." She turned to Jane. "This is your last chance to be sensible, my darling. Cease your foolish association with these *show business people*." Her nose wrinkled in distaste. "Come with me. Accept your place by my side, with your family."

Jane held her gaze. Then she drew herself up as far as the chains would allow and said, "These people are my people. They're my family. My place is with them."

"Then you're no daughter of mine," Al Swearengen said coldly.

"If that's how it is." Jane nodded. "I don't really want to be your daughter no more."

Al looked sad, so much so that Jane almost regretted saying such harsh words. Then the older woman lifted a gloved hand to stroke Jane's cheek.

"You always were a stubborn, stupid girl," she sighed. "I'm sorry it's come to this, but I'm afraid I must bid you a fond farewell. And, as I can't have you thwarting my plans again, I'll leave you with a parting gift. Goodbye, my dear." She stepped back, and Jack McCall came into view. The man grinned and placed a crude bomb made of dynamite and an old-fashioned alarm clock down on the floor of the stagecoach. He made a production of setting it for five minutes.

"Oh, but before I go, would you mind signing this for me?" Jack McCall pulled out a small leather-bound book and flipped through the pages until he found a blank one. He tried to hand it to Jane. "It's not every day you get a chance to get the signature of Calamity Jane, now, is it? And the Pistol Prince, too. And, what was your name again, miss?"

Annie squeaked and made a sound that could have been a muffled "Annie Oakley."

McCall shoved a pen into Jane's hand. She spit in his face. She only had something like four minutes and fifty-five seconds left to live, and she was determined to make it count. "Go to thunder, Jack McCall."

He wiped his face on his sleeve, all the while smiling that creepy smile of his. "All right, be that way. Bye, Jane." He shut the door of the stagecoach and jogged away from it (quickly, as the time was literally ticking away here—they now had four minutes and fifty-*one* seconds before they'd all be blown to kingdom come). Jane could hear Swearengen and McCall some distance away discussing which of the horses—Frank's, Annie's, or Jane's—they should take for the remainder of their escape.

Frank dropped his head and groaned.

Jane thought it might be time for prayer. "Lord," she said, "whatever I've done to piss you off, if you could get us out of this and somehow let me know what it was, I promise to rectify the situation."

Annie made a noise like a determined little grunt, but other than that, nothing happened. At least it would be over in four minutes and forty-one seconds, Jane thought. Forty. Thirty-nine.

"Any ideas for how to get out of this *now*?" The chains were chafing Jane's wrists something fierce. Frank's wrists must have also been chafing. But he had other things on his mind.

"Annie," he kept saying, "Annie, hang in there. This isn't the end."

Jane begged to differ.

Annie didn't respond. She was probably going crazy about that dirty handkerchief, Jane reckoned, what with her whole cleanliness-is-next-to-godliness bit. But now they were about to die in a pretty messy fashion, so Jane figured it was all relative.

"I'm so sorry about the dirty handkerchief in your mouth," Frank said, coming to the same realization. "If we could get out of this mess, I'd get a chance to tell you how I really feel about you. And maybe you'd feel the same way. And then we could get busy growing old together. We could have the whole thing. The porch, the rocking chair, our guns side by side on the wall, George at our feet."

Annie didn't answer, though if Jane knew Annie (and Jane felt she knew Annie pretty well after all they'd been through), Annie likely had a lot to say about such a declaration.

"Well, I guess this is goodbye," Jane declared mournfully, as this was obviously a time for speeches. "Annie, it's been real nice knowing you. Frank, I guess you know this, but you're like the brother I never had. I mean, I had a brother. I have one, actually. Did I tell you that I have a brother and three sisters, back in Salt Lake City? Swearengen said she was going to send for them in Deadwood, but of course now that won't happen seeing as how she has to change her identity again, and I'm about to be killed. I always dreamed that someday, somehow, I'd be able to send for them myself and we could all be together again, with some land, maybe, some horses. It sure was a pretty dream. I wish it could have come true. But, oh well."

"That's nice, Calam." Frank turned his attention back to his deep and abiding feelings for Annie. "Annie," he declared. "I've never been happier than the time I've spent with you . . ." He sighed. "I wish I could hear your voice one last time." He sighed again. "Annie, this might not be the appropriate time, or place, but would you consider . . . I mean, would you do me the honor of making me—"

"Geez, Frank, this is *not* the appropriate time," Jane interrupted. "How about when you're alone and maybe facing each other and when you're definitely not about to get blowed up in the next three minutes and twenty-nine seconds?" She could hear that bomb ticking, ticking, ticking away.

"As I was saying," Frank said, again ignoring Jane in favor of Annie. "The minute I met you, I thought, *Wow, what a girl!* And I still think that, Annie, every time I see you."

Then he and Jane both yelped, because right then Annie popped up in front of them, ungagged and unchained.

"Good news! We're saved," she announced.

"But how . . . ," Jane stammered. "When . . . ?"

Quickly Annie began to free Frank and Jane. "Many Horses and Walks Looking are here," she explained, pointing to the opposite door of the stagecoach, where, indeed, the two girls were standing watching them. "When I didn't show up where I said I'd meet them, they got worried. They tracked us here and saw that we were in trouble. Then they picked the lock here with one of my hairpins, and I shimmied out of the chains."

"Thank you," said Frank to the Lakota girls. "You two are lifesavers."

"Don't mention it. I mean that," said Many Horses. "Don't ever."

"Any time," said Walks Looking.

"Wait, you want to *help* us?" Jane said, scratching at her head. If this was true, she was going to have to rethink those stories she'd told about battling the Sioux all this time, as part of her being the hero-eene of the plains. Clearly it weren't so heroic to fight them, after all. She'd have to set the record straight.

"Yeah, don't ask me why," said Many Horses wryly.

"Stop it. Annie's our friend," admonished Walks Looking, smiling at Annie.

"What about the bomb?" asked Frank, which seemed like a more pertinent question.

"I disabled it," said Annie brightly. "It was only a matter of carefully disconnecting the dynamite from the detonation device.

First I cut the white wire, then the blue, then the yellow with black stripes. But everyone knows it's always the red wire you have to be really careful about. I ripped that one out, not cut it. Cutting it would have killed us all. It was simple, really."

(You, reader, may be wondering how Annie knew which wires to cut and in which order, especially since movies that depict those kind of bomb-disarming scenes had not yet been invented. But as you know by now Annie was ingenious and resourceful, and although we, the narrators, really don't know how she knew about the wires, we have since researched disabling bombs, and we can verify that, as usual, Annie was very, very right.)

Annie smiled triumphantly.

"Wow," Frank breathed.

"Now all we have to do is catch up to my ex-ma and that no-good, murderin', cowpie-lovin' Jack McCall," said Jane.

This turned out to be easy enough, as Swearengen and McCall were still working out the horse situation.

"I don't want that one," McCall was saying as Frank, Jane, and Annie quietly snuck out of the stagecoach and worked their way around the back side. "It nodded at me. That's weird."

"Well, make up your mind," sniffed Swearengen, already astride Bullseye (crud, she was even stealing Jane's horse) and ready to go. She glanced back at the stagecoach. "The imminent explosion is bound to attract attention."

"But the brown one looks grumpy, and it walks funny," complained McCall.

Next to Jane, Annie stifled her gasp of outrage at such an insult to Charlie's horse.

Frank met Jane's eyes and pointed at Bullseye.

She understood him completely. Al Swearengen was a horse's ass.

But then Frank was mouthing something.

The guns, she finally picked up on the fourth or fifth attempt, after Frank quietly pantomimed shooting with a rifle and Annie nodded and smiled and pointed at Bullseye's butt again. Where, tucked into a saddlebag, Jane finally noticed Annie's rifle poking out.

The plan, she understood then, was to get the guns. Which made sense, considering. And of course she should be the one to do this, since she was the stealthiest of the three of them. Jane moved silently forward toward her ex-mother and the horse. She could be like a shadow lurking in the corner of a darkened room. She could be a crow gliding through the silent air on a moonless night. She could—

"Quick!" barked Swearengen. "Someone's coming."

They all turned toward the road, where, sure enough, the sound of hoofbeats was fast approaching, maybe some kind of backup, Jane thought hopefully, but this was also bad because turning to look in that direction caused Swearengen and McCall to see Jane standing right there.

"Hey!" yelled Jack McCall.

"Look out!" yelled Frank.

"Why can't you ever stay where I leave you?" yelled Swearengen.

"Get me a gun!" yelled Annie at the same time.

It was too late. Jack McCall had his pistol out lickety-split. He cocked it and aimed it at Annie's head. The group froze, except for Walks Looking and Many Horses, who were still in the stagecoach for some reason. Something to do with the bomb?

"Well, drat," Jane tried out. "Nope. That won't do at all. Well, crud."

"I'm rethinking our decision not to kill you earlier," Annie said primly, wagging a finger at McCall as he stepped toward her, the gun still trained on her head. "I was trying to be accepting because you're a garou, and I wanted to be sensitive to your experience, but I think you may simply be a bad dog."

"Kill them," said Swearengen, lifting her own gun and pointing it at Jane. "I'm done with these games. Let's kill them all and be done with it."

This was really going to happen this time. Here it was: the meeting of the Maker. The kicking of the bucket. Giving up the ghost. Being called to a better place. Resting in peace. The end.

But then came a loud, horrible noise.

It was a whistle—a high-pitched noise that instantly made Jane's head feel like it was about to pop like a balloon. She screamed and clapped her hands over her ears, but it didn't block out the sound. The noise went on and on and on. It was hard to make sense of anything—but she saw Jack McCall writhing about on the ground like he was also in the same kind of pain. She saw Frank and

Al Swearengen clutching at their ears as well, everything else forgotten. Her eyes focused on Annie, who was standing up straight like she alone didn't hear the terrible whistling, staring off down the road.

"Put 'em up," said a low and gruff, distinctively male voice. There was the undeniable click of another gun being cocked.

"I said, put 'em up," came the voice again, a familiar voice that, even though Jane was half wild with the agony of the infernal whistling, made her cry out in amazement and wonder and sheer, incredulous joy.

Everybody, Swearengen and McCall, Frank and Annie and Jane, even, lifted their hands into the air.

The whistling faded.

Then Wild Bill Hickok himself stepped out of the shadows.

FORTY-FOUR
Frank

Bill put away the silver dog whistle (an ingenious way to subdue a bunch of werewolves, if we've ever heard of one) and removed two balls of cotton from his ears.

Frank could scarcely believe his eyes.

"Dad?" he said.

"Bill?" Jane said.

"Mr. Hickok?" Annie said.

In a flash, Bill drew his ivory-handled pistols (which he must have received back from Charlie) and pointed one at Swearengen and the other at Jack McCall, whose face had gone pale, as if he were seeing a ghost.

"I killed you," Jack McCall said incredulously.

"Guess it didn't take," Bill said.

Frank still had his hands up in surrender. "Dad? You're alive!"

"Yep," Bill said. "It takes more than a lead bullet to put me in the ground."

And then Frank understood what Bill meant by that. "You're a garou?"

Bill nodded. "We all have our secrets, I reckon, and we get to decide when to tell them. So I guess now I'm letting you know."

"Wait. You've been a woof this entire time?"

"Since you were a toddler," Bill confessed. "You went through a bit of a biting phase."

Frank's mouth dropped open. "You're a garou because I was *teething*?"

"I didn't take it personally. I was just relieved you didn't bite the nanny."

"Dad! You should have told me!"

Bill shook his head. "You had your own burdens. I didn't want you to carry mine."

"I don't care. You're here. That's all that matters." There weren't enough words in the dictionary to pin down all the emotions that were washing over Frank. His father was alive!

"I knew they'd never really get you down, Bill," sniffled Jane.

Frank glanced at Annie, who had been watching the exchange with her hands clasped beneath her chin and a wide smile on her face. She loved happy endings and family reunions, even at the most inopportune times. But then she frowned. "Wait a minute. Am I the only one who isn't a garou here?" she asked.

"You hate garou," Frank said.

Annie tsked. "I don't like being left out. Besides, I can

think of a few garou who I love."

Frank's breath caught. "Is that so?"

"Jane is my best friend," Annie said.

"Is that so?" said Jane. "That's nice."

"Oh," said Frank.

Someone in the stagecoach cleared a throat. It was Walks Looking. Still in there with her sister doing something with the dynamite.

Annie gasped. "Oh, and Walks Looking's a garou too, and also one of my best friends."

Bill chuckled. Then Annie gestured to him. "And Mr. Hickok. I don't really know him that well, of course, but I'm already growing quite fond of him."

Jack McCall cleared his throat.

"Not you," Annie said.

"And not me, either, huh?" Frank couldn't stop his smile.

"Well." Annie smiled right back. "You're growing on me."

Jane gave an exasperated snort. "Cut it out! Isn't this supposed to be the part where we all reunite with Bill?"

Oh, yeah. Frank strode over and threw his arms around his dad.

Then Jane came over and threw her arms around Frank and Bill.

And then Annie followed behind Jane, trying to throw her arms around all three, but really getting no farther than putting them around Jane and touching Frank with her fingertips.

"Okay, okay," Bill said. "That'll do, kids. That'll do."

Then they heard the distinct sound of a gun cocking. All that hugging meant that Bill hadn't been able to keep aiming his pistols at Swearengen and McCall.

"What a touching scene," Al Swearengen drawled.

The hugging quartet froze. Frank glanced over his father's shoulder to see Al Swearengen with a small shiny pistol pointed at the back of Bill's head. Not this again, thought Frank. He was getting so sick of this hostage situation that kept happening tonight.

"No, really, I'm shedding a tear." Swearengen wiped an imaginary tear from her cheek. "I've got a silver bullet right here with your name on it, Bill." Swearengen purred. "I guess if you want something done right, you've got to do it yourself."

Frank didn't want to imagine going through Bill's death a second time. He decided right then that he'd give his own life, to keep that from happening again.

"Enough of the group hug," Swearengen said. "Let go of Wild Bill."

Frank sighed. He was out of time. "Annie, I want you to know that I love you."

"Crick your leg up," Annie replied.

"Huh?" Frank said eloquently.

"I'm talking to Jane," Annie whispered.

"Huh?" Jane said just as eloquently.

"Bend your leg. So I can step on it," Annie said. "My best friend and I are working on a plan."

"It's nice that I'm your best friend, Annie, but now's probably not the time for stepping on legs," Jane said. "Swearengen's about to kill Bill. Again."

"Do it," Annie commanded.

"Okay," Jane grumbled.

Swearengen stepped closer. "Stop hugging." She cocked the pistol again, even though it seemed only for show.

Suddenly there was an explosion off to the side of the road. Fire bloomed into the night air. At the same time, Annie catapulted upward, somersaulting over the group hug, and kicked the pistol out of Swearengen's hand. "I did it!" she exclaimed upon landing. "Oh, and thank you, Walks Looking and Many Horses. That was a dynamite idea."

She would have continued to congratulate everyone on their success at disarming the bad guy, but Swearengen pulled a knife from her cleavage and held it to Annie's throat. "I've got your girl!" Swearengen cried. "Don't make a move."

"Not again!" groaned Frank. He and Jane were still facing Bill, and away from Swearengen. Bill quietly handed one of his guns to Frank. He looked at Jane, but Jane just touched the bullwhip at her hip. Bill gave a slight nod.

"Now, everybody is gonna settle down," Swearengen said. McCall grabbed the pistol from the ground and tried to cock it a third time.

Frank side-eyed Jane, who side-eyed him back. Jane glanced at the ground, where an empty sardine can lay in the dirt. (Littering was a problem in 1876, too.) She raised her eyebrows.

Frank winked.

With her toe, Jane kicked the can up, caught it, and put it in front of Frank, who used the reflection to target the perfect shot.

He swung Bill's revolver over his shoulder, aimed, and fired.

He missed.

But a small hole appeared in Jack McCall's hand. The creepy son of a biscuit then dropped the gun, doubled over, and cradled his fingers.

Then, while Swearengen was looking at McCall, Jane dove to the side, tucked into a roll, and cracked her whip.

Swearengen's knife went flying.

They all stood still for a few minutes, panting, reassessing the situation. It seemed (for the moment anyway) that the bad guys were down again. The good guys had their victory.

Walks Looking and Many Horses came out from inside the stagecoach, holding sticks of dynamite. Jack McCall moaned and clutched at his hand. Swearengen started to swear profusely. Jane stuffed the dirty handkerchief into her ex-ma's mouth. "This is going to hurt me more than it hurts you," she said.

Bill rubbed his hand over Frank's hair. "You did well, kids. Now let's tie up those dirty rats."

Jane hog-tied McCall and Swearengen in eight seconds and seven seconds flat, respectively.

"We're gonna need them to walk," Frank pointed out.

Jane untied their feet in five seconds and six seconds flat, respectively. "Now, you guys better get ready to walk."

In the meantime, Annie, Walks Looking, and Many Horses had gathered up the stagecoach horses. "I think there's enough for everybody," Annie said.

"So listen up, you prisoners," Jane amended herself. "You

guys better get ready to ride sheepishly into town, where you're gonna hang by your toenails."

"Trial," Annie whispered.

"Where you're gonna get a fair trial, this time with no obstruction or collusion. And then you'll hang—"

"If convicted," Annie whispered.

"Would you please just let me threaten?"

Annie held up her hands. "Fair enough." Then she turned to Frank. "Remember that time you used a sardine can to shoot the pistol out of Jack McCall's hand?"

"You mean, three minutes ago?" Frank asked.

Annie smiled. "That was so gosh-darn amazing."

Frank knew she meant it, otherwise she never would have used such harsh language.

"Looks like I missed out on all the fun." The voice came from Seth Bullock, who had just arrived on a horse, with Charlie Utter trailing behind on Silver the donkey. "I believe there are some arrests to be made," Mr. Bullock said.

"Too late," Jane said. "I already made the arrests."

Bullock pointed to the metal star on his chest. "I know you did the hard work. But we're going to follow the letter of the law."

"Which letter is that?" Jane asked. "I only know a few of them."

"And as for you two," Bullock pointed to Swearengen and Jack McCall. "I expect you will spend what little remains of your life in a tiny cell."

"I hope it's not the one I broke," Jane said.

FORTY-FIVE

Annie

Long story short, the town of Deadwood held a second trial for Jack McCall, and included Al Swearengen in that one too, and—this might not come as a surprise—both were found guilty of murder, conspiracy to murder, lying to the public, inciting mob violence, cheating at cards, and generally being unlikable people.

When the prison wagon slammed shut, both villains locked securely behind bars, everyone cheered. Swearengen and McCall were on their way to the USA for a real trial, where the real law would fall down on them like a ton of bricks. Someone would throw the book at them.

"We would have gotten away with it," shouted Jack McCall, "if it weren't for you kids and your pesky dog!"

George yipped angrily.

Frank translated: "George says he's not pesky, and that he barely helped at all. In fact, keeping track of him made things more difficult!"

All that was true, although Annie would never dream of telling George. She had too much respect for him. Plus, she wanted to keep his owner around a while longer.

Overall, she was just relieved to see the prison wagon jerk into motion, getting an early shot on the long road out of Deadwood.

When the prison wagon was out of sight, Sheriff Bullock led Deadwood residents to the cemetery, where Mr. Utter was going to bury Wild Bill Hickok. (And, in a year or two, his "remains" would be exhumed. He'd be moved over to Mount Moriah Cemetery just up the hill, which would be a neat trick for an imaginary body.)

It wasn't a long walk, not really, but it felt like one as the cheers faded into thoughtful discussion and a few tears. As far as the residents of Deadwood knew, Wild Bill Hickok really was dead, and Mr. Hickok had told our heroes already that he had no plans to come back to life. He just wanted to make it back to his wife, Agnes, before the news of his "death" reached her and he earned himself a slap for scaring her like that. After which, he'd retire both literally and figuratively.

"Not every day a man gets to attend his own funeral," Mr. Hickok said as Jane, Frank, and Mr. Utter walked along with him. He'd cut his hair and shaved his mustache, which was a pretty good disguise, since the hair and the mustache were so iconic. He'd also swapped his black hat and coat for brown ones, and that was all it took for no one to have any clue who he was.

The cemetery wasn't far away now, and Annie was about to ask him how he felt about all of this, but two figures appeared around the corner of the No. 10 Saloon, both wearing the borrowed hats and coats she'd left for them.

Annie peeled away from the group and wandered toward the saloon.

"I thought you didn't come into town," she said, once they were all safely out of sight.

"We made an exception this time," Many Horses said. "Because we wanted to say goodbye."

Annie's breath caught. "You're leaving?"

Walks Looking nodded. "We were able to find all the Lakota wolves Swearengen enthralled, and we're going to take them home."

"I thought this was your home," Annie said, even though she knew it was no use. "The Black Hills."

Many Horses offered a tight smile. "It is, but our *people* are our home. This morning, I got word my father has moved toward Wood Mountain to regroup. That's where we'll go."

Annie's heart broke with missing them already, but she nodded. "I understand. But I hope this isn't the last time we meet."

"I'd be surprised if it was." Many Horses and Walks Looking exchanged glances and smiled. "Besides, we want to see your show some day, and we expect the best seats in the house, considering all the times we've rescued you."

Annie laughed, snorted, and then covered her mouth. "I think we can arrange that. And if you ever need anything—*anything*—you can come to us."

"Good to know." Many Horses smiled a bit sadly.

"We will miss you," Walks Looking said. "Well, I will. My sister would never admit it."

Annie blinked away tears. "Be safe on your journey."

They all hugged, and then Annie watched them go. She waited long enough to make sure she wasn't going to cry before returning to the procession entering the cemetery.

(The sisters—and all the Lakota—had a hard road ahead of them. We wish we could change history here to make things easier for them, but some things aren't within our power. Even so, we hope that the bond Annie formed with Many Horses and Walks Looking was strong enough to bring them back together again, and that they had many more adventures.)

In the cemetery, Annie found Frank and Jane in the front row. (Mr. Hickok had moved elsewhere, so as not to attract attention.) Mr. Utter stood at the gravesite with the coffin, giving a long speech about how great of a friend Wild Bill had been.

It seemed like an awful lot of pressure when the man you were eulogizing was right there, listening to every word.

"Where'd you go?" Frank whispered.

"Many Horses and Walks Looking came to say goodbye."

"Oh." He took her hand and slipped his fingers between hers. "Are you okay?"

She nodded but couldn't say anything else about them—not

without crying. Which would have been wholly appropriate, given that they were at a funeral, but it seemed wrong to cry for losing someone whose funeral this wasn't, even if the "dead" person wasn't actually dead.

She looked up at Mr. Utter and the gravestone that had already been carved.

WILD BILL

J. B. HICKOCK

Killed by Assassin

Jack McCall

~in~

DEADWOOD BLACK HILLS

August 2nd, 1876

Pard, we will

meet Again

in the happy

hunting ground

to part no more.

Good bye

COLORADO CHARLIE

C. H. UTTER

Annie tilted her head. "They spelled Mr. Hickok's name wrong."

"Well," Frank said with a smile, "he's not really in there, is he?"

Annie squeezed his hand. "I've been meaning to ask you something."

"Oh yeah?"

"Back in the stagecoach, when you thought we were going to get blown up, even though I knew we were perfectly safe."

"Um."

"You were talking about how you wanted to grow old together. George and rifles were involved."

"Oh, right." Suddenly, Frank looked nervous.

"And then you said that you love me."

"Did I?" Frank's voice went tight.

"Yes," Annie said gently. "You did. And even if you've managed to forget it, I remember. I have the best memory out of my whole family."

"That's not at all a surprise. But I wonder what they'd say about you constantly claiming these things."

"You can ask them yourself," Annie said. "Since I'm going to insist that you meet them if we move forward. I mean, I suppose I've got a lot of explaining to do with them. I need to make things right with Mama and be sure my siblings know how important they are to me, but . . . Are you even listening?"

"Hanging on every word." Frank scratched his chin. "It's just, I'm not sure what we're talking about. What are we moving forward with?"

"With the wedding."

"What?"

"Yeah. That was what I was going to ask you: do you want to marry me?"

"I think there's only one good answer here," Frank said slowly.

"I agree."

"And that's to say . . ." He cleared his throat. "Annie Oakley, I asked you first."

"What?" The word came out a little too loudly, and everyone nearby glared at her. Right. They were at a funeral. "What?" she asked more softly.

"Don't you remember? I asked you after the competition. You said it would take more than a cute dog to impress you, so I've been trying to impress you this entire time."

"Does that mean you're saying yes?" she whispered.

He smiled. "That means I'm still waiting for you to say yes."

"Well, drat. I wish I'd realized that a long time ago. But in that case—" Annie stood on her toes and kissed him.

At once, Mr. Utter stopped his eulogy, and the rest of the mourners turned to stare.

"What in tarnation?" Jane said from the other side of Frank. "Get a room, you two."

"Oh, we will," Frank said.

Annie drew back.

"Once we're married, of course," he finished.

"Good save." Annie grinned.

"You're getting married!?" Jane shouted. "Since when?"

"Since two seconds ago," Annie said.

"That was fast," Jane muttered. "But romantical, I suppose. I'm glad y'all are getting your happy ending."

Annie grinned and hugged Jane. "This isn't a happy ending. This is a happy beginning, and you're getting one, too."

"I see. And how do I know that?" Jane stood totally still, like a cat unsure why affection was happening.

"Because Frank and I are going to make sure of it. We'll go on the road together. Perform our show. Mr. Utter will manage it, like before."

"Mr. Utter is trying to manage a funeral," Mr. Utter said. "In case you've forgotten."

"See what a good job he's doing already?" Annie squeezed Jane. Then Frank hugged her, too.

"I am uncomfortable," Jane said. "I'm exiting this hug."

Annie started to draw away, but not before Jane got a quick squeeze in. "After the funeral, we should all go practice for the show."

Jane sighed loudly, but she was grinning. "All right. You know what they say."

"There's no business like show business?" Annie said.

Jane rolled her eyes. "The show must go on."

Epilogue
Denver
One year later

"Look, Mama!" said a girl on the street as Jane passed by. "Isn't that Calamity Jane?"

"I think so, sweetie," said her ma.

"She's a hero, isn't she?" said the girl.

"She sure is," said the mother.

Hero-eene, Jane wanted to clarify, but instead she tipped her hat to the pair and continued on down the road. It was odd now when people recognized her. They all smiled at her, for one thing, and said things like, "Wowee! There goes *the* Calamity Jane!" and they talked like she was some kind of inspirational figure. Times were definitely changing.

She walked over to a post and smoothed a flyer over it. It was a new flyer, and front and center on the paper was a drawing of Annie with her rifle and the words *Little Miss Sure Shot* under her feet, then a smaller picture of Frank and those good teeth of his, and Jane with her bullwhip.

Jane lifted her hammer, but before she could nail the flyer to the post, a breath of wind came up and stole it from her hand. "Oh, rocks," she said, and chased the paper down the street, almost catching it a few times before it stopped and fluttered against a pair of shiny black boots.

The owner of the boots bent and picked up the flyer. Jane squinted at her—a young woman wearing a white dress with lace at the throat and a pair of black spectacles. The sun made a halo out of her pale hair.

Jane still thought she was the prettiest thing she'd ever seen. "Thanks," Jane murmured.

Winnie straightened and read the flyer out loud. "'Come One, Come All, to the *New and Improved Wild West Show*!' Oh my goodness," she said, smiling impishly. "You're Calamity Jane, now aren't you?"

"That's me," Jane said, grinning right back at her. "And you are . . . ?"

Winnie held out her gloved hand, and Jane shook it.

"Katie Brown," Winnie said, because Katie Brown was the new name she'd decided on for when she wanted to dress as a woman. She'd also chosen a different name for when she was a man, seeing as how she'd sold the name Edward Wheeler (and the notoriety that went with it) to Ned Buntline before the group left Deadwood. She wanted a completely fresh start, she'd said, and Jane couldn't blame her. Winnie still wanted to be a spectacular writer, mind you, but she was done penning stories about Calamity Jane. So Edward Wheeler had become Edward Burke, and Edwina Harris—who had been known as the traveling companion of Mr. Wheeler—had become Katie Brown, although Jane would never be able to think of her as anything but Winnie.

Jane grabbed the flyer to read it herself. (Annie had been teaching Jane to read for the past several months, and Jane had finally learned her letters past *G*.) "'Exhibitions of Peerless Sharpshooting by Annie Oakley. Trick Shots by Frank Butler, the Pistol Prince! Mar—marvel—'"

"Marvelous," prompted Winnie.

Jane nodded. "'Marvelous Feats with the Bullwhip, Performed by Calamity Jane! Hear Tales of the Terrific Three's Thrilling Adventures in the Black Hills!'" She lowered the paper. "I still say that 'the Magnificent Three' has a better ring to it." This had been her suggestion when the group was trying to come up with a new name. The others had said it most definitely did not have a ring, and Annie had thrown out something like "the Sharpshooting Trio," which lacked sparkle, Jane argued, and Frank had come up with "the Terrific Three," to which Annie had shaken her head and said, "Terrific? We're not trying to scare them, are we?" (Reader, hey, it's us, one last—or is it the last?—time. It turns out that *terrific* didn't always mean "excellent." *Terrific* was more on par with "terrible" and "terror." Basically, it was a bad thing, hence Annie's worry that "Terrific Three" would send customers running for the hills.)

But then Winnie had wisely chimed in with, "Language is a living thing, you know. It changes all the time. If we want *terrific* to mean something good, we just have to persuade everyone we ever meet."

"That sounds like a tall order," said Annie. "But I like a challenge." So the group went with Terrific Three, and Winnie turned out to be right: people did accept their new meaning of the word.

Now Jane and Winnie walked back to the post, and Winnie held the flyer down while Jane nailed it on. "Are you nervous?" Winnie asked.

Jane pshawed her. "I'm never nervous about the show."

"No, I mean, this is the last town before we head to Salt Lake City," Winnie said. "You're so close to home."

"Haven't you figured out by now that my home is with you all?" But Jane's heart did start to beat faster at the mere mention of Salt Lake City and the notion that she'd finally get to see her brother and sisters again. "But yeah, I'm a little nervous, I guess. What if they've forgotten all about me?"

"Nobody could forget you, Jane Canary," said Winnie, and took Jane's arm, and together they strolled around the city posting up flyers, until it was time to head back to get ready for the show.

* * *

In the dressing room, Annie finished putting on her show dress. She'd sewn it herself—of course—and matched it with her favorite stockings (so she never accidentally showed leg). She liked to pin the medals she'd won in various shooting competitions in the past year to the bodice, even though Frank sometimes said she'd blind the audience with the shine of all of them. And to top it off, she put on her hat, the one with the star on the underside of the brim.

"You're lovely," Frank said as he walked in. "As always."

Annie blushed and finished pinning her hat. "You look very dashing as well."

Frank grinned. "That's what your mother called me."

"Can we not talk about my mother?" Annie asked with a groan, but it was mostly in jest.

As Annie had, ahem, demanded, after the events in Deadwood, the two of them had gone back to Ohio to meet Annie's family. Annie had been pretty nervous, considering how she'd left things with her mama and everyone else. Mama had all but forbidden her to return if she didn't return with a man, and here Annie was—returning with a fiancé.

"All my dreams have come true!" Mama cried. "You've got a man! And a handsome one!"

It would have been embarrassing if Annie wasn't so happy that Frank had agreed to marry her.

Sarah Ellen, Huldy, and John had all loved Frank immediately, partly because he had a nice dog and their requirements for a good-for-Annie husband were pretty limited: must have a nice dog.

Mama had been thrilled, of course, but Grandpap Shaw had gotten right to the interrogation.

"So, young man." Grandpap Shaw stroked his beard. "Annie will be an assistant in your show?"

"No, sir." Frank glanced around the doorstep where they'd been since Annie had knocked. (Yep, knocked on her own door. That's how strained things were.) "Do you think we can come in now?"

Mama looked at Annie. "If you're not the assistant, what do you do?"

"She probably manages the books," said Grandpap Shaw.

"Annie is the talent," said Frank. "The star of the show. The headliner. People love her."

Grandpap Shaw's mouth pulled down into a frown. "Show business is no business for a young lady like Annie."

But Annie's mama had different thoughts. She lowered her voice—although not so much that everyone three farms down didn't hear the exchange—and asked, "Aren't you worried about outshining him with your talent? You should probably miss a few shots if you want to keep him around."

"Mama!" This was worse than Annie could have predicted.

"Why should I be jealous of Annie?" Frank had mused. "I knew I wanted to marry her the moment she beat me in a competition. If anyone's an assistant, I should be hers."

"Wait," Mama had said. "Tell us how you met?"

"Only if you let us inside."

And so Annie had finally been allowed back in her house, where she and Frank told the whole family about the competition, that first proposal, and all the things Annie had included in her first letter—the one they'd returned unopened.

Before Annie and Frank left a few days later, Mama had agreed to take some of the money Annie had earned. They'd be able to pay off the farm, and no one would go hungry without Annie there to shoot game for them. And when Annie and Frank presented the trinkets—paints, a pendant, and a small book for the children called *Goodnight Garou*—everyone had descended on the gifts like vultures.

That had been several months ago now, and Annie wrote to her family regularly. (And, even better, they wrote back to her. No more returned mail.) Postage was still terrifically expensive, but the show made them enough money now.

"Are you ready for your closeup, Miss Oakley?" Frank asked, holding the tent open.

"You know it."

The show, as always, was an overwhelming success.

It began with Calamity Jane making a tin can walk across the main floor, striking it with her whip just so. The crowd loved it, cheering every time the can did a spin before flipping over. Little did they know, the real show had hardly begun. Because after she walked the can across the floor, Jane shifted into her wolf form and performed the same trick.

The first few times she'd done this, people had screamed and there'd almost been a stampede out of the theater, but when Agnes Thatcher Lake—the show's ringmaster—called for order (and everyone obeyed because no one dared disobey Agnes), the audience took their seats again and watched wolf-Jane whip the can back across the floor, the same as she'd done as a human.

After that first show, when the audience had realized they weren't about to get eaten up by a garou, ticket sales went through the proverbial roof.

Once wolf-Jane left the stage—to wild applause, we should add—Annie and Frank took their places. Annie with her gun. Frank with the targets.

This is what really happened, and to be perfectly honest, it kind of freaks out your narrators here. But Frank's job was to hold cards *in his hands* and Annie would shoot out the hearts. He'd also toss dimes into the air—which Annie would shoot—and every so often he'd balance glass balls on top of his head . . . and, you guessed it, Annie would shoot them, too. It all seems extremely dangerous to us, but the crowds loved it. (Although Annie never had silver bullets in her gun, so it wasn't *quite* as dangerous for Frank. . . .) They cheered and called out for more, so at that point, Annie got up on Charlie's horse and stood on his back like she had during the stagecoach chase. Instead of axles, this time she shot more glass balls, apples, and anything else the audience tossed up into the air.

When she was finished, Frank offered a hand and helped her down off Charlie's horse (not that she needed help; it was all part of the show). Then, he gave her a quick kiss—and like every time, Annie's foot popped back—and the audience cheered and whooped.

"How do you do it, Annie?" yelled a reporter from the front row. "How'd you get so successful so quick?"

"Aim at the high mark and you will hit it," Annie replied. "No, not the first time, not the second time, and maybe not the third. But keep on aiming and keep on shooting, for only practice will make you perfect. Finally you'll hit the bull's-eye of success."

He hurried to write that down.

At the end of the show, Annie, Frank, and Jane (who was human once again) stood in the middle of the floor and took one another's hands. Agnes encouraged more and more cheering as everyone in the audience stood, clapping and clapping.

When the audience was gone, the stagehand helped disassemble the set, and by stagehand, we mean Wild Bill, who was now calling himself Ted.

"A fine show, my dear," he said as Agnes approached him. "How did we do?"

"Charlie has the final numbers," she said, "but we sold out here, and we've sold out all our shows for the next three months."

Frank and Jane whooped.

"In fact," Agnes went on, "a few cities have been building stadiums so we can get even larger crowds."

"Amazing." Annie could hardly comprehend all of this. It was just such a huge thing for a farm girl from Darke County, Ohio.

"Annie?" Charlie approached with an elderly man in tow. "You have a visitor. He says you've met before."

The man in question was tall and quite hairy, and a good decade older than the last time Annie had seen him, but she knew him immediately. He was the gentleman from the train, the one who'd listened to her story and given her sweets and bought her ticket home.

"Mr. Oakley!" Annie cried. "How did you find me?"

"Well, you've been using my name. But I'm glad to see you again. You've done well for yourself." He motioned around the show floor. "And after what happened to you, I never thought I'd see you working so closely with garou."

Annie blushed. "It wasn't easy, but some very smart friends helped me understand that I can't judge all garou based on that one experience, even if it was really bad."

"I'm proud of you, Miss Annie. You're doing good work."

Annie and Mr. Oakley talked for a while longer, as the set went into trunks around them, and finally it was time to say good-bye. "I'll write to you," she promised, and only as they parted did Annie catch the way his eyes reflected the light.

The stagecoaches packed and sent off ahead of them, there was only one thing left to do: mount up and ride, seven horses for seven heroes: Frank and Annie in the lead, Jane and Winnie riding close together, Bill/Ted and Agnes, and Charlie bringing up the rear. Jane's heartbeat quickened again at the thought that in a short few weeks, they'd reach Salt Lake City and she would come full circle. But this time she had a bunch of money saved up, more and more with every show, and could afford to buy her siblings some shoes. Someday soon, she thought, she'd have enough to quit show business for good, as it had never really given her the thrill it gave to Frank and Annie, and settle down somewhere. Montana Territory, maybe, as she'd heard it was beautiful up that way.

But first, she had a show to do in Salt Lake City.

"Let's go," she said.

And with that, the Magnificent Seven (we had to point that out) rode off into the sunset, not because it was a cliché of Westerns, but because it was late afternoon, and they were heading west.

"Well, drat. It sure is bright," Annie observed.

"My eyes are burning," cried Jane. "Gah!"

Frank put a hand to his forehead and squinted. "It really is the worst spot, where it's not blocked by our hat brims, but it's not low enough for the mountains on the horizon."

Bill/Ted groaned. "You'd think I raised a bunch of daisies," he said.

"I have to pee," said Jane.

"I told you to go before we left," said Charlie.

"I did!"

And so it went on for hours. Every ride was like that.

But none of them could have imagined a happier ending.

Acknowledgments

Writing this book involved no fewer than five, ahem, calamities. (Be careful what you name a thing. . . .) We've taken a blood oath not to talk about some of them, but you can be assured it's something of a miracle this book made it to your bookshelf. (Although we will say, many laptops died to bring you this information.)

There were a lot of miracle workers involved with this book, including our agents: Katherine Fausset, Holly Frederick, Lauren MacLeod, Michael Bourret, and Jennifer Laughran; our editors: Erica Sussman and Stephanie Stein; and a whole ton of behind-the-scenes Harper folks like: Jenna Stempel-Lobell, Olivia Russo, Alexandra Rakaczki, Louisa Currigan, Sabrina Abballe, Ebony LaDelle, Cindy Hamilton, and Jennifer Corcoran.

As Jane discovers her family in this book, we are grateful for ours. Thanks to Carter, Beckham, Sam, Joan, and Michael; Jeff,

Sarah, and Jill; and Will, Madeleine, Dan, and Carol and Jack, who graciously let us use their house to hide away and write.

For this book, we made our own journey to Deadwood, where we had lots of adventures that included having dinner at the Gem, watching the trial of Jack McCall, and visiting Wild Bill's and Calamity Jane's graves in Mount Moriah Cemetery. The Deadwood of today is pretty different than the Deadwood of 1876 (it's a lot cleaner, for example), but we definitely felt the spirit of the Old West while we were visiting. Thanks to Justin Coupens, our Air-Bob guy; we loved staying in the jailhouse, our awesome and weird home away from home. Thanks to Jena Sierks, the actress who walks around Deadwood dressed as Calamity Jane; this chance meeting was a highlight of our trip. And thanks to Wyatt and Misty Morse, the owners of Raspberry Hill, who let us look around their beautiful raspberry (not pink!) house.

In this book, we adjusted a few ages, combined various historical figures to create our own characters, and generally messed around with things to suit our purposes. Yes, we usually do this, but in *My Calamity Jane*, we did it a *lot*. Presenting a full list of what we changed would take another full book (and this one is already pretty long), so we encourage you to do some research on your own to see what we kept and what we, ahem, improved upon. A few resources to get you started:

The Life and Legends of Calamity Jane by Richard W. Etulain
Searching for Calamity: The Life and Times and Calamity Jane
    by Linda Jucovy

Bury My Heart at Wounded Knee by Dee Brown

Native Peoples of North America, the Great Courses series
    by Professor Daniel M. Cobb

Wild Bill: The True Story of the American Frontier's First Gun-
    fighter by Tom Clavin

Missie: The Life and Times of Annie Oakley by Annie Fern
    Swartwout

An Indigenous Peoples' History of the United States by Rox-
    anne Dunbar-Ortiz

"All the Real Indians Died Off": and 20 Other Myths About
    Native Americans by Roxanne Dunbar-Ortiz and
    Diana Gilio-Whitaker

The Real Deadwood: True Life Histories of Wild Bill Hickok,
    Calamity Jane, Outlaw Towns, and Other Characters of the
    Lawless West by John Ames

This Land podcast hosted by Rebecca Nagle

The Oglala Sioux Tribe Official Website: www.oglalala-
    kotanation.info

The Northern Cheyenne Tribal Historic Preservation
    Office: www.ncthpo.com

Also, thank you to our fantastic sensitivity readers, Elise McMullen-Ciotti and Ruth Hopkins. Your feedback was invaluable and we are so grateful for your knowledge, your work, and the time you took to read our book.

We also want to acknowledge some of the incredible people who read and push our books. OwlCrate and LitJoy Crate are two book boxes we love and support. The amazing Sarah Kershaw of

Your Book Travels, who works so hard to promote our books; gosh, you're great. Also, Tiffie van Bordeveld, who drew some amazing *My Plain Jane* art: thank you!

And, of course, we're grateful for all the librarians and bookstores who share our books with readers. Special thanks to our local indies, One More Page, Rediscovered Books, and King's English Bookshop.

And, as always, our readers. Thanks for being so gosh darn wonderful.

More can't-miss books from the Lady Janies
Also by Cynthia Hand
The Afterlife of Holly Chase
The Last Time We Say Goodbye
The How & the Why

Unearthly
Hallowed
Boundless
Radiant: An Unearthly Novella (available as an ebook only)

Also by Brodi Ashton
Diplomatic Immunity

Everneath
Everbound
Evertrue
Neverfall: An Everneath Novella (available as an ebook only)

Also by Jodi Meadows
Before She Ignites
As She Ascends
When She Reigns

The Orphan Queen
The Mirror King

The Orphan Queen Novellas (available as ebooks only)
The Hidden Prince
The Glowing Knight
The Burning Hand
The Black Knife

Incarnate
Asunder
Infinite
Phoenix Overture: An Incarnate Novella (available as an ebook only)

YOU MAY THINK YOU KNOW THEIR STORIES . . .

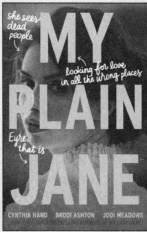

Go on these fantastical and romantical adventures through the past with stories you won't find in any textbook.

ALSO FROM
CYNTHIA HAND

 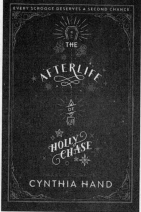 

Insightful standalone novels about love, life, and family.

READ EVERY NOVEL
IN THE CAPTIVATING
UNEARTHLY SERIES
by CYNTHIA HAND

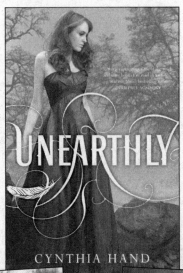

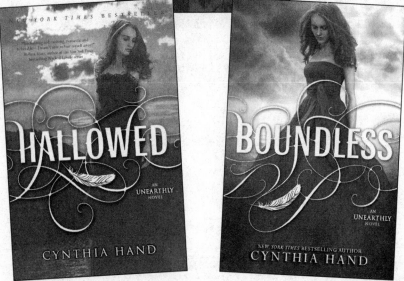

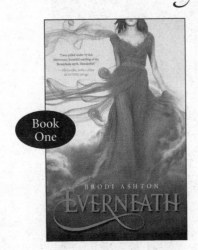

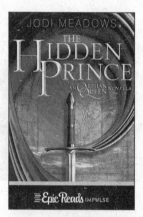
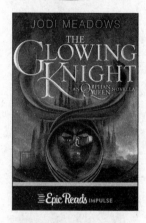

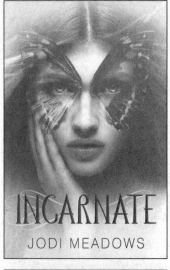

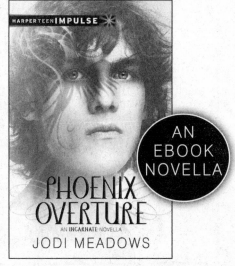

JOIN THE

Epic Reads

COMMUNITY

THE ULTIMATE YA DESTINATION

◄ **DISCOVER** ►

your next favorite read

◄ **MEET** ►

new authors to love

◄ **WIN** ►

free books

◄ **SHARE** ►

infographics, playlists, quizzes, and more

◄ **WATCH** ►

the latest videos